CHASM

CHASM

A novel based on a true story from the Civil War

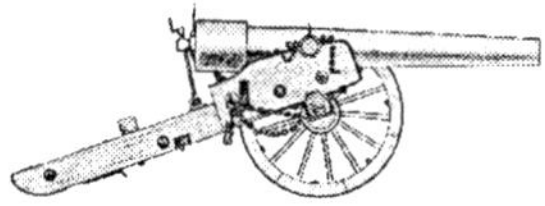

Elaine Evain

JAMES A. ROCK & COMPANY, PUBLISHERS
ROCKVILLE • MARYLAND

Chasm: A Novel Based on a True Story from the Civil War by Elaine Evain

JAMES A. ROCK & COMPANY
PUBLISHERS established 1973

JAMES A. ROCK & COMPANY, PUBLISHERS

Address comments and inquiries to:
James A. Rock & Company, Publishers
9710 Traville Gateway Drive, #305
Rockville, MD 20850

E-mail:
jrock@rockpublishing.com lrock@rockpublishing.com
Internet URL: www.rockpublishing.com

Trade Paperback ISBN-13/EAN: 978-1-59663-629-3

Library of Congress Control Number: 2008920283

Printed in the United States of America

First Edition: 2008

In memory of my husband Jean

C'est pour nous, mon amour

And to my mother Wini

Thanks Mom

Acknowledgments

This work could not have been written without the cooperation of many people.

Primary among those are three descendants of the families paramount to the story who opened family scrapbooks and allowed this writer access to old letters, memorabilia and photographs. All have expressed a desire to remain anonymous and I must respect those wishes, but I am sure you know heartfelt thanks goes out to each of you.

Deep appreciation goes to the librarians of the Ashe County Library in West Jefferson, North Carolina: Vickie Milam, Jo Green, Lee Faust, Joanne Kemp, and Karen Riddle, who were of tremendous aid in helping uncover historical documents, diaries, letters and books. Your dedication and unending patience was invaluable. Thanks also to the staff of the Appalachian State University Library, Boone, North Carolina, who helped uncover music and lyrics of the period.

Bud Altmayer, a native North Carolinian and author of several books about the region lent insight and little known information about the families and history around which the story revolves.

Appreciation is expressed to the members of The Blue Ridge Writers' Group, West Jefferson, North Carolina, who gave support and encouragement when it was sorely needed, as did early readers, Barbara Sacchetti, and Lorraine Bettencourt.

My gratitude to all those at Rock Publishing who gave immense support and especially to editor Lynne Rock for her patience; always there to hold my hand and never too busy to answer my off-the-wall questions.

My love and appreciation to my four children; Peggy, Leslye, Michael and Eric. Always there for Mom. My love and gratitude to my late husband, Jean, who contributed so much to this work in research and early editing, and who was so strongly dedicated to the work. And to my late mother, Wini, whose emotional support and belief in me made it possible.

Thank you all.

FOREWORD

The people and main events in this story are true. In one instance a composite of two characters has been made, and in two other instances fictional characters were introduced for dramatic impact. The major portion of the story is torn from little known pages of recorded history. Other parts were gleaned from conversations with descendants of the principal characters and from family memorabilia.

Interpersonal relationships are not found in the pages of history books, and when a writer takes on the responsibility of defining relationships which existed in a bygone era, logic, supposition, and imagination become intertwined. Was Keith Blalock a Robin Hood or a rogue elephant? The answer depends on where your feet were planted on the Mason/Dixon line.

—Elaine Evain
Center Harbor, New Hampshire

PART ONE

THE SEEDING

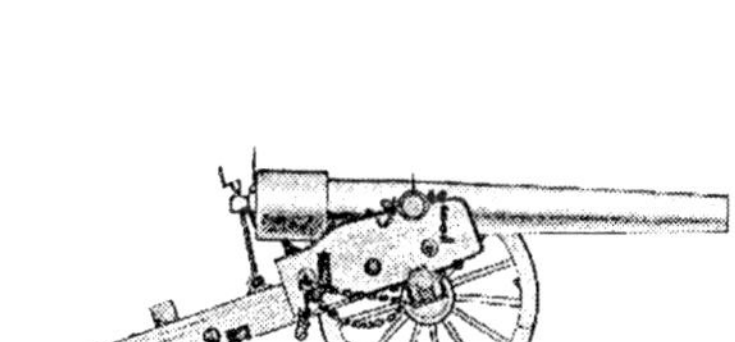

The Globe Valley

Caldwell County, North Carolina

December 1859

☆

CHAPTER 1

"I will marry him! I will marry Keith Blalock! I will, I will, I WILL!" Malinda Pritchard pounded the goose feather pillow with knotted fists as she muttered her affirmation into its soft depths. A moment later, frustration bubbling over, she seized the pillow and hurled it into the deep darkness of her tiny loft. The pillow hit the rafters with a soft thud and plopped to the floor. Outside, the winter wind whipped the branches of the old chestnut against the shingled roof.

Malinda's breath was now coming in short angry puffs. She bolted from her pallet, covered the three feet to the ladder with a single stride and grabbing the top rung propelled herself forward far enough to look down on her parents who were seated before the dying fire. "I don't care what you say, Ma, I'm marrying Keith. And you can't stop it. Nobody can stop it!" As the words flew from her lips the tears sprang from her eyes. Angrily, she swept them away with the sleeve of her muslin gown. "You best listen, 'cause I'm meaning what I say!" She stomped back across the cold, rough floor to the pallet, slipped into it and pulled the quilt over her head. Settling into her warm nest, she closed her eyes tight in an attempt to stem the tears. "No use crying like some milksop baby," she scolded herself aloud. "You're near being a woman now." As if in answer, the wind howled again and beat the branches against the roof. Pa'd been talking about chopping down that ole tree forever it seemed. Never did get around to doing things anymore like he used to. "Oafish." That's what Ma called him the other day when she was steamed over something he'd messed up.

Below, Elizabeth and Alfred Pritchard sat silent before the remaining embers of the supper fire. Alfred's eyes were closed. Not even his daughter's outburst had pried them open. Elizabeth's hands rested on her swollen belly and the flannel shirt she was patching; the stitches were large and clumsily made.

Elizabeth Pritchard was a contradiction. Her lineage was gentle, but the hand of fate had made her into a mountain woman, carved and honed by the rocks and forests of her home. Her gnarled fingers knew the icy rush of the mountain stream where she pounded cloth against rock, and they knew too the searing heat of the iron kettle where she cooked her family's meals. The strong hands also knew the hard pull of a musket. Elizabeth could drop a deer as well as any man.

Elizabeth's chest swelled with a sigh as she fastened her gaze on the last tiny ember. Her toughened heart was soft now with the weight of her daughter's pain, for she still held the bittersweet memory of a young girl's passion. But how, she wondered, could she let Malinda marry Keith Blalock? It wasn't right. On the other hand, how could she stop her? Malinda was as strong willed as an iron horse, and there didn't seem to be a way *of* stopping her short of tying her to the bedpost. In Elizabeth's opinion, Keith was a troublemaker. It seemed he was always smack dab in the middle when things were busting loose. Malinda, of course, defended him. Made excuses. It wasn't even a subject they could talk about anymore.

Secretly, Elizabeth had hoped her daughter would marry one of the young men from town. Town living was an easier life, and she had encouraged Malinda to appreciate fine things. Things she wasn't likely to have if she married Keith Blalock. Oh, there was love enough between them. And there had been precious little in Malinda's life to love. No siblings or grandparents. A stray kitten or two that were soon killed by wild animals. She could still see the tears streaming down that tiny face when they'd buried the mangled remains of the last of them. Malinda had asked God to make it whole again and screamed with rage when He didn't comply. Yes, Malinda was ripe for love all right. But did it have to be Keith? There was an angry current running through that young man … a roll of thunder just waiting for lightning. Maybe that's what made him so irresistible to Malinda. Surely that was part of it. The excitement.

The fire was settling now. Soon the room would be cold as the grave. All seemed quiet above. Perhaps the tantrum had spent itself. Elizabeth placed a hand on Alfred's arm. "Time for bed, Pa."

* * *

In the loft, restless, sleepless, her young face turbulent with anger, Malinda lay staring into the darkness. She knew she'd hurt them. Especially Ma. And she didn't want to hurt anybody. Least of all Ma. She had grief enough without her adding to it. But why couldn't Ma understand how much she loved Keith? She'd always said, "Now Malinda, you've got some education, as much as I could give you, and you need to find a husband whose got some education, too. Isn't easy living with a man whose got less learning than you." But Keith *is* educated! His stepfather, Austin Coffey, had seen to that. And wasn't Ma always saying, "A person would be hard put to find a finer man than Austin Coffey?" And all her talk about there being another man who'd come along. A better man. That only made the pain worse. Only made her want Keith all the more! Couldn't she see there'd never be another man for her. *NEVER!!!*

From below, Malinda heard the sound of her father's muffled voice as they bedded down for the night. "Lizzie, she's just a child. She don't mean no harm. Malinda just can't think beyond herself. That'll change with time. I know she pains you. But you gotta be thinkin' of that other youngin you'll be hatchin' soon. I'm wishin' with all a my heart I could make it easier for you. You deserve better than what you got, losin' seven babies as soon as they was birthed. But maybe this time it'll be different. Maybe we'll be gettin' a son. A strong one. Sometimes I wonder how you put up with it Lizzie, comin' like you do from such genteel folk. Toughin' it out up here on this mountain when you been brung up to have better."

It was a familiar chant. One both Elizabeth and Malinda could recite by heart. When Alfred was faced with a situation he couldn't handle, he leaned heavy on his wife.

Reaching now for sleep, Elizabeth's back was turned to Alfred. His hand rested on her hip, giving an occasional pat. Another sigh swelled her chest but she let it go softly. It was true. She did come from a line that could be traced all the way back to Scotland. Moneyed people. Landed people. Big important thing, that was! One of her direct forebear's claim to glory was being pressed to death for being a witch! After that messy event most members of the clan had escaped to America and settled around Charleston. Later, some drifted North. Her great grandmother Dorcas had headed inland with her family in search of farming land. Stories had it Dorcas had been kidnapped by a drunken Cherokee, raped and left to die. But neither Dorcas nor the seed of that dastardly union succumbed, and Elizabeth's mother, Margaret, was born into disgrace. As soon as Margaret was old enough she'd escaped to the mountains, away from the humiliating stares and whispers of the neighbors. And there, she'd met Sam Whitehead, a mountain man. They'd married and Margaret bore Sam seven children. Elizabeth was the middle child and the only girl. Tales had it there was Cherokee in Sam's veins as well.

Malinda had heard the story of her privileged bloodline more times than she could count always from Pa. Ma seldom mentioned it. Malinda also knew the limb from which her father had sprung: English, mountain folk for generations, religious, independent, not too strong on education.

Pa never talked much about his beliefs, though lately she knew they included anti-slavery. And he never stood in the way of Ma's educating. But there were times when Malinda found all the preaching and teaching to be a pain. She was grateful though that Ma had taught her reading and writing. It would no doubt come in useful somewhere up ahead. But for now there didn't seem much use for it. It did bring her joy though when Keith took up a newspaper or poster and started reading, and she'd look over his shoulder and read right along with him. Pleased him too, she could tell. If the truth be known, Keith sometimes made mistakes in his reading, but she would have died before letting on she knew better. Keith was awful sensitive that way. Touchy even. *Keith.* Even his name brought a kind of settling to her spirit. Malinda wrapped her arms tight around herself, pretending the arms were Keith's, then slowly she began exploring her secret places, the way he did, remembering his touch ... at first gentle, then turning to fire. Oh dear Lord, there was no escaping thoughts of Keith. And there was no wanting to. He filled her mind and body totally. Without Keith there was nothing. Without Keith she would sooner off be dead.

And what did Ma mean anyway, saying she wasn't ready for marrying? She'd be sixteen in a couple of weeks! Near past the marrying age! It was that ... that *knowing thing* Ma had. Came down through all those generations, all the way from Scotland. Maybe they *had* been witches. Maybe the curse *had* been passed down. She wondered about that because there were times when she had *the knowing* too ... a knowing what was going to happen before it ever did. Sometimes it was scary. Most especially it was scary when Ma talked about Keith and there being something in him that was going to bust loose one day. Truth to tell, she sometimes felt that about Keith, too.

First light stole through the slit between the logs where the straw and clay chinking had fallen away. Malinda stretched catlike, reached up, untied the cowhide at the window hole, and peered out. The angry winds of night were slowly being replaced with the bright hope of sunrise. She loved this ever changing view. For now, the winter bare trees lining the top of the ridge looked like a giant injun headdress, sticking up all tall and feathery like, their tips coated with a layer of white. She craned her neck and looked down on the cold forest still wrapped in black. Her most favorite place for "looking" was from the front door of the cabin. From there you could see The Grandfather, stark and bald, the cold, gray rock reaching 6,000 feet into the sky. "Etched by God's own hand," Pa'd said. The giant mountain rock was in the form of an old bearded man lying with arms folded across his chest, toes pointing to the heavens; staring up at the Creator with a kind of cold defiance. Nothing was more comforting to look at than The Grandfather.

Keith would be waking up now, too. Was he thinking of her? Surely so! Surely, he must be feeling the same yearning she was feeling.

* * *

An hour's ride away, out where the Morganton Road snaked around the base of The Grandfather, in a place called Coffey's Gap, Keith Blalock was indeed awake. For the moment, however, his thoughts were not of Malinda or of love making. As he groped about his dark room looking for matches to light the oil lamp his thinking was centered on the political events that were sucking him down like a pig in quicksand.

No one talked about anything except the war. All the neighbors blabbered secession, trying to protect slavery when they didn't have slaves. Never *would* have slaves! Hell! What did a mountain man need slaves for anyway? Most didn't have fields big enough to feed their own families, much less slaves. There weren't more than ten dozen niggers in the whole county anyway, and they were owned by the rich lawyers and doctors in town. Maybe some merchants, too. They were the only ones with enough land to support slaves. Didn't make sense, mountain folk getting all riled about slavery. And seceding sure didn't make sense!

Keith tightened his belt, blew out the lamp, and climbed down the ladder to the kitchen. He drew kindling from a box beside the fireplace, banked it, lit it, and fanned the flame to life. His movements were as automatic as his train of thought.

Any man with the mind of a monkey could see there was plenty the North had to offer the South, and vice versa. Can't raise rice or cotton in the North. Too damned cold. And doesn't that Reynolds fellow over by Durham have over 3,000 tobacco acres in North Carolina alone? Never mind Virginia! By God, money could be made by shipping Southern crops North. And that fancy machinery from those big factories in the North could be shipped down here to the rich people in the South. Why in the hell did they build a railroad if they aren't going to ship anything? Wasn't ANYBODY thinking?

Keith ran his fingers through his hair and shook his head. The pitiful part was, this whole cat fight was meaningless to mountain people. Mountaineers didn't have crops to sell or a need for fancy machinery, but by God, mountain men would be called on to do the fighting! You could bet your pants on that one!

But Keith's real concerns were far more personal than political. If *when* war broke out, he would be forced to fight for the Confederacy. The thought brought a taste to his mouth as bitter as Aunt Lincha's herb tea. If he was going to fight, and fighting wasn't something he was apt to run from, it sure wasn't going to be for a noaccount Confederacy! He picked up four logs from the firebox and stacked them on top of the kindling.

Much of Keith's political leanings came by way of his stepfather, Austin Coffey, the man who had married his mother when Keith was an infant with no father in sight. There had been no questions asked, and Austin had done his level best to give the boy a good home and whatever education he could. He'd tried to instill a set of values in him, but sometimes feared he had instilled more of his own stubbornness instead.

Austin was a devout Unionist. Whenever talk of war between the states surfaced, as it so often did, in defiance of his three brothers, all avid Confederates, Austin made his sympathies known. He was a calm man, deliberate in action, thought and words, but not one to be coerced into accepting viewpoints he disagreed with. This made interaction with his brothers something less than pleasurable, but for the sake of family unity they usually managed to keep the peace.

Keith ran his fingers through his long, light brown hair, stooped his lanky frame and stared at his reflection in the cracked mirror hanging above the washstand. The gray eyes, the color of thunderheads, stared back, analyzing the stubble at his long jaw line and cleft chin, searching for errant hair growing from the faintly hooked nose. Unlike most men of his time he wore no beard, just a mustache. It was thick and well shaped, the hair surprisingly soft. It covered his upper lip and spread out another quarter inch, curling rakishly upward at the ends. It was a good face. Strong, if not actually handsome. The eyes, which took in a whole scene in a single glance, reflected a sharp intelligence. Maybe he would grow a beard one day, he mused. Maybe after he and Malinda got married. He stroked the razor across the strop while continuing to study his reflection, then dropped the sharp instrument into the icy water as he lathered his neck and chin with soap.

Gradually, another face, a phantom face, drifted into the mirror... Malinda ... Ah, sweet Malinda! Malinda who could turn all thoughts of anger into an ache of longing. He envisioned the dark, lustrous eyes, big as ripe prunes, banked by rich thick brows and row upon row of dark lashes. He could almost see the Cherokee cheekbones, high and chiseled, the elegant narrow nose, and the thin lips that grew plump with desire. He smiled at his own thoughts. How could a man with blood in his veins think of war when there was so much lovin' to do?

From the adjoining room Keith heard the sound of soft humming. Austin was awake, and like most mornings he awoke singing. In a minute now, the rich baritone would build until it filled the house. But first, there was the sound of the chamber pot, followed by a sigh of release. "Ahhhh ... "

"Mornin' Mary." Austin bent to kiss his wife who was still snuggled in sleep. "We'll have the fire goin' in a minute. You rest till the house is warm." Austin lumbered into the main room, pulling the strap of his blue denim overalls over his shoulder, rubbing at his small, birdlike eyes as he yawned.

"Mornin,' Will. How's that fire going? Your Ma's still got that danged cough. Don't want her gettin' any sicker than she already is." He patted Keith on the shoulder as he moved toward the cupboard.

Austin was the only one who still called Keith by his childhood name. It was a bond between them. A private thing. Born Lyle McKesson Blalock, his mother had taken one look at him and said he looked like a "William." And so it was. Then, by age nine, the boy was showing such ability as a scrapper, friends, neighbors and soon family began calling him "Keith" after the famous pugilist Alfred Keith. As he'd reached further into boyhood, the name began to stick as he pummeled one opponent after another into the red clay dirt. By age eleven even his mother called him by the nickname.

Keith laid the razor aside and picked up the iron poker, probed again at the fledgling fire. "Don't want to catch this morning," he mumbled. Then as a few promising flames licked upward he returned to his basin and mirror as Austin's humming grew into a whistle that soon erupted into a tune.

As I went out walking for pleasure one day
in the sweetly creation to while time away
As I set amusing myself in the grass,
oh who should I spy but a fair Indian lass.

Austin hugged the wooden coffee grinder between his knees, twirling the handle in time with the rhythm of his song.

"Pa, I ain't never figured out how you can be so damned cheerful in the morning." Keith wiped at his face with the towel and moved closer to the mirror to make sure he'd gotten everything he was after.

Austin chuckled. "Coffeys all wake up singin.' Least ways we did when we were youngins. We used to bandy around Uncle Webb while he played his jew's harp and we'd all sing our hearts out. Singin's natural. If more folks would sing instead of moan, the world would be what the good Lord intended it to be. A happy place."

Keith rinsed the razor in the pan, walked to the door and pitched the water outside, paying attention not to let any fall on the stone step where it would ice. No use saving the water for Austin. Austin's hand hadn't held a razor in more than twenty years. He had a white mustache that curled downward into a white beard, that curled halfway down his chest.

Keith closed the door and leaned against it, his eyes suddenly wary. "Pa. Me and Malinda will be getting married soon."

Austin looked up from his grinding. His pink lips, barely visible through the tangle of white hair, opened into a smile. "Isn't that why we've been buildin' you that cabin?"

"I mean, sooner than we were talking about. Her Ma is well, we're thinking of doing it the twenty-first. She'll be sixteen that day, and that being four days before Christmas, we could make it a kind of double celebration." Keith studied his stepfather with sharp, probing eyes.

"Mary and me will be mighty pleased; you can be sure of that. And I agree, there's no sense in waitin.' Malinda's a fine girl. Besides that, her Pa's a Union man." Austin winked at Keith as he poured the ground beans into the blue speckled coffee pot, hung it on the iron handle above the fire, then poured water from a black kettle over it. "It can't be more than two days ago when Mary was sayin' how happy she'll be to see the two of you settled."

Keith felt a sigh rising in his chest. "Guess I'd better be riding over to see the parson then." He grinned broadly.

"That you should, I reckon." Austin returned the grin.

Keith had counted on Austin's approval, and along with Ma's, those were the only opinions that mattered. To hell with what Malinda's parents thought of him. And to hell, too, with what his uncles thought. Especially, William and Reuben. Yeah, and that went for McCaleb, too! Damned Confederates all of 'em! And all of 'em saying a man shouldn't be getting married in times like these—what with the war coming and all. Well, by God, Keith Blalock was going to do what he was aiming to do, and *no man* was going to stand in his way.

☆

CHAPTER 2

Nervous, Keith pulled at the unfamiliar shirt collar. Ma had put so much stiffening in it the blamed thing was starting a rash on his neck. He hadn't wanted to wear it, didn't seem necessary not being a church wedding, but Ma said a wedding day belongs to the bride and that it would make Malinda happy. Probably so. But what did that make him then? An onlooker? Wasn't it his wedding, too? Truth was, Malinda could get anything she wanted from him just by flashing one of her sweet smiles. He knew it and she knew it. Better that way, he figured. Everybody knowing where everybody stands. Not that he was going to be the kind of husband who was pussy whipped by his woman! Not like Malinda's Pa. No siree, no woman would ever do that to Keith Blalock. Not even Malinda.

Lord, but it was hot in here! Ma had been cooking since before sun up, but he had to admit it did make the house smell sweet. Sweeter than he could ever remember. Must be that brown bread with all the raisins in it.

He ran his hands down the sides of his Sunday pants and wondered if other men felt like this on their wedding day. Partly wishing the whole thing was over and done with; the ceremony, the gathering, the damn gushing and talking—while another part was just waiting for it all to begin.

Of course the thing he was really looking forward to was tonight when he could truly claim his bride. Where in the hell was the parson anyway? Damnation! He was supposed to have been here a half hour ago. The ice storm two nights back had slickened the roads. Best thing when the weather was like this was an ox and dray. But the parson didn't have an ox, or a dray, just that worn out ole buggy with a horse to match. Hell! The parson hardly had food to put on his table. Now why would any man get himself into a position where he had to live off the bounty of other folk? Keith shook his head. Maybe there was something in The Bible he didn't understand. He chuckled. Something? *Hell!* I don't understand *most* of it! Especially that part about the "meek inheriting the earth." Ask any nigger slave about that one! And damnedest, hardest reading book there ever was!

"Son? Do … do I look all right?" Keith turned from his place at the window to see his mother standing beside the fire. Her chill blue eyes looked oddly intense. She was a handsome woman with strong, even features. Keith had often wondered why he hadn't taken more after her than he had his Pa—

whoever the hell *HE* was! And on the Pa subject, he'd spent a goodly bit of time mulling that one, all right! When he was younger he used to study each of his features; eyes, nose, mouth, ears, then try to measure them up against the men he knew. Never did come up with anything though. One thing about Ma, she was closed mouth on the subject. He'd fought a lot of scraps over that, starting when he was still in knickers. Never told Ma why he sometimes came home bleeding and dirty. More'n likely she knew anyway.

Pausing to study her now, he answered finally, "You look real pretty, Ma." His lips opened into a wide smile. Mary Coffey's hand moved nervously, smoothing the gray streaked hair back toward the tight knot at the nape of her neck. Keith read her nervousness. "Pretty dress too. Don't remember seeing it before."

"It belonged to Ma. It's a little big. Does it show?" She turned so he could get a full view.

Keith crossed to her, bent and brushed her cheek with his lips, surprising them both by the unusual show of affection. "There was never a prettier lady," he said awkwardly, then in an effort to cover his ill ease, he added, "but don't you go telling Malinda I said so."

He moved again to the mirror; brushed at his mustache. "You just watch when Sally and McCaleb get here. That woman will turn green as a frog with envy when she gets a gander at you."

"I don't want to start trouble," Mary said, putting her hand to her mouth as the perpetual cough rattled her lungs. "There's trouble enough between your Pa and his family without adding more to it. Besides, this is a happy occasion, a wedding *and* Christmas. There'll be no feuding today."

Keith glanced around at the decorations she'd made from newspaper and stained red with berries and hung about the room. In the corner, the fir tree held a dozen candles, as yet unlit, and a shiny, tin cutout angel peered down from the top. Yes, sir, it *was* going to be a happy occasion.

"Better get out here, Son!" Austin called from the front porch. "Somebody's comin.'" Keith stepped outside onto the covered porch that ran the length of the frame house. Across a large clearing was a weathered, wind whipped barn that listed slightly to one side. To the right of it was the pig sty and a small shed; to the left a garden plot, tangled now and winter weary. In the middle of the clearing was a hitching post. The entire compound was enclosed by a split rail fence, and the gate that opened onto the gutted, dirt road stood open in welcome.

Keith made his way out into the yard, feeling the bite of the wind against his face as he listened to the beat of horse's hoofs. The rider was in a hurry. His pulse quickened as a moment later Malinda rode into view. He wasn't surprised to see she'd come alone. So her Ma had held out to the bitter end, had she? And of course Malinda's Pa wouldn't have come without her say so. Well, if that was the way they wanted it, that was just fine with him. They didn't need the Pritchard's blessing anyway.

He hurried forward as Malinda drew her horse to a halt. Taking the reins, he tied them around the hitching post, then reached up for his bride. My God, she was beautiful! The frigid air had rosied her cheeks till they looked like fresh apples.

"Oh wait! First take my dulcimer." Malinda unbuckled the strap from her shoulder, slid the narrow instrument off her back and handed it to him. "Sure hope that blanket I wrapped it in was enough protection. Hate like crazy to damage my dulcimer."

"Don't fret. We'll unwrap it soon as we get inside and make sure it's all right." Keith slipped the strap over his shoulder then lifted Malinda from the horse, his hands lingering about her waist longer than necessary. Soon the whole world would know she belonged to him.

"Don't worry about your horse," Austin called as he walked toward them. "I'll take care of him."

"Thank you, Mr. Coffey."

"It must have been a hard ride." Keith looked down at her green gingham dress noting how it was splattered with pellets of ice and mud.

"Old Tim knows the way here by heart." She smiled up at him as she gently patted the horse's nose. "I think he knew this was a special occasion 'cause he did his best to keep under the trees so I wouldn't get so wet." She linked her arm through Keith's as they headed for the house. "Wish I could've afforded a new dress," she said, smiling up at him. "But there'll be time for buying new things and such after we get settled."

"I surely hope so, Sweetheart. But new dress or not. You look mighty good to me."

"And I must say, you look mighty handsome yourself, all decked out in your Sunday best."

"I hate this damned shirt." He wedged a finger between his neck and the stiff collar. "Can't wait to get it off."

"Am I late?"

"No, Sweetheart you're not late. Dern parson ain't even here yet. We still don't know about Uncle William and Reuben. Aunt Margaret said she'd be here though." He guided her toward the porch. "I think Ma's a little nervous. But God bless her, she was up before dawn doing the cooking."

"That's all right," Malinda giggled. "That just means I'm not the only one who'll be nervous."

"Uncle McCaleb and Aunt Sally are coming, and so are Carroll and Zinnia Moore. It was Pa's idea to invite the Moores. Don't know how he proposes to get all these people inside this house though."

Malinda looked up at him with astonishment. "Don't tell me Jesse Moore is coming to our wedding!"

Keith rolled his head back and laughed. "No, I don't suppose they'll be bringing son Jesse. Every time he shows his face seems I just feel an itch to change the shape of it for him."

"Then it'll just be Carroll and Zinnia?"

"Yeah, I don't think any of the boys will come. But you know how Ma and Zinnia have always been close, even if their sons do try to kill each other, and their menfolk battle over politics." He grinned down at her. "Zinnia's been right helpful to Ma since she's been sick. And I suppose, too, Pa's trying to keep peace with the Confederates."

"Well, that sure enough surprises me! My Pa would never allow a Confederate in his house, and he isn't near the Unionist *you*r Pa is."

They were interrupted by the rattle of a buggy turning in off the main road. Keith glanced over his shoulder to see the parson's bay pulling to a halt beside two figures who were just then emerging from around the bend. "Well, it appears the parson has arrived! And Uncle McCaleb and Aunt Sally."

Sally was carrying a huge basket in one hand while fighting the wind to keep her shawl around her with the other. Keith saw McCaleb reach up to shake the parson's hand, then both he and Sally climbed in and rode the remaining few yards through the gate into the compound.

Austin greeted them warmly, shaking the parson's hand, then his brother's, while offering his other hand to his sister-in-law. Sally accepted it with a look of disdain, and once free of the buggy rushed forward to greet Keith with a smile that could have been carved in river rock. "My, my, don't you look handsome today Keith," she purred, then turned to Malinda who was now standing on the porch. "And doesn't the blushing bride look lovely, too! You are still blushing aren't you dear?"

Keith ignored the remark, hoping Malinda would do the same. Everyone knew what a witch Sally was. Keith walked over to the carriage to help the parson down. The old man suffered from rheumatism; so crippling one leg was nearly lame. As Keith shook his uncle's hand, he read in McCaleb's face a look of friendliness. Maybe they would get through the day without a fight. He hoped so, for Ma's sake. And for Malinda's as well.

Malinda and Sally moved into the house where Mary Coffey was setting out dishes on the long, plank table. The aroma of roast turkey mingled with the spices from the brown bread and the fresh pine of the tree.

"Oh, Child, you look so lovely!" Mary embraced Malinda tenderly as she helped her with her shawl. "Welcome to the family, my dear."

"Thank you, Mrs. Coffey. I'll be proud to be a part of it."

Mary was too wise to inquire about Malinda's parents, and Malinda offered no explanation.

Sally opened her basket, carefully lifting out a large pie which she handed to Mary. "It's pun'kin. With nutmeg." Then she dove into the basket again and withdrew a corn bread pudding.

"Why, thank you, Sally," Mary murmured as the two women quickly busied themselves with the food in an attempt to avoid a more intimate greeting.

Margaret and Zechariah, Austin's sister and her husband, arrived a few minutes later, straddling the backs of two mules. Margaret was a comical sight, her long legs dangling nearly to the ground, but once inside, as usual, her towering presence lent warmth and humor to the gathering. Gangly like her brothers, Margaret possessed a special knack of putting others at ease with her outlandish wit. She loved her brothers equally, and walked a fine line in an effort to maintain harmony when the subject of politics raised its head. Both she and her husband were what was termed, "Moderates," a stand intended to be neutral, but one which garnered suspicion as well as condemnation. From both sides.

* * *

Austin again took up his post on the porch and lit his pipe. Hunching his shoulders against the gusting wind he eyed the road, waiting without too much hope for his older brothers, William and Reuben to show. They should do it for Mary, if for no other reason, he stewed. She, more than anybody, with the possible exception of Margaret, has tried to restore harmony to this family. And she being sick like she is ... Again the sense of dread washed over him at the thought of his wife's physical condition. He didn't care a whit if the Moores came or not. Carroll Moore's patriotic pride was sometimes more than he could stomach. What made it even harder was back before "the trouble" began he and Carroll had been friends.

Austin pulled out his pocket watch for the tenth time just as two more figures, struggling against the wind, came into view. The towering form was Carroll; the short, rounded one, Zinnia. Austin heaved a sigh. Well, Mary would be pleased. She loved Zinnia like a sister.

They waited another twenty minutes, but neither William or Reuben appeared, which made no difference at all to the bride and groom. The simple ceremony was short on time, but long on religious fervor.

Keith barely had a chance to kiss his bride before Mary began shooing everyone toward the table. The chairs were reserved for the women. Austin brought up wooden boxes from the root cellar for the men to sit on, while Mary placed the roast wild turkey, acorn squash and sweet potatoes in the center of the table along with her brown bread. The fresh churned butter was a gift from the Moores, and Margaret had brought foxglove jelly, along with another pumpkin pie.

When dessert was served it quickly became apparent that Margaret's pumpkin pie was prized over Sally's. Noting this, Sally took a mincing bite of her opponent's pie, then looked at her sister-in-law with rounded eyes. "My, my, Margaret, what is that peculiar taste in your pie? Reminds me of something I've tasted before, but I just can't place it."

"I think you must mean clove." Margaret smiled, readying herself.

"Ah, that's it! I knew it reminded me of the doctor's office. I believe he used oil of clove to relieve the pain I suffered with my wisdom tooth."

"I got the recipe out of the Knoxville Daily Register."

"Oh well, that explains it then. Tennesseans are such a strange breed now ain't they?" Sally laughed as if everyone approved of her little joke.

Margaret glanced across the table at her husband and winked. Everyone present knew that if Sally had any wisdom at all it had to be in her teeth because there wasn't any rattling around farther up in her head.

Zechariah managed to cover a smile. He was a third cousin to Margaret and long acquainted with the bitchiness of McCaleb's wife. It seemed a shame, Sally being such a pretty woman, all that flaming carrot colored hair and big green eyes, and that tiny build that made a man's thinking stray. But real unpleasant to be around, she was. Sometimes he even felt sorry for McCaleb.

"Parson, I thought your readin' from Scripture was inspired." McCaleb leaned across his plate and peered down the table at the parson who was seated on the other side of Sally. "Yes sir, if more people would remember the sacrifice of our Lord Jesus Christ, and his sufferin,' and the way they tormented his body, piercin' his side, and offerin' him gall to drink while he hung there agonizin,' why this world would be a much better place."

Mary took a fit of coughing just then and Keith caught her eye when she did it. This time, the cough was contrived. God Almighty, Keith steamed silently. If McCaleb wasn't trying to pick a fight by talking politics, he sure enough was going to make everybody sick by talking about drinking piss. Why couldn't he just eat his dinner and go the hell home? Another minute and he'd have Sally going, and she was something else when it came to ranting religion!

Keith reached over and squeezed Malinda's hand as it lay resting in her lap. She looked at him with a knowing smile. Encouraged, he probed deeper, getting in a poke at her groin. She slapped his hand, and passed him a "don't-do-that" look. He withdrew, but chuckled inwardly. He knew she wanted it as much as he did.

"Why, I thank you Brother McCaleb," the parson was saying, "Yes, I agree, if we would all pause to ponder—"

"Would you mind passing that corn bread pudding, Parson?" Austin interrupted, and Keith knew that he was trying to plug whatever was building behind Sally's vulturous stare. Another minute and she'd break loose like a musket ball.

"McCaleb, I suppose you heard that nigger lover John Brown got what was comin' to him." Carroll Moore pushed the wooden box he was seated on back from the table and folded his arms across his massive chest. He was a big man, yet wiry as a fox, and although he was addressing McCaleb, his eyes never left Austin.

"Yep, hung him up like a dead skunk," McCaleb smiled, also tilting back from the table.

Keith winced. Next to a bleeding Jesus, secession was McCaleb's favorite subject.

"Can't say the sucker wasn't begging for it after what he did at Harper's Ferry, excitin' the niggers and gettin' white men killed," Carroll continued. "We can expect more of that kind of thing before this is over, I reckon. Once them Unioni—"

"Well, boys," Austin rose and moved to a corner behind the chimney from which he removed a large, corked jug. "Parson?" Austin lifted the jug to show his intent. "I won't be insulting you if I offer you a sip from the fruits of my labor, will I?"

Keith joined in on Austin's ploy. "Fruits of *your* labor? Why Ma and me not only tended those apple trees, but we did the picking and the sorting, and the pressing, too. And you're saying the fruits of *your* labor?"

Everyone laughed, including Sally, but when the jug was passed to the men around the table, she turned her nose away as if finding the odor of fermented cider repugnant. Margaret, on the other hand gave a lingering sniff as Keith poured himself a glassful.

"I'd like to offer a toast to the newlyweds." Austin raised his glass. "May you always be as happy as you are this day, and may your lives be blessed with peace and tranquillity."

Carroll Moore frowned but said nothing as the men all stood and took long deep pulls from their glasses. After a brief pause McCaleb lifted his glass a second time. "May your days be filled with as much happiness as the good Lord will allow." Again, the men took strong pulls of the fiery liquid.

Malinda looked up at her new husband and abruptly tugged at Keith's sleeve. "Aren't these toasts meant for me, too?" she asked sweetly.

"Why sure they are Malinda." Keith grinned down at her through eyes that were beginning to look glassy.

"Then I reckon I'd better have a taste!" Malinda rose, reached for Keith's glass and lifted it to her lips. The remaining drops of liquid burned like a hot poker as they trickled down her throat, making her stomach lurch when they hit bottom. She'd no idea cider could burn that much, but her smile stayed in place as she set the glass down and hooked her hands on her hips. "There now!" she said. "That's a toast to the groom *and* his bride!"

The gathering erupted in laughter at Malinda's spirit, if not her good manners, each eyeing her with varying degrees of bewilderment and amusement. Margaret's smile of approval was tinged with envy. Here was a woman who would never stand in the shadow of any man. She wondered if Keith Blalock realized just how *much* of a woman he was getting.

CHAPTER 3

Malinda twisted the wide gold band round and round on her finger. Just think of it! Keith had ridden all the way to Lenoir to buy it for her. And paid a handsome price no doubt. She'd told him she didn't need a ring. Not yet anyway. She'd told him she'd be willing to wait till they were settled and able to put some money away. But he said he wanted everybody to know she belonged to him. Like as if there were so many other suitors knocking at her door. She stifled a giggle. Well, best Keith didn't know about Jesse Moore, and how he'd hung around like a cat waiting for milk. Her lips were sealed on that and she'd sworn Ma and Pa to keep it secret, too. Not that she'd ever in this world consider anybody but Keith. Surely not any of those town fellas Ma was so hot about. Besides, Jesse was only trying to court her because he knew she was Keith's girl—*WOMAN!* That Jesse was a treacherous one, all right!

Malinda shifted the corn husk pillow under her head thinking how it wasn't nearly as comfortable as her own goose down one back home. Grandma Whitehead had given it to her for her fifteenth birthday. But sleeping in a real bed instead of on a pallet was nice. More than nice. It was *WONDERFUL!* Especially with her man beside her. She turned to look at her sleeping husband just as a tree limb brushed the roof. Gentle as an angel's wing. Keith's hair was falling across his forehead so that it nearly covered his eyelids. Observing him secretly, she was filled with wonder at the depth of her feelings. How could she ever have been so lucky as to be the bride of Keith Blalock?

His eyelids were twitching. She'd heard somewhere that that meant a person was dreaming. Maybe he was dreaming about last night. Maybe he was remembering how they had made love most all night long until she had to beg for rest. Married loving was sure different from unmarried loving! Before they'd had to hide out, usually in the barn or woods, then forever be wondering if somebody would come by and catch them. Of necessity it had generally been quick, and kind of rough ... but nice, too. But last night! *Whew!* Last night was different all right. There wasn't a part of her body that hadn't been kissed, and stroked and satisfied. Over and over and over again. Ma was wrong about one thing. Not that she'd ever said much about love making, but she had said that when a man was full of whiskey—and that no doubt included cider as well—he couldn't perform like usual. That he'd lose his manliness. Well, that sure wasn't true of Keith!

Stealthily, so as not to wake him, Malinda crawled to her knees and pushed open the injun shutter above the bed. The first slim threads of light were stealing their way to the ridge, but a bank of rich dark clouds was fighting to hold them back. Didn't feel nearly so cold as yesterday. Nice having a real window to look out of. This house was almost twice the size of her cabin at home.

HOME! Oh Ma! Malinda turned her head away in case Keith should wake and catch her with her eyes full. I wish with all my heart you could love Keith even a smidgen as much as I do. She pushed the heels of her palms against her eyes and wiped away the wetness. Beside her, Keith was beginning to stir. When she was certain the tears were gone, she snuggled down beside him again. His eyes were still closed and his cheek laying against the pillow made the end of his mustache stick up almost to his eye. He looked kind of … gentle. Almost like a little boy wearing a fake mustache. Was this really the man who had ravished her last night? She stifled another giggle. Then taking the corner of the quilt between her fingers she rolled it to a peak, and ever so carefully reached out to tickle his nose.

She had almost reached her target when suddenly Keith's eyes snapped open and his hand grabbed her wrist.

"Caught you, didn't I?" he leered. "Don't you go trying to poke things at me, Mrs. Blalock, else I'll have to do some pokin' of my own." He wrestled the quilt from her hand and pulled it over their heads. Then his hand found her breast, fondled it until the nipple thrust upward like a red raspberry.

"Oh Keith, honey, not again," Malinda moaned. "You've got to give me a chance to heal up. I swear my privates are swollen shut."

He smiled down at her as he placed his hand between her legs and began stroking. Gently at first, then gaining in intensity. "I'll just see about that," he said huskily, and Malinda moaned again. Only this time it was different.

Afterward, Malinda lay back against the pillow. It was soaked with sweat, and her body was still feeling quivery. "If we keep this up I'll soon be in the same fix Ma's in." She looked over at him as he sat on the edge of the bed, his broad shoulders still heaving from exertion.

Keith turned and looked at her. "I hope we can wait a while for youngins. Everything's so uncertain now. I wouldn't want to leave you with a baby on the way while I'm off fighting somewhere."

The familiar spasm hit her stomach; the one that felt like a dulcimer string ready to snap. It happened every time he mentioned leaving, or even talked about the war. "I don't know why you keep saying you're going off to fight somewhere," she snapped, sounding harsher than she'd intended. "I've heard war talk all my life, and it doesn't mean anything. People talk about a war. But that's *all* they do. Talk!" She swallowed back the tears before they could rise again.

Keith reached over and patted her hand, then reached for his pants. "I hear Pa moving about. Guess I'd best get down there and see to the fire."

"I don't hear anything."

"Oh, you will. Any minute now. He starts out slow with his humming but before long he'll have the cocks a crowing." He reached over and tousled her hair. "I ... Malinda, I want you to tell me the truth. I didn't truly wear you out last night, did I? I didn't hurt you?"

"Of course you didn't hurt me. You made me happy." No sense in going on again about how her privates were a throbbing.

"That's one thing I'll always be aiming to do Malinda, is to make you happy." His face was suddenly serious. "If there ever comes a time when I'm not, I want you to tell me. That's real important."

Not trusting herself to speak, she merely nodded and caught his hand. Lifting it to her lips she kissed his fingertips. He bent and pressed his lips to her forehead, then pulled on his shirt and went down to the kitchen.

Malinda had feared she'd feel embarrassed around Mary and Austin since they knew what she and Keith had been up to all night, but somehow she didn't feel that way at all. Mary was just as sweet and easy to be with as always, and Austin, singing his head off like some happy spirited bird. He had to be the grandest man she'd ever met. Next to Keith. Pa never sang. Not even when Ma played her dulcimer. He didn't even whistle.

"Hey Pa," Keith looked up from his plate. "Tonight after supper maybe Malinda will keep you company in your singing. You know she plays the dulcimer real well."

"Now that's something I'll be looking forward to." Austin cleaned up the last of his egg with a twist of bread. "I always liked a dulcimer. Pretty as a harp. I reckon it beats a banjo or a fiddle anytime."

Malinda cleared the dishes from the table, then walked to the open window and peered up at The Grandfather. Although the view was different from here he was still the same; looking as if he was inviting you to come up and stroke his beard. Guess Ma was doing breakfast about now, too. Had she gotten the crying over with yet?

The image of her last hour at home danced through her mind. It had been awful leaving Ma standing there in the doorway looking like the end of the world had come ... tears running down her cheeks. And Ma was sure no crier. She hadn't cried since her last baby died, and that was near three years ago. Maybe they could go over there this afternoon. Do some patching. She'd ask Keith about that.

But as it turned out the day was too filled for visiting. After breakfast Keith said he wanted her to go with him and Austin when they went over to the new cabin. Always before Keith had said he didn't want her to see it until it was finished, but it was near enough ready now for her to make plans about linens and such.

Austin had given them a parcel of land at one corner of his property. It was around the bend, south toward Morganton. They were overjoyed with the gift, and as Keith put it, "It's just about perfect, except for one thing. It's within spitting distance of the Moore place." The Moore's house sat diagonally across the road and around the bend on a large spread surrounded by trees and a split rail fence.

Keith had been so secretive about the particulars of the new cabin she'd had no idea what to expect. When they rounded the bend and she saw for the first time what he had built for them, her breath caged in her chest. *Merciful heaven!* This was so much more than she could have *ever* imagined!

Fifty yards back from the road, nestled in a clearing between two banks of tall pines, stood the cutest little log cabin Malinda had ever seen. And wonder of wonders, there was a window with real glass, sort of ripply and tinted a soft shade of blue! There was no porch, but there was a kind of peaked little roof above the front door. The high roof was about half covered with pine shingles, the other half still bare frame. On the side where the stone chimney was reaching for the sky, and about twenty feet in front of the pines, was a thicket of mountain laurel. *Oh won't they be glorious in the Spring!* In back of the house the land rose sharply, its banks dense with pine, oak and chestnut. At the left, as though it had been put there to make things complete, a mountain stream tumbled down over stones of white granite and dark slate. *Dear heaven, our own waterfall!* "It looks like something from a picture book," she murmured finally, reaching for Keith's hand.

"Truth is, I got the idea for that little roof over the door out of the children's picture book Ma keeps on the shelf. The one we can't read 'cause it's written in German."

"What a wonderful idea, Keith! The best you ever had!"

"I'd have liked to make a regular porch, but we've got lots of shade from all the trees, and a porch does cut the light from coming in through the window—"

"Keith, a glass window! Just like in town. Only prettier. How did you ever—"

"The Moores have got one," he said firmly, "and I'm not to be outdone by a damned Confederate."

Malinda couldn't wait a moment longer. Lifting her skirts high she took off at a run toward the house; Keith a step behind her. When she reached the open doorway she stopped dead and looked around. Standing on the threshold behind her, Keith put his hands on her shoulders. "This will be the kitchen," he explained, "and over there's the bedroom. I'll put up a wall and a door later, but for now we can hang a curtain if you want … " He pushed passed her, then taking her hand, he pulled her along behind him.

"The ladder to the loft will go here. That's where the youngins will sleep when they're old enough. Pa and me will be finishing off the flooring in the loft and kitchen this afternoon if the weather holds, and maybe we'll get some more shingling done on the roof—which reminds me—"

Keith walked back to the door. "Pa? Did we bring the froe? I think we're going to need to cut some more shingles."

"Yeah, Will, we got it."

Turning again to Malinda, Keith opened his arms. "Well, Sweetheart, do you like it?"

This time as she ran to him she wasn't ashamed of the tears. They streamed over her cheekbones and dribbled from her chin. "What woman could ask for more?"

"Hey wait! You haven't seen this!" He took her hand and directed her toward the back of the house. "This is the root cellar." He pointed to a door set deep into a bed of rock and opening into a cavern below the cabin floor. "We'll put in a ladder and a trap door up to the kitchen so you won't have to go outside when it's cold. And out here," still dragging her behind him he rushed up a gentle incline, "is where we'll put our vegetable garden. I'll have to clear and terrace it of course, and then when we harvest we just carry the vegetables down here a few steps and ... "

"Oh Keith!" Malinda placed her hand across his lips to stay the onrush of words. "Don't say anything more. My poor heart can't hold it. I feel like heaven opened its doors and the angels are singing just for me."

Austin, who had remained on the road with the ox and dray, came toward them now, carrying the froe. "Son? While Malinda takes a look around and decides what she wants for curtains and all, we'd better get cuttin' on these shingles. I'm thinkin' it looks like snow."

"Sweetheart," Keith brushed her wet cheek with his lips. "You go on inside and do your measuring. Ma said she'd make up whatever you decide you want."

"But your folks have done so much for us already. The house, the wedding ..."

"Listen up, wife! This here is no ordinary family you got yourself married into. This is the best damned family in the whole state of North Carolina. And we do things right!" Grinning, he nudged her gently. "Now you tend to your woman thing while we men get to work."

Malinda spent most of the morning mentally arranging things. The pine table Keith was making would go here, and the rocking chair that was a wedding present from Margaret and her husband would go there. And they were going to bring over Keith's bed and set it up ... maybe here ... and the stove they hoped to find at auction next week would go there ...

At noon, Zinnia Moore made a surprise visit. She came carrying a kettle of hot chicken soup, a pan of fresh baked corn bread, and a basket of dishes. "I can't stay," she said, handing it all to Malinda, "but I want y'all to know I'm—we're mighty happy to have y'all for neighbors."

Malinda was touched by the act of neighborliness. No wonder Mary liked Zinnia. She was one good woman. Now if only their menfolk could see eye to eye ...

Zinnia insisted she couldn't stay because she had things to do at home, so Malinda spread the food out on the floor of the cabin and they all sat around it and warmed their bones with the hot soup.

After the meal Malinda took the dishes down to the stream and rinsed them off in the icy water. Good thing about the stream; she mused. No need to even dig a well.

Austin had been wrong about the weather. By one o'clock the sun began to splinter the gauze-like clouds, bringing not only light, but a degree of welcomed warmth as well. Malinda picked up the kettle, hooked the basket over her arm and headed up the road toward the Moore place.

Their neighbor's house was a large frame with two full stories. From its size, Malinda guessed it had at least one parlor. Maybe even two. The Moores were better off than most in the valley. Keith had told her that Carroll had inherited a goodly portion of it from his Pa. The glass window Keith had mentioned was on the left front side of the house. The second story had two shuttered windows at the front and one on the side, which meant there could be more than one room upstairs.

As Malinda drew nearer she saw a horse tied at the hitching post in front of the house, and two more poking their noses out of the barn. It appeared that all three of the Moore boys were at home. She felt certain the roan in the barn belonged to Jesse. And Jesse wasn't anybody she wanted to see. Never did like seeing him for that matter! For reasons she couldn't explain, Jesse always made her feel uncomfortable. Kind of crawly.

But ... there was no way around it, the dishes had to be returned. She took a deep breath, stuck out her chin and trudged ahead.

Zinnia opened the door as Malinda came through the front gate. "Thank you ever so much Mrs. Moore," Malinda called. "We really do appreciate you being so neighborly. The food was delicious." Malinda climbed the two steps to the porch and handed the kettle to Zinnia who was standing on the threshold. "Austin and my husband send you their thanks and appreciation, too."

"It's the least I—we could do." Frowning, Zinnia glanced over her shoulder as if fearful of being overheard. She was a rotund woman and her bulk filled the doorway.

Malinda was surprised at not being invited in, but at the same time relieved that she didn't have to linger. She handed Zinnia the basket and turned to go. "I'm sure we'll be seeing a lot more of each other as soon as we get moved in. Once we're settled we'll be having you over for supper."

Zinnia's gray eyebrows knitted together in a single line. "Well, yes ... yes we'll see. Y'all have a nice afternoon." She closed the door before Malinda was off the porch.

Now wasn't that the strangest thing! Friendly as a stray dog at noon and by two o'clock colder than a witch's broomstick!

* * *

Back at the house, Malinda and Mary began working out the details for curtains and other linens. By dusk Mary had stitched up several flour sacks for dish drying and cut out pieces of muslin to make a curtain for the window. Malinda couldn't help noticing how delicate Mary's stitches were. She had the patience of a true mountain woman, not like Ma who did her chores out of necessity, with very little pride in the results. The one thing Ma did do in a delicate way was play her dulcimer—and finger the china she'd inherited from Grandma Whitehead.

As light began to fade, Malinda lit the oil lamp and offered to prepare supper. "Why thank you," Mary smiled. "That'll give me time to finish up this curtain. There's a pot of turkey soup simmering on the stove. Maybe you could cut up some leftovers and make dumplings to spiffy it up."

Nervous, Malinda set about her task. This was the first meal she would prepare for her new husband and his family. *Oh, please Lord, let it come out right!*

Keith was jubilant when he and Austin returned shortly after dusk. Bursting in the door like a hard wind, he strode across the kitchen and grabbed Malinda by the waist. "Sweet wife, I am happy to announce your new home will be ready by sundown tomorrow." Scooping her up in his arms he spun her around like a rag doll. "McCaleb and two of his friends came by this afternoon and finished up the loft, so Pa and me got the best part of the roof shingled. Another day's work and we can start moving in."

"Oh Keith, I can hardly believe it!"

"To tell the truth neither could we! McCaleb's been none too friendly of late. And getting two of his Reb friends to pitch in was sure enough a surprise." Then putting his lips to her ear he whispered, "I worked myself so hard today you'll not get any use out of me tonight."

Lord that was sweet enough news! Maybe now she could catch up on her rest. She'd nearly fallen asleep over her stitching. Grinning up at him, she said, "If you want your supper you'd better unhand me so I can get it to the table."

Keith laughed and let her go, patting her rump as he put her down.

The meal turned out better than Malinda had hoped, and Mary complimented her on the dumplings. "Looks like your wife knows her way around a stew pot," Austin commented, giving Malinda a long wink.

"Well now Pa, you didn't think I married this woman for her looks, now did you?"

After the supper dishes were put away, Keith coaxed Malinda to bring out her dulcimer, and for more than an hour she accompanied Austin in one song after another. Keith hummed along and so did Mary as she bent over her stitching.

When the fire began to fade Malinda finally put her instrument aside.

"Awe, Sweetheart, play just one more. Please? That one your Ma always sings. The one she says comes down to her by way of Scotland."

"Oh yes dear, please do," Mary encouraged. "I so love the Scottish ballads." She laid her stitching aside, and went to the stove to prepare a bowl of scraps for the cat.

Malinda again picked up the dulcimer and began plucking out the tune, although her heart wasn't in it. The song reminded her too much of Ma ...

There was a fair lady in Scarboro did dwell
She was courted by a sailor, whom she loved full well
They were promised to marry when he did ret—"

"Oh Austin *LOOK!*" Mary stood in the open doorway, the bowl of scraps still in her hand. *"It's a fire!"*

Austin and Keith rushed to her side. "My God," Keith cried. "It's our cabin!"

For a moment Malinda was too stunned to react. She stared blankly at the gaping black hole into which Keith had just vanished—then heard him shout from the yard. *"Pa! Bring the musket!"*

Austin's hand was lifting the gun from its resting-place before Keith's words had left his lips. Then Austin too disappeared into the night.

For a moment longer Malinda stared gape-mouthed at the open doorway before leaping to her feet. "I need to go with them!" she cried. "Oh merciful heaven this can't be happening!" She grabbed her shawl from the peg and an empty bucket that had been left beside the door, and dashed out into the darkness.

☆

CHAPTER 4

The wood was green so the fire burned slowly at first. But once it generated enough heat the flames devoured the structure like a wild animal gorging prey. Keith rounded the bend in time to see the roof crash inward, sending fingers of flame leaping for the trees. He stood motionless. Helpless. Gasping. A second later when the exterior walls folded in on themselves his chin dropped to his chest and a shudder ran through his body.

How could this have happened? Had they left something behind that caused it? A lantern? An oil lamp? No! They left when the light began to fade. They hadn't used a lamp. Not once the entire day. And the fire he'd lit in the morning while Malinda was in the house had gone out by mid afternoon. The last thing he did before leaving was to check the fireplace.

He took a step backward, reeling from the heat, the flames sending contorted images dancing across his face. Along with the popping and crackling came sizzling noises that sounded like fireworks. This was coupled with an intermittent roar as the flames found something new to eat. It won't live long now, he thought, there isn't much more left to burn.

The noise from the fire outdistanced all other sound, and Keith failed to hear Austin as he approached. He jumped, startled, when his stepfather touched his shoulder. The older man, gasping hard for breath, was momentarily speechless. Keith stared at him with questioning eyes. "Pa!" he shouted above the cry of the flames, "I ... don't understand it."

Still struggling for breath, Austin shook his head.

Then as reality came into focus, Keith erupted like a cannon, a white hot rage ripping his gut. He shook a fist at the sky as he shrieked, *"Jesse Moore, you son-of-a-bitch! HE* did it, Pa! *JESSE!* I'm sure he did it! Who the hell else would do such a thing? This is no damned accident!" Keith grabbed the musket from Austin's hand. "I'm going to kill that bastard!"

"*WAIT!* Will, hold on a minute!" Austin's cry was barely audible as he still fought for breath. "You don't know for sure—"

"I know he's mean enough to do anything!" Keith yelled. "He lives across the road. If he's so fucking innocent why the hell ain't he out here? Why ain't any of 'em out here? If we could see the flames from our place, why couldn't they see 'em?" Gun in hand Keith started for the road.

"Son, *WAIT!*" Austin grabbed his arm, but Keith shook himself free.

"Let go Pa. Jesse's going to pay for th—Who's there?" Keith raised the gun as he sensed, rather than saw, a figure moving toward him from out of the shadows.

"Keith, it's me!" Malinda dropped the bucket and ran to him, arms outstretched. "Oh, Keith!"

He folded her to him. Stood between her and the flames. They held each other for a long moment, locked in despair. Finally, Malinda pulled away and peered around him. He felt her body tremble. "My God! . .Oh my God," she murmured.

Keith placed a protective arm around her shoulder as together they watched the flames. Momentarily, his rage gave way to grief. It was as if everything had dropped out of him. There was a vacuum in his stomach and he felt dizzy. His voice was barely audible as he vowed. "I'll build our home again, Malinda. So help me God I *will* build it again." Her face was upturned to his and he could see little flecks of black ash sprinkling her cheeks and hair. The pungent smell of charred wood permeated the night. As they stood mesmerized the flames began panting for breath. Within minutes only the stone chimney remained, a lone and stalwart sentinel amid the ruins.

"Hey! What's going on?"

Keith whirled to see Carroll Moore, wearing a night shirt and clutching his wife's shawl around him, come running out of the shadows. He carried a lighted lantern.

"My God!" Carroll cried. "What happened?"

Keith's mood swung like a weather vane. The white hot rage engulfed him once more. *"Your son-of-a-bitchin' son, Jesse, burned my house down. That's what happened!"* he shrieked. *"Where is he Carroll? I'm going to blow his fucking brains out!"* Keith lifted the musket and took two menacing steps toward Carroll.

The older man reacted with astonishment. Malinda fell back in dismay.

"Son!" Austin stepped between the two men. "There won't be any killin.' Everybody needs to calm down."

Keith nudged Austin's arm with the butt of the gun. "You'd best be taking Malinda on home now, Pa." He made an heroic effort to contain his anger. "There ain't any use in her being out here catching her death—or you either for that matter. You two go on back to the house. Carroll and me here, we've got some talking to do."

"I've got nothin' to say to you, you Yankee scum," Carroll growled. "You're goddamned crazy if you think Jesse had anythin' to do with this!"

"Think he couldn't have done it alone? Yeah, maybe you're right. Maybe your other two son-of-a-bitchin' boys helped him!"

"Keith?" Malinda wailed, "I think we ought—"

"Get on back home, Malinda! I'm not saying it another time! Pa? Take her back to the house. There's nothing to be done here anyway. It's over. Our home is gone."

Austin looked from Keith to Carroll, then put an arm around Malinda who was staring at her husband in disbelief. Absently, she reached for the fallen bucket, picked it up and handed it to Keith. "You may need this," she said. It was a pitiful gesture.

"Come on Malinda," Austin motioned her to him. "He's right. There's nothin' to be done here. We need to get on home. Mary will be anxious." He paused and looked deeply at Carroll, then nodded. "We'll be talkin' tomorrow, Carroll."

Austin took a step toward Keith, and in an almost casual gesture, reached for the gun. With equal casualness, Keith drew it backward out of his reach. The two men's eyes locked briefly, then Austin turned and guided Malinda toward the road.

Silent, jaw jutted, Keith watched them go. He now held the musket in both hands, pointing it at the ground. As Malinda and Austin faded into the night his gaze returned to Carroll. "I want to know where Jesse is. It's not my intent to hurt you Carroll, but I need to know where that noaccount son of yours is hiding out." His voice was raspy, his hands trembling.

Carroll looked at him with disgust. "I don't know how you come off sayin' Jesse is responsible for this. He ain't even home. All three of my boys went to Wilkesboro this afternoon. They're gonna spend the holiday with Zinnia's Ma. She's been poorly. Won't none of them be back till the day after Christmas."

"I don't fault you for covering for your son, Carroll. I'm just saying that both you and me know it's God's honest truth that Jesse had a hand in what's happened here. Maybe he didn't do it alone, but he *did* do it! And I intend to make him pay."

Carroll shook his head. "You goddamn hot headed Yankee! There's no tryin' to talk sense with you 'cause you ain't got none."

Keith ran his tongue over dry lips. Adrenaline was pumping so hard he could feel his own heartbeat. "You're talking mighty brave for a man whose only holding a lantern."

"I'm goin' home now, Keith. If you want to shoot an unarmed man in the back, that's up to you." Carroll turned and took two steps in the direction of the road.

"You want to go home, Carroll?" Keith's laugh bordered on hysteria. "Well, I'll just walk right along behind you. And no, I'm not about to shoot a man in the back—unless he gives me reason to, that is. You just walk on ahead and hold that lantern high, so we can both see where we're going."

They crossed the road in silence, Keith three paces behind, the musket pointing directly at Carroll's back.

As they neared the gate, Keith heard a horse whinny. The noise came from the barn. At that same moment the front door of the house opened and Zinnia stood on the lighted threshold. "Carroll?" she called, lifting an oil lamp. What's goin' on?"

"It's Keith Blalock, Zinnia. He wants to talk to Jesse. He thinks Jesse set fire to his house."

"*WHATTT?* But y'all know Jesse ain't home! You know Jesse's in Wilkesboro."

Carroll turned toward Keith. "Are you satisfied now?"

"I sure as hell am not satisfied!" Keith screeched. "You think I'm such a damn fool I can't see you already had your story cooked before the match was lit?" He spat on the ground. "Don't be an ass Carroll, 'cause you ain't dealing with one." Keith stepped from in back of the older man where he could be seen by the lantern light; still keeping the gun on Carroll.

"Mrs. Moore? This is Keith Blalock. I'm going to let Carroll come back in the house now while I take a look around. I need to see Jesse, and if he's in there it'll be best if you tell him to come on out. Are you hearing me?"

"Yes, Keith. I'm hearin' you all right. But y'all ain't gonna find Jesse around here tonight. He sure enough went over to Wilkesboro with his brothers this afternoon. And I'm awful sorry about your house."

"I thank you for that, Mrs. Moore." Keith nudged Carroll with the nose of the gun. "You go on inside now. I'm going out to the barn and count horses. If Jesse's roan is there, I'll be back."

"Listen you Yankee bastard, the only horse you'll find in that barn belongs to me!"

"Well, I don't imagine you'll mind me taking a look for myself then, now will you Carroll?" Lowering the gun, Keith began walking across the yard in the direction of the barn.

Keith's hatred of Jesse Moore went back a long way. As a child he'd been outnumbered three-to-one by the Moore boys. The taunts he'd received stung to this day. "Bastard Blalock," they'd called him; long before he had any idea what the word meant. He'd suffered terrible beatings at the hands of the three of them. Beatings that tore his skin and burned humiliation into his soul. There was one day in particular, a steamy, July afternoon, the summer he was seven. A day he would never forget …

* * *

Before he even sensed danger the three of them were on him—Ben, Cal and Jesse. They emerged from a thicket like a hound after a rabbit. They slugged him, kicked him and tied his hands behind his back. Ben, who was fourteen and lanky like his father, looped one end of the rope around Keith's neck while Jesse tied the other end around his ankles. Cal, the strongest of the three, yanked him to his feet.

"Run nigger, Run! Yer our slave now!"

But he couldn't run. He could only shuffle. When he fell, face down in the dirt, Jesse grabbed a tree limb and began beating him with it. At first he could hear the crack of the branch as it tore at his skin, and he could hear himself crying ... then ... the only sound was their laughter.

He came to when they stuck his head in the creek. He was lying face down, struggling to raise his face from the cold water, but one of them was sitting on his back and Jesse had his foot on the back of his head pushing his face into the water.

"Better not hold him under too long Jesse," Cal said. "He might drown."

"Let the bastard drown. No more'n what he deserves."

The water was black. Strength fading. Lungs bursting. He stopped struggling.

"Hey! What's goin' on here?"

"Run! Run! It's McCaleb!"

"My God, boy! Whata they done to ya?"

Out of the water. Coughing. Retching. Someone pounding his back.

Ma told him he'd been unconscious for a day and a half. McCaleb had come along just in the nick of time. Austin had gone to see Carroll and all three of the boys got lickings.

Lying in the bed, staring at the ceiling, he swore no one would ever do that to him again. When he was on his feet again he hung a gunnysack filled with potatoes from the tree out back and beat the livin' bejesus out of it with his fists for more than an hour every single day. Soon his knuckles were as callused as a horse's hoof. By the time he was ten people were starting to call him "Keith" after the prizefighter. At fifteen he had drummed Jesse's pimply face into the dirt so many times his nose was permanently misshapen. It looked more like a hot pepper than a nose. And nobody in the county was willing to take on Keith Blalock one-on-one.

* * *

Now, as Keith drew near the barn he heard a horse whinny nervously. He stopped, holding his breath; listening for other sounds. Nothing. Reassured, he stepped inside the arched opening; felt around for a lantern. The light cast faint glimmers into the empty stalls.

Carroll was telling the truth about the horses. The only one in the barn was his. Then where in the hell was Jesse? He wasn't buying the story about Wilkesboro—not for one minute. The son-of-a-bitch was probably hiding out somewhere laughing his pimply head off. "Well listen up little fucker," Keith muttered aloud. "You've had your last laugh on Keith Blalock. When I get my hands on you, you're going to wish to hell you'd never laid your hands on that match."

Keith started to lower the wick on the lantern. Paused. The dry straw had all the makings for a nice fire. He considered it a moment—and decided against it. Destroying the Moore's barn and killing a horse wasn't what he wanted. He wanted Jesse's balls, and by God, he was going to get 'em! As he walked back across the front yard he knew he was being watched. Carroll and Zinnia were no doubt peeking out through the cracks in the shutter. Who else but stinking Rebs would come to your wedding one day, fix a meal for you the next, and then hatch a plan to burn your house down?

He crossed the road and headed in the direction of the smoldering ruin. As he walked the grief he'd been blanketing finally surfaced. A sudden sob raked his chest as tears gushed down his cheeks. Groping, he found a stump and sat down. Resting the musket across his knees, he hunched his shoulders and cried. Cried like he hadn't cried since that day he was seven.

It was a long time before he was empty. He hadn't known he had that kind of grief inside him, nor could he remember ever feeling this kind of pain.

At last spent, he lifted his head and looked around, wiping his face on the back of his sleeve. By God he *would* build again! Nobody, especially not a Moore, was going to rob him of his home! Weary to his marrow, he picked himself up, along with the futile bucket Malinda had left, walked to the stream and filled it. Carrying the water back to the dying embers he dumped it and smoke spewed up like a gush from hell. Retracing his steps, he refilled the bucket again, and again, and again.

Finally, he felt cold. He shuddered once ... twice ... then dropped the bucket, picked up his gun, and headed for home.

A dozen steps away from the opening to what had been the root cellar, he slipped and nearly fell. Righting himself, he took two more steps, hesitated and turned. He lit a match and bent down to take a look. Then a slow, bitter smile crossed his lips. Horse shit. *FRESH* horse shit! He stood and waved out the match. The only animal they'd brought to the site was the ox, and he'd been left out on the road. This confirmed what he already knew in his gut was true. And the little son-of-a-bitch left his calling card.

Somehow he felt better.

CHAPTER 5

More than six hours after her labor began Elizabeth's body gave a final convulsion and expelled the child. Regina Blevins, a neighbor and a midwife, caught the squirming infant, lifted it by its heels with one hand and tapped it on the back with the other. The baby responded with a lusty cry. Regina Blevins heaved a sigh, and for the first time in several hours, almost smiled.

The delivery had been difficult, but not any more so than Elizabeth's other eight deliveries had been. This time, however, things looked a little brighter. The child appeared healthy, not scrawny and feeble like the others.

"Y'all got yourself a son, Elizabeth," Regina said, as she laid the child on his mother's stomach then picked up a butcher's knife and deftly cut the umbilical cord.

"A *boy?* I can't rightly believe it."

Over near the fireplace Alfred Pritchard stared with disbelieving eyes at his wife and newborn. His lips remained closed.

"Well you best believe it, 'cause he sure 'nuff has a manhood." Regina wiped the baby's face free of blood then wrapped him in a blanket and carried him to his father.

Alfred's face was ashen, his eyes puffy. His mind had been wracked from the hours of piercing screams, and at one point, he'd been sure his wife was going to die. Twice he'd ventured out into the frosty dawn to vomit. Now, scarcely able to believe it was over, he gazed in wonder at the bundle Regina placed in his arms.

"Keep his head up and keep him near the fire so's he'll stay warm," Regina instructed. "I need to get Elizabeth cleaned up. And for Lord's sake Alfred sit down. Y'all are shakin' so you'll likely drop him." Then the midwife returned to her patient's side and gave one final push on the tortured belly to make sure all the afterbirth had been expelled.

"He's … all right?" Elizabeth's eyes searched Regina's face for the slightest sign of a lie.

"As fine a babe as I've seen." Regina wiped her hands on her bloodied apron. "I'd say this child was full term, not early like them others."

Elizabeth struggled to sit up. "I want to see him. I didn't think it was possible we'd have a son. And a healthy one at that." Her voice was filled with wonder.

"Alfred, bring your son over here to his Ma so she can take a look at him before I get him cleaned up. But mind now, keep him covered good. It's drafty in here."

Obedient, Alfred carried the baby to Elizabeth, placing him in her arms. "Nine times, Lizzie," he said smiling, "and we finally got us a boy. Healthy one, too!" Glancing up at the midwife. "You think he looks healthy, don't you Regina?"

"Healthier than any of them others she's birthed, 'cept maybe Malinda. Looks like a fighter too. He'd a been here a lot sooner if his shoulder hadn't got stuck on his Ma's pelvis bone."

Solemnly, Alfred placed his hand on his wife's shoulder. "This won't happen to you again, Lizzie," he vowed. "I promise you no more child bearin'. It's over and done with. No matter what happens with this one."

Elizabeth examined the red-faced infant, counting fingers and toes; turning him over, she checked his back, the shape of his head. "Don't see any birthmarks. That's a good sign." Then she wrapped him up again, covering all but the tiny face. *Will God let you stay awhile?* The thought she'd carried for the last nine months surfaced once more. *Or will He lash out at me again? Rob me again? Dare I let myself love you?* But the child's breathing *is* steady, her mind argued, and his little hands *are* strong … As she nuzzled him to her the baby broke free of the confining blanket and thrust one tiny arm upward; batting the air as if waving to an unseen visitor.

Gently, Elizabeth kissed the fingertips, then tucked the little arm back inside the blanket. "I want to name him Jacob," she said. "It's a strong name, and he's a strong boy."

Alfred placed his hand on the baby's head. "Then Jacob it is," he said solemnly.

They heard the sound of a rider arriving in the dooryard. Alfred hurried to the window slit and pulled back the rawhide. "It's Malinda. I sent Regina's boy Billy to fetch her." He turned back to his wife. "Didn't seem right, her not bein' here. I thought she'd be some solace to you."

"Solace? *Malinda?"* Elizabeth almost chuckled.

"Are you distressed that I sent for her?"

Elizabeth managed a smile. "I reckon not. Time we did some mending, and this is as good a time as any.

* * *

It had been a torturous ride for Malinda, and not only because of the cold temperature. Concern over her Ma and the baby weighed heavy on her mind, as did wondering if her folks had forgiven her for running off the way she had. *Although Pa wouldn't have sent Billy to fetch me if they were still peeved. Would he? But what about Ma? Oh, please God let this be a happy occasion. Let this baby live and grow strong, and let Ma and Pa welcome me.*

The other tormenting thought centered on Keith and his threat to kill Jesse. Surely, that's all it was. A threat. He wouldn't do anything so crazy as that. But never in her life had she seen a human as angry as Keith was last night! Why had he immediately thought it was Jesse who set the fire? He hated Jesse, all right; had ever since they were boys. He'd never expanded on the reasons though. Except to say Jesse was a noaccount coward, and there was nothing Keith despised more than a coward.

She thought about the way he'd looked when he came home last night. As if he'd been crying. Eyes all swollen and red. But never in this world would Keith admit to crying. And of course she would die rather than ask. How many times had she heard him say, " … tears are for womenfolk; they're allowed to be weak on occasion." There were things you didn't question Keith Blalock about. And crying was one of them!

It had been hard leaving Keith in the state he was in—not for him so much as for her. She surely hadn't wanted to. But when Billy Blevins came riding up—poor child's chest puffing like an iron horse—there wasn't anything else she *could* do but go. She'd sort of stalled around waiting for a sign of Keith's intentions. He was acting so strange … almost as if he was relieved she would be gone for a day or two. That didn't seem natural. But there was no way of telling what was in Keith's mind. He did that sometimes. Shut himself away like a mud turtle in its shell.

No denying the fire was a set back. And a heartbreak. Their beautiful home and all those long hours of work that had gone into it—wasted. But it was only a building. Not like as if it was a dead child … Oh, please Lord, please let Ma's baby live! No woman should have to bury as many babies as she has. Why did God keep testing Ma's faith like He did? Taking her babies? And why me? Why was I the only one to survive? So far anyway.

This was not a new question in Malinda's mind. It had been there since she'd learned the family history and been old enough to understand. Ma's explanation was because Malinda was the seventh daughter and almost born on Christmas. A seventh daughter born on Christmas Day was supposed to have special powers. Well, she'd beat Christmas by a few days, but maybe it was close enough. Sometimes she did have that "knowing thing." Like Ma.

As Malinda dismounted, the front door opened and Pa rushed out toward her.

"It's a boy! You got a brother!" Alfred grabbed the reins looping them around the hitching post as Malinda reached for her saddlebag.

"How's Ma?"

"She's doing okay now. Tired though. The boy seems healthy. Breathing real good!"

Malinda lifted her skirts and darted for the house. There was no rancor coming from Pa, and that was a load off the heart! Maybe they'd gotten over the hurt. A boy! A healthy boy! It hardly seemed possible!

"Hurry in!" Alfred pushed open the door. "Gotta keep the house warm."

Malinda stepped into the darkened, familiar room. It smelled dank and pungent with blood. On the bed, Ma was sitting up holding a bundle in her arms. Her smile was the most tender Malinda could ever remember. She opened her mouth to say something when Regina Blevins startled her by stepping out of the shadows.

"It's nice to see y'all again, Malinda. I hear there's been a weddin'. Congratulations."

"Thank you Mrs. Blevins. And I want to thank you for allowing Billy to come fetch me. He sure is a fine young boy. I gave him a hot meal before he started back. He should be getting home about now; he left before I did."

"Malinda?" Elizabeth's voice was unexpectedly weak. "Come take a look at your brother."

Malinda hurried to the bedside and knelt on the rough floor. "I'm so happy for you Ma. Pa says he's healthy."

Elizabeth pulled the blanket away from the baby's face. "I'm almost afraid to hope," she murmured. "Here take a look and tell me what you think." Gingerly, she handed the tiny bundle to Malinda.

"Oh dear me," Malinda whispered, a strange and unexpected wash of warmth flooding over her. "Oh how darling you are." The tiny face puckered, then relaxed into what resembled a smile. "You truly are an angel, aren't you!" she cooed.

"We need to get him back by the fire." Regina's large frame appeared at the bedside. "It's chilly in here."

Reluctantly, Malinda handed the baby over to the midwife who carried him to the cradle beside the hearth.

"It's good Mrs. Blevins could come to help. I'm sorry I didn't get here in time. Things ... well ... things were kind of busy you might say this morning." Malinda touched her mother's cheek with her palm. "You look weary, Ma. Did you have a hard time?"

Elizabeth rolled her eyes upward. "I can't honestly say I didn't. But Alfred promised there'll be no more youngins. And I'm thinking he's right. I'm getting too old for this. It isn't so bad when you're young and strong, but when you get old like me, it takes a toll on a woman."

"Oh, Ma, you aren't old. You haven't reached forty yet."

"I will in April. God willing. And forty's too old to be bearing young." She reached up and gently touched Malinda's hair. "You're cold, Child. You should warm yourself by the fire."

"I'm fine, Ma. Truly. I just want to stay here beside you awhile and know that you're all right." She bowed her head into the mattress, shaming herself with tears. "Ma, I can't tell you how happy I am about the baby. And that you're both all right. What will you name him?"

"Jacob. We've named him Jacob."

"I'm so thankful. Not just for little Jacob, but for you not being mad at me anymore. It's pained me so, knowing you were angry with me."

"Malinda, I'm not going to tell you that I think what you've done is right. I don't. And I'm not going to say that defying Pa and me the way you did was right either. It near broke my heart. But children do that to their parents, and you learn to take it. You take it because you love them. It's your life, Malinda, and you've made up your mind. And your bed. I only ask that your husband be good to you; that he keeps that temper of his in check, and does you no harm."

"You're right Ma. About Keith having a temper. There's no denying that. But with me, and with his Ma too, he's gentle as a kitten. It's like there's two people inside him; the gentle, and the ... the angry." She wiped the damp hair back from Elizabeth's forehead. "Keith's a strong man, Ma. In more ways than one. And maybe that's good. I need a strong man because I'm no pussy cat myself." She smiled down at her mother. "He's a man I can lean on, Ma. And he's wise. Now he isn't perfect by a long shot," she lowered her voice, "but then what man is?"

"Well," Elizabeth said, a twinkle lighting her eye. "I'm thinking maybe Jacob is just about perfect. And he'll be a man someday."

* * *

While Elizabeth dozed, Malinda sat by her brother's cradle, gently rocking him as he slept. Regina Blevins had left instructions regarding the baby's care: "Keep him warm, put a speck of alcohol or whisky on the umbilical cord, and if he should stop breathing put your mouth over his and breath hard into him to get his lungs movin' again."

Then while Pa saddled the horse, Regina had packed up her things, which included a quarter side of beef in payment for her work, and they rode out the front gate. Malinda watched them go, Regina's gray hair whipping behind her like a giant spider web, one powerful arm around Pa's waist and the other holding for dear life to the side of beef.

Later when the baby awoke and began to fret, Malinda picked up Elizabeth's dulcimer, and rocking the cradle with her foot, quietly strummed a song she remembered from her childhood.

Oh Father, oh Father, go build me a boat
That on this great ocean I may afloat
And hailing great ships as they do pass by
Inquiring for my prentice boy bye-and-a-bye
Crying, 'Captain, oh Captain, please tell me true
Does my sweet Willie be asailing with you?

"Malinda?" Elizabeth pulled herself up on one elbow. "Are you all right, Child?"

Malinda was instantly on her feet. "Yes, Ma. I just dozed for a minute. Can I get you someth—"

"The baby's fussing. I'm sure he's hungry."

"Oh, of course." Malinda picked up the wiggling child, tightening the blanket about him and nuzzling him tenderly as she carried him to the bed.

Elizabeth put the baby to her breast, helped him find the nipple, then winced as he eagerly did so. "Nothing weak about him," she laughed.

Malinda sat on the edge of the bed, smiling as she watched the baby suckle. "I sure am looking forward to the day when I can have one of my own. Maybe before too long I'll—"

"Malinda," Elizabeth interrupted. "I don't think it would be a good idea for you to have a child now. Bearing them is only the beginning. Bringing them up is a lot harder than you think. With things so uncertain— the war coming and all. These are dangerous times, Malinda. I'd hate to see you having to raise a child alone, while Keith's gone off to war."

"Ma!" Malinda leaped to her feet. "That isn't going to happen! Keith isn't going off to war because there isn't going to be any old war. If people would just stop talking about it; stop spewing hateful words over things that doesn't matter to anybody—" She broke off, consciously stifling the rush of anger begging for release.

"Malinda," Elizabeth's voice was gentle. "The world can't be the way you want it to be, just because you want it so much. Maybe I've made mistakes by encouraging your dreams. Reality, is sometimes very different from what we want … or even expect. But when it's handed to us we have to take it all the same."

"I know, Ma, I know." The combative glint began to fade from Malinda's eyes, and she sighed deeply. "Riding over here today I was telling myself that very thing, and I keep telling myself there are some things I can't control. Most times I can accept that, but this talk about a danged war gets me so riled. That's all I've heard all my life; the war, the war, and nothing has ever come of it. And I don't want you thinking for a minute that Keith will be leaving me—because he won't! I … oh let's not talk about it. You've got a baby to feed and I've got a supper to cook."

* * *

Malinda busied herself with setting the table and preparing a meal, and gradually the anger melted. She decided to stay the night to make sure Ma could manage, then she would head home tomorrow. Home. She'd been born in this cabin; lived here all her life, yet now, home and heart were in another place. How swiftly things changed.

She knew there was no keeping what had happened back in Coffey Gap a secret. News spread through the mountains as quickly as the fire had spread through their home. Nor had she actually intended to keep it from her folks, but finding a way to explain it was difficult. Married twenty-four hours and your house burns down. Not a good omen. And Ma, bless her, and sometimes even Pa, put a lot of stock in omens. Well, just spitting it out was no doubt the best way.

The problem, however, was taken out of Malinda's hands. When Alfred returned from taking Regina Blevins home he had already heard the story from Billy. The boy met someone along the road who'd told him about the fire at the Blalock place. Fortunately, Malinda mused, Jesse's name hadn't been mentioned. She fended her parents' questions as best she could, explaining that the cause of the fire was still a mystery, and that Keith and Austin would do some investigating and everyone would know the full story real soon.

That night, bedding down on the familiar pallet in the loft, visions of the fire and Keith's raging voice filled her dreams. She saw Jesse's face, bruised and bloodied, and Keith standing over him, laughing. Twice she awoke, and twice she fell back to sleep only to return to the same dream.

Malinda was up early the next morning, fixing breakfast, and tidying the cabin. She boiled water and washed the baby's diapers, then carried the soiled bed linen down to the icy stream and washed away the blood stains. Back at the cabin she boiled these linens too, and hung them out in the yard to dry. After lunch she prepared a rabbit stew for her parent's supper, and when she was convinced there was nothing more to be done, she kissed Ma and the baby, hugged Pa, and headed home.

The promised snow was soft and feathery. It lay gently on Malinda's shawl, making glistening pools of white in the folds of her dark skirt. By midnight the mountains would be bedded in a deep quilt. As she approached the main road she spurred her mount to a trot. It was Christmas Eve and she wanted to be home before dark. Besides, her spirit would know no peace until she was with Keith again. Safe in his arms.

CHAPTER 6

Keith sat alone in front of the fire; his parents had gone to bed right after supper. He could hear Austin's intermittent snores and the muted cough of his mother as she tried to muffle the sound in her pillow. Every time Keith thought about her illness his blood began to boil. That damned Doc Petersen refused to treat her, saying there was nothing more he could do. He hadn't done piddly shit for her anyway. Just gave her some cough syrup. The real reason for the neglect was because they were Unionist and the Doc was a stinking Reb. That seemed to be the dividing line on everything these days. Including people's lives.

The candles on the Christmas tree were out now. Ma had lighted them just before supper. Didn't seem right, Malinda not being here to see it though. Well, there were a few stubs left. Maybe they could light them tomorrow. If she was home by then. He was surprised at how much he'd missed her. Seemed as if part of himself was missing.

Keith had returned to the cabin site only briefly after Malinda left. There was no reason to poke further; Jesse wasn't stupid enough to leave clues laying around. He chuckled. Only his horse was. He looked at the cider jug still sitting on the table. Maybe he'd have a mite more. Maybe another swig would help put the snake to sleep—the snake inside his belly. The snake named Jesse.

If there was even a thread of truth to what Zinnia and Carroll had said—and it was beginning to look like there might be—the Moore boys ought to be showing their hides the day after tomorrow.

Keith drained the glass and stretched his legs. He was tired. No wonder Pa had tucked it in early, he'd ridden as far as Keith had—most of yesterday, all last night, and all today—and with no luck. They'd searched every rock and ravine of the mountain, every cave and deserted cabin, and not a trace of Jesse.

It was possible Carroll and Zinnia didn't know what Jesse'd been up to. Possible, but not likely. But then you couldn't dismiss the idea that the boys could have left home in the afternoon, told their parents they were heading for their grandmother's place, then hung around till dark, done their deed, and then gone on to Wilkesboro. Could be too, that Jesse had acted alone. It wasn't like a fight. Jesse didn't need help starting a fire.

Pa was still saying he didn't think Jesse had done it. Mainly, because he couldn't figure out a reason. There was a lot Pa didn't know about Jesse. The little son-of-a-bitch didn't need an excuse to be mean. He just was.

He'd never told Pa about the rotten things Jesse was saying—not only about him, but about Ma, too. It was shameful enough for him to hear it. No sense in shaming Pa as well.

The cider was just beginning to talk to the snake when Keith heard the sound of an approaching rider. He glanced at the clock: 6:57. Peering out the window he saw a mounted figure entering the dooryard. Malinda. Instantly, the warm urge rose within. Sometimes just hearing her laugh could do that to him. He opened the door and rushed out into the snow. "Sweetheart! I was hoping you'd get here tonight, but I wasn't really expecting you till at least tomorrow."

"I wasn't going to be away from my husband on Christmas Eve," she said breathlessly.

Keith helped her from her mount, kissing her hungrily as she came into his arms. "Go on in and warm yourself," he said huskily. "I'll take care of the horse." He grabbed the reins. "How's your Ma doing?"

"She's fine. I'll tell you all about it inside."

"Oh! Best be quiet, my folks are sleeping."

"Already? What time is it?"

"About seven, but they were both dogged. Ma's not been feeling so good and Pa and I were—well, I'll tell you about that later. Now you go on in and get yourself warm."

By the time Keith had unsaddled the horse and rubbed him down, Malinda had changed from her wet clothes into her flannel nightdress. She was drying her hair before the fire when he came in, the light behind her outlining the gentle curves of her body. He lowered the wooden bolt on the door. Shutting out the world. "Well? Tell me what's happened."

"Everybody's fine." Malinda's face was luminous. "It's a boy! Can you believe it? She named him Jacob. It's an honest to goodness miracle, Keith! And he seems so strong. Regina Blevins was there to help out, and she says he's healthy as a horse."

Keith took the brush from her hand and began brushing her hair. "I'm pleased things worked out all right. Healthy you say?" Her tresses felt like silk in his callused hands.

"Appears to be." Malinda let her head fall backward, and looked up into his eyes. "It took me longer than I thought it would to get home. I left before supper. Wonder if I might have a bite to eat? My stomach thinks my throat's been cut."

Keith leaned over and kissed her, their lips meeting upside down. It was different than they'd ever kissed before. Again, there was the rising stiffness. "Ma fixed a piece of pork for supper. There's some left and it'll be good cold."

"Sounds wonderful!"

As Malinda ate, he watched her carefully. Even tired and hungry she was a delight to the eyes. "Did your folks have anything to say about our wedding?"

"Not much." Holding the pork rib in her fingers she took a big hungry bite before continuing. "Ma chided me a mite, but ended up saying she only wanted me to be happy—and ... "

"And what?"

Swallowing hard. "And that she hoped you wouldn't let your temper turn against me."

Keith threw his head back and laughed. "Your Ma thinks I'm a woman beater, does she?"

"Now Keith, I never said that. Stop making up things. Ma doesn't think you're a woman beater. She just knows you've got a powerful temper and sometimes you've been known to get into scraps. That's all."

Wincing. "Sometimes? Why I find my reputation to be outstanding! I'll have to talk to her about that. I should let her know that her daughter is married to the hardest fighting man in these mountains."

Malinda gave a rueful nod. "Oh, I think she already knows that."

They talked a little more before heading upstairs to bed, but it wasn't until after the lovemaking that Malinda broached what was really on her mind. "You haven't said anything about the fire. Or Jesse."

"There's nothing to say. The little Reb weasel is hiding out somewhere. But he'll be back. He'll have to come home to his Momma one day. And I'll be waiting for him when he does." He held a strand of her hair between his fingers. Toying with it. "Then your Ma will no doubt hear what a brute her son-in-law really is!

"What did your folks say when you told them about the fire?" Twisting the strand around his finger.

"I didn't have to tell them. Somebody told Billy Blevins as he was riding home, and Billy told Pa. Actually, my folks didn't say much. But you know how superstitious Ma can be. I'm sure she thinks it's a sign."

"The only sign is the one I'm going to carve in Jesse's hide," Keith smirked. "If I decide not to kill him, that is."

* * *

An hour after Keith was asleep Malinda lay owl-eyed, listening to the murmurs of the night. The peace she had so looked forward to during the long ride home, was not to be. There didn't seem to be any way around it. Trouble was a brewing. But what would Keith actually do to Jesse once he found him? That ... was what she didn't know. Maybe even Keith didn't know. She wondered what Ma would say if she knew what was going on? *"Let it go, Malinda. It's a man's business, and nothing a woman is supposed to deal with."*

"Yeah, Ma. I suppose you're right," Malinda whispered into the stillness. Then she let out a wrenching sigh and snuggled up to Keith's back. Draping one arm around his middle, an unexpected smile touched her lips. In the last three days there'd been a wedding, a baby and a fire! Life with Keith Blalock sure wasn't dull. No doubt about that! But hadn't she known it would be like this? Life filled with excitement? She fell asleep with the soft smile still playing at her lips.

* * *

Keith was up long before the sun, rising quietly so as not to wake Malinda. His mouth was dry, his body cold, but he was too intent on his mission to take time to either drink or make a fire. Silently, he pulled on his brogans, put on his coatee, gathered up his musket, lariat, and Bowie knife, and slipped out the door.

The air was frigid, the snow almost six inches deep. Unfortunately the wind was picking up. If it got much stronger it would be hard to track prints. Outside the gate he turned left and cut across the brambles and ditch until he reached the road. The moon was peeking through the scurrying clouds, offering narrow shafts of light. Somewhere a wolf howled. Keith lowered his head against the wind, tugged reassuringly at his musket strap, making sure to stay close to the edge of the road. Jesse wasn't the only one who could leave tracks in the snow.

Once around the bend Keith trudged another eighth of a mile before seeing the dark outline of the Moore homestead. The house was in shadows, but moonlight was shinning directly onto the open entrance of the barn. He left the road and hopped the rail fence that bordered the pasture, picking his way through the bank of trees and tall laurel bushes that lined the fence. As he edged up on the back side of the barn the wolf howled again. Inside, a horse snorted. And then a second time. One horse or two? There was no fury in him now. Only giddy anticipation. He paused a moment before jumping the fence that separated the pasture from the barnyard. Then keeping to the downwind side of the building, back against the barn wall, he edged his way toward the front. The moon was still lighting the clearing near the entrance.

Holding his musket with both hands Keith took a deep breath and stepped out of the safety of the shadows. The wind had drifted the snow, erasing most of the tracks. Only a few remained, but it appeared that more than one horse had made them.

With one swift motion he was inside the barn. A horse neighed, sensing a foreign presence. And then another. Definitely *TWO* horses! He groped his way past the first empty stall, and from the light sifting through slits in the wall he could make out Carroll's horse in the second. The frightened animal pawed the ground, and Keith gave him a reassuring pat to the flank.

On the opposite wall, another horse snorted. Keith edged toward him, hoping for enough light. The nervous animal stomped and pulled at his tether. Keith slipped into the stall beside him, touching the animal's neck and head.

He was wet and cold. A blanket had been thrown over him, but he hadn't been rubbed down. Only Jesse would do that to a horse. Keith raised the blanket and from the muted light, he saw the markings of Jesse's roan.

There came a sudden shout from the house. "Who's out there? What's goin' on?"

Carroll.

Another voice. "What is it Pa?"

JESSE!

The wind gusted and the wolf cried again. The horses responded with neighs of fright. Keith slipped out of the stall and dashed for the inside wall near the entrance. He waited; musket at the ready.

Through a slit in the boards he could see the outline of a figure on the porch, then a lantern light blazed and he saw that it was Carroll.

From inside the house, Jesse called again. "It's only a wolf, Pa."

"I dunno. Could be. I'll check it out. You get yourself to bed."

"Hang on, I'll do it. I've still got my pants on, and you're in your nightshirt."

"All right. But here. Take the lantern."

"Keep it. I'll use the one in the barn." Jesse stepped out onto the porch, pulling on his coatee.

Keith saw him hook his musket over his arm and begin heading in his direction. *Come on little Jesse. Walk right over here to Keith and get what's coming to you.* Quickly, Keith looped his gun over his shoulder and crept silently up the ladder to the loft. He removed his lariat from his belt, made a noose and tied the other end of the rope around an overhead beam. Then he crawled to the edge of the loft, noose in hand, and waited.

"Carroll?" Zinnia's voice.

"Go back to bed. Jesse's takin' care of it."

The wind abruptly died and there was only the crunch of approaching footsteps in the snow. Nearer they came. And nearer. Abruptly, they stopped at the entrance. Keith held his breath. He could see Jesse clearly now. Musket raised. Alert. Listening.

Two more steps little fucker. Come on … just two more steps … come on now. Come to—

Keith dropped the noose. It fell over Jesse's head and landed on his shoulders. Keith yanked, tightening the rope around Jesse's neck. Jesse dropped the gun as his feet left the ground. His legs kicked frantically. His airway shut off, he made no sound, but he managed to grab the rope above his head and relieve some of the pressure on his neck. Keith pulled him upward with two mighty yanks on the rope and dropped him onto the floor of the loft. Clawing at the noose, Jesse hooked his spurs into the floor; fighting for leverage, twisting and writhing in an effort to get air.

Keith bent over him, lips inches from Jesse's face, Bowie pressed to his victim's throat. "Don't even think about making a noise," he whispered, "or you won't have to worry about choking 'cause I'll cut your fucking throat."

Fighting to stay conscious, Jesse managed to wedge his thumbs inside the noose, loosening it enough to get a gasp of air. Keith stood up and loosened the rope from the overhead beam. Jesse struggled to his feet, thumbs still inside the noose.

"Now we're going down that ladder and we're going to do it real quiet like," Keith instructed. "If you make a sound, you're a dead man."

Obediently, Jesse groped for the top rung of the ladder with one hand, keeping the fingers of the other wedged inside the noose. He descended slowly, while above, Keith held the rope tight in his hand.

"Son?" Carroll's gravely voice boomed through the night.

At the bottom of the ladder Jesse stopped and waited. "Now take two steps to the right," Keith ordered. "Put your hands behind you. Do it now, Jesse."

His prisoner obeyed without hesitation, and Keith tied the end of the rope around Jesse's wrists, tightening the length between neck and hands. The only way Jesse could ease the tension on his neck was to tilt his head backward and lift his bound hands behind him.

"Now we're going to make it look as if everything out here is just fine and dandy," Keith said softly. "I'm going to light a lantern and you're going to call to your Pa and tell him everything is okay. Do you understand me, Jesse?"

A frenzied nod.

Keith reached for the lantern on a shelf beside the entrance, lit it, then turned and again put his face inches from the eyes of his prey. He gave a tug on the rope. "Now tell your Pa everything's all right."

Jesse lifted his arms and opened his mouth but no words came. His eyes grew to the size of boiled eggs and he shook his head, gasping.

Keith's jaw thrust forward as he grabbed Jesse's arms and pulled them upward in back of him until they were nearly wrenched from their sockets. "Speak, goddamnit!"

"It's all right, Pa," Jesse shrieked. "Go back to bed. It's all right!"

Keith lowered his victim's arms and Jesse slumped to the floor moaning.

"Now we'll just give it a minute and see if your Pa's smart enough to do what he's told." Keith peered through the slit. The lantern was still burning on the porch. "Go back in the house Carroll," Keith muttered. "I don't want to hurt you. It's your son here I've got to settle the hash with." But as he watched, the lantern moved, and Carroll stepped off the porch, carrying the light high in his left hand, a musket in his right.

Keith motioned Jesse against the wall. "Get over there and be as still as death. I won't hurt him if you keep your mouth shut." To insure his orders were carried out, he gave another tug to the rope, then crouched down beside the open entrance. Waiting. Again the wind died. And again the only sound was of footsteps on the snow. Keith sunk to his haunches, and with both hands held his musket steady six inches from the ground.

Carroll's view was eye level as he entered the barn. Keith thrust the gun barrel forward and Carroll stumbled over it, pitching forward on his face. His firearm discharged into the air, the lantern skidded along the floor landing in a pile of hay. Keith was instantly on him, swinging the butt of his musket into the back of Carroll's head. The older man twitched once, then lay still. Keith looked at the terror stricken Jesse still crouched against the wall. "Get on your feet," he ordered. "We're out of here."

At that moment there was an indistinguishable shout from the house, and the sound of a shutter banging open. The horses were pawing at their stalls now; trying to rear on their hind legs. Keith turned to where the lantern had landed and saw flames lapping the wall of the barn. He made a dash for the stalls and untied the horses. The animals reared, then ran screaming from the barn. One hoof barely missed Carroll's inert form. Keith grabbed the unconscious man by the heels and pulled him outside into the clearing.

Back in the barn Jesse was making a fruitless dash for freedom. Laughing, Keith grabbed the rope trailing behind him and tugged, pulling him away from the entrance and back into the shadows as Zinnia came running across the yard.

"Carroll! *Carroll!*" Reaching the still body of her husband, Zinnia collapsed over him, sobbing. The rising wind whipped at her shawl.

Keith, his prisoner in tow, slipped unnoticed from the barn and escaped into the darkness. At the rail fence, Keith vaulted it easily, then grabbed Jesse by the shoulders and pulled him over after him. Jesse landed face down in the snow; quickly struggled to his feet, his arms raised in back of him, head tilted backward. His tongue lolled hideously from his open mouth.

"Walk ahead," Keith commanded. "We're heading for the road."

Desperate, Jesse trudged through the rocky, gutted pasture. Unable to see where he was going he lifted his feet high in order to keep from stumbling. They had gone a bare twenty yards when Jesse encountered a huge rock and went sprawling.

Mercilessly, Keith yanked on the rope, again cutting off his prisoner's air supply. Too weak to rise to his feet Jesse plunged forward on his knees.

"That's more like it," Keith taunted. "You look more like the dog you are when you're leashed and crawling on the ground."

Behind them the crackle of the burning barn was coupled with Zinnia's wails. Keith felt a tantalizing sensation of power; a rush shooting through his body that was almost sensual. "Sounds like your Ma's upset about her barn burning down. Wonder how she'd feel if it was her house?" Keith paused and looked back. The flames were licking through the roof. "Take a look Jesse. Second fire this week. Sort of an epidemic, wouldn't you say?" He tugged and Jesse toppled over onto his side. "Now we know how this fire got started, don't we?" Keith prodded Jesse with his boot. "Your Pa got careless with a lantern. But there's still sort of a mystery about that other fire. You know the one I mean. My cabin. The one I just finished building. The one that was vacant and didn't have any lamps or lanterns in it. Or kerosene. Yet somehow it caught fire. Strange, wouldn't you say? Now Jesse, you're reasonably intelligent for a dog. How do you suppose that fire got started? You got any ideas?" Keith's voice was as hard as granite.

Looking up from the ground, Jesse raised his arms behind him so he could speak. "I don't know nothin' about your cabin. I swear to God I didn't set it on fire. I didn't know about it till I got home and Pa told me what had happened."

"You are a lying, yellow cur, son-of-a-bitch!" Keith shrieked. "Get on your fucking feet, we're going across the road to where my home used to be, and that's where I'm gonna kill you." Grabbing Jesse's shoulder he yanked him to his feet, and shoved him forward. "Now get over that fence or I'll kill you right here."

The moon frolicked with the clouds as the two men made their way across the ribboned road and trudged through the open field to the cabin site.

Keith laid his musket against a stump and pulled his Bowie from its sheath. Jesse watched with tormented eyes. "Don't do it!" he screamed. "Please don't do it!"

"Shut your fucking mouth," Keith railed, and reaching in back of his prisoner he cut the rope linking his neck to his wrists. Next, he sliced the knots holding Jesse's hands together. Then he put the knife to Jesse's throat, and leaned close. "Hanging's too good for you. And so is slicing your fucking Reb throat. I'm going to do it MY way. A little at a time. And I'm going to enjoy every second of it."

Keith lifted the noose over Jesse's head and tossed it to the ground. "Now I'll even give you a minute to get your breath, and then right here in the ruins of my home, I'm going to pound your worthless brains out. Real slow like."

Jesse's chest heaved. His eyes darted around the shadowed periphery, sizing up his chances for escape. Keith moved back a few paces, took off his coatee, folded it, bent over and laid it neatly on the stump. He came up swinging, connected with a powerful right to Jesse's jaw that sent him reeling as three teeth spewed from his mouth amid a stream of blood.

The beating was slow and methodical. Each time Jesse went down, Keith waited patiently for him to regain his footing before knocking him down again. As he pounded away the moon danced above the trees, offering glimpses of the progression of his work.

Jesse's eyes were soon swollen shut; his attempts at connecting blows mere tokens of defiance because he could no longer see. Keith bounced from side to side, taunting the blind man with calls of, "Come on you Rebel cur. Pretend you're a man for once in your life."

Jesse swung wildly as Keith ducked to the side, and called again. "This way little fucker. Over here."

Jesse swung again aimlessly; this time his arm dropping to his side before the thrust was even completed. He stood for a moment more, tottering, then fell to his bruised and bleeding knees; raking sobs wrenching his body.

Keith stood above him, glaring with a hatred so deep his gut seemed to catch fire. "Now I want to hear it! I want to hear you say you burned my house down. I want to hear you confess. And I want you to tell me if your brothers had anything to do with it."

A shake of the head.

"Say it, damn you! *Say it!"* Keith roared. "Say you burned my house down! Say it or so help me I'll kill you before you take another breath!"

Jesse's chin sunk to his chest, his body crumpled until his forehead touched the snow covered earth. "My brothers had nothin' to do with it," he gasped. "I did it. I did it because I hate your fuckin' guts, and I wish to hell you'd been inside when it burned!"

"And where the shit were you hiding out? We covered every inch of this mountain."

Jesse wheezed.

"Tell me goddamit! Tell me or I'll cut your lying tongue out of your mouth!"

"In back of Austin's barn mostly. I figured you'd never look there."

The little son-of-a-bitch was right. They hadn't looked there. Keith raised his boot and gave a hard kick to the chin.

Jesse tumbled backward, unconscious before he hit the ground. Keith stood over him, breathing hard, savoring victory. Then he looked across the road. The barn was nearly gone now. Lucky for the Moores the winds were blowing away from the house.

He saw Zinnia, pools of white whirling about her, dragging Carroll across the snow by his feet. Maybe the old buzzard wasn't dead after all. Probably best. No sense killing a man because his son is rotten. Keith looked down at Jesse's still body. He studied him a moment then bent down and grabbed him under the arms. He dragged him to a spot near the root cellar, rolled him over and pushed his face into the horse manure. Then placing his boot on the back of Jesse's head he applied pressure. "Wallow in it you little son-of-a-bitch," he muttered. "It's where you belong." Keith was sweating from exertion. He wiped his sleeve across his forehead. "Merry Christmas little fucker. You got your present. I'm letting you live. This time."

The wind had stilled as Keith made his way back to where he'd left his coatee and gun. He picked them up, and headed home. The knuckles of both his hands were torn and bleeding, but he scarcely noticed. Within him there was a feeling of satisfaction. A sense of peace. At least for the moment.

CHAPTER 7

Malinda sat upright in bed staring blankly at the window. She held the corner of the brown woolen blanket between her fingers, twisting it around and around and around. Paralyzed with fear. She'd heard the shot … watched the panorama of color; black to purple to shades of red, yellow and orange. The colors were gone now. The sky was gray. It was fire of course. She could smell the charred wood. She had heard the shriek of frightened animals; the drum of hoofs. It must have been hours ago when she'd heard Austin shuffling about in the kitchen. But he didn't go out. She would have heard the door squeak if he had.

How long had she been sitting here wanting to run with no place to go? Where was Keith? Why hadn't he come home? Was he still alive? Who had fired the shot? Desperate to know she'd tried forcing the "knowing thing," closing her eyes and concentrating. Trying to find Keith's face. But it wouldn't come. It never worked that way. It came when it wanted; unbidden. And so she waited. Cold. Empty. Twisting the blanket.

How much time had passed? Impossible to tell. Then … she heard the door open; heard the sound of the musket being settled into its place on the wall; heard the shuffle of feet across the puncheon floor. She held her breath. A moment later there was the creak of a footstep on the ladder. She shuddered. Then Keith's head appeared. Only his outline was visible, the light too dim to read his face.

"Merry Christmas Sweetheart," he whispered softly. "I'm sorry I woke you."

"Keith?" she croaked.

Then he was at her side, taking her in his arms. "Sweetheart, you're freezing." He tucked the blanket around her. "Here, get back under the covers until I can get a fire going."

She grabbed his shoulders as he lowered her back into the bed. "Where have you been? What's happened? Please! *Please!* I need to know!"

"Sweetheart, there's no reason to get upset. I've been taking care of business. Now you just lay here and—"

"TELL ME!" She no longer cared if she woke the others. "I need to know what happened! Did you … did you ki—find Jesse?"

Keith sighed as he leaned over and lit the bedside lamp. "It's all taken care of, Malinda. The score's settled. There's nothing for you to be concerned about."

"N … n..nothing for me to be concerned about?" She pushed back the covers and hopped to her knees. "I want to know where you've been and if Jesse is … Did you kill Jesse?"

"Noooo, I didn't kill Jesse." Keith ran his fingers through his hair, and when he turned toward her his eyes were ugly. "Least ways he was alive when I left him. It's a man's business, Malinda. It's not for you to concern yourself with. I gave the little fucker a fighting chance before I beat him into kingdom come. It was nothing more than he deserved. He admitted to setting the fire."

"I heard a shot."

"That was Carroll's gun."

"He shot at you?"

"No. His gun misfired."

"I saw flames." Why was she having such a hard time getting her breath?

"Carroll dropped a lantern and the barn caught fire. I pulled him out."

Malinda felt her body go limp; felt as if she might vomit. The room began to sway. She opened her mouth but found no words.

Again, Keith laid her back against the pillow, tucking her in. "I'm going down and start the fire," he said firmly. "It's over, and there'll be no more talk about it. I'll tell Pa, and that's the end of it." He rose and headed for the ladder. Without turning around he added, "I need you on my side, Malinda. You're my wife, and I'll not have you taking up sides against me."

Still fighting the black wave, she could only nod. Exhausted, she closed her eyes, longing for a peace she sensed might never come.

* * *

Downstairs, Austin was fully dressed and waiting for Keith. For a long moment neither man spoke, their eyes poking at each other. Then Austin broke the silence. "I take it things are settled now."

"Yes, Pa, it's settled." Briefly, Keith explained what had occurred.

Austin had only one question. "Are they still alive?"

"I'm not sure. Probably so. I reckon I hit Carroll pretty hard, and Jesse … well …"

Austin pulled on his blue coatee and walked to the door. His steps were as deliberate as his words. "You see to your Ma, and if she asks where I am tell her I'm out in the barn. I'm going over to the Moore place. We need to know what shape things are in."

"There's no need for that."

Austin's gaze was stern as he reached for the door latch. "I waited while you settled your score. It wasn't easy but I knew you'd do whatever needed doin.' Carroll used to be a friend of mine and he's still my neighbor. I want to know if he's alive or dead." With that Austin opened the door and bent his head into the whirling wind.

Austin's concern over the state of his neighbor's health was more self serving than he had admitted. If Carroll and Jesse were alive it might be possible to get things straightened out, but if one of them was dead that opened up another set of problems. One that had a direct bearing on the welfare of his own family.

Jesse's brothers wouldn't hold still for a killing, and the Moore clan was a big one. Every one of them a Reb. If somebody had died a lot of people would be out to defend their kin. A great deal hung in the balance over what might—or might not—be settled this cold Christmas morning.

Austin knew, and to some degree understood, the hatred between his son and Jesse. He knew how Jesse and his brothers had tormented Keith with taunts about Mary. Although it didn't give him pleasure to know his son had the reputation of being the bully of the county, he'd often wondered how he might feel if Keith hadn't defended Mary the way he did.

Carroll had tried to do his duty as a father, tried to straighten out his boys, and to some degree it appeared Ben and Cal had learned their lesson. But Jesse. Now Jesse was another case. His hatred of Keith went so deep there wasn't a whipping in the world that could beat it out of him. Neither from his Pa or from Keith. No matter how many times Keith pummeled him, he always came back for more. If there was a word deeper than hatred, that was what Keith and Jesse had for one another.

As Austin plowed onward, his thoughts gyrated like the swirling snow, settling on a time years before when he'd overheard a conversation between the Moores. It was early Autumn and the boys were out in the field harvesting corn.

* * *

The air was filled with the redolence of fresh fallen leaves and the crisping of wild flowers. As Austin came to retrieve a cow that had wandered off he overheard voices. The corn was so high his presence went unnoticed.

"Maybe we can jump him when he goes out to haul the wood I seen him cuttin' up a couple a days back. I heard his Pa say he had to get it to the woodshed right soon." It was Jesse's voice.

"Jesse, I done told you we ain't gonna be layin' for Bastard Blalock no more. If'n he comes after you, that's different, but Pa's threatenin' to kick Cal and me both outta the house and not give us a piece of land when we marry if we go after him one more time. And Pa means it. Cal and mes of an age where we need to be thinkin' about such things."

"That's right, Ben! You don't give a damn about me! You don't give a shit if that Yankee bastard pounds me into the dirt, now do ya?"

"You're talkin' stupid, Jesse. But I reckon it's about time you start learnin' to defend yourself. Cal and me ain't always gonna be around to do your fightin' for you."

"And just how the hell am I supposed to defend myself against Bastard Blalock? He's stronger than a fuckin' bull. Got muscles on him like they was made from iron."

"Oh for chrissakes, Jesse," Cal intervened. "Stop your whinin.' If you did a little more work around here instead of always playin' sick, you'd have muscles, too. You got Ma believin' you're plum puny. And that you ain't! You're just plum lazy."

"Stop pickin' on me, Cal!" Jesse spat. "Lest I'll be tellin' Ma."

"Listen up, Jesse," Ben broke in. "We both know you're pissed off at Blalock 'cause of Suzanne Sheets. She's been all lovey dovey over him, and you got an eye on her for yourself. Now go on, admit it."

"You shut the fuck up, Ben. I don't give a shit about Suzanne Sheets. She's nothin' but a no good whore anyways. I know she's been lettin' that Yankee bastard poke her, and after what she said to me, I wouldn't put mine in hers if she was the only female on the face of this earth!"

"Whadda she say?"

"She made fun a my clothes. 'Cause they're hand-me-downs from you and Cal, and then she said ... she said she'd never kiss nobody with pimples, 'cause she might *catch* somethin'! She's a no good little piece of shit, and I don't care nothin' about her at all!"

"The trouble with you Jesse is you're jealous of Bastard Blalock!"

"You shut the fuck up, Cal. You shut the fuck up right now! I ain't neither jealous! Who the hell would be jealous of a piece of shit who ain't got no real Pa, and a whore for a mother?"

"And whose tall and strong and doesn't have pimples and is pokin' Suzanne Shee-"

"THAT'S ENOUGH!" Austin pushed through the cornstalks with his walking cane and faced the three of them down with one blazing glare.

Without his having to say another word they ran off like the devil was at their heels.

* * *

The events of that day hadn't crossed Austin's mind a half dozen times in a dozen years. Jealousy was a heavy burden to carry. Heavy for any man. Eats away at you like a dog gnawing a bone. He'd learned that lesson a long time ago when he and Mary were first married. And he'd gotten past it. Too bad Jesse Moore never had.

Austin saw a light in the front window as he neared the Moore place. Out back, there was only an occasional wisp of black smoke rising from the charred patch of earth where the barn had stood, but the wind still carried the acrid smell of burnt wood and hay.

Two horses were huddled against an oak in the side yard. Austin recognized them as belonging to Carroll and Jesse. It looked as if Ben and Cal weren't home. That was good. He was too tired for a fight … and too darned old.

As Austin's foot hit the porch the door flew open and Zinnia stood on the threshold, a raised musket in her hands. He found himself staring straight down the barrel as she screamed hysterically. "Y'all come back to finish the work your bastard son didn't get done?"

Austin could feel the blood drain from his face. In all the years he'd known Zinnia, he'd never seen her in such a state. "Zinnia, I mean no harm. I've come to see how things are with Carroll and Jesse. Keith told me what happened. I'm sorry about your barn. Really sorry."

"SORRY? That bastard half killed my husband, and I don't know from minute to minute if Jesse's alive or dead. He ain't got his senses, and his head's swolled up near the size of a watermelon. His knee's shattered and an arm's broke. I found him crawlin' in the road more dead than alive, and I like to died myself gettin' him in the house. And now y'all come askin' how things *IS?"* She lowered the musket poking the muzzle into Austin's chest. "When my other boys get home they'll be payin' y'all a visit, I reckon. And I figure there's gonna be a hangin' party for Keith." She pushed the musket harder against Austin's chest and he took a step backward, raising one hand in a sign of peace.

"Zinnia, please. I'm not here to cause more trouble. There's been enough of that already. Is there anything I can do to help you?"

She stared at him a moment, glassy-eyed, then lowering the musket until it pointed at the porch floor, she burst into tears. "I don't know what to do. Carroll just lays there moanin,' and Jesse ain't even moved at all."

"Can I come in, and see if there's something I can do?"

Zinnia bent her head to one side and bit her lips into a thin line. "All right," she sobbed. "Come ahead. There's nothin' more y'all can do to us. Our barn's gone. So's the horses … "

"The horses are down by the oak tree," Austin said. "Now let me see Carroll."

Zinnia nodded toward the parlor. "He's in there." She closed the door behind him with one hand while holding the musket with the other.

Carroll lay on a serpentine-back sofa, one heel resting on its curved back, his head supported by two pillows. His nightshirt, visible above the blanket, was splattered with blood. The kerchief that encased his head was soaked with it.

When Austin entered the room Carroll blinked at him in disbelief, but an instant later his eyes blazed to life. Raising a menacing hand he gestured to his wife who stood in the doorway. "Get this Yankee scum out of my house or else shoot him. One or t'other."

"Carroll, maybe he can do somethin' for you. Or Jesse."

"Zinnia can use some help," Austin interjected. "And I'm offering it."

"We don't need your damned Yankee help!" Carroll raised his head from the pillow as if wanting to lunge, but quickly fell backward. "Keith burnt our barn down and near killed Jesse and me both. We don't need your goddamned help!"

"Keith didn't burn your barn, Carroll. It was an accident. You tripped over the musket, and dropped the lantern." Austin was forcing his voice to remain steady, but there was a weariness in him that went to the bone.

"Is that what the lyin' bastard told you?" Carroll sneered. "Well, it ain't true, but that's no surprise. The truth ain't in him! He damned near bashed my brains out. Did he tell you that? Then after he knocked me senseless he set fire to my barn and near killed Jesse. Did he tell ya that? He's a crazy Yankee bastard, and you're no damned better. Now get outta my house or so help me God I'll kill ya." He reached toward Zinnia. "Hand me that gun!"

"Carroll, *NO!*" Zinnia drew back, clutching the gun to her breast like a prize. "Austin you'd best go. If you'll fetch Doc Petersen, I'd— "

"ZINNIA!" Carroll bellowed.

"All right, I'll go." Austin moved toward the door. At best Carroll was an unreasonable man. Wounded he was a maniac. "I'll fetch Doc Petersen."

In the yard Austin paused long enough to tie the horse's reins around the oak tree. It would be awhile before Zinnia would have the presence of mind to see to them.

Austin's steps were leaden as he headed for home. Each one heavier than the one before. No use wondering when a war between the states is going to erupt, he mused bitterly, there's a clan war to be dealt with right here and now. Once blood was spilled on one side, there would be no rest until blood was spilled on the other. It was the creed of the mountains.

Austin felt an emptiness in his stomach that had nothing to do with hunger. It was regret—coupled with fear. With all the trouble there was between he and his brothers, he wondered if he could depend on them now? Would they rally to his side—or Carroll's? He'd no doubt know the answer to that question soon enough.

Mary and Malinda were preparing breakfast when Austin returned. There was a hush over the house, a heaviness of spirit. He felt it the minute he opened the door. He kissed his wife and said "good morning" to Malinda, then took Keith aside where they couldn't be overheard.

"You stay here with the women in case more trouble erupts. I'm going to fetch Doc Petersen. Things over there are more than Zinnia can handle. When Ben and Cal get back and word of this spreads, we'll be in for a time of it. There's no doubt about that. Carroll will probably pull through, but Jesse may not make it, and if he doesn't ... well ... you know what that means."

"I don't agree with you getting help for Jesse, Pa. Let the little fucker die. It's no more than he deserves. I should've finished him off when I had the chance."

"If Jesse dies, you go to jail. More than likely you'd get hung before you got there. I back you up on what you did, Son. You're right, he deserved it. If he dies that'll leave more fresh air for decent men to breathe. But he's got kin that don't see it that way. My goin' for a doctor is the human thing to do. Even in war you help the wounded."

Austin turned, making sure his wife couldn't see what he was doing, and quietly opened the top drawer of the bureau. Withdrawing a shooting iron he stuffed it inside his overalls before turning around. "The musket's loaded of course, and you know where the ammunition is. I think you'd better have it ready."

With that, Austin kissed Mary on the cheek. "I don't have time for breakfast," he said. "I'm riding into town to fetch Doc Petersen. It appears Jesse got his face rearranged again." He said it jauntily in an effort to lighten his wife's concern, but one look at her face and he knew he'd failed. Austin began his mission with a feeling of deep apprehension. There was no joy in this Christmas morning.

Behind him, the shuttered window was left open and the door ajar, and three sets of eyes were trained on the gently falling snow. Keith, Malinda and Mary all watched for an emerging figure. But none came. No enemy. No friend. No family. Six times Keith took the musket and went outside; searched the barn and woodshed. Even the pig sty. Christmas dinner was eaten in almost total silence. No one suggested, or even thought about, music.

PART TWO

THE GROWING SEASON

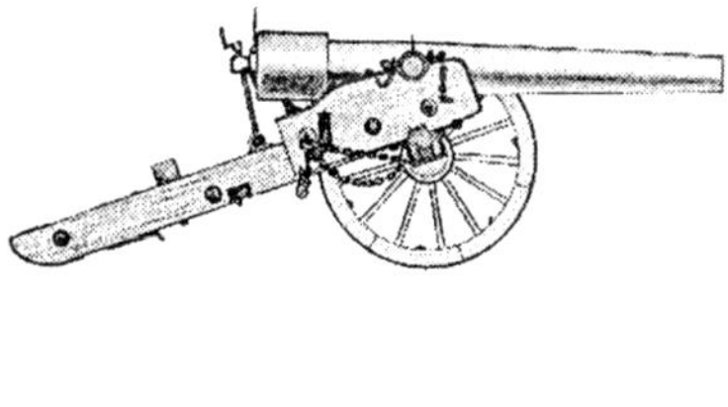

Caldwell County, North Carolina

March 1862

☆

CHAPTER 8

Malinda lifted the lid on the stew pot and took an educated sniff as she poked at the chicken with a wooden spoon. You're sure a spindly little critter, she mused. Another ten minutes and you'll be done. Hope there's enough of you to go around. She glanced again at the window. Land Sakes! Where *are* they? Ma's letter said they'd be here by noon. It isn't like them to be late. Could they have run afoul of the Moores? she wondered.

The war with the neighbors had quieted some since the other war had started—the war she thought would never come—the war everyone else said would last a month and was more than a year old now. Once South Carolina seceded and things really got heated up, Ben and Cal Moore had rushed off to join the Confederacy. Folks said it nearly broke Zinnia's heart. But she still had Jesse at home. And Carroll. They had both survived that terrible night two years ago, though Jesse never had healed right. The few times Malinda had seen him, once eye-to-eye in the General Store, his face looked like it had been run over by a plow. He had a bad arm, too. But like Keith said, "You can't kill the Devil!"

My! What a terrible time that had been! All the while Keith and Austin were rebuilding their cabin, she'd had to sit on a stump in the yard with a musket in her lap. She'd fired a few warning shots, never hitting anybody, but then she'd never intended to. Keith kept telling her to take better aim. He wouldn't have cared if she'd blown a few heads off, but she just pretended to be a poor shot. Which was a long way from the truth, and Keith knew it. What a sorry state of affairs, shooting at your neighbors!

Keith had insisted that the new cabin be exactly like the first one. Down to the tiniest detail. And it was. But the joy wasn't built into it this time. She could tell. It was all work, and hurry up and get it finished, and grumbling when things went wrong.

During that first year, there'd scarcely been a night that somebody wasn't shooting at somebody else. Sleep was something you did in shifts. It was nothing short of a miracle that no one got killed. Austin was winged once in the left forearm, but it turned out to be only a flesh wound. Then they stole his mare. That was when Keith got hold of two of Carroll's cows and butchered them. They'd had a good lot a meat that first winter!

From Malinda's point of view the whole thing had turned into more of a scrap than anything else, but all the tension had taken its toll on Mary. She'd mourned the loss of Zinnia's friendship like you'd mourn the dead. Her weight had dropped until she was nothing but a bag of bones and the cough was a lot worse.

The truly awful thing about the fight with the Moores was the way Austin's brothers had acted. William and Reuben, even McCaleb, sided with Carroll. They chose to believe Carroll's story about Keith setting his barn on fire on purpose, and they didn't believe that Jesse had set fire to their cabin either. Well, there wasn't anything you could do about what people carried inside their heads, and at least the brothers never did any harm to Austin's property, or to theirs. But! They never came around either. Keith said the one time he and Austin ran into Sally and McCaleb in Morganton, McCaleb had been real cold. Barely spoke to Austin, and didn't speak to Keith at all. Of course, Sally never spoke to anybody Union after the war started. Two of their three boys were fighting with the Confederacy up in Virginia. It had hurt Austin though, McCaleb turning on him like that. He'd expected it from the other two, but not McCaleb. Keith said he didn't give a good damn one way or the other, so long as his uncles kept their distance, and didn't get mixed up in the trouble.

Malinda smoothed back the wisp of hair that kept falling about her face; tucked it behind her ear. There was a biting March chill outdoors, but the heat from the stove was making the room uncomfortably warm. She opened the front door to let in some cool air. This was the ugliest part of the year. Nothing greening yet, and bits of snow still caught in the dark patches where the sun didn't touch. The beaten clay path leading up to the door was gutted with frozen pools of gray ice, and even the mountain laurel out front looked dejected.

Malinda paused in her wondering and looked up at The Grandfather. He was still snoring away with his arms folded across his chest. Sometimes the whine of the wind through the pines made it sound as if he really was snoring. And his toes still pointed to heaven. It was comforting to know that *something* never changed. No matter what the season The Grandfather was always the same. And he would always be there. Even a hundred years from now.

Malinda closed the door and looked around the room. Everything was in place. She was anxious to show off the changes they'd made since her folk's last visit. Which was right after Christmas.

Keith had put up a wall, separating the bedroom from the main room, and he'd made a second terrace out back on the mountain so they could plant several more rows of corn and maybe some squash and sugar beets. Last winter they'd nearly run out and had to skimp to get through. Keith said he planned to set up some of that new fencing stuff they called barbed wire that was supposed to keep the deer and critters away. Of course she hadn't told Keith, but when things got so bad last winter, she'd felt sorry for the poor starving animals and put some sugar beets out for them. That's why they'd run short. Keith would have sure had a fit if he'd known about that one!

Malinda's eyes rested on the mantle clock, the one Ma had given them. Nearly one o'clock. Her gaze traveled to the book lying beside it; Nathaniel Hawthorne's, *The House of Seven Gables*. She'd found it a few weeks back at the General Store and talked the proprietor into swapping him her copy of *Jane Eyre* for it. She'd found it so interesting she wanted to give it to Ma to read. Keith hadn't liked it though.

Malinda was suddenly conscious of the loud tick of the clock. Maybe they *had* run into trouble. But Keith said the main roads were fairly safe. Busy enough, that was for sure. Reb soldiers running back and forth like an army of ants! Ever since Fort Henry fell to the Union last month it seemed things had been in more of an uproar than usual. When you considered it though, the presence of the soldiers did afford some semblance of protection. Even if they were noaccount Rebs.

She turned as she heard Keith come in through the back door. His face was flushed from exertion. As always, just looking at him brought a smile to her lips. Unconsciously, her hand moved to cover her stomach, and she wondered again if this time she might truly be pregnant. She was three to four—could even be five days late now. But then that had happened a couple of times before. Best not to dwell on it and get her hopes up.

"I'm going to wait another week or two until the ground thaws some," Keith said. "No sense breaking my back trying to turn it when Mother Nature'll soften it up for me." He dropped wearily into the chair beside the stove.

"No sign of your folks yet? I figured they'd be here by now."

Malinda wiped her hands on her apron, and tried to still the small seeds of worry—then hearing the pound of horse's hooves she drew a sigh of relief. "They're here!" she cried, and hurried outside to greet them.

* * *

Malinda preened as her folks admired Keith's latest improvements to the house. It had taken time, but they really did seem to like him better now. Especially Pa. Whenever they got together they always talked politics. That was one good thing that had come out of this miserable war. Instead of people being so independent and distant, everybody chose up sides and supported each other. About the only "neutral" Malinda could think of was Austin's sister Margaret and her husband, Zechariah. Of course, they didn't have any youngins to send off to do the fighting either, and Zechariah was too old to be called up.

"Sissy, play wiff me?" Jacob reached up imploringly.

Malinda put the hot pan back on the stove and picked him up. "Sissy can't play now, Jacob," she said, nuzzling his neck until he squealed. "I have to get your food on the table. I stewed you a chicken and it's got dumplings in it. And we've got mashed potatoes—"

"You make cookie for Jacob?"

"Yes, darlin'. Sissy made you some gingerbread cookies. You can take them home with you."

"I want cookie now."

"Not till after you eat your chicken, then you can have a cookie." Malinda lowered the child to the floor, and he toddled off in search of more instant pleasures.

"His chest seems cleared up, but he does look a trifle wan," Malinda said, returning to the stove.

Elizabeth shook her head. "He's better now, but for awhile there we thought we might lose him."

"Ma! You've got to stop thinking like that. Jacob is basically a healthy boy. He's not puny like the others you lost."

"I know. I know." Elizabeth heaved a sigh. "But you have no idea what it's like hearing him choke and wheeze and struggle for breath."

"He's fine now. So stop worrying."

As expected, the minute the blessing was over, table conversation turned to the latest events in the war. Doesn't anyone ever talk about anything else? Malinda thought bitterly. If there wasn't any damned war would everybody suddenly turn mute?

"Lizzie and me, we been wonderin' what your plans are, Keith?" Alfred spooned another dumpling out of the bowl and plopped it onto his plate. "Zeb Vance's Rough and Ready Company is looking for volunteers, and we hear they're after anybody strong enough to hold a gun. How much longer you think you can hold out?"

"More potatoes, Ma?" Malinda offered the bowl.

"Not much longer I'm afraid," Keith replied. "I was hoping this damned mess would be over by now, but it doesn't look like there's any end in sight. And the Rebs keep talking Conscription. I've got a plan though whereas I may be able to put on a Union uniform instead of a Reb one."

Plan? Union uniform? Malinda's stomach dropped to her toes.

Elizabeth shook her head. "No thank you dear, no more potatoes for me."

Malinda turned to Jacob. "Eat your meat like a big boy and Sissy will give you that gingerbread cookie she promised you."

"Mind sharin' it with us?" Pa was still fishing. "Lizzie and me, we're pretty concerned about what'll happen to Malinda once you're gone off." He cut the dumpling in two and shoved half of it into his mouth. "From what we've been seein' around our parts, some of the womenfolk are havin' a hard time of it with no man to do the plowin' and plantin'." A piece of chicken found its way into Alfred's beard, nestling near his lower lip. "Over in Boone, Lila Sheets' homestead's been raided twice. The damn Reb soldiers took her pig and cow, and then if the Unionists didn't drop by and take all her chickens. The poor woman's got no crops and no livestock now. And no man to protect her."

Keith shook his head. "Is she Reb or Union?"

"Her man's fighting for the Union," Elizabeth responded. "But it doesn't matter which side you're on, these people aren't anything more than thieves, if you ask me. We don't want to see Malinda suffering through anything like that."

"Here now Jacob," Malinda raised a spoonful of potatoes to the boy's lips. "One more bite and Sissy will get you the cookie."

"I got hold of the Richmond paper last week," Elizabeth continued. "That Confederate Treasury Secretary Memminger is warning Jeff Davis to stop printing notes to raise money. And did you know inflation has been going up 12% a month! Can you believe that? Why it said flour is selling for eighty-five dollars a sack in Richmond! For once city folks are having it harder than we are. Poor souls. They've got no food, and no money to buy it with if there was any."

"Here you go, Jacob! Here's your cookie!" Malinda untied the baby from his chair, placed the cookie firmly in his hand and lowered him to the floor. "Ma, would you like some more apple juice?"

"No thanks."

"How about coffee?" The knot in Malinda's stomach was tightening.

Out of the distance came an ominous roll of thunder. It rumbled through the valley, bouncing from one mountain to another. Malinda rose on the pretense of checking on Jacob.

"You don't have to be worrying about Malinda," Keith said, casting a reassuring smile in her direction. "She can pretty much take care of herself. Besides my Pa's just up the road and he'll be watching out for her."

Malinda returned Keith's smile with glassy eyes. Whatever was he talking about? She knew he was being pressured to join the Rebs. Everybody was after him, not only neighbors, but merchants and townspeople, too. Reb recruiters had been by last week, and Glory Be, even the parson! But what was this about having a plan to take care of her? He wouldn't actually leave, would he? Walk out that door and leave her behind?

Jacob waddled up to Malinda and raised his hands. "Cookie? Cookie?" he pleaded.

"You just had a cookie," she snapped.

Elizabeth looked up with surprise, belatedly aware of her daughter's discomfort. "If everyone's finished I'll clear the dishes," she said softly.

"I'm thinking that if I have to, I'll join the Rebs and bide my time till there's a battle," Keith continued. "Then afterwards when everything's still confused and all, I'll just hop myself over to the Union lines. I've heard about others who've done it."

"Yeah, I've heard them stories, too," Alfred said. "But here in this community you're surrounded by Rebs, except for John Boyd and a couple of others. How do you think the rest of these people are goin' to treat Malinda once you've run off and joined the Union?"

The crash of thunder drew nearer and Keith reached for the jug of cider; poured a glass for Alfred and another for himself. "I guess I didn't explain myself clearly," he said. "I'm hoping to have the Rebs think I've been killed. That way they won't be looking for me. I could leave a bloody shirt or something with my identification on it behind so they'd think I'd died a hero for the Confederacy. Folks here will be nicer to Malinda, when they think I died to save slavery!" Keith lifted his glass and laughed loudly as Malinda lit an oil lamp and placed it on the table.

As soon as Keith's glass was empty he refilled it, and Alfred's as well.

"Ma," Malinda whispered, as the two bent over the dry sink. "I'm thinking maybe you should spend the night and get a fresh start in the morning. You'll never outrun this storm."

At that moment thunder again crashed overhead, this time causing the house to rattle. A flash of lightning lit the darkened sky.

"I think you're right," Elizabeth said. "We'll be staying the night."

* * *

The following day dawned bright; the air gloriously fresh and clean. Alfred and Elizabeth left immediately after breakfast and Keith was relieved to see them go. It wasn't that he didn't like the Pritchards, he didn't have strong feelings one way or the other—although he did have to admit the sting of the wedding boycott was still with him. That rejection rang bells from childhood. Bells he didn't want to hear. Oh, Alfred was all right, he supposed. Weak though. Always seeming to be bested by his wife. And Elizabeth all the time flaunting how she reads so many books and newspapers. It was a good thing he and Malinda didn't have that problem. Playing second fiddle to a woman was something he just wouldn't tolerate. Not that they hadn't had their share of problems, Malinda always wanting to get inside his head, while he was trying to keep her happy and still have some thoughts to himself. Folks were right when they said married life isn't easy. But Lord a mercy, whenever he thought about leaving her and going off to fight some noaccount war, he got a pain in his heart that almost threatened to burst it. How could he get through a day without her sweet presence beside him?

* * *

Keith was bending over the pig sty and looked up to see his wife coming toward him. She seemed in a hurry, and she was wearing her pink dress, his favorite, but it wasn't the same one she'd had on at breakfast. For Malinda to change clothes in a single day was rare. "What's going on, Sweetheart?" he called.

"Keith!" As she drew nearer, he could see her cheeks were crimson, and her voice had a breathless quality. "I'm … I'm thinking we need to go over to your folks place."

"Why's that?"

Malinda raised her shoulders in an exaggerated shrug. "I don't rightly know. It's a feeling. But it's strong, and I truly do think we need to be getting over there. We haven't seen them in nearly two weeks, and … I've just got this feeling something isn't right."

Keith dumped the last bit of food into the pig trough, opened the gate and closed it securely behind him. "I reckon we can do that," he said. "Guess maybe it has been a spell since we've seen my folks."

* * *

It was mid morning by the time they arrived at Keith's parents' home. Austin's face was haggard when he opened the door. "Mary's in bed," he said softly. "She's been there five days. Her strength's going. And that damned, hacking cough gives her no rest. She only sleeps a few minutes at a time."

"Has Doc been by to see her?" Keith asked.

"That no good Reb bastard won't look at anybody who isn't wearing gray!" Austin's face flamed. "If his own wife was dyin' he'd throw a mule blanket on her before he'd give her a look!"

"I'll fix some tea," Malinda offered, and went outside to pump water into the iron pot.

Keith and Austin sat down at the long pine table as Austin pulled out his pipe; stuffed tobacco into it and lit it. "Doesn't seem to bother her anymore," he said, sadly. "Time was when she'd complain to heaven about the smoke." He looked at Keith with a level stare. "I don't think your Ma's goin' to be with us much longer, Will. She's …" He coughed nervously. "She's wore out."

Beads of sweat broke out on Keith's forehead as he fought the sweep of panic flowing through him. "Ma's a fighter. She always has been. She'll rally." From out of nowhere he was aware of the cow mooing in the pasture, the chickens clucking in the dooryard. The sounds of life.

"Pa?" Keith lowered his voice so Malinda wouldn't overhear. "There's something I have to ask you. I know this may not be the right time, but everything is moving so fast and—I need to know—"

Austin saw the tic beside his son's left eye begin to work. "What is it, Will?"

Keith looked down at his hands, spread them wide on the rough surface of the table. How could he just ask it so simply when everything—his whole life—depended on the answer? Although the room was chill, the shirt under his armpits was soaking wet. He lifted his gaze and looked deeply at Austin. "I need to know Pa—I've needed to know for a long time. You know what I'm talking about. I need to know who my real father is. I need a name. I don't mean to say that you haven't been the best father any son could ask for, because you have, but I need to know who sired me. I want to look that man in the face and hear from his lips why he disgraced my mother and threw me away … Pa?" Keith wiped the sweat from his forehead with his shirt sleeve, and out of the corner of his eye he saw Malinda carry a steaming cup of tea into the bedroom. "I don't rightly like saying this, but time was when I thought it was you. I … I need to know if you *are* my real Pa?"

Austin's face was the color of ripe cotton as he stared at Keith. "No Son," he shook his head slowly. "I'm not your natural father. I wish to God I could say I was, but it ain't so … " He reached out and covered Keith's hand with his own. "I couldn't feel more for you if I *was* the one who sired you. I think you know that."

Keith shook his head, humiliated by the rising wetness in his eyes. "I do know that Pa. But I'm not talking about feelings, I'm talking about siring. Don't you see how important it is for me to know where I come from? I've asked Ma so many times, but she won't tell me. She says people would get hurt. Pa, if you know, you've got to tell me!" He placed his hand on top of Austin's. "I have a right to know who my real father is."

Austin's head dipped low. Slumped into his shoulders. He stared at the table for a long moment, and when he finally lifted his head, his eyes held a distant look. "I wish to heaven I could answer that for you, Will. But I can't. Plain and simple, I don't know. It's a question I never asked Mary, and it's one she never volunteered to comment on. It'll go with her to the grave."

Keith bit his lips and felt the sting of blood. "I … have … a … right … to … know!" He accentuated each word with a pound of his fist on the table. "When she dies, there'll be no one to tell me the truth."

Austin rose, weary as the grave, and heaved a sigh. "I've got some work to do out in the barn." As he walked past Keith's bowed shoulders, he patted him gently. "We'll not be talkin' of this again."

"Pa?" Much to Keith's dismay his voice broke as he spoke the word. He swallowed hard before continuing. "There … there is a resemblance between us. I got your build and … and some of your ways."

Austin managed a smile. "I reckon that comes from living together all these years. Hell, even ole Nellie looked like me. And she was a horse."

Keith nodded. "Yeah, Pa. I guess you're right. She did at that." He cupped his head in his hands as Austin headed for the barn.

* * *

The following Monday, Keith was plowing the final row on the newly terraced land. Although there was still an early Spring chill in the air, he'd had to pause often to wipe sweat from his brow. The recent rains had turned the ground muddy, but it had also helped it to thaw. Another week to ten days and they could plant some peas. He interrupted his own thoughts. Rather, Malinda could plant the peas. There was no telling where he would be ten days from now.

He looked at the willow tree beside the creek. There was a faint hint of yellow in its limbs. Then his gaze moved to a newly turned patch out front, the one Malinda had designated as a flower garden. He'd laughed when she'd been so hell bent on putting it in, told her nothing would ever grow there, it was too rocky. But damned if there wasn't a purple crocus poking it's head up, and close by a couple more spikes of green that looked like they might be jonquils. Quite a woman, his wife! He removed the wide brimmed straw hat and wiped his forehead with his bandanna.

There was no urgency to go inside, although he could hear Malinda puttering with supper preparations. The time had come to tell her, and there couldn't be anymore putting it off. Things had been a little strained since that Sunday when her folks were over and he'd made known his plans. It had seemed easier, laying it all out in front of others; less likely of a fight. Malinda was far too proud to fight with him in front of her parents. The strange thing was though, she hadn't even mentioned it after they'd left. Hadn't talked about it at all. Sort of like nothing had ever been said. But she had been awful quiet and withdrawn. That was the strain he was feeling, all right. The being cut off from her.

He looked skyward. Thunderheads were building again over The Grandfather. They were due for more rain. What must it be like, he wondered, fighting a war in the mud? It was going to be harder to leave Malinda than he'd thought.

And Ma! Dear God, Ma truly looked like death when they'd been over there last week. Malinda was going there every day now, doing the cooking and cleaning that Ma could no longer do. And Ma kept insisting she was feeling better, but that was just to make everybody else feel better. He'd stop by and see her tomorrow to say good-bye. There wasn't anything he could do for her. Probably nothing anybody could do. Well, Pa would be here to look after her. And Malinda.

At least the clan war had quieted to the point where he could feel comfortable in that area about leaving. The older Moore boys were off fighting; so there was only Carroll and Jesse at home now. Carroll was getting too old to do much fighting, and he'd heard that Jesse had twice been turned down by the Rebs because of his health. Which told you he was *really* in rotten shape! The Moore's would more than likely back off completely once he was gone. He could just picture the smug look on Jesse's face though when he found out he'd joined up with the Rebs. Damn! It was just about more than a man could stomach! But there was no way around it. At least he wouldn't be running into that pimply, pitted puss of Jesse's anymore. Lord Almighty! If Jesse wasn't ugly before that last beating he sure enough was now! His nose looked like a turnip, and his bottom lip was all sucked in from losing so many teeth! It made his heart glad to know he was responsible for that.

Keith rose, glanced at his shoes and scraped some of the mud off on a large rock. His choices were few; hide out for the duration and no telling how long that would be, make that trek to Kentucky and enlist as a Federal volunteer and likely get nabbed on the way and thrown into a gray uniform, or join the bastards and try to escape to the Union side. Doing nothing was asking for trouble. All the Reb neighbors, *and* relatives were making it known that if he didn't join up, they'd take matters into their own hands. Just last week he'd gotten that note from charming Uncle William:

Get into uniform or get burned out, and your Pa's place, too.

The old son-of-a-bitch. Never could stand that man! And that goes for Reuben and McCaleb, too. They're all just about the most worthless individuals a man could think of. Shit! When they were handing out relatives, Pa sure didn't get the pick of the litter!

Keith walked to the stream, knelt and put his hands into the icy water and splashed it on his face. Trickles ran down his neck onto his chest, and he shivered.

"Supper's about ready!" Malinda was calling from the back door.

She brushed his cheek with her lips as he entered. "My, you do look tuckered," she commented. "How come you're working so hard? We've got time. Planting season isn't for a few weeks yet. No sense in killing yourself."

The words spilled out before he could stop them. "I won't be here to do the planting, Malinda. You'll be doing it without me."

She stopped in mid motion. Still as a statue.

"I'm joining the Rebs. I'll be leaving tomorrow."

The disbelief and then the pain in her eyes was almost more than he could bear. He shuffled to the table and dropped into his chair. "There isn't going to be any debating because it's a decision I *had* to make, not one I wanted to. I'm putting us all in danger by not joining up. I hope you understand that, but if you don't it won't make any difference, because my mind's made up."

When he found the courage to raise his eyes and look at her, it struck him that her face was the color of fresh snow. Silent, she placed his plate before him, poured a tin cup of water from the pitcher and sat down at the table across from him. He could barely swallow his food, and she didn't even try. Not once did she raise the fork to her lips. Neither one of them had the courage to look at the other.

After dinner, Keith went outside to chop wood. Malinda would need an extra supply if it didn't soon warm up, and God knows when he'd be back to chop any more. Every time the ax hit the stump he felt a surge of power. He would get through this night and tomorrow, and yes, life was going to change, but the war *would* end one day, and things *would* be back to normal.

Half an hour later as gray shadows settled in, the chopping was finished. He drew a deep breath as he put the ax to one side and walked slowly back to the house. He pulled open the door, stepped inside and stopped dead in his tracks. His breath catching somewhere in the middle of his chest. Malinda was standing in front of the fireplace. She was wearing one of his old loose fitting shirts and a pair of his pants that although attached to a pair of suspenders, were gathered in at the waist with a rope. On her feet she wore her work boots and generally looked as if she'd been swallowed up by clothes. But the most unbelievable thing was her hair. It was gone. What was left ended just above her ears. He found his breath but not his voice.

As he continued to stare, Malinda picked up his old wide brimmed cowhide hat and plopped it on her head. Then she hooked her thumbs through the rope at her waist and began strutting about the room.

"Howdy! I'm Sam Blalock," she grinned. "Me and my big brother Keith are joining the Confederacy."

CHAPTER 9

Keith finally found his voice. "Malinda, you are nuttier than a chestnut! Look at you! Why you look like—"

"A boy? " Malinda said hopefully. "That's what I'm intending to look like."

"But … your hair … Sweetheart, your beautiful hair! My God woman, what have you gone and done to your hair?"

"I'm … I'm sorry about that." Malinda glanced at the fire where the last locks were turning to ash. "But it'll grow back. You'll see! When this silly war is over I'll be your woman again. But don't you see? For now, if we're going to be together … " Her voice dropped to a whisper, "I'll have to pretend to be your brother."

"This is so crazy, I don't even know what to say." Keith looked at her with a mixture of anger and astonishment.

Malinda lifted her chin defiantly. "While you were making your plans, I've been making some plans of my own, Mr. Blalock." She saw him flinch and knew her words had found their mark. "I've heard stories about other women going to war with their men, and there's no reason why I can't be going with you." She resisted the instinct to place her hand on her belly. You're always saying you need me by your side. Well, I'll *be* by your side! And when you escape to the Union lines, I'll be by your side there too, and not sitting at home waiting for news and going half crazy when I don't get any."

"Good Lord Malinda what makes you think you can handle army life—even if you could get by posing as a man? The mud and the filth and the sleeping in trenches and everybody sleeping in the same tent—"

"There isn't just one big tent. There's a whole mess of little ones. They're allowing family members to tent together. How many times have we heard that? Been told that too many times by too many people for it not to be true. And since I'm your younger brother, they'll put us together."

"Sweetheart, there's more to war than tenting. There's people shooting at each other. I don't want my wife being shot at!" He began to pace the room. "Christ, Malinda! Give this a think!"

"Keith," she reached out to him, the cuff of the sleeve almost covering her hand. "I'm asking *you* to give this a think. Now you tell me how shooting in the army is any different from shooting at the Moores. Shooting people is shooting people, and I can shoot as straight as any man. You know as well as I do that I missed blowing the heads off the Moores because I wanted to miss. You've seen me level more than one deer. And if you're worried about people shooting at me, how about the Moores shooting at me? Glory be, they came mighty close a couple of times! If shooting is your argument you'll have to come up with something else because that one doesn't hold water."

Abruptly Keith stopped pacing and turned to face her. "Don't you think this is hard enough for me without you going and pulling one of your damned harebrained stunts just to get me off center? Damnit Malinda! Sometimes I think you are plum crazy!"

The look in his eye was one of doubt rather than anger, and a secret part of her breathed a sigh. "Keith, the truth is, I can't face being apart from you. I know other women have been left behind while their menfolk go off to do the fighting, but I'm not like them. I can't live without you. It's the God's truth, Keith. I can't." Her voice dropped an octave as she stared miserably at the clouded window. "If you go and don't take me with you, I'll surely die. I know I will. And all you'll have to come home to is a grave."

He ran his fingers through his hair as he slowly shook his head. "Malinda, I don't even know if *I* can handle military life. How in the hell do you think you're going to do it?"

"With your help," she said softly.

Over the next quarter hour Malinda pleaded her case. They would be told—or taught—what to do. She was young and strong and she could keep up. As far as her sex was concerned, she could pass as being a sixteen-year-old, that would explain the lack of a beard. What reason would anyone have to suspect otherwise? Of course, the main thing was, they would be together. No matter what duties they were assigned during the day, at night they could be man and wife.

In the end Keith reluctantly conceded, not out of reason, but out of his own desire. He wanted her with him as much as she wanted to be there, and the thought of not having to be parted from her was like a load of bricks being lifted from his shoulders. "I think your plan is full of holes," he said wearily. "When you get caught—and it'll only be a matter of time—then you'll have to come back home on your own, and God only knows where we might be when you do get found out. But if you're willing to take that chance ... then okay." He took her in his arms and kissed her hungrily. "It's going to seem mighty strange kissing a boy. Maybe I ought to practice some."

After supper they packed their most prized possessions; the mantle clock, the rocking chair, a few pieces of china Elizabeth had given them, and two of their books. Malinda moved with precision, doing what needed to be done; keeping her mind focused on their being together, and away from the dismantling of their home. They would come back here someday. Together. And if the

Moores or some other Rebs burned it down then they'd build it again. Together. They would live a long and happy life here when all this foolishness was over.

The following morning, under an overcast sky, they set out for Austin's place driving the cow and pigs before them. Once there, Keith explained their intentions to Austin, who, after recovering from his initial shock at Malinda's appearance, agreed that she could pass for male.

"I never would have believed it," Austin said, stroking his white beard, "you always lookin' so girlie and all, but dern if you don't look just like a young whelp." He slapped her lightly on the shoulder as he would a boy. "I admire your spirit, Malinda."

They borrowed Austin's ox and dray and returned home to collect their belongings. Malinda penned up the chickens, and Keith loaded the pens on the wagon along with everything else. At the last minute Malinda removed her wedding ring and wrapped it carefully in a piece of cloth, then slipped it inside the iron pot along with the china.

When they returned to Austin's house they unloaded the wagon and carried everything to the root cellar. As long as they were busy with the preparations, she had little time to think about what her parents would have to say, but the closer the time came to departure, the more she dreaded telling them. She could picture her mother's face when she saw her daughter dressed as a boy, could almost read the fear in her eyes when she heard that she was going off to war. Oh God, why was it she always seemed to be causing her folks pain?

In the end her courage failed her and she wrote a note instead. "Please see my folks get this after we're gone." Malinda pressed the note into Austin's hand.

"Then you'll not be tellin' them direct?"

"No. We'll be heading in the opposite direction."

"I'll see they get it," Austin said solemnly, then turned to Keith. "Don't you be worryin' about your livestock. They'll be here when you get back. Bigger than ever."

"I appreciate that Pa, but if you need 'em, I want you to use 'em."

"Won't be a need. We got pigs of our own and two cows. Could be we fry up a chicken or two though."

"I hope you will, Pa." Keith pulled out his pocket watch. "Well Sweetheart, I guess it's time we get going." He gestured toward the door to the bedroom. "I think I ought to go in first and tell Ma. Sort of prepare her to meet Sam Blalock."

* * *

Ten minutes later when Keith opened the door and motioned Malinda to come in, there were unmistakable tears in his eyes. Quickly, Malinda looked away. Mary lay propped up in bed, looking more like a corpse than a living person, but there was the beginning of a smile on her pallid lips.

"Keith told me about Sam," she said, the smile widening. "I'm happy to meet you, Sam." Mary reached out her hand to Malinda. "I'm glad you're going with him. If I was young and it was Austin going off to war, I hope I'd have the courage to do what you are doing. I'm proud you're my son's wife."

Malinda leaned over and kissed Mary's forehead, then kneeling beside the bed she took the wasted hand between her own smooth, strong ones. "I'll watch over him, Mary, I promise. And we'll be praying for you each night. We'll be back real soon. You'll see." She raised the claw-like hand to her lips and kissed it tenderly, then placed it back beneath the covers and left the room.

Moments later she and Keith hugged a subdued, but stoic, Austin, and headed out the door. A sliver of brilliant light was caught between The Grandfather and the gray mass of clouds as they strapped their saddlebags, along with Malinda's dulcimer, to their mounts. That bright streak of sunlight is a good omen, she thought as she climbed slowly into her saddle. And whatever this new life holds, at least we'll be facing it together.

The horses moved out into the road at a leisurely pace, in no hurry for what lay ahead. Nor was Malinda. Things would unfold as the good Lord meant them to. Who was she to battle fate? A deep sigh of contentment welled up from within and she never looked back.

* * *

"Yes Sir, my name is Sam Blalock. I'm Keith Blalock's kid brother." Malinda gestured with her head toward Keith who stood a few yards away in front of an adjacent tent talking with another recruiting officer. The officer standing across the table from Malinda was scarcely older than she was, but the gray uniform gave him an air of authority.

"How old are you Sam?"

Consciously trying to keep the pitch of her voice low, she answered, "Sixteen, Sir."

"Do you know how to handle a gun?"

"Yes Sir. I'm a pretty fair shot."

"Do you understand what this war's all about?"

Malinda thought the man's eyes could have frozen running water. "It's about seceding from the Union, and having the right to own slaves if we want to."

"Does your family own any slaves, Sam?"

"No, Sir. We don't have much land. Sure not enough to support slaves." She gave a quick sideways glance at Keith, wondering if they would check their stories against each other. They'd never thought beyond the lie of "brotherhood."

"Are you aware you are obliged to supply your own mount?"

"Yes, Sir."

"Do you own a horse, Sam?"

"Yes, Sir."

"You realize that should your horse be killed, you will be expected to supply yourself with another at your own expense."

Malinda nodded.

"Can you play that thing?" The recruiting officer gestured to the dulcimer strapped to her shoulder.

"Yes, Sir. I can play it."

"That's good. Music helps men feel better after a battle."

Malinda nodded again, wondering how many battles those cold eyes had seen.

The recruiter bent over the table and wrote something on a piece of paper, started to hand it to her, then paused. "How's your health, Sam? Any medical reason why you can't serve?"

"No, Sir. No reason." *Besides maybe being pregnant.*

"I'm asking because our medical officer is not here at present. He'll be rejoining us in a few days and will be giving you your physical then."

He handed Malinda the paper as she felt the color rising in her face. *Dear Lord we're going to have to figure some way around that one!*

"Can you sign your name, Sam?"

"Yes Sir, I can." She signed Sam Blalock at the bottom of the sheet of paper and handed it back to him.

"Raise your right hand. Do you swear to uphold the Confederacy? Answer by saying, I do."

"I do."

"Do you swear allegiance to the Bonnie Blue Flag of Secession?"

Malinda swallowed. "I do."

The recruiter reached for her hand and shook it, smiling for the first time. "Welcome to the Confederate Army, Mr. Blalock."

"Thank you, Sir." Malinda's knees were knocking so hard she was sure he could hear them.

The recruiter motioned to the officer who was talking with Keith. "When ever you're finished with Mr. Blalock, his brother is ready."

"We're finished now."

Keith turned toward Malinda and she could read a sense of relief on his face that no doubt mirrored her own. The first hurdle was passed, the next would be the physical. But with luck, they'd be far away on the Union side by the time that little problem arose.

As anticipated they were assigned to the same tent, one barely two yards from the next, and part of an encampment that covered almost a full acre. Recruiting was having a harvest, but as Keith commented once they were alone, "From what I've overheard, a lot of men who have been joining up aren't doing it anymore willingly that I—we did. Everybody figures that damned Conscription Act is going to be signed any day now, and then you could be stuck for as much as three years. From the look of things I'd say they're expecting this skirmish to last a spell."

Malinda snuggled closer to Keith, his arm, beneath her head shifted slightly, and drew her even nearer. A soft wind rustled the tent. They had used their saddles for pillows, and placed one of their two wool blankets beneath them on the ground to keep out the damp cold, while covering themselves with the other.

"I'm sure Conscription has something to do with it," Malinda whispered, "and like you say, a lot of people are signing up because they've been forced to. There's this young fella from Deep Gap—Lonnie Coones, I think he said his name is. Maybe you saw me talking to him down by the paddock. Kind of pale like, with a whole thatch of auburn hair and a mess of freckles that nearly covers his nose? Well, poor thing isn't too bright. He was telling me he's a Unionist—and me a perfect stranger, mind you! He says he joined up because his neighbors gave him till noon on Sunday or they'd make him the center of attraction at a hanging party. He's scared out of his wits."

"Well, I reckon your friend's bright enough to know hanging is permanent, and joining the Rebs is temporary," Keith chuckled. "But it does beat all now doesn't it? Expecting loyalty from people who are forced to fight?"

Malinda smiled and lifted her hand to Keith's hair, stroking it away from his forehead. He responded by cupping her face in his hand and kissing her warmly. "I'm glad you're here, Malinda," he said. "I can't even begin to tell you how glad I am."

"Probably no more glad than I am," she said softly.

Their love making that night held echoes of the past when they'd had to worry about discovery. The proximity of the other tents lent a hushed, and hurried element that was also exciting. Afterward, Malinda lay in Keith's arms listening to the sounds of the New River tumbling over the rapids. From far off came the haunting cry of a wolf, and from a distant tent, a harmonica played a mournful rendition of *Dixieland.* A grim reminder that they were, after all, in enemy territory.

* * *

They awoke to the cry of a bugle and the aroma of brewing coffee. Malinda heard someone pacing outside the tent, and then came the call, "Anyone wanting a bath fall out now. We'll be moving out in exactly forty-five minutes." She peered out through the slit and saw men in varying stages of undress, some naked as newborns, running headlong for the river. From the look of some of the bodies they hadn't seen water, much less soap, in a long while.

While Keith joined the others in the frigid river water, Malinda remained behind, collecting their belongings and waiting for an opportunity to sneak off privately into the woods to relieve herself. There, amid feelings of joy and regret, she learned she was not pregnant. At least, that's one less thing to worry about, she counseled herself, as a sweeping sadness engulfed her. It's for the best. There'll be time for babies when this damned war is over. Nonetheless, there was a heaviness of heart and an inexplicable feeling of loss for something she never really had.

Back at the tent Malinda protected herself with the clean rags she'd brought along 'for just in case' and had a smile ready when Keith returned. No sense mentioning the near miss, it might cause him needless worry, or make him cautious about coming near her again. And *that* would never do!

After a breakfast of flapjacks, boiled beans, and coffee, served from the back of a chuck wagon, a short, towheaded officer, wearing a uniform that was two sizes too big for him, stepped up onto a small wooden crate. His blond head was barely level with the gangly recruits gathered before him.

"Welcome to the 26th North Carolina Regiment of the Confederate States Army, under the command of Colonel Zebulon Vance," he shouted. "Many a y'all have been wonderin' for several days where y'all will be assigned. Well, the assignment is to the garrison at Kinston, and we'll be movin' out in exactly fifteen minutes. We'll be ridin' in files of two, and if y'all have got any canteens it's best to fill 'em with fresh river water before departure. At Kinston y'all will get your military trainin' and maybe some uniforms."

Malinda, who was standing next to Keith in the midst of the group, turned when someone tugged at her sleeve.

"Hey, Sam," a voice whispered. "What's he mean, maybe some uniforms?" The auburn haired Lonnie Coones sidled up beside Malinda, his freckled face twisted into a look of concern.

"I don't know, Lonnie. Maybe they don't have enough to go around."

"That there was one of the reasons I signed up. So's I could get me some new clothes." He glanced down at his bare feet and tattered overalls. "I'm thinkin' this here's a BIG mistake I'm makin'." He shook his head sorrowfully. "Where is Kinston, anyway?"

Malinda shrugged as Keith folded his map and slipped it inside his shirt. "It's a looong way from here," he commented. Almost to the coast."

The words did nothing to lift Lonnie's apparent sense of impending doom. He squinted up at Keith, the freckled nose wrinkling until it resembled a small carrot. "I'm regrettin' this already. He wiped the red nose on the back of his sleeve. "I knew I shouldn't a done it. If'n I have to fight, the way I figure it is, I want to be on the winnin' side, and I got a feelin' this ain't it."

Malinda took her canteen from her shoulder and reached for Keith's. "Give me your canteen Lonnie and I'll go fill it for you."

Lonnie wrestled a sheep's bladder from his knapsack and handed it to Malinda. "I thank you, Sam. Say, do yeh mind if I ride with y'all? I don't know nobody else."

Keith stuck out his hand. "Course you can ride with us. I'm Keith Blalock, aaahh ... Sam's brother."

"Happy to make your acquaintance." Lonnie's face brightened as he pumped Keith's hand. "I'm Lonnie Coones. From Deep Gap." Then he lowered his voice. "I'm a Unionist."

Keith nodded. "That's what Sam tells me, but I don't think you ought to be mentioning that to anybody else around here. Somebody just might take offense."

The ride began at a brisk pace. Malinda felt a sense of exhilaration as they galloped down the main road, their mounts hurling mud in every direction. The uniformed men were riding at the head of the line. It was easy to forget the colors they wore and merely enjoy the rush of blood through your veins, the feel of your mount's muscles between your legs.

The morning air was clear and filled with the aroma of breakfast fires from the cabins they passed. The blue haze hovering over the mountains was familiar and reassuring. Riding side by side, Malinda and Keith exchanged intermittent smiles of pleasure and expectation. So far, the Reb Army wasn't all that bad!

It came as a surprise when a bare two hours after the ride began, they left the main road and branched off onto a trail that wound through a mountain pass. This necessitated a single file, and the pace was slowed to a walk as horses picked their way over rocks and underbrush. The men ducked and dodged to elude overhanging branches.

This route continued until noon when they reached a small gap neatly laid out beside a briskly flowing stream. They dismounted, and led the horses to water. Lonnie, trailing like a lost puppy behind Malinda, was still worried.

"There's no way a chuck wagon got through that trail. I'm just wonderin' what they got in mind to feed us?"

Malinda and Keith exchanged glances, and Keith nudged Lonnie good naturedly. "I reckon they're going to let us get these animals watered then choose one 'em for a meal and shoot it and roast it. Think I saw a spit back there aways."

Lonnie looked at Keith in wide eyed terror. "Y'all are just kiddin', ain't ya?" He looked at Sam for reassurance. "They won't be killin' none of our horses, now will they?"

Keith laughed and pushed farther. "Don't you know anything about Rebs? Why they'd eat their mothe—"

"Keith!" Malinda broke in. "You're frightening him." She turned to Lonnie. "My brother's a big tease. Don't pay him any mind. He gets that way sometimes." She shot Keith a meaningful look, and received a remorseful shrug in return.

Moments later a uniformed corporal walked up and offered them each a package wrapped in newspaper. "I'd rinse it in the stream first," he said. "Unless you like your salt pork REAL salty."

Before Malinda and Keith could unwrap their packages, Lonnie had torn his open and taken a huge bite. "Ain't too salty fer me!" he grinned, obviously enjoying the meager offering.

They rested briefly, then mounted again and continued following the twisting trail for the next several hours. Behind them, the sun was beginning to kiss the mountain tops as they again emerged onto an open road. It was well traveled and far less muddy than the trail. Bordering the road was a narrow strip of meadow covered with a thick layer of kudzu and backed by a rich forest permeated with evergreen. The tangled vine blanketed many of the barren trees, creating an eerie, seemingly impenetrable wall of green. The horses, now tired, traveled at a slow trot.

They had been on the road only a few minutes when Keith, riding on Malinda's right, leaned toward her and said in a low tone. "Keep your musket handy. I saw an injun, and where there's one there's a score."

Malinda gasped and gave a quick look around. "Where? Where did you see him?"

"Back a ways. He's been tracking us. *Don't look*!"

"Are you sure it was an injun?"

"This is not the time to question my eyesight! I'm telling you we might have to do some shooting, and likely some fast riding. Stay ready."

"But the horses are tired," Malinda said feebly. "Besides, injuns wouldn't attack this many men would they? We must be a hundred or more."

Keith's eyes darkened as they turned narrow. "Depends on how many of *them* there are now doesn't it! Stay ready." He then righted himself in his saddle, briefly fingering the Bowie knife at his belt. Malinda shifted her gaze in a 180 degree arc and saw nothing. She turned on the ruse of saying something to Lonnie and caught the unmistakable glint of sunlight on metal. She was sure she also saw a feathered head. "Getting tired Lonnie?" She pumped cheerfulness into her voice even as her throat constricted with terror.

"Not near as tired as these horses," came the unreassuring reply.

Suddenly, the officer leading the march held up a white gloved hand and cried, "Halt." He waited a moment until the end of the line had rounded the last curve, then called out in a loud voice. "We will be camping tonight with Thomas's North Carolina Highland Legion. Every man is expected to be courteous." With that, he waved to the right, and spurred his mount forward.

Within minutes they were fighting the tangled vine and entering the dense cover of forest. The fading sun pierced the overhead canopy in narrow shafts of light, casting a ghostly glow that seemed almost dreamlike. Riding in and out among the trees made it impossible to maintain any sort of file, but less than a quarter mile in, there was no longer a need. They had reached a clearing, one unlike anything they could have expected.

Malinda felt the blood drain from her face as her bowels turned to water. The officers who had been leading the column were nowhere to be seen. But before and around them; some dressed in buckskin, some in loin cloth, a few in Confederate uniforms, were a hundred or more Indians. Many wore war paint and all were armed. But by far the most frightening were the ones who had bayonets affixed to their rifles. Each bayonet was topped by a scalp covered with dried blood. The hair of these scalps ranged from gray to blond to shades of brown and black, and there was no mistaking that the previous owners had been white men.

☆

CHAPTER 10

Time was frozen. Malinda sat her mount, eyes lifted to the canopy of pines, not daring to look around, afraid of what she might see. Sweat was drenching her shirt and trousers and running in rivulets from her hairline. She neither flinched or attempted to wipe it away. Remaining stone still seemed the only safe thing to do.

Something touched her arm and she jumped as if hit by lightning. Keith was looking at her, his hand reaching to cover hers which were wrapped in a talon grip around the saddle horn.

"I think they're Rebs," he whispered. "A few of 'em are wearing Reb uniforms. I've heard about a company of Cherokee. This must be it."

A company of Cherokee? Why was Keith's voice coming from so far away? Like out of a cave. Her vision was going blurry. My God, I'm going to faint! *No!* I can't faint! If I fall off this horse they'll find out I'm a woman. *Oh God!* Malinda forced herself to take deep breaths; fought to keep her eyes in focus. In a few moments will power conquered fear, and slowly her head began to clear. Keith's hand, still covering hers brought a small sense of comfort.

There was movement through the pines ahead. She could hear men's voices and the sound of barking dogs. A spotted mongrel came toward them wagging his tail. As if emerging from a dream, three officers whom she recognized, appeared out of the haze. The thought crossed her mind that she'd never been so happy to see anyone in her entire life. These officers were followed by a fourth, a stranger, and immediately following them were six Indians dressed in Rebel gray.

The towheaded officer from the recruiting camp jumped up onto a tree trunk that had fallen across a footpath. "Gentlemen," he shouted. "It is my honor and privilege to present to y'all Lieutenant James W. Terrell, of the soon to be organized, Thomas's Highland Legion. Lieutenant Terrell wants to speak a few words."

Towhead stepped down and the lanky Lieutenant Terrell took his place on the fallen tree. His uniform appeared brand new. The gold braid on the sleeves and brass buttons on his tunic glistened as they were touched by shafts of sunlight filtering through the trees. He raised his white-gloved hands above his shoulders in a plea for silence, but there was no need. The only sound was an occasional snort of an exhausted horse, or the intermittent bark of a dog. Everyone was holding their breath.

The lieutenant cleared his throat and let his gaze sweep the assembled crowd. "Some of you may have heard of us, but for those who haven't let me explain that you are this evening the guests of Captain William Thomas's Highland Legion, the only Cherokee Company in the Confederate States Army. Our camp here on the banks of the beautiful Yadkin River will offer you respite from what I am sure has been a long and arduous day. As you have already been told you are headed for the garrison at Kinston, which is a few days ride from here. Let me again assure you that you are our welcome guests. As you wind your way through our midst this evening you will no doubt find some of our company who speak English. I hope you will exchange pleasantries with these brave men who have sworn allegiance to the Confederacy.

"I think you should know, that this day, these brave soldiers of Thomas's Highland Legion met in combat with Union forces in an area known as Baptist Gap. Our Confederate forces were victorious. We repelled the scheming and deceitful attack by the enemy, but regrettably not without the loss of life. Our distinguished Second Lieutenant, John Astoogatogeh gave his life in defense of the Confederacy, and we mourn his loss, as we honor his sacrifice. Two other gallant men fell with him, and we honor their memory as well. Again, I bid you welcome. Thank you, that will be all."

Lieutenant Terrell stepped down as an Indian, dressed in a Confederate gray frock coat and buckskin trousers, gestured for the line to move single file down a narrow tree shrouded path. Malinda ventured another glance at Keith, and received a reassuring wink.

Breathing easier now, she looked around for Lonnie. He was directly behind her, his white face streaked with tears. "It's going to be okay," she encouraged. "They're friendly. We don't have to be afraid."

Lonnie moved his head slightly in what substituted for a nod.

The path through the woods was short. Within moments they entered what appeared to be an Indian village, or what Malinda thought an Indian village would look like, except there was an absence of squaws. The area was peppered with teepees, some painted with animal symbols, others were only bare hides with no color on them. In the center of the compound was an army regulation tent, large enough to accommodate ten to twelve men. The flap to the tent was open and as they rode past Malinda saw a table spread with papers, and several uniformed men, red and white, pouring over them. A short distance away, smoke was rising from a roasting pit, along with a delicious aroma. From nearby came the sound of rushing water. The Yadkin River the lieutenant had mentioned.

As their horses moved slowly through the encampment, their progress was monitored by a host of Indians on either side. They stood motionless, faces seemingly carved from stone. Again they were moving by twos, and a few rows in front of them, their guide raised his hand, held up four fingers and gestured toward a teepee. Four men dismounted, secured their mounts and entered the tent. Two stops later it was their turn. Their guide again gestured toward the nearest teepee, holding up four fingers. Malinda and Keith dismounted and Lonnie literally slid off his horse in an effort to join them. A fourth man, tall and quiet, who'd been riding beside Lonnie also dismounted. Appearing relaxed and not at all shaken by the savage faces surrounding them, he introduced himself simply as Harold.

They tied their horses to a stake beside the opening of the tent, and went inside. They'd barely had time to enter and look around before another red face, this one painted with bright streaks of yellow and red, and forehead brushed with ashes, pulled back the flap and motioned them outside again. He first pointed to their horses and then toward the river. So where are the ones who speak English, Malinda wondered?

Silent, Keith untied his horse and headed for the river bank where others of their party were watering their mounts. Malinda, Lonnie and Harold followed. In unison, they dropped to their knees beside the animals, and sticking their own faces in the rushing water, drank greedily.

After a moment or two, Lonnie lifted his head and gave a quick look around. "Ssss ... Sam," he sputtered, "do you think we're gonna get ourselves scalped? I seen it happen once. A scalpin.' My granpappy got killed by a band of maraudin' injuns. They let me go. Guess 'cause I was a youngin. No more'n four. I seen them take the top of granpappy's head right off with their scalpin' knife, while he was a screamin' and a shriekin'. Do y'all think that's what's gonna happen to us? Do ya think so, Sam? Huh? Do ya?"

Malinda searched for words of comfort. Looking to Keith for reassurance she saw the makings of a smile, and felt suddenly angry. Couldn't he see the poor boy was scared half to death? "The way I see it," she said, patting Lonnie's hand, "if these injuns are thinking of scalping us, they're sure going to a lot of trouble, now aren't they? Giving us a tent and a chance to water our horses, and unless my nose is lying to me, there's something good cooking for dinner. I think we're safe enough. I don't think we have anything to worry about."

"Yeah, I'm thinking this isn't near as bad as what it first looked." Keith tried a look of confidence on Lonnie that didn't go unnoticed by Malinda. "Sam's right. If they're intending to do us harm they sure are going to a lot of trouble to make it look otherwise. And that officer who talked to us, he seems to feel everything's as it should be. I don't reckon we have much to worry about."

"I heard about that fella John Astoogatogeh," Harold interjected. "The one the lieutenant says got hisself killed." The tall man pulled himself to his feet, leaned back against the trunk of a willow tree and rubbed back and forth scratching his back. From the smell of him Malinda felt certain there was something besides Harold living inside his shirt.

"This here Astoogatogeh was the grandson of Chief Junaluska," Harold continued. "Real honored among his tribe. Smart, and strong as an ox. Weren't no heathen either. He turned Christian and even tried to convert the Cherokee."

Keith rose and opened his saddlebag, withdrew a brush and began grooming his mount. "Do you suppose that's why they had the scalping party? Because the Yankees killed this John Astoo—this injun lieutenant?"

"That's what it sounds like to me." Harold spat on the ground and with his tongue moved the wad of tobacco from one cheek to the other. "When a Cherokee, no matter how unheathenized he pretends to be, gets all heated about something, he's been knowed to do some down right devilish things."

Malinda looked at Keith with raised eyebrows. Talk about an understatement, she thought.

Once the horses had been watered and groomed and their own thirst quenched, they returned to their teepee to find four wooden buckets filled with grain sitting outside the entrance. As the animals began to feed they saw other members of their group moving toward the center of the compound and the smell of supper cooking.

* * *

Later, after dark, Malinda, Keith and Lonnie were alone in the teepee. Harold had wandered off somewhere following supper. Keith handed Malinda one of the wool blankets, indicating she should sleep apart from him, and she nodded in silent agreement.

"Wonder what that was we had fer supper?" Lonnie sat with his elbows resting on his knees, chin cupped in his hands. He appeared less fearful since his belly had been filled. "Sorta tasted like groundhog, didn't it? Only different. Good though."

Noting where Malinda was laying out her blanket, Lonnie rose and pulled his closer to hers, leaving only a few inches between them.

Abruptly, the flap of the teepee parted and a small dog's head appeared. Its ears were rounded, its heavy coat a mixture of gray and white. Keith, lying on his blanket and resting on one elbow, pointed at the dog and laughed. "I'll bet that's what we ate for supper, Lonnie. Probably this pup's mother."

Taking the words as an invitation, the dog wagged its way into the teepee immediately heading for Keith and licking him full in the face. "Gol Dang it, get away!" Keith lifted his arms to protect himself as Malinda giggled.

"Looks like you got yourself a new friend, Keith!"

"Get him off me, Mali—Sam!" Keith flailed his arms wildly as the amorous dog continued his licking.

"Come here girl." Lonnie emitted a low whistle. "And it ain't no he. She's a she. Come on girl." Instantly, the dog left Keith and found new pleasure in licking Lonnie's freckles. "We probably still got food on our faces," Lonnie snickered, also holding up his arms in defense. "Hell, I know you do, Keith. Half your supper's still in yer mustache."

"Well, the bitch can go get her victuals somewhere else," Keith snapped. "I don't need a wolf dog sniffing around here licking my whiskers."

"Ah, she's a nice dog. Ain't she Sam?" Lonnie gave the bobbing head a tender pat. "Look! See how's she's waggin' her tail?"

"Well she can wag it on your side of the tent! Look at her. She's half wolf. She's only licking 'cause she's a pup. If she was bigger, she'd be eating you!" With that Keith pulled his blanket high over his shoulder and rolled onto his side, his back to Malinda and Lonnie.

"Good night, Keith," Malinda said softly, feeling neglected.

"Nite, Maa—Sam," came the muffled reply.

Apparently convinced there was nothing left to glean from Lonnie's face, the new arrival dropped to her stomach, nestling tight against her adopted master's side. "Y'all know who your friend is, don't ya?" Lonnie patted the soft head. "Y'all just stay right here nice and close and tomorrow ole Lonnie boy'll get you something right fine to eat."

It was past midnight when Malinda heard Harold return to the teepee. He moved quietly, unrolled his blanket and minutes later she heard him snore.

The call of a bugle marked the beginning of a new day, and Malinda thought how much nicer it was to awaken to the crow of a rooster. Lonnie, accompanied by his new four legged friend, was the first out of the tent and first in line at the chuck wagon. Malinda, Keith and Harold, moved more leisurely. Harold, silent until now, became suddenly talkative. His night reconnaissance had offered up information he seemed eager to share.

"The Captain came in late last night and from what I'm hearin' he ain't none too pleased about the scalpin' party."

"The Captain?" Malinda asked.

"Captain Will Thomas of Thomas's Highland Legion." Harold removed his hat and scratched his head, then plopped it back in place. "He's the one in charge."

"I don't know what you mean by a legion."

"Fancy name for a company if you ask me. It appears Thomas is tryin' to get officially mustered in as a real company—er legion—and he figures when word gets out his men had themselves a scalpin' party, some people jest might frown on it." Harold took a large bite of tobacco and stuffed it in the upper corner of his mouth, arranging it with his finger.

"I reckon he's right there," Keith nodded. "But how the heck did this Thomas—I'm presuming he's white—get to be heading up a company of Cherokee anyway?"

Harold took a couple of determined chews and spit a stream of brown juice on the ground before answering. "Story is when he was a youngin he somehow got right friendly with Chief Yonagushka who was chief of the Oconoluftee Cherokee, and the old chief adopted him. Called him Wil-Usdi, that's injun talk for Little Will. Made him a chief jest afore he died. They say he's the only white man to ever be an injun chief."

Malinda tucked her shirt into her pants and tightened the rope at her waist. "Well, I never heard of such a thing! A white man leading a tribe of injuns! Just think of it!"

"Little Will gets around in high places. He ain't jest a injun chief, he's a real dandy. Big noise up in Raleigh. Word has it he tried to get some kind a treaty and some land for the Cherokee. They say he's more injun than white, though nobody knows for sure if he's got injun blood in his veins. Doubt it though, 'cause he's cousin to Jeff Davis's wife, and she's Ole Zach Taylor's daughter, which means he's related to two presidents." Harold scratched his head again and chuckled. "They say Little Will's smoother than a tiger's eye. Why if that man tells you to go to hell, you'll look forward to the trip."

As the line moved closer to the chuck wagon, Malinda pressed for more information. "Do you know how it happened? The battle, I mean."

"The injuns were up near a place called Baptist Gap, and a Union advance party, out of Indiana, and no doubt lookin' for volunteers fer the Boys in Blue, seen 'em and set up an ambush. Now that's a pretty tricky thing to do to an injun, but talk is they were able to do it because of the land lay. They was high up and they seen the injuns comin' from far off, so they sets up this ambush and the first one they picked off was this Lieutenant John Astoogatogeh. Well, that made them injuns plum wild and they started war hoopin' and brandishin' their knives and bayonets, and shootin' their rifles, and they rode smack dab into the middle of that Union party, and before the Yankees knew what hit 'em, they'd all been slaughtered. That was when they took to scaplin' 'em for good measure, 'cause they was all upset about loosin' the lieutenant."

With the chuck wagon now in sight Keith leaned closer to Harold and spoke softly. "I hear what you're saying about this guy Thomas, but just because he's an honorary injun don't make him a good soldier, now does it?"

Harold spit on the ground again and wiped his mouth on the back of his hand. "They say Will Thomas knows these mountains as well as any injun, and he's been assigned to the North Carolina/Tennessee border to keep them damned Yankees from maraudin' and kidnappin' men to press into service fer the Union. There's been some bushwackin' goin' on, too. But after what happened yesterday, I reckon it'll be awhile before anymore Yankees'll be showin' their faces in North Carolina."

"Is this their main camp?" Keith prodded; and from the glint in his eye Malinda knew he was digging for information that could be useful when they made their escape to the North. "Seems to me this here's a long way from Tennessee."

"Their main camp's near Quallatown, over by the Tennessee border," Harold gestured toward the west. "This here's not much more than a scouting party."

Scouting party? Malinda gave a quick look around. *If this is only a scouting party, how many Cherokee are fighting for the Rebs?* She thought of the grisly scalps and involuntarily shuddered.

* * *

After breakfast the bugle sounded again followed by shouted orders to, "Mount up." The band left the forest by the same route they had entered, again passing silent sentries still displaying their souvenirs of battle. If what Harold said was true about Captain Thomas being upset over the scalpings, why were his men still carrying them? The discomforting thought came to her that Captain Thomas didn't have as tight a rein on his "legion" as he should have.

With the horses rested and back on a well traveled road, they continued their journey at a faster pace. The sun was bright, dispelling all traces of morning dew and rime. Before long the terrain became less winding, the inclines more gradual. Malinda looked back wistfully at the high country they were fast leaving behind. She had heard stories about the flat lands, how the summer heat was so intense it could scorch a man's skin in a matter of minutes, and how the air could sometimes weigh so heavy it was hard to breathe. She hoped they would be further north, behind Union lines, before the summer heat arrived.

Malinda's thoughts turned to her parents and she felt an immediate stab of remorse. Had Austin told them yet? What must Ma be thinking by now? How would she feel about her daughter riding off to war disguised as a man? And what would she tell Jacob about his sister? Maybe it was better not to think of such things. When her thoughts turned to Austin and Mary she found no solace there either. Best not to think about what lay hidden back there in the mountains … not family … or crocus peeking tiny heads through the snow … or the long plank table sitting idle in the kitchen … or their warm, comfortable bed …

When the pace slowed to give the animals a break, Malinda turned to Lonnie riding faithfully behind her. Harold, at Lonnie's side and directly behind Keith, was again silent, eyes fixed to some distant point. To Malinda's surprise, the dog who had spent the night with them, was curled up in a sling that swung from Lonnie's neck and shoulder. Only the small face was visible, eyes closed, obviously in a state of total contentment.

"Lonnie Coones what ever are you doing with that injun dog?"

"I ain't doin' nothin' with her. She wanted to come along. I didn't coax her none, she just tagged along."

Keith looked back at Lonnie and grinned. "Sure hope that scalping party doesn't come tracking their dog. I hear injuns are pretty attached to their animals."

Although Keith's tone was teasing, Malinda could see the fear once again rising in Lonnie's eyes. "Now don't you pay attention to Keith's teasing. Those injuns aren't going to come looking for any stray dog. They have other things to think about."

"If you're going to keep her," Keith added, "I reckon you oughta give her a name."

"I done named her already." There was an impish smile on Lonnie's rosy lips. "Her name's Fart."

"*FART?*" Malinda put one hand on her hip, immediately realized it was a feminine gesture and placed it on the rear of her saddle instead. "What kind of a name is that for a dog? Poor thing deserves a real name."

"Well, I was thinkin' 'bout the injuns and all, and how they name people after their natures. You know, if'n you're short they call you 'Little Somethin'-or-Other,' and if y'all are fast they name you 'Swift So-and-So,' well her bein' an injun dog and all, I sure enough named her after her own nature." He patted the dog's head and was rewarded with a lick to his palm. "I'm namin' her Fart, 'cause that's what she does real good. It's the most outstandin' thing in her nature."

Even Silent Harold chuckled at that one.

By the time they stopped for the noon meal, the land was nearly flat and the Blue Ridge a misty outline in the distance. "They look as if somebody painted them there, don't they?" Malinda's tone was pensive, a longing she had never known before was rising within. Where, she wondered, was that grim determination she'd felt earlier? All she wanted to do now was cry from homesickness. She let out a deep sigh. No doubt, she'd find her courage again ... But it would sure take some looking.

* * *

That night they bedded down in a woods beside a lake. There was no tent or teepee for cover, and they stretched their blankets out on a bed of leaves and pine needles. Malinda lay between Keith and Lonnie. Harold, who'd said he didn't like wolf dogs who farted all the time, had found himself another spot.

"Don't like Harold much, anyway," Lonnie said, cupping his hands behind his head as he stared up at the stars. "Somethin' about him makes me think of a snake."

Lonnie's words echoed Malinda's own thoughts. There *was* something sneaky about Harold. He always seemed to know things before anybody else did. And there was something about his eyes ... She was curious too, as to where he got all his information? Eavesdropping, probably. He seemed to be the type who would do so.

The night air carried a chill, and when Lonnie's dog changed sides, snuggling down between Malinda and Lonnie, Malinda welcomed the warmth and gave the animal an appreciative pat. "I'm going to find you a more respectable name," she whispered conspiratorially. "Any animal that is as faithful as you are deserves something better than Fart. Hey! Maybe that's it. Maybe I'll call you Faithful. How'd you like that?"

The dog responded with a thump of her tail, which Malinda took as a positive reply. "Faithful, it is then." She settled back, listening to the rush of the wind through the pines, the occasional sound of an animal plowing the night. Above, the mantle of stars, swept by occasional gray clouds, reminded her of something she'd read in one of Ma's poetry books, the one by that doctor fella, Oliver Wendell Holmes:

Day has put on his jacket,
And around His burning bosom
Buttoned it with stars.

Malinda reached out to touch Keith's shoulder and felt immediately reassured. They hadn't talked a lot since this journey began. Not private talk like they were used to. But once they got to where they were going things would settle down. Hopefully, they'd have their own tent, and some private time. At least for awhile. And soon—it couldn't be soon enough to suit her—they'd be heading North.

☆

CHAPTER 11

Austin was feeling uncomfortable as he stood on the Pritchard's porch. He disliked being the bearer of bad news and he was certain that was how Malinda's parents would view her letter. Again he wished she would have found it in herself to tell them direct, but maybe if they had seen her all decked out like a boy that might have been even more painful. It had sure come as a surprise to him. And to Mary. There were a lot of things to be admired in Malinda; her spirit bein' one of 'em. She was some woman, all right. He chuckled to himself. Brave enough to go to war, but not brave enough to stay behind.

Elizabeth answered Austin's knock. Jacob, twining himself in her skirts, peered out at him with a shy, mischievous grin.

"Afternoon, Elizabeth." Austin removed his hat, poking the brim of it at the child's stomach in a teasing gesture. "And good afternoon to you Jacob." The boy hid his face in his mother's skirts. "Hope I'm not disturbing you, Elizabeth." Reading the strain on her face he quickly explained his mission. "Malinda's all right. I … I have a letter for you. From her." He dug into his pocket and withdrew the folded piece of paper.

Elizabeth took the note and stepped back, allowing her visitor to enter. "Come in Austin. Come in and sit down. Alfred's out in the barn. I'll call him. He probably didn't hear you ride up. He's getting deaf as a doornail of late."

Austin took a place on the milking stool beside the fire, twisting his hat between his hands. "No need to bother him, Elizabeth. I'll not be staying. Mary's been poorly, and I don't like leaving her alone too long."

"Yes, I've heard. I'm sorry to hear that." Elizabeth stuffed the note into her apron pocket. "Surely you have time for a cup of sassafras tea?"

Austin shook his head and gestured with his hat toward the door. "Elizabeth, maybe it's best if you read your letter before I head back. That way if you have questions, I'll try to answer 'em. I'm not sure of the particulars of what's in there, but I reckon I know the meat of it."

Elizabeth wet her lips then closed them between her teeth until they disappeared. She sat down at the pine table and pulled the note from her pocket.

Jacob, still pulling at her skirts, raised his hands to be picked up. She lifted the child to her lap, unfolded the note and cupped her forehead in her hand as she silently began to read:

Dearest Ma and Pa,

I'm sorry to be writing to you like this, instead of coming to tell you of our plans face up, but we decided in such a hurry it's necessary to tell you through this letter. Keith is being forced to join the Confederacy and I'm going with him. I've changed my appearance. That way we'll be able to tent together. As soon as possible, most likely within a few weeks, we'll be carrying out Keith's plan, if you know what I mean. He told you about it during your last visit. I'll be with him.

Please pray for us, as we will be praying for all of you. Pray too, that this awful war will be finished and over with soon, so we can all be together again. Please don't worry about me. Or Keith. We'll be fine, so long as we're together.

Love, M.

Please kiss Jacob for me and tell him I love him.

Elizabeth slowly folded the paper and placed it back in her apron pocket. "She … she went with him? Surely, the army wouldn't take a woman—" Her voice faltered. "She … says she's changed her appearance."

"She sure did just that, Elizabeth. She cut off her hair and fixed it man style, and wore Keith's shirt and trousers, and if you didn't know beforehand it was Malinda, you'd never in this world guess she was anything besides what she's posing to be. Just a young whelp. Did she say there that she'll be sayin' her name is Sam?"

"No. No, she didn't say that."

"She's sayin' she's Keith's kid brother. Sam Blalock." Trying to soften the blow. "Seems now I got myself two sons instead of one."

"Malinda has joined the Confederacy. She's a Rebel soldier." Elizabeth said the words aloud, trying to make them real. Her eyes were trained on Austin but she seemed to be looking straight through him. Jacob reached for a lock of his mother's hair with one hand and stuck his other thumb in his mouth as he leaned back in her arms.

There was a sound from the porch. The door opened and Alfred stood on the threshold. "Afternoon, Austin. Thought that was your horse. Everythin' all right?"

Austin rose and stretched out his hand. "Mary's ailin,' but I'm doin' just fine thank you. You're lookin' well Alfred."

Elizabeth lowered Jacob to the floor and the child began to whimper. "He needs his nap." Lifting him to her shoulder she carried him up the ladder to the loft and settled him on the pallet.

The two men studied each other awkwardly for a moment until finally Alfred broke the silence. "Well, Austin I reckon you best be tellin' me what brings you such a long way. Got somethin' to do with Malinda, now ain't it?" He dropped heavily into a chair at the other end of the table. Expecting bad news.

Austin leaned forward, knees apart, stared down at the hat he was still twirling between his hands. "I brought a letter from Malinda. Elizabeth's read it." He glanced up at his host who sat motionless, studying the fire.

"A letter now is it?" Alfred said after a long moment, then shook his head. "How are things over your way, Austin? Better than here, I hope."

"I can't say they're good. The Rebs are after anybody healthy enough to hold a gun. They even took Jones, my brother McCaleb's boy, and he only now turned fifteen. Nearly killed his mother, I hear. Him bein' the youngest, and the favorite."

"We got the same thing here. The Rebs are out collectin' anybody who's breathin,' and let me tell you, they sure as tarnation are makin' it hard on anybody who doesn't back 'em up. I been figurin' on doing my plantin' in the next couple of weeks, but I don't imagine I'll be seein' the harvest. Them bastards have been takin' livestock and robbin' barns from anybody who even thinks Union. They already cleaned me out of hay. I've had a helluva time tryin' to find enough feed for my cows, and to tell the truth I'm expectin' they'll be takin' them any day now, too. When them cowards come on their raidin' parties they don't come one or two at a time. They come by the handful so's a man ain't got a chance to defend his property." Alfred lowered his gaze to the floor. "Tom Decker tried to hold 'em off when they came after his chickens, and they shot him dead right there in his own yard."

"Good Lord! Did they catch the ones who did it?"

Alfred chuckled ruefully. "If they did, they more'n likely pinned a medal on him. Tom was Union."

"Oh! I didn't know."

"Yeah, he always kept his opinions to hisself. But young Tom run off up to Kentucky and joined the Union a few weeks back. That's the reason they was gunnin' for him, I suppose."

Alfred looked up as Elizabeth descended the ladder. "Lizzie? Austin here tells me we got news from Malinda."

"Yes." Elizabeth looked toward the stove. "I was just going to make some tea for Austin. Would you like some?"

Alfred shook his head. "I reckon you'd best be bringin' out the cider jug instead. I'm thinkin' this ain't news to be taken with no tea."

* * *

Austin hadn't wanted to stay for the rereading of the letter, but Alfred had insisted on his having a glass of cider with him, and considering the chill of the late afternoon, and the long ride ahead, he'd agreed.

Now, heading out onto the main road he tapped his mount lightly on the flank in an encouraging gesture to hurry. As so often of late, his thoughts turned to what life would be like when Mary was gone. Try as he might he couldn't dispel the tormenting thoughts. What would be the reason to go on alone? For that matter, did he even want to? Perhaps it was these very thoughts that helped him to understand Malinda's recent actions. There couldn't be many things much worse than being left behind. He had been a one woman man all his life. Except for those two haystack adventures when he was fourteen or so, and that one visit to a bawdy house in Lenoir when he was nineteen, the only woman who'd shared his bed and body was Mary. And that was the way he'd wanted it.

* * *

After Austin's departure, Alfred didn't return to his work in the barn. Instead he poured himself another glass of cider and continued to stare into the fire. It wasn't long before the bleary-eyed homily began. "Wonder what your family would think of this, Lizzie? All those well read and well wrote relatives a yours are no doubt turnin' in their graves at the thought of one of their own females joinin' the army. Ain't somethin' respectable folk do, now is it? They'd be layin' the blame at my feet, probably, and rightfully so. Educated people don't have their girl children runnin' off to war. Malinda's got some of my blood all right. Just common old mountain folk, who ain't never been much on the fancy things in life. You shoulda had an easier life, Lizzie. You should a married one of them city guys who coulda give you the things you deserve and not wasted yourself on the likes of me. Then your daughter wouldn't be off fightin' in no war."

Elizabeth sighed and looked up from the pot of boiling turnips. "I'm thinking Alfred that we might be concerning ourselves with the living instead of the dead. I'm thinking we ought to be sending our prayers out to Malinda and asking God Almighty to protect our child." She walked to him and placed a warm and comforting hand on his shoulder. "She'll no doubt be needing some prayers coming her way, but she's a good melding of the two of us, you know. She's got your mountain strength and fortitude and my daring and logic. I'm thinking that for the first time I'm glad she's got Keith Blalock at her side. Keith isn't a man to be messed with, and he'll look after Malinda."

She leaned Alfred's head against her breast; gently stroking his hair. Keith Blalock or God Almighty, one or the other would have to look after their daughter now because there wasn't anything more she could do. Dear God she felt so helpless! *Oh, Malinda, Malinda, my willful, willful child! Whatever is to become of you?*

* * *

As the new recruits continued their ride east, news of the war was delivered periodically. Keith was never quite sure who was bringing it, since he and Malinda were riding in approximately the middle of the company. But he reasoned the news must be coming from scouts who had been dispatched ahead.

If this ill assorted group, many who supported the Union, was any indication of the military power of the Confederacy, he was amazed the war had lasted this long. He had envisioned military life as restrictive and disciplined, but this group of mountain men seemed as fiercely independent as he was, and just as determined to do things their own way. The hell with taking orders from any officer. Before leaving the induction center they had been told that drinking anything intoxicating was strictly forbidden, and that everyone was to be in bed by eleven o'clock. Yet every night since the trip began five days ago, there had been raucous noise, loud music and drunken laughter from various quarters of the group long after curfew. The only exception had been that first night, the one they'd spent with Thomas's Highland Legion. Mountain men respected injuns far more than they respected anything military.

Keith was proud but not surprised at how well Malinda was holding up. In spite of the soft exterior there was an iron will buried inside his woman. He'd sensed that the first moment he'd laid eyes on her, and his intuition was proving correct. There were times since this journey began when she'd actually seemed to be enjoying herself. How many other women would or could—do what she was doing? Except for those first few minutes when they'd met up with the Cherokee—when he too, thought they were marked for slaughter—she hadn't flinched. Actually, she was holding up better than that kid Lonnie who kept tagging after them.

Now that was one scared kid. Probably lying about his age. Seemed more like fourteen than the sixteen he claimed to be. But like Malinda said, Lonnie was a trifle on the dull side. His Ma probably hadn't been able to run fast enough to get away from her brother.

The man riding directly in front of Keith slowed his mount and turned to shout over his shoulder. "Over in Tennessee at Pittsburg Landing we surprised Grant, and overran his ass. We lost General Johnston, though. Pass it on."

Keith tipped his hat acknowledging he'd heard the message, then turned and shouted it to Harold who was close in back of him. When he glanced at Malinda he read her look of concern, and risked a reassuring pat on the thigh. "No sense worrying about trouble before it gets here," he said lightly.

Since the trip began, with the exception of the night they'd spent with the Cherokee, they had camped every night in the open air. And it appeared tonight would be no different. Their route had been easterly, veering occasionally in order to stay close to a lake or river, but for some reason the site chosen tonight was far from the water. Keith found this strange, especially so since the air had turned unseasonably warm. Added to this was a feeling of tension among the group that hadn't been present since their encounter with Thomas's Legion. It was hard to define.

Malinda posed the very question Keith had been thinking. "Wonder why we're stopping so far from the river? The horses need water, and I could sure use a dip myself."

"Well, you'll be doing your dipping in private, I reckon," Keith said firmly. Two nights before when they'd camped beside a waterfall, everyone had stripped and taken a swim. Malinda had stationed herself on the river bank, watching, and when he'd seen her enjoying the view, he'd sent her back to tend to the horses. Along with a few choice words.

Now, as Malinda pulled her brush from the saddlebag and began grooming her mount, she gestured with the brush. "Look! Here comes one of the officers."

As a rule the officers had remained aloof, and only when necessary had they spent any time with the new recruits.

"Wonder what *he* wants?" Keith's tone dripped with antagonism.

"Gentlemen." The pale faced lieutenant, who normally carried himself with such a pompous air, now greeted them with a worried frown. "It is imperative that the following order be carried out in its entirety. There will be no fires, no music, no noise and above all no drinking. The enemy is camped directly across the river from our location, which is why we are not closer to the river. It is unlikely our presence will be discovered because of the terrain, but only if the orders are carried out in full. We have sentries posted near the river. In the event our presence is discovered, the bugle will be sounded and everyone will mount up immediately. Do not unsaddle your horses. Water will be provided for the animals. It will be up to you to supply food for yourselves and for your mounts from any provisions you may have brought with you. And remember there will be no fires. If you see any man violating these orders you are to use whatever force necessary to stop him—while still retaining the integrity of silence, of course."

"How many are they?" Keith asked.

"That is not your concern," came the sharp reply.

"Well, why don't we stand and fight? That's what an army is supposed to do isn't it?"

Without answering the lieutenant moved on to the next group of men, and Keith turned to Malinda. "This may be our chance," he said softly.

"You mean ... ?"

"Yes. If that's the Tar River, and my calculations say it is, we can't be far from Union lines if anything we've been hearing is true. I'll go scout around and see how it looks."

"Keith? Be careful!"

He gave her a wink as he slipped away into the cover of trees and bushes.

* * *

Malinda busied herself by grooming her horse, and when she'd finished with her own, she groomed Keith's. As expected Lonnie wandered up, accompanied by his dog. He seemed more nervous than usual, and it was obvious he intended to bed down with them as he had done every other night.

Malinda was finding it hard to disguise her own feelings of uneasiness, and Lonnie's presence would certainly complicate things if Keith decided they should make their escape tonight. Could they take Lonnie with them, she wondered? He would be willing, no doubt about that, but how dependable would he be? Could they count on him if things went amiss, or would he panic? While Lonnie chatted aimlessly as he played with his dog, Malinda pondered the question. Reluctantly, she decided that Lonnie would be too great a risk. He would have to stay behind.

Two hours later Lonnie lay sleeping, but Malinda was wide-eyed, straining to hear every sound the night offered up. Suddenly, she sat upright. Listening. The night was thick with silence. Maybe it wasn't anything. She tucked her knees to her chin. And waited.

Although Keith's step was soft, she heard it before he reached the clearing. By the filtered light of the moon she saw his shadowed form standing beside a tree. He raised one hand and motioned her to follow.

Being careful not to wake Lonnie, Malinda crawled to the edge of the clearing and crept into the brush. Once there she stood up and reached for Keith's hand. He led the way quietly through the dense cover of trees.

When they were far enough away not to be overheard, he paused and shook his head. "It won't work. It's too risky. We'd have to take the horses, and that river is so still there's barely a ripple. The Rebs have got sentries every 50 yards on this side, and it seems more than likely the Union has sentries posted too. We'd be sitting ducks with that moon shining down on us. I think our original plan to wait for a skirmish is still the best. While everybody is otherwise occupied we'll stand a better chance."

"Whatever you say." Malinda felt a rush of relief. Nothing had to be done for now; they could both get some needed rest. And she wouldn't have to abandon Lonnie. Not yet, anyway.

* * *

It was a hazy dawn swathed in layers of fog. The hush of the previous evening still hung over the camp like a smothering blanket. Men moved silently back and forth, in and out of the brush and bushes relieving themselves, but no one whispered a word that wasn't necessary. The enemy was still close by. They could hear men laughing and talking, splashing in the river, and the tantalizing aroma of coffee brewing hung as heavy as the fog.

Within the hour the Union troops began crossing the river, heading toward them up the steep, rocky incline. They wound their way through the woods, sometimes passing within a few hundred yards of where men lay hidden under fallen trees and behind rocks.

From a vantage point high up at the mouth of a cave, and well hidden by bushes, Keith estimated there were between two hundred and two hundred and thirty men, all neatly uniformed, all carrying heavy weaponry. Most had Spencer rifles, and some had what he thought might be 16-shot Henrys. He'd heard tales of this weapon, but had never actually seen one. Some of the Reb boys in Morganton who had seen them said the Yanks loaded the Henrys in the morning and shot the damned things all day without ever reloading.

Keith counted three 24-pounder siege guns and two flatbeds of canisters filled with ammunition. Although his vision was somewhat limited because of the trees, he felt sure there were other small cannons, too. Maybe Napoleons. There was no mistaking the wisdom of the Reb officers' decision to lay low. If they'd stood their ground against those weapons nobody would have lived to see Kinston.

The last of the Union detachment had been gone a full hour before there was any activity in the camp. Finally, leaning with her back against the cave wall, Malinda nudged Keith. "I smell coffee."

"Yeah, I think you're right."

All around them men were beginning to emerge from hiding places; from behind jutting rocks and trees, beneath logs, even from treetops. Lonnie, whom they hadn't seen for some time, suddenly reappeared through the brush, his dog at his heels. There was a broad smile on the freckled face, an indication that his belly was full. It was a condition both Keith and Malinda envied.

"The little fucker's been foraging," Keith chuckled.

"Probably not in the woods either," Malinda giggled. "More than likely in somebody's saddlebag."

After a welcomed breakfast the company moved out again on what rumor said would be the final day of their journey. They were now moving almost due South. As the uniformed soldiers rode into position, Keith noted that while the officers were wearing their usual wide brimmed hats, the non commissioned men were wearing havelocks over their kepis, an indication the sun was expected to be hot. There was no doubt about there being a major weather shift. The last two days the temperatures had risen far above the 75 degrees said to be normal for these flatlands during the first week of April.

The terrain had become monotonous. There were long, open stretches where a man could see for miles, occasionally broken by a small incline that could hardly be called a hill. Trees were scarce, too. And real woods, where a company of men could take shelter, were fewer and farther apart. Although this open space made their group a sitting target, the opposite was also true. They could see what was coming long before anyone was within shooting range.

"Keith! Look!" Malinda stood upright in her stirrups in an effort to see above the heads of the riders in front. "Would you look at that! I've never seen anything like it! Can that be somebody's house? Look at all those windows!"

Keith pulled slightly to the right to get a better view. Up ahead lay a huge plantation. The house, the biggest he'd ever seen, was made of brick and had six white pillars and a veranda that ran clear across the front. It was set back from the road a quarter mile or more on a raised knoll. There were four chimneys and twelve windows on the front of the house alone, each framed by white shutters. A bank of towering trees sheltered the structure on both sides, and at the back there were two enormous barns. As they drew nearer he could see that also at the back, and to the side of the main house, was a row of small buildings, wooden, weather worn, and all leaning slightly in the same direction like saplings caught by a strong wind. Apparently, these were slave dwellings.

What was most fascinating, however, were the fields. In the front and to the side of the house, were row after row of plowed land that seemed to stretch for miles. Sprinkled among the treeless fields were a half dozen or more mule drawn wagons, each with a black driver up front, seated between two enormous barrels. Two more slaves sat on the back of the wagon with a pile of green plants in their laps. Every foot or so the driver would release a small amount of water from one of the barrels and as the mule moved forward, one of the slaves at the back would reach down and plug a plant into the wet spot.

"Looks like it's 'puttin-in-tobaccy-time'." Keith removed his hat and wiped his brow with a kerchief. "Now that's what I call one helluva plantation!"

"I could never have imagined one house could be that big!" Malinda marveled. "Those two we passed yesterday weren't near half this size, and there sure weren't this many slaves either."

As they watched, a massive black man appeared on the front porch. He was dressed in tight, gray knickers, knee high white socks and matching shirt. His entire costume was topped by a gray vest adorned with several rows of brass buttons, and a wide brimmed triangular hat of the same gray. He took no note of the passing parade but went straight toward two magnificent horses tied to the hitching post in front of the house. He untied a black stallion and began leading the animal toward a side portico that was draped heavy with wisteria vines.

The pace of the column began to slow, and to everyone's surprise, they turned into the winding dirt road that led to the house.

"Whatever is going on?" Malinda cried in astonishment.

"Looks like we're stopping to call on somebody," Keith answered. "Sure as hell hope they're expecting us."

While the line of men waited, two officers dismounted and approached the front porch. The black man who had led the horse to the portico and secured the animal, reentered the house through a side entrance. A moment later, reappearing at the front door, he opened it wide for the officers to enter then closed it behind them.

"What's going on Sam?" Lonnie prodded. "Lord a mercy I never seen so much tobaccy at one time in my whole life! An' did y'all see that buck nigger? Lawzy! He's the biggest damned thing I ever seen! Why I bet he's bigger'n an elephant!"

It wasn't long before the mystery was solved. One of the two officers returned to the head of the line, spoke briefly with another man and then the signal to move ahead was given. The line moved slowly to the rear of the house.

In back of the mansion was a graceful, sloping lawn just beginning to green. It was surrounded by a variety of fruit trees. At the bottom of the incline was a narrow brook. The men were ordered to dismount and water their horses.

While they did so, several slaves, women and children mostly, appeared from rear doors of the house bearing chairs, stools and small tables. Two male slaves carried a small awning and quickly erected it beneath a willow tree at the water's edge. Within minutes other slaves appeared carrying white tablecloths which they laid out on the grass at various places throughout the yard. Then they quickly returned to the house, only to reappear bearing baskets of Johnnycakes, sourdough breads, jellies and pitchers of water and tea.

"Are you believing this?" Malinda gasped, addressing no one in particular. "They are going to feed us! *All these men!* They are going to feed us!"

The officers remained inside the house. Two sergeants and three corporals took seats beneath the awning, while the remainder of the group lounged on the lawn beside tablecloths. Stacks of dinner plates had been placed on the tablecloths.

"I can't believe one house could have this many dishes," Malinda stared at the display with open mouth wonder.

"Probably had to borrow some from the neighbors," Keith commented dryly.

Malinda nudged him with her elbow. "You damned idiot, there aren't any neighbors! And you haven't ever seen anything this grand before either, now don't go pretending you have. I wonder who in the dickens lives here?"

A female slave bent near Malinda offering a basket of fried chicken. Malinda reached in and took two pieces.

"Da pickaninnies be 'long wif da chitlins and taters most di-recly, Massa," the slave said, offering the basket to Keith.

A few steps behind the woman were two young boys; one a mulatto. They were carrying a large pot. The older one, maybe ten, lifted the lid and pulled out a ladle of boiled potatoes, while the smaller boy wrestled with holding the pot upright.

Once Keith and Malinda were served the boys quickly moved on, saying not a word, their huge brown eyes fixed on the ground. Another young boy arrived with a steaming pot of chitlins, followed by another carrying a tray of condiments.

Malinda took another bite of chicken, laid the bone on the plate and began licking her fingers one by one as she grinned up at Keith. "I have to say that right here in this place, in the yard of the richest house I ever did see, owned by somebody I don't even know, is one of the best meals I ever ate in my entire life!"

Feeling something move in her lap, she looked down to see Lonnie's dog stealing the chicken from her plate. "You aren't going to get much from that," she said. "I ate it clear down to the marrow."

As the men were finishing their meal the officers reappeared. There had been no sign of their host, but as the line mounted up and began heading back toward the road, Keith noted the black stallion was missing and saw in the distance a rising cloud of dust traveling in a straight line. A rider in a hurry.

When they reached the main road and turned South in the direction of Greensboro, Keith looked back at the house. "I wonder who owns that place?" he mused. "I'd sure like to know how one man ever got so much money."

The ever knowing Harold supplied the answer. "That's Hardin Reynolds' place. If you think this one is big you outta see the one he's got up in Rock Springs, Virginia. Pissed as hell he is, too," Harold grinned. "He jest found out this is his last year for raisin' tobaccy. Jeff Davis says he's got to plant edibles fer the rest a the war."

"I'd sure like to have a picture of this," Keith said.

"I don't need a picture," Malinda sighed. "This isn't something I'm likely to be forgetting." She looked at Keith with a wistful smile, then leaned toward him and said softly so no one else could hear. "One day, after the war is over, when we've had a chance to put some money away, I'd like to have a place like this. Oh, lots smaller, of course. Nothing that would require slaves. But something sort of like it, you know, with a veranda and nice dishes and all."

Keith stared straight ahead without responding. What was there to say? It was moments like this when he remembered that Malinda, however strong willed and courageous, was in some ways, still very much a child. And very much a dreamer.

* * *

By mid afternoon the sky had darkened. In the distance a storm was building. By the time they reached Kinston, it was raining.

CHAPTER 12

"This here's the Confederate Garrison at Kinston. Y'all are members of the 26th North Carolina Troops under the leadership of Colonel Zebulon Vance. Y'all will be issued firearms and receive training on how to shoot, load and care for these here firearms. Training in the use of these here firearms will begin as soon as the rain stops. At that time y'all will gather at the rear of the mess hall and be divided up into squads and be assigned to training officers. Uniforms will be issued when and if we get 'em."

Malinda and Keith edged their way toward the front of the gathering, nearer to the wooden staging where the baby-faced lieutenant stood holding an umbrella over his head. Malinda didn't want to miss anything he had to say. If there was something she needed to do well, it was follow orders. Getting it right meant she wouldn't be singled out for attention.

It was a bitter morning. Rain had poured like a waterfall throughout the night and showed no signs of stopping. There weren't many times in Malinda's life when she could remember being more physically uncomfortable. They had no cots and the ground was a literal mud hole. Her clothes were drenched, her boots so filled with water they squirted with each step. She had tried to dry them out overnight by turning them upside down on a rock she'd drug inside their tent, but one step into the deep mud this morning and her efforts had been wasted.

The lieutenant climbed down from the staging, still protecting himself with the umbrella, as Keith grabbed Malinda's arm, ushering her in the direction of the mess hall.

"I guess that Nancy-boy lieutenant is finally finished with his half-assed orders," Keith growled. "Jesus I can't stand seeing a man carry an umbrella! He's supposed to be a soldier, and he looks like a damned girl!"

Malinda shot him a sharp look but said nothing. Ever since Keith had opened his eyes this morning his mood had been a long way from good. She put it down to physical discomfort. Though he'd be the last to admit it, in spite of her husband's strength and toughness, there was one thing that bothered him more than he let on. Keith called it "the bone aches." Doc Petersen said, "rheumatism." But whatever you called it, being wet sure didn't help. When they were putting their boots on this morning she'd seen him rubbing his legs and knew he was paining. But as Mary had advised, when Keith was in one of his moods, it was best to walk gently and say little.

Malinda decided she wouldn't have shared her current thoughts with Keith even if he was in a good humor. He didn't want to hear *anything* good about the Rebs, but she was finding herself pleasantly surprised by what they'd seen so far at the Kinston Garrison. And if the pissing rain would ever stop they'd be able to see a lot more!

A high log wall surrounded the compound and on the inside wall was a narrow platform. Sentries, the army called them "pickets," marched back and forth on the platform keeping their eyes trained on the open field outside. The garrison was well fortified with cannon, too. They'd seen a dozen or more of what Keith called 10-inch Columbiad, and Malinda was sure there were others. It made a person feel well protected—if you were a Confederate, that is.

Outside the wall and beyond the field lay a long stretch of swamp backed by a deep forest. They'd been told there were pickets posted in those woods who weren't only looking for Union scouts, but deserters as well. From both sides. There were six frame buildings within the compound, the main one being the Company Headquarters. This building also served as the mess hall and had a ceiling high partition separating the two areas. The second building was the armory where weapons, ammunition, and certain provisions were stored, and the third served as a barracks for junior officers. Another smaller building was both a hospital and the sutler's shop.

The new recruits had been warned about the sutler. He was a merchant, and a dishonest one. It was said he could get you whatever you wanted. Anything from a horse, to a hand mirror, *if* you were willing to pay his price.

The smallest of the buildings was the jail, and the remaining one was Colonel Vance's residence, which he shared with other high ranking officers. It was rumored that present activity inside that house centered on Colonel Vance's efforts to get both General Catlin and General Branch removed from their posts after the disastrous Confederate losses at New Bern a few weeks back. Keith said he had talked with some of the soldiers who fought at New Bern, and they all said General Branch deserved to be hung. They had high praise for Colonel Vance though, especially since he'd restored their spirits with a keg of brandy they'd uncovered.

To Malinda's delight the enlisted men were housed in two man tents. *Thank you Jesus!* No doubt when Keith was rested and his bone aches were doing better they would resume their man and wife activities. She was certainly looking forward to that!

* * *

As Keith and Malinda entered the mess hall they paused at the door to stomp their feet and pour water from their hat brims. Buckets had been placed on some of the tables to catch an occasional leak, but the place was essentially dry.

They had just filled their plates and taken seats at one of the long tables when Lonnie approached and settled down on the bench next to Malinda, his thigh touching hers. Fart, as usual, was trailing after him and settled himself beneath the bench. Lonnie wiggled his bare feet under the dog's furry coat in an effort to get them dry and warm.

"Danged rain's got a chill to it now, ain't it?" Lonnie dug into the food on his tin plate without looking up.

"I'm beginning to think anything resembling food is about as scarce as hen's teeth in this Reb Army," Keith griped. "Look at this! They're calling it stew! It isn't anything but boiled cornmeal with a hunk of bacon thrown in. No wonder they're saying everybody around here has got the shits!" He pushed his plate away and glared at the cook and the two young slave boys who were ladling plates full of the steaming cush into outstretched tin plates.

Lonnie, who wasn't about to cross Keith by disagreeing with him, wasn't about to let food go to waste either. He reached gingerly across the table and scraped the remainder of Keith's food into his own plate. After he'd swallowed as much as he could hold he put the plate on the floor, offering what was left to his dog.

At noon the next day the rain finally stopped. A cheer went up throughout the camp, and as ordered, everyone assembled for firearms training. They were told that whatever knives they had they could keep. Most, like Keith, had Bowies.

Targets were set up and each man was told to fire his own gun. Flintlocks, which the army called "Kentucky Rifles" were standard among the new recruits. They were commonly used for hunting, which was what most mountain men used them for, but their accuracy and loading time made them a hazard in a military situation against the breech loading rifles known to be used by the Union.

Keith breathed a sigh of relief when a wagon with Sharps rifles and a few Jennings was brought out. He was very much surprised when a dozen or more Spencers were produced, too. The training officer gave a brief lesson on the proper use of these firearms, and he felt a surge of pride when he overheard the officer congratulating Sam on his marksmanship.

On the third day, assignments were handed out. Some would be heading North to engage the enemy, others, who would be leaving the 26th, would head toward the coast to join another company. Others were to be relief troops for men stationed around the railroad junction at Goldsboro, while still others were assigned garrison duty and would remain at Kinston.

There were some uneasy moments while names were being called, but Keith noted that the best marksmen were the ones singled out for garrison duty. He placed a casual arm around Sam's shoulder while they waited to hear their assignments, and they heaved simultaneous sighs of relief when both Blalocks were called for garrison duty. Although this was the last assignment Keith wanted because it meant they would be far removed from the fighting, at least they were still together. Lonnie, who was also a crack shot, was assigned to the garrison as well. Keith assumed the Army's reasoning was that poor shots were expendable.

"We've got to come up with a new plan," Keith said glumly when they were finally alone in their tent. "All we're going to be doing here is parading around that damned wall holding a gun."

"When we get picket duty out in the woods can't we just slip off and join up with the Union like we planned? We won't need to be going through a skirmish."

Keith ran his fingers through his hair as he paced the tent. "Even if we are assigned duty out in the woods the chances of finding Union lines is pretty slim. We don't have any idea where they are! We could roam those woods for weeks before we find 'em. And the chances of not getting shot, either from one side or the other, is just about zero!"

"But Keith, don't you think it looks as if they're expecting the Union to attack the garrison? Otherwise why would they be putting so many pickets around it? And their best shots at that. Don't fret, Sweetheart, we'll find a way." She reached for his hand, but he jerked it away. "I figure we just have to wait it out," she continued, ignoring the slight. "It only makes sense for the Union to attack here. It's where the guns and ammunition are stored."

"Not being privy to their plans it's a little hard to figure out just how long that may be, now isn't it?" Keith snapped. "Face it, Malinda, we could be stuck here for months!"

"I don't see there's much else we can do *but* wait."

"Well, maybe you can wait, but I can't! Goddamnit, I *won't* wait! We've been here four days now, and I can't think of a more miserable four days in my entire life." He stopped pacing and turned to her with a pleading look. "Malinda, I don't think you have any idea how *much* I hate the Rebs. It's … I can't even put it into words." He gave a helpless shrug. "But I'll tell you one thing. I'll go nuts if I don't get out of here soon. I know now how a slave feels. Some asshole with the brains of a toad barking orders all day long. Telling you what to do, just because somebody with more gold braid on his sleeve told him to say it. These people don't have any idea of what they're fighting for, they're just doing it because some other asshole told 'em to."

* * *

Keith's lament came as no surprise to Malinda. If there was one thing Keith Blalock hated, it was anybody telling him what to do. And he also hated being a tiny cog in a big wheel. Back home, people had generally looked up to Keith. Or feared him. In any case he was shown respect. There, everyone knew who he was. Here, he was just another raw recruit. So how, Malinda wondered, did he think the Union Army would be any different?

Over the following days she watched Keith during drill practice and several times had to stifle a giggle. He reminded her of that little wooden soldier of Jacob's, his uniform so proper and all. The only thing was it looked like they'd run out of material before they got the pants done. Evidently somebody didn't know mountain men grew tall. Keith's pants stopped three inches above his boot tops. Good thing there wasn't a mirror around because he would have had a fit if he could see what he looked like!

The uniform issued to Malinda consisted of boots and a kepi. She was told to check back next week and maybe they would have the rest of it. Lonnie too, had been bypassed except for boots and a hat. But the boots he'd so yearned for were turning out to be a grave disappointment.

"I swear Sam, I can't walk another step in these damned things," Lonnie moaned. "I'd figured they'd feel right nice and friendly on my feet, but Lord's truth, I ain't never had nothin' to pain me so in my WHOLE life!" He dropped to the ground beside the barracks wall, unlaced one boot, and held his blistered foot up for Malinda's inspection.

She winced and pulled away. "Maybe if you'd wash some of that grime off your feet before you put them in the boots, they'd fit better. You've got at least an inch of mud caked on the bottom of your foot. Socks would help."

"Ain't got no socks, Sam. I'm thinkin' maybe I just won't wear the danged boots."

"But you've been assigned picket duty just like Keith and me," she argued. "And if you get sent to the woods you sure as blazes better be wearing boots. There's a whole swamp of poison oak outside this compound, and that's no place for a human to be walking barefoot. I was telling Keith that just this morning, because he's allergic to poison oak. All he's got to do is look at it and he breaks out."

Lonnie offered the wounded foot to his dog for licking, then grinned as the dog's tongue tickled his toes. "Guess you're right, Sam. But I ain't sure I can do much walkin' on these poor feet a mine, and we got all that instructin' stuff to do this afternoon."

"You'd better be planning on doing some walking if you know what's good for you," Malinda cautioned.

Reluctantly, Lonnie pushed his foot back into his boot, rose and limped after Malinda out into the compound for "Picket Instruction."

* * *

That night Keith wrote a letter to his parents.

Dear Ma and Pa,

Sam and I are here in Kinston at the garrison, and there isn't much going on. Everything is so quiet, we figure the Union Army must be hiding out somewhere. We are both fine and hope you are the same. They tell me you can write to us here at the Kinston barracks,

but it may be a spell before your letter gets through. Please let our friends the Pritchards know we're fine. You know what I mean, I reckon. Hope you're feeling better, Ma.
Love, Keith

They had been at Kinston less than a week when one evening Malinda returned to their tent to find Keith seated on the edge of a cot. Harold, whom they hadn't seen for awhile, was seated on a second one.

"Well, now isn't this a surprise!" Malinda exclaimed. "Wherever did you find the cots?" She nodded to their visitor. "Howdy, Harold. Haven't seen much of you lately."

"Harold got 'em for us," Keith said. But Malinda read something in his eyes besides gratitude. "He found out which troops were moving out, and he borrowed their cots, since they won't be using 'em."

"Now wasn't that thoughtful!" Malinda forced a smile. "That was real Christian of you, Harold, thinking about us like that." Now why in the name of heaven, she wondered, was Harold being so considerate? He'd all but abandoned them since they'd arrived in Kinston.

"Harold says these latest stories we've been hearing about what happened in Tennessee are true. It seems that little skirmish over at Shiloh didn't exactly turn out the way we first heard it did. Seems General Grant turned things around some, and it's now being considered a major victory for the Union. Looks like the Yankees are getting ready to march on Corinth in Mississippi to try to take over the railroad."

"We had over 11,000 dead and wounded," Harold added. "But the Yankees lost at least that many, maybe more."

"Eleven thousand men?" Malinda shook her head as if to clear it. "In one battle? ... How ... how can they count that many dead? Where do you bury that many bodies? And *how*?"

"Sometimes there ain't enough left of a man *to* bury," Harold scratched at his shoulder. "Them cannons do a pretty fair job of separatin' a man from his parts."

Malinda felt her eyes filling with unexpected tears and went outside without saying anything more. The pure savagery of those numbers made her physically ill. She needed fresh air. And she needed to get away from Harold. That was one thing about that man. You could generally smell him before you could see him. As she walked Harold's words played over and over again inside her head. "We had over 11,000 dead and wounded, but the Yankees lost at least that many, maybe more." It was incomprehensible.

She walked briskly up and down the lines of tents, then circled the entire encampment. "I don't care what Keith says," she muttered aloud. "I sure as hell would rather be inside these walls than out there somewhere on an open field being shot at with a cannon!"

Twenty minutes later as she neared their tent her pace was slower, her mind clearer, but her heart remained heavy.

Surprisingly, Keith had little to say about their visitor's message or his unexpected gift, but as they were getting ready to bed down he said, "I'd look out what you say around Harold. I get the feeling he tells us things in the hope we'll tell him something back."

"Yes," Malinda answered as she turned down the lamp. "I feel the same way about him. And where on earth do you suppose he gets all his information?"

In spite of her misgivings, as Malinda settled into sleep she couldn't help feeling a sense of gratitude to Harold for commandeering the cots. It was sure nice not to have to sleep on the ground. However, instead of the restful night she'd anticipated, her sleep was fitful. By the time the bugle sounded she realized why. Harold had left something behind besides the cots. "That bastard!" she wailed, clawing at her hair. "He left us his vermin!"

* * *

Picket duty was proving tedious. Four hours on, two hours off, then four more hours on, shouldering a heavy rifle and walking back and forth behind the log wall in the now oppressive heat. The monotony was beginning to tax Malinda's disposition as well as her stamina.

Cannon duty was easier. There was a three man team whose duty was to make sure the weapon was clean, and to change its position occasionally to verify its maneuverability. The only tough part was handling the cannonballs. They were heavy as well as cumbersome. Each cannon was fired once a day to ensure its readiness, and occasional rifle shots could also be heard coming from the wooded area outside. Malinda was told that these shots were more likely to be aimed at a deer or other wildlife, than a human.

After three weeks Keith and Malinda still remained untested. There hadn't been a single occasion when the firing of their guns was necessary. Since their arrival at Kinston, a half dozen or more so called Union deserters had been brought in. No one was taken at face value, and several hours of interrogation by numerous officers was necessary before anyone claiming to be a Union deserter was accepted into the Confederacy. If there was the slightest suspicion that the man was a Union spy, he was shipped off to a prison camp. From all accounts that was a place no human wanted to be.

Forest duty was by far the favorite among the pickets. There a man could sit down in the shade of a tree, have a smoke, or a chew, or a swig of white lightning without anybody telling him not to.

Although Keith and Malinda seldom pulled the same assignment, one or the other of them nearly always ended up with Lonnie.

It was a Tuesday evening, coming up on eight o'clock. Finally a breeze was building, a welcome relief from the relentless afternoon sun that had pounded the treeless compound. Malinda, on wall duty, heard a rifle shot from the woods. She turned in the direction of the sound, leveling her weapon on the top of the wall and straining to see if anything was moving near the black backdrop of trees. Two more pickets quickly came to her side.

The encroaching darkness made it almost impossible to see anything. Then came a shout, followed by some shadowed movement and the sound of muffled voices. When the men drew close enough for her to make them out she recognized Lonnie. He was walking toward the gate which was now beginning to swing open. He had his hands over his head and he looked scared as all get out. Another uniformed picket was following with a rifle aimed at Lonnie's back. Two others were behind him.

A moment later Malinda had a further surprise. Three more men followed the first group, one appeared to be wounded, and one of the pickets helping the injured man was Keith. As they passed through the gate Keith looked up and sent her a broad grin. She stared after him, completely baffled.

An hour later, alone in their tent, Keith could barely tell his story. Each time he tried he erupted with laughter. Finally, gaining a degree of control, he said, "You know we've always said how Lonnie's a little slow? Well, he isn't just slow, he's downright stupid!"

"Oh, Keith! That's not nice. He can't help it."

"You remember during picket training we were told that when we're out in the woods and we hear or see something and don't know what it is for sure, we're supposed to say … 'Halt there' three times, and if they don't answer, we shoot." Keith again groaned with laughter, doubled over and clutched at his stomach.

"*Keithhhh!* Stop laughing and tell me!"

"Well good ole Lonnie, did just what he was told, all right. He said—and so help me God it's true 'cause I heard him with my own ears. He said, 'Halt there three times.' And then he shot one of our own pickets!"

Malinda's mouth fell open. "Oh Keith, that's not funny! Was the poor man hurt?" Then, mentally picturing the situation she too doubled over with laughter.

"If it isn't funny then why are you laughing? Lucky for the guy it was dark and the shot just grazed his shoulder. But that poor little son-of-a-B's got some explaining to do over that one."

In spite of the seriousness of Lonnie's situation Malinda couldn't control her laughter any better than Keith could. "Poor Lonnie," she blubbered. "What will happen to him?"

"I don't know. But the next time you're on picket duty with him and somebody says halt—Duck!"

* * *

A week later Lonnie had paid his penance with twenty extra hours of picket duty and a lacing down by the captain. For Malinda the welcome relief of their evening of laughter had soon faded as she realized they were facing a serious problem.

Keith was growing increasingly restless and irritable. He snarled at the slightest affront to his independence, and complained relentlessly about the body lice. Malinda tried everything to relieve them of the continuing torment of the vermin, but when nothing worked she finally decided the only thing to do was accept it as a common trial of military life and somehow live with it. However, her change of mind had little effect on Keith. She remembered her mother's evaluation of Keith's temper and sensed that something was indeed about to bust loose.

Late one night Keith confronted her with his newest plan for escape. As thunder rolled in the distance he laid out his plan. "I know of two men who have been released from the army because of medical problems." He paced the tent as the oil lamp flickered, casting huge shadows on the canvas walls. "If there's one thing this army is worried about it's an outbreak of a contagious disease. An epidemic could wipe them out."

Malinda sat on her cot, knees hunched to her chin. "You mean you think we ought to play sick?"

"No. They'd see through that. What I'm suggesting is, I actually *do* get sick."

"But—"

"Now listen!" He stopped pacing and sat down on the cot beside her. "You mentioned how the swamp out there is filled with poison oak, and you know how it affects me. Well, if I was to get infected, I mean *really* infected, so bad the doctor can't tell what it is, I could tell him this is something I get every now and then and how my poor ole uncle died from it, they might let me go."

At mention of the doctor Malinda caught her breath. Everyday she'd been expecting to be pulled in for that physical the recruiter had mentioned, and she knew time was running out. Maybe Keith was right. They needed to do something in a hurry. "So you're saying, you get infected, then you pass it on to me?"

"No, that won't be necessary. Once they decide to let me go, you can go to the captain, or maybe the colonel, and tell 'em you're my wife and you need to be let out so you can go home and nurse me."

"And you think they're going to believe that? After I've been passing myself off as your brother?"

"Well, there *are* ways you can convince them, Malinda!"

"You mean?"

"I hope it won't come to that, but if it does, they can't help but let you out, now can they?"

The sky suddenly lit up, followed by a piercing crack of thunder, and seconds later the clouds burst open. "Yes, I guess it might work." Malinda stretched out her legs over the side of the cot. "But if it doesn't, then what?"

"If it doesn't, I'll think of something else. But it *will* work, Malinda. You'll see."

"Don't you remember how sick you got the last time? You ran such a fever and started talking crazy and all. And how it hurt when I had to bathe you in brine water? You said you'd never hurt so bad in your life."

"I'm not saying this is going to be pleasant, but neither is being in this damned Reb Army. This way I—we—won't have to be in *any* army. We'll be free!"

Malinda looked deep into her husband's eyes and read his misery. What he was saying was true. He hated being a Reb soldier. He hated it beyond all reason. And if he wasn't free of it soon ... "If this is what you're willing to do then I'll go along with it. Sure enough, I will."

Keith heaved an audible sigh of relief, then leaned over and kissed her tenderly on the lips. "It *will* work Malinda. I promise you it will." His hand touched the soft curve of her breast. "Have I told you how proud I am of you, little brother?"

"I don't see anything to be proud of here. It's you who'll be doing the suffering." She looked down at her hands. "When are you planning to do it?"

"I've got woods duty tomorrow night. I'll hang back after the others come in. It won't take long, and if they question me I can always say I fell asleep. They'll believe that."

Malinda leaned over and blew out the lamp. In the darkness she reached for Keith's shirt and slowly unbuttoned it. "If I recall correctly," she whispered, "it took you some time before you were able to do any loving after that last spell. I think maybe we ought to get a start on things. Don't you?"

* * *

The following night at the end of Keith's watch he waited for the sound of the gate rumbling open which signaled the next watch of pickets leaving the compound. The night was exceptionally dark, the sky cloud covered and almost totally black. The only light came from the lanterns and oil lamps within the compound, along with the one the gate keeper was waving to light the way for those entering and leaving.

Earlier, Keith had selected a tree abutting the swamp, one that would be easy to climb. He now scaled it and lay motionless among the covering branches as members of his squad passed below, chatting and laughing; exchanging greetings with the group coming to take their place.

"Hurry on," the gate keeper called. "It's time for y'all to get to supper. Cook's wantin' to be closin' up."

Keith waited until the sounds in both directions had died away, then he slid serpent-like to the ground.

Wading deeper into the swamp, movement became more difficult. His feet stuck in the thick ooze, and to his dismay, created soft popping sounds with each step he took. He reached down and removed his boots. The only sound now was the drone of tree frogs, and the chirp of crickets, accompanied by the intermittent screech of an owl.

He sank to his knees, and crawled on all fours to the base of a giant oak. There he sat with his back against the tree. Resting. Listening. Then slowly he stripped off his clothes and laid them on a nearby log. He placed his boots, rifle and Bowie on top. Naked, he lay down in the poison slime and began slowly rolling from side to side. After several rolls he turned over onto his stomach, and keeping his head raised, repeated the procedure. Over and over. Finally he picked up two handfuls of the poison goo and rubbed it on his face and head. He climbed a few steps to higher ground and again rolled over and over in the drier leaves.

At first, the sound was so soft he thought it was an animal he had disturbed. But a beat later he heard it again and instinct told him it was no animal. Whatever it was, was coming closer. An animal would be moving away. Keith held his breath. There it was again! The same soft popping sound his own steps had made. Silent as a snake, he reached for the log, felt along the top until he touched the handle of his Bowie.

Suddenly, a whispered voice called, "Hey come on out. It's okay."

Keith rolled effortlessly, silently, to his side, then to his knees, Bowie clutched tightly in his right hand. WHISH! There was a sudden movement and a gun butt struck the spot where he had lain an instant before. Keith lunged in the direction of the barrel, grabbed a leg with his left hand, and yanked. The man fell hard on his back, emitting only a muted cry of surprise. Keith's right arm came up and plunged downward. Again there was a muted sound. This time though it was air escaping through a ruptured lung, a heart surprised in mid beat, struggling for a breath already gone.

Keith rose, dipped the Bowie in the slime, then wiped it on the bushes. He dressed quickly; silently. Sitting on the log to put on his boots, the lifeless body lay at his feet. He leaned over, trying to distinguish the features, but all he could see were the white, glassy eyes staring upward in eternal surprise.

He picked up his gun and headed for the gate.

Of all the fights he'd ever had, none had ended so quickly. Or so effortlessly. But then, he'd never fought with a weapon before either. He'd always used his bare hands. And of course he'd never killed anyone. Changed their faces around a little. Like Jesse's. But where was the thrill, the feeling of power over a victim? It was missing. Was it the lack of physical contact? He'd only touched the man's ankle ... before slipping the knife between his ribs. There had been no fight. Not a real one anyway. Funny. He'd known this would happen one day—that he would kill a man—but he felt ... nothing. Well ... relief maybe. Yeah, that was it! Relief! Relief at not being caught. Or killed. But still ... something was missing. What the hell was it? He paused and slipped the Bowie back into his belt. *Cheated! That was it!* Damned if he didn't feel *cheated!* There'd been no challenge. He allowed himself a deep sigh. The thing that surprised him most was just how easy it was to kill a man.

Before he reached the gate Keith had decided not to tell Malinda about the incident. What good would come from upsetting her? There wasn't anything that could be done to change it. People get killed in a war.

"Hey! Charlie! It's me! Keith Blalock. Sorry I'm late. You see I met this cute little injun lass out there in the woods and we—"

"Good thing I like you Blalock," the gatekeeper growled, opening the gate just far enough for one man to enter. "Y'all better skedaddle if you want some supper. Even them nigger boys stop workin' at ten o'clock."

* * *

Three days later the infection had ripened and Keith presented himself at the hospital. He knew his fever was high because he was having trouble focusing. Black spots were spinning before him and try as he would he couldn't keep from staggering.

The young corporal who asked his name winced when he looked up from his desk and saw Keith's face, neck and hands covered with giant red blotches, some swollen, others festering and emitting a greenish puss. The corporal rose, ashen-faced and knocked on the closed door behind him. "Captain, Private Keith Blalock to see you, Sir."

The medical officer opened the door and glanced out over the corporal's head. His face lost its color. Without a word he motioned Keith to enter his office, stepping aside so as not to touch him.

Ten minutes later the medical officer again opened the door and placed a paper on the corporal's desk. Keith followed him out of the room, buttoning his shirt.

"Prepare a medical discharge for his man, Corporal. He has a virulent disease which I consider to be potentially contagious." He nodded to Keith. "Good luck, young man."

The corporal immediately began filling out the paper then pushed it across the desk for Keith to sign. "Put your mark, there, Private," he said, quickly withdrawing his own hand.

Keith picked up the plume and signed his name with a flourish even though the paper was dancing before his eyes. "Thank you Corporal." He turned and walked unsteadily toward the door. Then, unable to conceal his delight any longer, he paused and looked back at the corporal. "Enjoy your war!" he said. And he saluted.

CHAPTER 13

Malinda lifted her chin defiantly as she walked up the steps and entered the door beneath the sign reading: COMPANY HEADQUARTERS. She hoped her brazen manner would hide the quaking nervousness within. Her insides felt like churned butter.

The young sergeant behind the desk looked up with a weary glance. "Yes, Private?"

"I want to see the Captain."

"Captain's busy now."

"Then I'll wait."

"Come back later. Captain's occupied with a serious matter. He can't see you today."

"This matter is serious too." Malinda knitted her eyebrows together and glared at the young man. Hard.

The sergeant leaned forward over his desk, reached for a paper with one hand while he swatted at a fly with the other. "What's the nature of this serious matter?"

"It's private business."

Swatting again at the fly, and picking up a quill. "If you don't tell me the nature of your business you're not going to see the Captain. Today or any day! Do I make myself clear Private? What's your name?"

"Blalock."

"Do I make myself clear *Private* Blalock?"

"It's clear you're making an ass of yourself."

The sergeant's eyes bulged from his head like cotton popping from a boll. "Get out of here before I have you thrown in jail for insubordination!"

"You don't have that authority *Sergeant*."

The chair crashed to the floor as the sergeant leaped to his feet. "Private Blalock, you are under arrest!"

Before Malinda could reply the door to the inner office swung open and Captain Jonathan Scott stood on the threshold. He was tall, imposing, with a thick, dark mustache and graying goatee. "What in thunder is going on out here? What's all this noise about?"

"I'm sorry Sir," the sergeant righted the fallen chair. "I've just placed Private Blalock here under arrest."

"What for?"

"For asking to see you!" Malinda snapped. "And if you won't see me, I'll go to the Colonel."

Captain Scott met Malinda's steady gaze, looked at the sergeant, and gestured with his head for her to enter. "I'm in the middle of a very important matter. I'll give you five minutes. No more. And believe me it had better be important."

The captain walked behind his cluttered desk, dropped heavily into his chair, and began stroking his goatee. "Now what's this all about?"

"I want to be released from the army."

A smile emerged. "You and a hundred other men."

"I have a very good reason."

"I'm sure you do. And what might it be?"

It was nothing she had planned beforehand but the thought jumped into her head and she acted on it. "Because I'm pregnant."

Captain Scott leaned his head back and roared with laughter. "I'm sure now I've heard it all."

"I'm a woman. I lied when I joined the Confederacy. I said my name is Sam Blalock. My real name is Malinda Blalock, and I'm Keith Blalock's wife, not his brother."

The smile was still there but the laughter had ceased. Captain Scott stared at Malinda meaningfully. "Are you prepared to substantiate your claim?"

Malinda stared back, but didn't answer.

"Can you prove what you are saying is true?" he continued.

"I can't prove I'm pregnant, but I can prove beyond any doubt that I'm a woman."

"This Keith Blalock, the man you say is your ... husband, wasn't he discharged for medical reasons?"

"Yes Sir, he was. This morning."

"Refresh my memory. He received a medical discharge, didn't he? What's the matter with him?"

"I don't know Sir. That's why I need to go with him. He has a terrible rash with open weeping sores. The doctor doesn't know what it is, but he thinks it may be contagious."

The Captain's eyes suddenly narrowed. "Private Blalock did you have a physical examination when you joined the Confederacy?" He rose and walked toward her around the desk.

Malinda bit her lips. "No Sir, I did not."

"And why not?"

"I was never called."

"I think it's time you had one." The captain strode across the room, opened the door and motioned to the sergeant. "I want you to escort Private Blalock to the medical officer immediately for a complete physical examination. You are to wait while this is being done, and then you are to report back to me immediately with the doctor's findings."

"Yes, Sir!"

Malinda's manner was still defiant as she followed the sergeant across the compound, but once inside the examining room her courage began to fail. Would she really have to completely undress before this man? No other man besides Keith had seen her naked body since the day she was born. The quivering in her stomach gained momentum and she needed desperately to find an outhouse.

"Well, Private, what's this all about?" The doctor motioned Malinda to the examining table.

"I don't think I have to get up there, S ... Sir," she stammered.

"Of course you do. I've been ordered to give you a physical examination. Now unbutton your shirt, take off your pants and get up on the table."

Malinda squeezed her eyes shut to hold back the tears as she began unbuttoning her shirt. "I truly won't need to get on the table," she said, eyes still closed. "I'm wanting to get out of the army because I lied my way into it to be with my husband. You see," she opened the shirt wide, "I'm a woman."

There was a moment of stunned silence before Malinda opened her eyes and saw the doctor staring at her with a look that was both amused and incredulous.

"Yes," he said firmly, the corners of his lips threatening a smile. "I am in complete agreement with your diagnosis. You are indeed a woman."

"Is this all I have to do then?" Malinda bowed her head as she buttoned the shirt. "I mean, I don't have to—"

"No. I've seen quite enough. But I really do have to ask why you did this?"

"Sir?"

"Why this pretense? Why did you join the army?"

"I told you. I wanted to be with my husband. And now he's sick and he's getting discharged—"

"Wait a minute! Is Keith Blalock your husband?"

"Yes Sir."

"Do you have any signs of the same malady?"

A sharp intake of breath. "Well, no Sir, not exactly. As yet." She decided to take the gamble. "There's just one or two little red spots—"

"That's enough." The doctor was suddenly brusque. "I'll let the sergeant know that I'll have the medical records ready for the proper signatures immediately."

* * *

Colonel Zebulon Vance picked up the paper one more time. Reread it. Sighed. Picked up a pen and signed it. He'd lost a good man. Harold Miller had been a valuable part of his command. It was a job not everyone could do.

Spying required a certain skill, an expertise that necessitated a definite type of character: someone who appreciated the value of money; someone who was totally dedicated to the Southern cause; and someone who had the intelligence and cunning to be able to ingratiate himself into a crowd of men and withdraw information from them. How many Union sympathizers had Miller uncovered? It was hard to count. And how many troop movements, encampment locations, and names of Union loyalists had he produced? Now he was dead. Murdered in the swamp. And probably by someone under his own command. What mistake Miller had made would likely never be uncovered. Replacing him would be difficult, and now he was faced with the unpleasant task of writing a letter to Miller's family. A letter of lies that would tell how he died heroically in battle. There were many things Zebulon Vance hated about this war, and lying was one of them.

The tap at the door was welcomed. Anything to get his mind off this latest problem, as well as the larger problem concerning the miserable mess the generals were making of this war! Every time his mind returned to General Branch and the way he had behaved at New Bern, Vance's blood boiled. The stupid man had literally evacuated all the troops except Vance's regiment to the other side of the river and then burned the damned bridge, leaving Vance and his men totally at the mercy of the enemy. What kind of a war were they fighting anyway, when a spy like Harold Miller could be counted upon, and a general could not? How much better it would be if Branch were the one in a grave instead of Miller.

The colonel pushed the report on Miller to one side as the knock sounded again. "Yes, come in."

"Colonel, Sir, I have a few papers here that require your signature." The sergeant laid a small stack of papers on the colonel's desk.

"Anything urgent?"

"Well, yes Sir. We are trying to avoid an epidemic and we need to get a couple of the men—er people, released from service immediately before they can contaminate the rest of the troops."

"What kind of epidemic? My God it's not smallpox, is it?"

"I'm not sure, Sir."

Colonel Vance picked up the new stack of papers. "Which one?"

"The two on top, Sir."

Vance read the medical officer's report about the possible contagion of an undetermined disease by one Private Keith Blalock. Vance signed the paper and handed it to the sergeant. "Get that man out of here as quickly as you can."

The colonel picked up the next piece of paper, read it, and looked up at the sergeant with a broad smile. "Private Keith Blalock is being dismissed from the army because he has an infectious disease, and Private Sam Blalock is being dismissed from the army because he is a woman?"

The sergeant tried unsuccessfully to suppress a smile. "Yes, Colonel. That does seem to be the case."

Colonel Zebulon Vance, elbows now on his desk, ran his fingers through his thick, dark hair, then placed his hands over his eyes. "Sergeant, do you have any knowledge as to how this Private Sam Blalock," he looked down at the paper, "also known as Malinda Blalock, ended up in the Confederate Army?"

"No Sir, I do not."

Colonel Zebulon Vance chuckled. "Well, Sergeant, I've heard about a Union woman who joined up. Vermont, I think it was—and all I can say is I'm proud as thunder that a Southern woman has that same kind of guts. Tells you something about our people now, doesn't it?" He lifted the pen, signed the paper and handed both to the sergeant. "I'd like you to tell her for me, that I wish both she and her husband well."

* * *

Keith was lying on his cot, his anguish evident with each movement of his body. He had finished his task of packing the saddlebags, except for Malinda's dulcimer which still needed to be wrapped. And he was exhausted. The only thing they were waiting for now were the signed papers. "When did they say they'd bring 'em?" he asked feebly.

"No one said, but it'll be soon. Colonel Vance himself has to sign them."

"Jesus, I wish they'd hurry!"

"There's no use fretting. We won't be leaving until daybreak anyway. It's far too late to be starting out this evening." Malinda was trying not to let her concern show. They had a long ride ahead of them, and Keith's condition had worsened over the last two hours. His fever was climbing and his discomfort intensifying. It wasn't only the itching, it was the awful weeping sores. Harold's vermin seemed to enjoy feeding on them. And the flies were another source of torment.

Malinda had managed to steal some salt from the mess hall. She hadn't even considered asking for some because it was in such short supply. She had begun bathing Keith's wounds with brine water, and just like the last time, the treatment was excruciating. He had to bite his lips each time she dipped the cloth and laid it on one of the sores. When it became too unbearable she handed him a stick to sink his teeth into so he wouldn't scream.

The journey home would not be made quickly, and there was a strong doubt in her mind if Keith could even make it. They might have to stop somewhere along the way and wait until he healed. She planned to stay close to rivers and lakes so she could bathe him regularly with the brine.

There was only enough room in the saddle bags for two days supply of food, which she'd managed to get from one of the slave boys, but the horses would have to be fed, too. She had talked the livery man out of a bag of oats, by explaining the situation to him. She figured he'd only let her have it because he knew she was a woman.

Keith was dozing as Malinda again picked up the rag from the basin and placed it on his forehead. Please God, she silently prayed. Please let his fever break before we start out of here.

She heard footsteps approaching and turned expectantly, but when Lonnie stuck his head through the flap, she couldn't hide her look of dismay. Raising her finger to her lips she stepped outside.

"I ain't botherin' y'all none am I, Sam? I ... I heard y'all was leavin', so I came to say good-bye." Lonnie hung his head and reached down to pet his dog in attempt to hide the tears welling in his eyes. "Fart wants to say good-bye, too."

"No Lonnie, you're not bothering me. I was just expecting it to be our discharge papers. We can't leave until we get them." Malinda leaned over to pet the dog, her face now on a level with Lonnie's. "How did you know we are leaving?" She had dropped the pretense of lowering her voice, and realized what a relief it was not to have to do that anymore.

"The whole camp knows y'all are leavin'."

"Do they know why?"

"Yeah, 'cause Keith's sick and you're a girl."

"I'll bet that came as a surprise to you," she smiled. "About me, I mean."

"Not to me it didn't. I knowed it all along."

"You did?" Malinda straightened, looking at him with astonishment. "And you never said anything? But how did you know?"

He shrugged. "I dunno. I just did. Maybe because you smell girlie ... oh I dunno. I just knowed. Is what they're sayin' true? Are y'all really Keith's wife?"

"Yes, Lonnie, I am," she said gently. "My real name's Malinda."

"I was kinda hopin' y'all was his sister. I was figurin' maybe you weren't his wife."

"Well, I am."

"I'm gonna miss you Sam. Y'all are the only friend I got around here. Sure wish I could go with you."

"I wish you could too, Lonnie. But, maybe we can write to each other, and when the war's over—"

"I don't know nuthin' about writin'." He moved so quickly he caught Malinda off guard, grabbing her in an awkward hug, his narrow chest heaving with sobs.

"Oh, Lonnie!" Malinda returned his embrace. They stood for a long moment with their arms locked about each other. Finally, she gently pushed him away, her lips brushing his cheek as she did so.

"I'll write and you can find somebody to read it to you." She took him by the hand. "Now come on in the tent and I'll draw you a map of where we live and you can come visit when you get out of the army. Deep Gap isn't all that far from The Grandfather, and that's right where we live. Beneath The Grandfather."

When Malinda finished with the map she handed it to Lonnie and he carefully folded it and tucked it inside his shirt. Keith was still dozing, so Lonnie left without saying good-bye to him. Tears were running freely down his freckled cheeks as he walked slowly outside and down the line of tents. Malinda stood watching him go, her own face bathed with tears. Poor Lonnie. He still wasn't wearing his boots.

Before it was time to light the oil lamp, the sergeant arrived with their discharge papers. While Keith continued to doze, Malinda opened hers and read it.

Mrs. Malinda Blalock is hereby discharged from the Confederate Army for being a woman.
Signed at Kinston, North Carolina by Colonel Zebulon Baird Vance, 26th North Carolina Troops, Company "F", Confederate States Army, April 30, 1862.

They had served in the Confederate Army a little over a month.

* * *

The following morning, on a day that promised to be sweltering, Keith and Malinda mounted up for the long ride home. They made it to Goldsboro, a distance of seventeen miles, before Keith tumbled unconscious from his horse. Malinda revived him by dragging him into the nearby river. When he was again conscious, she transferred both saddlebags to Keith's mount then helped him up onto her own, and rode in back of him, literally holding him up, for the remaining mile and a half into town.

At the railroad station Malinda bartered their horses, saddles, and the bag of oats, for two one-way tickets to Morganton. They waited three hours in the broiling sun for the train, then climbed aboard and found straight backed wooden seats in the front of a car that was suffocating and crammed with Confederate soldiers.

There was no where to stretch out and she had to hold the saddlebags on her lap, as well as her dulcimer. Ashes and cinders rained in on them from the open window as the train rattled down the track at an incredible twenty miles an hour. But at least they were going home.

PART THREE

HARVEST

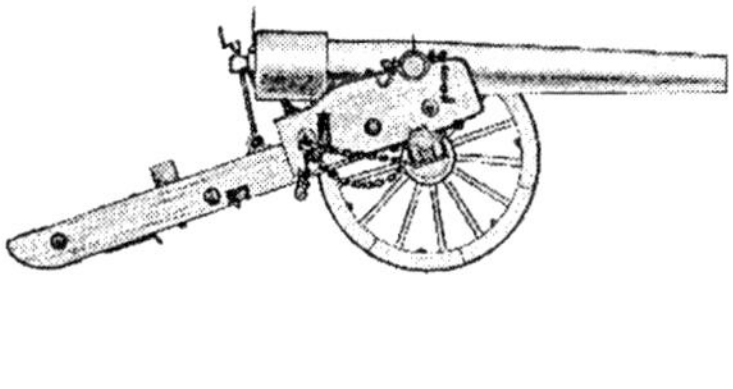

North Carolina

May 1862

☆

CHAPTER 14

The train stopped at Raleigh for refueling and to take on still more Confederate soldiers. Amid the sweltering heat, many who had missed the earlier hospital train hobbled aboard on crutches—a few on sticks; implements used to replace missing legs and feet. Although the faces were young they were lined with deep, gray ridges that seemed to have been carved into their flesh. All wore the same macabre mask; eyes stared straight ahead, dimmed by images that would haunt them to the grave. There was no way of knowing where they had been, words, when spoken, were merely mumbled. When the train at last began to rumble its way westward, any hope of conversation was lost in the roar of the engine and the relentless clatter of the iron wheels. The cacophony was punctuated by the occasional clang of the engine's bell when they drew near a station.

Malinda mopped at her forehead with her sleeve. At least the air gave some relief while they were moving. Even if it did feel like a breeze from hell. She glanced at Keith who was slumped beside her. Everyone else who had looked at him had quickly turned away, as much from disgust as from fear of contamination. The cinders and ash pouring in through the window were clogging the weeping wounds in Keith's face and hands, turning them into hideous black crusts. Although his eyes were closed, he intermittently let out small whimpering sounds. *Dear Lord, how much longer until they were home?*

It was nearly midnight when the train clanged into Greensboro where they were to change to the North Carolina, Richmond and Danville Railroad. Malinda was told it would be several hours until the next train arrived, however, so she found a grassy spot beneath a willow where Keith could stretch out. She didn't dare sleep for fear their scanty possessions would be stolen.

When their train finally arrived Malinda had to half drag Keith on board. Not one person reached out a helping hand. They left Greensboro in a gray dawn, riding a little more than three hours before changing trains again at Salisbury, this time to the Western North Carolina Railroad that would take them to Statesville and finally on to Morganton.

A few hours west of Statesville the air began to cool, and although Malinda couldn't yet see the mountains, her vision being blocked by a bank of bandaged bodies, she could sense the gradual change in altitude. Her heart quickened with the thought of home as a litany began inside her head. "Oh God, please, p*lease* let our home still be there."

It was late afternoon when the train at last chugged into Morganton, screeching to a stop that sent scarlet sparks flying past the window. "Keith?" Malinda nudged him gently. "Keith, we're nearly home. We have to get off the train now. We're in Morganton."

He roused slightly, looking at her with uncomprehending eyes. "Home?" His lips were so caked and swollen the word was barely audible.

"Well, nearly." Malinda rose precariously to her feet, shifting the saddle bags to her shoulder with one hand and reaching to help Keith with the other. "Come on now. On your feet, Sweetheart."

A soldier standing nearby reached out to help, then drew back when Keith raised his head. Malinda forced a smile. "It's all right, we'll manage."

Pushing her way through the throng gathered at the open door she climbed down the iron steps then reached back to help Keith. Once on the platform she headed for the farthest corner where they would be out of the way. She dropped the saddlebags and eased Keith to a sitting position, his back resting against the bags. "You wait here a minute or so while I go into the station and find a way to get us home. I won't be long."

He looked up at her but didn't respond.

Malinda paused, taking in the familiar surroundings; the station house, and across the road the blacksmith's shop, next to that the general store, and a few steps farther on, the bank. She recognized faces but none that were friendly. Were there no Unionists left in Morganton?

She pushed her way into the station house, now teeming with the gray uniforms from the train, and their welcoming, weeping families. As she aimed for the ticket counter the first face she encountered was Cal Moore's. Malinda's pulse quickened. Cal gave her a puzzled look, taking in the male clothing and boyish haircut, then the dawning of recognition came into his eyes and his lips curled into a snarl. Before he could utter a word Malinda pushed past him losing herself in the crowd. She thought of Keith, defenseless on the platform, but hopefully unrecognizable.

"Please! Please, Mr. Shatley?" Malinda reached across the narrow counter for the ticket agent's arm. "I know you may not recognize me, I'm Malinda Blalock, and my husband Keith is very sick. He's just been discharged from the Confederate Army because he's real sick and we need to get home. Are there any wagons or coaches heading up the Morganton Road toward Coffey Gap?"

The diminutive ticket agent dropped his head and peered at Malinda over his pince-nez. "Who did y'all say you are?"

"Malinda Blalock. Keith Blalock's wife."

"I heard Keith had joined the Confederacy."

"Yes Sir. He sure enough did, but he's been discharged because he's mightily sick and now I need to get him home."

Ambrose Shatley batted away the other hands waving in his face. "Wait a minute! Wait a minute!" He turned again to Malinda. "There ain't no horses. Nowheres! The army's got 'em all. Best thing is to hitch a ride on one of them ox pulled wagons headin' up your way."

"Where do I find one?"

"Well, I reckon, you best start walking up the road and when one comes along, just hop a ride."

"But my husband is very sick. He can't do much walking."

The ticket agent again peered over his eyeglasses and his bird-like glance swept the room before returning to Malinda. "Ain't many others in here who can walk neither. Terrible thing war." With that he turned his attention to one of the waving hands, and Malinda found herself being elbowed away from the ticket counter.

Outside, she gathered up a smile along with their belongings, and pulled Keith to his feet. "I don't like telling you this Sweetheart, but we're going to have to do a bit of walking till that wagon heading up towards our place comes by. Shouldn't be long though, and good thing it's not nearly so hot now, so it'll be easier walking."

Like an obedient child Keith followed her off the station platform and into the road. Malinda was staggering under the weight of trying to support him and carry the two saddlebags as well.

Over the next hour, two drays, overflowing with uniformed men passed them by, refusing to stop. Nearing exhaustion, Malinda heard a third wagon approaching and planted herself in the middle of the narrow road, saddlebags on each side blocking the way.

The driver pulled his ox team to a halt and glared down at her. "Git yer ass outta the way boy, or I'll run ya down sure as I'm born."

"I'm no boy, I'm Malinda Blalock and my husband here is near dying, and I plan to get him on this wagon so he can do his dying at home. Now you shove over and make room or so help me Hannah you'll have to run down a defenseless woman."

The driver glanced at Keith slumped against a tree, then looked back at the heap of humanity piled into his wagon. "I guess these brutes can pull two more without breakin' their backs. But he ain't sittin' up here. Y'all climb on back yonder."

Malinda pushed Keith onto the rear of the wagon, reaching gratefully for the helping hand that pulled her aboard. She lay half covering him as they bumped their way down the gutted road. The wagon stopped occasionally to let men off, then slowly continued on its way. It was a little more than an hour later when she finally caught a glimpse of the chimney of their cabin, barely visible through the trees. Again she silently prayed … *Oh God, please, please let our home still be standing.*

A moment later, through a clearing, the cabin came into view. *Oh thank you Blessed Jesus! Thank you! The Moores didn't torch it after all!* She called to the driver to stop, then jumped to the ground, pulling the now unconscious Keith after her. She tried to catch him but his weight was too much for her and he pitched forward out of the wagon landing face down in the middle of the road. She dropped the saddlebags and dulcimer, and weeping, fell to her knees as the wagon rattled out of sight around the bend.

* * *

"Malinda? Malinda where are you? I can't see you! I can't find—" Ah, there she was, standing in the doorway, dressed in that soft green velvet gown she'd seen in the catalog. Her long, dark hair tumbling about her shoulders. Behind her the chandeliers glistened with a thousands sparkling candles, and the orchestra played a waltz while hundreds of people, all dressed in finery twirled around the dance floor. Slaves dressed in full black skirts and white starched aprons stood behind a long elegant table set with gleaming crystal. One slave, a massive man in tight gray breeches and matching jacket with rows of brass buttons, carried a silver tray to Malinda, bowed and offered her a tall crystal glass. She lifted the glass to her lips, then turned again to face him. Thirsty. He was so thirsty. She was walking toward him carrying the glass, lifting it to his lips and smiling her sweetest smile …

"Drink it, Keith. Wake up now and drink it."

The vision faded as he struggled to open his eyes. Were they weighted with stones? Finally he managed to open them and the crystal glass evaporated in a mist of steam. The taste of hot broth moistened his lips. The green velvet dress faded into brown muslin. He looked up into Malinda's worried eyes, then opened his mouth for the spoonful of soup. It tasted good. It was only then he realized the pain and closed his eyes again, longing to escape back into the dream.

"I'm going to bathe you again," Malinda said softly, poking at his lips with the spoon, "so you'll be needing your strength to handle it. Here now. Open wide." She pressed harder against his clenched teeth.

When he opened his mouth to sigh she inserted the spoon again. Oh God, his body was on fire! The itching was maddening! He lifted his hand, holding it before his eyes and saw the weeping sores, smelled the stench of decaying skin. "My God!" he murmured.

"It's better now," Malinda encouraged. "Much better than it was. Three days of baths have helped a lot. Your face is almost cleared up. Just scabs now."

"I want to see."

"Maybe later."

"Now. Bring me a mirror."

"You best wait."

"Please. I want to see."

Malinda placed the bowl and spoon on the bedside table and crossed the room to retrieve the mirror. Keith's eyes followed her and suddenly he realized they were in their own home. He strained to lift his head. "Malinda? We're home. How … how did we get here?"

"You don't remember the train ride?"

"Train?" Dim images danced into view then vanished as quickly.

"You weren't able to ride so I sold the horses and saddles to buy us train tickets. We've been back three days, but I reckon you don't remember much of it."

He fell back against the pillow. "You sold the horses? I … can't … I don't remember."

Malinda returned to his bedside, the mirror in her hand. "I know you're still paining, but you truly are better now. You've come through the worst of it." She brushed the hair back from his forehead. "You're looking a lot better than before." She held the mirror above his face. He took one look, winced and turned his head away. "It's all right Sweetheart. You'll soon be the handsome devil you always were. Probably won't even be any scars to speak of."

"I don't know how you can stand to look at me like this. And … I smell."

"It's the infection, Sweetheart. The flies and the vermin were feeding off you. But that's getting better, too." She placed the mirror face down on the bedside table.

"What about my folks?"

"Your Pa came by two days ago. I'd been heating water for your brine baths and he saw the smoke from the chimney. I hadn't been able to get over there to tell them we are back; you were too sick for me to leave you alone." She stopped short of repeating what Austin had said about Mary—that he was expecting her to die at any time. "Your Pa said he'd send John Boyd's boy with a note to my folks so they'd know we're back."

She poured hot water from the kettle into a tin pan and methodically pulled back the sheet, dipped a rag into the hot brine then placed it on Keith's chest.

He let out a scream and fainted.

* * *

On the fifth day Keith managed to get out of bed and climb into the tin tub Malinda had dragged up from the root cellar and filled with the healing brine water. She had been right about the scarring. There were only two places on his face that bore witness to his ordeal; one small round spot on his forehead, and a second elongated scar below his lower lip.

* * *

Two days later Austin appeared at their door. One glance told Malinda why he had come.

"Will, if you're able you'd better be comin' now to see your Ma. She's failin' fast." Austin gestured with a toss of his head. "I brought the wagon 'cause I know you're still weak and don't have a horse. No need for you to be walkin.'"

"I'll be right there, Pa." Keith slipped clumsily into his denim shirt, rose and hobbled toward the gun rack.

"No need for that, Son. Things have been quiet around here for several weeks now. Besides, the Moores won't be causin' trouble when they know about Mary. Zinnia will see to that."

"Who's going to tell 'em?"

"I reckon McCaleb will. I'll be goin' over to his place as soon as we get you up to see Ma."

"You think that's wise? I didn't think McCaleb had been what you can call friendly of late."

Austin nodded, and managed the ghost of a grin. "Yeah, but there'll be some prayin' to do, and you know how he and Sally never miss out on an opportunity to talk to the Lord."

"I've got a pot of soup cooking," Malinda moved toward the stove. "I'll bring it along."

* * *

Keith stood beside his mother's bed, unabashed tears streaking his cheeks. Beneath the blanket the thin chest still labored for breath but the rhythm was erratic. The dark hair, swept with gray, lay limp about the skeletal face. Keith turned to Malinda. "If you don't mind Sweetheart, I want to be alone with Ma for a spell."

"Of course." Malinda leaned down and pressed her lips to her mother-in-law's forehead. "I'll be right outside, Mary, if you should be needing me for anything." She slipped quietly from the room, pulling the door shut behind her. In the main room she took a seat beside Margaret and Zechariah.

Keith knelt at the bedside and raised his mother's fingers to his lips. He reached out to touch her hair and at that moment a sound was heard from the dooryard. The sound of voices raised in anger.

"I tell you Austin we'll be needin' the parson!" It was Aunt Sally. "You send somebody over to fetch him."

Keith touched his mother's cheek with the back of his hand. The skin was cold and clammy. "Don't you pay any mind to Aunt Sally. You know how she is ... Ma? Can you hear me, Ma?"

Mary's eyelids fluttered open. "Yes, Son. I hear you."

"You have to fight, Ma. You have to fight this. You've never been a quitter. Never. And there's no reason to be starting now."

"I'm tired, Keith. I want to go home." The words were whispered, but the intent was firm.

"Ma ... I need you Ma. Pa needs you."

"It's the nature of things, Son. There's no call for being sad. The Lord's ready for me, and I'm ready to meet Him."

"Ma!" Keith leaned nearer and slipped his arm beneath her shoulder, cradling her against his chest. "Ma, please don't go without telling me. Please Ma! Don't go without telling me about my Pa. I need—"

There was more commotion outside and the drum of horse's hooves as another rider pulled into the dooryard. A horse neighed loudly, and several pigs squealed in reply.

Keith heard his father's voice. "No! Not now! Keith's with her!"

There was the sound of heavy footsteps in the outer room and suddenly the bedroom door burst open. William Coffey stood on the threshold. He wore a gun on each hip. His tall frame filled the doorway. "I've come to say my farewells to Mary." The long white beard and full mustache nearly covered his lips, but the gray eyes were as sharp as honed knives.

Keith glared up at him. "You've got no business here," he rasped. "Get out!" He felt his mother's body tense and watched astonished as she stretched out a trembling hand to William. He reached out to take it just as her mouth opened, body stiffened, arched … and went limp. William dropped her hand and Keith watched with dismay as the light faded from his mother's eyes.

"Oh merciful heaven," Keith whispered, feeling as if the spirit had left his own body as well. He pressed his lips to her cheek, and laid her head back on the pillow before looking up at William. "You're too late for apologies, Uncle Will." He eased himself to a standing position.

"I didn't come here to apologize for anythin' you arrogant little son-of-a-bitch!" William Coffey's face was as red as a rose.

For a moment speechless, Keith glared at him. Then abruptly he lunged at his uncle like an animal suddenly set free. "You fucking bastard! Get the hell out of here!" William took a step backward, and off balance, Keith crashed headlong to the floor.

"*KEITH!*" Malinda rushed through the open doorway, and fell to her knees at Keith's side. Sally and McCaleb stepped over them, hurried into the bedroom, and knelt beside the deathbed. Sally instantly began to wail as McCaleb prayed loudly for the redemption of his sister-in-law's soul.

William Coffey gave a final look of disgust at Keith's crumpled form, then stormed out the front door. Austin was at his heels. "Hold on there, Will!"

William spun like a top and faced his younger brother. "You goddamned Yankee!" he shouted. "You and that so called son of yours are just alike. Neither one worth the powder to blow you to hell!"

"Get off my property and don't come back!" Austin shouted, arms windmilling, breath coming in short puffs. "If you show your face here again so help me Will, I'll kill you!"

"Why you son-of-a-bitch!" William swung at Austin, as Zechariah jumped between them, taking the punch to his own chest. Reeling, yet managing to maintain his balance, Zechariah stretched out his arms in an effort to keep the two men apart.

"Stop it! For God's sake, stop it both of you! Don't you have any respect for the dead?"

Austin slumped. Dropped his arms to his sides as he gave his brother a thunderous look, then turned and silently reentered the house. Without a word to Zechariah, William jumped onto his mount, whipped the startled animal into a run and stormed out the gate.

Inside, Malinda and Margaret had managed to get a dazed Keith onto a chair at the kitchen table. Malinda applied a wet towel to his forehead where an angry gash was oozing blood. Austin lumbered past them into the bedroom, stopping short when he saw his dead wife laying with her arms folded over her chest; Sally and McCaleb kneeling at her bedside imploring the Almighty to "be kind to this sinner."

"All right, that's enough prayin,'" Austin said sharply. "Mary's gone and it's up to God now. There isn't anythin' more we can do."

Sally interrupted herself long enough to respond. "We can pray for her soul, Austin. She fornicated. She bore a bastard child."

"I said that's enough!" Austin roared.

Abruptly silent, Sally and McCaleb exchanged knowing glances, then rose in unison and left the room. In the outer room Sally walked over to Keith and placed a hand on his shoulder. "The Lord works in mysterious ways his wonders to perform. We must not question. But know that we will miss her," she said sadly.

Keith looked up at his aunt. "That's the most hypocritical thing I've ever heard you say, Aunt Sally. You haven't spoken to Ma for more than two years and you live within spittin' distance. You knew she was sick and dying and you never once called on her. As far as I'm concerned you can take your pious puss and put it somewhere else. I sure as hell don't ever want to see it near me again."

"Now see here, Keith, I won't have you talkin' to my wife that way," McCaleb sputtered. "You've got no right—"

"I've got every right." Keith rose unsteadily to his feet, holding the wet towel with one hand, supporting himself on the chair with the other.

"Speakin' of right," Sally sneered. "Why the hell ain't you in the army?"

"I was *in* the goddamned army!" Keith bellowed.

"Well from the looks of you you're well enough to serve now. If you don't fall down and hurt yourself again, that is!"

Malinda put out a staying hand as Keith made a move toward Sally. "Keith has a medical discharge."

"I've seen boys in worse shape than he's in still proudly wearin' their uniform," McCaleb said, easing Sally toward the door. "It appears to us that you're nothin' more than a shirker, Keith."

"That's enough," Austin said from the bedroom doorway. "You'd best be goin' now."

Silently, McCaleb ushered his wife out the door and onto their wagon. They left the compound without a backward glance.

* * *

The following day, Mary McKesson Blalock Coffey was laid to rest on a green hillside in the shadow of The Grandfather. Along with the parson, her husband, son, and daughter-in-law were present, as were her in-laws, Margaret and Zechariah. Also present were Unionist neighbors John Boyd, his wife Nell, and their thirteen-year-old son, Andrew. No one else came. William Coffey, followed by his brother Reuben, thundered by on their horses, but they didn't stop.

☆

CHAPTER 15

Mary Coffey was in her grave less than a week when Confederate agents again came looking for her son. Malinda opened the door.

"We're here to see William Blalock."

The speaker was a stocky man dressed in a gray suit. Behind his thick spectacles his pig-like eyes looked around Malinda and above her, but not *at* her. Of the four well armed men, two wearing the cinnamon colored Rebel uniform known as a Butternut, Malinda recognized three. Weasels every one. She kept her voice steady as she stood with her hands touching the door frame on either side. "My husband isn't here. May I inquire as to what it is you want with him?"

"The new Conscription Act has been passed and we're here to make sure your husband fulfills his duty to the Confederacy." As the stocky man spoke the other three nodded their heads like puppets.

Malinda glared at the agent contemptuously. "My husband has already fulfilled his duty to the Confederacy. He served with the 26th North Carolina Regiment, Company F. He has a medical discharge."

The agent brushed his suit jacket aside to make certain Malinda saw his firearm as he returned her look of contempt "Oh does he now? We have a report that his strange malady has suddenly disappeared and he is in good enough physical condition to fulfill his responsibilities. I'll ask you again, Ma'am. Is your husband here?"

Malinda pressed her hands harder against the door frame, determined these men would not enter her home. "And I'll tell you again he is not at here." She stemmed her desire to glance at the road. Keith had gone to visit Austin and to sort out whatever things of Mary's they might be able to use. He'd been gone for a lengthy period and should be returning at any minute.

"Can you tell us when he's expected?"

"No."

The stocky man pulled himself erect in an effort to appear more commanding as he slapped his gray riding gloves against his thigh. A crimson flush began at his collar and rose quickly to his hairline. He raised his hand and pointed a pudgy finger in Malinda's face. "You tell him he has two choices. Reenlist or be branded a shirker. We'll give him a few days to think it over. And you can tell him we'll be back."

The agent turned and stalked across the yard to his waiting horse. The other three marched after him in single file as if practicing for a parade.

Malinda watched from the doorway until they were out of sight, disgust welling in her throat; so mad she felt sick at her stomach. She turned sharply when she heard the creak of the back door. "Keith?"

"Yeah, it's me. I reckon I know what those sons-of-bitches wanted."

Malinda was still fighting to remain calm. "They're not going to let you alone. They know you've regained your health and they said you either have to reenlist or be branded a shirker under the new Conscription Act."

Keith dropped heavily into a chair and folded his arms on the pine table. "Which means if I don't reenlist they'll either throw me in jail or shoot me, which ever they feel like doing."

Malinda moved to his side, cradling his head against her breast. "Oh God this isn't fair! This just isn't fair! You didn't go through all the hell of those brine baths—and near dying—just to have them put you back in the army!"

"You're right on that one, Malinda. There is no way in hell I am ever putting on a Rebel uniform again. They'll have to hang me first." He pulled away from her and propped his elbows on the table, head in his hands. "As I was coming back from Pa's I saw the horses, and I figured the sons-of-bitches were after me again. It wouldn't surprise me one bit if it wasn't dear old Uncle William who put them on to me. Could even have been McCaleb for that matter. They're the only ones who've seen me since I've been feeling better, except for John Boyd and he's Union." Rising, Keith moved to the ammunition chest behind the door, opened it, and began filling a cloth bag with gun powder.

Malinda raised a hand to her lips. "What are you going to do? Oh God Keith, please don't go gunning for them!"

"I may be mad as hell but I'm not crazy," he said wearily. "If I pick off these four, they'll send eight others. I can't stay here Malinda," he said without turning around. "They'll be back."

"Yes," she murmured, "they said they would be … in a few days."

Keith straightened, opened the door and stared out for a moment before again looking at her. When he did turn around, she read the fearful determination in his eyes she'd come to know so well. And dread. "I've thought about this. Things are different now than they were before I—we joined the Rebs. When I disappear, and I sure as hell am going to, they'll know I've gone to the Union side. When they can't get me, they'll come looking for you. Lord knows what they might do. It's certain they'll burn the house down. Pa can't look after both places. We'll be lucky if they don't burn him out, too. But, no matter what they do, it isn't safe for you to be here. I want you to go stay with your folks. At least there you'll have your Pa to protect you. I'll be heading for Tennessee. There's a lot of Unionist there, and I'll be joining 'em. I shouldn't have any trouble traveling since I've got my discharge papers, and as soon as I'm out of this region, I'll not likely encounter anybody who knows me."

Emotion gave a sharp edge to Malinda's voice. Sharper than she intended. "If you go without me Keith, don't bother to come back because I won't be waiting." For an instant she wondered where she'd found the courage to say the words, but was immediately thankful she had.

He looked startled, then his lips settled into a thin, firm line. "Don't threaten me, Malinda. You know damned well I don't *want* to go. I *have* to go."

"I'm not about to beg. I want to go with you, wherever in this world you go, but if you leave me behind, I'll not wait for you to come back. I won't be tossed aside like a bag of soured oats."

The few moments of silence that weighted the room seemed to last forever. She knew that the rest of her life was being decided right here. Right now. The light suddenly faded as a dark cloud embraced the mountain. The corn bread she had put to bake before the agents arrived was beginning to send an acrid odor and soft wisps of gray smoke spiraling upward from the stove. Keith was running his fingers through his hair as he paced the room. She caught her breath when he finally turned to face her.

"This won't be as easy as last time," he said. "There's no guarantees of a bed or food. Least ways not till we get where we're going. I reckon you'll be wanting to see your folks before we leave. If you go there tomorrow we can leave the day after."

Malinda ran to him, wrapping her arms around his neck, the long held tears rinsing the tense lines from her face. She felt dizzy with relief. "I love you Keith Blalock. I love you with all my heart."

His voice was husky. "So far our life together hasn't been exactly what you thought it would be, now has it, Malinda?"

"So long as we're together our life *is* what I want it to be. Being together is all that matters. The one thing I could never stand is being apart from you."

The following day when Keith told Austin they were leaving again; the old man's eyes dimmed and the white head dipped low. "This year's not been a good one for this family, I reckon," he said sadly. "Maybe the good Lord's got some real fine things in store for us for next year. Good luck to you Will. To you and Malinda, too. Get in touch when you're able. I'll keep fresh flowers on Mary's grave, and I'll look after your place best as I can."

* * *

Meanwhile, over in The Globe Valley, Malinda was saying good-bye to her family. Elizabeth's first burst of relief at seeing her daughter was quickly replaced by concern and disappointment when she learned of the latest plan.

Seated now in her rocking chair, sewing basket on one side, her dulcimer on the other, Elizabeth moved to and fro, clutching her elbows under her breasts. Jacob, lolled happily on the floor, his head in Malinda's lap, listening to conversation he scarcely understood, but delighting in the presence of his adored sister. Alfred, sensing Malinda had not come bearing good news, had left the two women alone.

The toughness that had gotten Elizabeth through difficult times before was readily apparent in her eyes now as she looked down at her daughter who was seated on the hooked rug at her feet. Malinda recognized the look. She'd seen it when Ma's last baby died, and again when she'd told her she was marrying Keith. She braced herself for what was coming.

"Malinda, there are things I need to say. Things I've long held in my heart without letting them go, but the time has come to get them out."

"Ma, I know you're upset about our leaving again, but truly, there's nothing else we can do."

Elizabeth fastened her gaze to a spot on the far wall and stared at it fixedly. "You've been a disappointment to me, Malinda, but in many ways I feel responsible for your behavior. If I'd been a different kind of mother to you perhaps you wouldn't be so headstrong. If I'd been firmer and not indulged your fantasies, not given you false hope, maybe things would have turned out different. I've defended your actions to your Pa and to others too; taken your side even when I knew you were wrong, but this time I'm not doing it. First you ran off and married Keith Blalock. Then you ran off and joined the Confederate Army, and now you're running again. This time to the North. Malinda, it's time you stop running. It's time you stop long enough to look at your life and the way you're living it, and ask God to help you change it for the better. The road you are on leads straight to hell."

"Oh Ma!" Malinda rose, reached out her arms to heal the gapping chasm between them, but Elizabeth stiffened at her touch and Malinda's arms fell away. "What ... what do you want me to say, Ma? I ... I don't know what to say."

"I want you to say you will ask God for guidance, and I want you to turn away from this destructive path you're on. I want you to tell me you'll stop running. I have a 'knowing', Malinda. You know what I mean. Something terrible is going to happen if you follow Keith Blalock to wherever he's off to now. Tennessee or wherever it may be. You're obsessed Malinda. Keith is going to hell and you're going to follow him there."

Malinda bowed her head. "He's my husband, Ma," she whispered. "The bible says a woman should leave her family and follow her husband."

Elizabeth sprang to her feet. "Not if he's riding into hell!"

Malinda rose too, and for a moment the two women's eyes locked in mutual distrust. Then Malinda turned and walked slowly toward the door. Ma didn't understand! Wouldn't understand! She could never see that the only place for her was at Keith's side. Always and forever!

Jacob toddled after his sister, pulling at her skirts, begging for attention.

At the door Malinda paused and patted him on the head. "I have to go now, Jacob," she whispered, then bent and kissed the upturned face. "I'll be gone for awhile, but … but I want you always to remember how much Sissy loves you."

She left without saying good-bye to her father; sobbing brokenly all during the long ride home; losing her way once because Austin's mare was not used to the road and she'd neglected to guide her. How much more heartbreak could she bring to Ma? Maybe it was best that this be the last one. Maybe it was best not to remember that she had a Ma who was so disappointed in her that her heart had turned to stone. Maybe she should just forget she even had a Ma. Never once did she question the advisability of her mother's request. In fact, it never entered her mind.

* * *

By the time Malinda returned home Keith had filled their saddlebags with a change of clothing, enough food for three days, and a large bag of salt to be used for preserving any game they might find. He'd also packed the gun powder.

"You forgot blankets," Malinda said, surveying the provisions laid out on the pine table.

"By golly you're right!" Keith walked to the bedroom and pulled the two woolen blankets from the bed.

"Mind telling me why we're taking saddlebags instead of knapsacks?" Malinda asked when he reappeared. "Knapsacks are so much easier to handle and since we don't have horses—"

"Pa loaned us his mule. But we'll get horses."

"But … "

"Malinda, it's a long way to Tennessee and I sure as shit don't intend to walk. We can borrow horses from some nice Reb farm somewhere along the way."

"You're telling me you intend to steal horses?"

"I'm telling you we're going to need them for the trip and what we need and don't have, we take. Just like the Rebs do."

Malinda nodded an agreement she didn't feel, but she was too tired to argue. The weariness seemed to come from someplace deep within—a place she hadn't touched before. "That's nice of your Pa to loan us his mule," she said.

Keith secured the strap on the saddlebag. "What did your folks have to say about our leaving?"

"Not a whole lot," she lied. "Actually, I didn't talk much with Pa. Ma mostly. And saying good-bye to Jacob, of course." There was no use in telling Keith how Ma had reacted to the news. What good would it do? She had made up her mind that Keith was a no-good who would never amount to anything, and that was that. All the time she'd spent hoping that Ma would eventually accept Keith was nothing more than foolishness. Some things a person just has to let go of. She looked around the shadowed room. Such as this house. From now on it was going to be just the two of them: Malinda and Keith Blalock. No home and no family. Better to travel light.

* * *

The new day was lighting the ridge when Keith pulled the cabin door shut behind them, loaded the mule with the two saddlebags and put his arm around Malinda's waist as they walked out of the yard. They each carried muskets on their shoulders. They headed upward onto The Grandfather and within minutes of leaving their land were swallowed up by the dense green of the forest.

☆

CHAPTER 16

Robert Green was a prosperous Caldwell County businessman. He owned two homes, one in The Globe Valley, and a larger one in the nearby town of Blowing Rock. He also owned more than forty slaves, some of whom maintained his homes and property while others worked at a variety of tasks involving his varied business interests. Green was a devout Confederate, exempted from military service—along with others—because of his affluence. However, Green contributed to the Confederacy in other ways; primarily through his zealous efforts to see that other able bodied men shouldered guns in defense of his comfortable way of life. He was a strong, well built man, with heavy features and blond hair, gifts from his German ancestors. The fact that Green did not wear a uniform did not mean he was ignorant of military activities. Indeed, he was a trusted confidant of Colonel John B. Palmer, Confederate Commander of the Western District of North Carolina. He was also a close personal friend of Robert Vance, Commander of the 29th North Carolina Regiment, brother of Colonel, soon to be Governor, Zebulon Vance.

Green had recently made a visit to Camp Vance, the Confederate military training camp at Morganton, and reported his findings back to Palmer. He made several suggestions for improving conditions at the camp, highlighting the fact that there were next to no sanitation facilities, which left the place a breeding ground for transmittable diseases. Dysentery was rampant. Thus far, Palmer had not acted on any of his recommendations. A situation which irked Robert Green mightily.

Along with everyone else Green knew what was happening on the great battlefields, but he was also privy to written accounts of the lesser known military operations, such as the burning of Winston by the Union in late February, and the Union charge by Hawkins Zouaves against the Confederate battery at South Mills in April. Both highly unnerving. Green's interest in all aspects of the war was entirely personal. Without free labor his empire would crumble, therefore, nothing was too trivial for his attention. He had set up a network of what he termed "reliable sources," an acceptable phrase for men who spied on their neighbors and reported back to him any activities even remotely tinged with Unionism.

On the morning of June 26, Green was in the study of his Blowing Rock home reviewing a written report that had just been handed to him by one of his slaves.

Coffey's Gap, North Carolina, June 24, 1862

There is a band of shirkers hiding out in the forest on Grandfather Mountain. As near as we can tell, there are eight of them, including Keith Blalock. It appears Blalock's wife is with him. Others in this band of renegades are either shirkers or deserters from nearby areas. We have the names of: Tom Gumby, Joe West, Will Harmon and his brother Jim, along with two others. We don't know for sure who they are.

We've been tracking Blalock for a month, and finally located his hideout two days ago. That's when we found out he had these others with him. On the back of this letter is a map detailing as near as possible where Blalock's hideout can be found. You'll need a good size posse, they are well armed.

Haste is encouraged if these shirkers are to be found since they move every few days or so. That's why it took us so long to find them. This information was given me by a man named William Coffey, Blalock's uncle.

Yours truly, Morris Townes

Robert Green folded the note, slipped it into his vest pocket and smiled. So Keith Blalock was hiding out on The Grandfather. Spitting distance away. Everyone had figured him to be in Tennessee by now.

A smile touched Green's full lips. What the letter didn't say, but what he already knew to be true, was that there was now a price on Blalock's head. Yes indeed, this was one manhunt he would head up personally. And not just for the money. Rising from his chair Green rubbed his left jawbone. The one Keith Blalock had broken with his iron fist more than a dozen years ago.

* * *

"Malinda?" Keith stood in the doorway of the hut, straining to see through the heavy downpour. Vision was limited to less than six feet due to the unusually heavy rain. He could barely make out the bank of pine trees surrounding the narrow clearing. Damnit anyway! He'd told her it was going to rain, but NO! she had to go berry picking, and now it was really coming down and as slippery as these mountains could get she could easily fall into a ravine. Damn that woman, anyway!

Tom Gumby, who'd just come in from lookout duty, sidled up to Keith and put his hand on his shoulder as he leaned forward and spit out a long stream of brown juice from the space between his front teeth. "She'll likely be back directly. If'n for no other reason then she knows y'all will be worryin' about her."

"I'm *not* worrying! Malinda's a big girl. She can take care of herself." Keith moved away from the open door and strode the six steps that took him across the room. If there was one thing that bugged him about Gumby, it was his never ending prying into other people's business. Damned gimp! Who the hell would want him besides the Rebs? One leg two inches shorter than the other. Never had a woman he hadn't had to pay for, so how come he was such an expert on females anyway? And it sure as hell was not pleasing the way he kept eyeing Malinda when he thought nobody was looking.

Keith slouched into a chair, started to lean back, then remembered it was broken. It was coming up on five o'clock. Nearly supper time. She should have been back by now.

"Chrissakes Tom, close the goddamned door! Yer gettin' everythin' wet!" Jim Harmon, a fuzz-faced boy of sixteen was feeling his oats and his easy target was Gumby; a man he could out run and out shoot without even thinking about it.

Gumby slammed the door and immediately it swung open again. He put his shoulder against it, and slid the makeshift bolt into place. Then he looked at Keith. "Want me to go look fer her?"

"What? Hell no!"

Gumby limped to the pot bellied stove, and leaned sideways toward the heat in the dim hope of drying his shirt.

Joe West picked up the skillet of corn pone and placed it atop the stove. "Sure would like to have some nice berries to go with this," he mused almost to himself. "Course a rabbit would be good, too."

"She'll be back soon." Keith rose and walked to the window slit, pulled back the rawhide and peered out. A second later he saw a figure emerge from the drenched forest. *Thank God!* He dropped the cover into place and moved back to the chair.

A moment later there was a banging at the door. "It's me! Malinda!"

Will Harmon, Jim's older brother, was seated on the floor beside the door. He paused in the chewing of a long reed, reached up and released the bolt. Malinda tumbled into the room; saved from hitting the floor when Will grabbed her hand.

"Lord have mercy, it's coming down in buckets!" Malinda set her basket on the table and immediately water poured from it like a sieve.

"For Chrissakes, Malinda, look what you're doing!" Keith snapped. "Just 'cause you want to drown doesn't mean the rest of us do!"

Malinda removed her shawl and set the basket on top of an empty bucket as she shot Keith a meaningful glance. "I would think you'd be grateful that I was willing to go out in the rain to get you something nice to eat."

Ignoring the remark Keith returned to the window slit and peered out. They had had sharp words on this subject just this morning. She had been complaining again about the way he talked to her.

"I know what you're doing," she'd steamed, her eyes snapping like a fiddle string. "You're trying to make yourself look big in front of the others by talking to me as if I'm your damned slave. Well, I've got news for you! What you really sound like is a snot-nosed little boy trying to fit into a man's britches. Just like that Harmon kid when he talks to Gumby!"

It was the first time Keith had ever really wanted to slap Malinda. By God, he sure enough had wanted to, but he'd held back from doing it. Didn't she understand he needed to maintain some air of authority if he was going to lead this band? He couldn't very well go around looking like some pussy whipped idiot! *Damn!* Well, she'd get over it. She always did. Whenever they had a spat, she was always the one to start the making up. One thing about Malinda, she couldn't stay mad long.

"By God this rain is turning day into night and it doesn't show the first damned sign of letting up," Keith grumbled. "If it doesn't stop soon we won't be leaving tomorrow, that's for sure. The mountain will be so slick a horse could break a leg. Well, maybe another day won't matter. We've waited more than a month now before striking out for Tennessee. They probably won't even be looking for us. They'll be figuring we're already there."

From Keith's view, meeting up with these other men had been a mixed blessing. First one arrived, then another, then a couple more. All meandering through the woods trying to find their way to Tennessee. Finally, there were six of them. The good thing was, the more men, the more guns. But on the other hand, the more men, the more likely there was to be somebody tracking them. Each man had his own horse though. That was good.

Keith chuckled to himself remembering the easy hit he and Malinda had made on the Baker place when they took their roan and pinto. Ma or Pa Baker hadn't raised an eyebrow when he'd said he was taking 'em. They just shrugged their shoulders and went on inside and closed the door. That pinto was perfect for Malinda. Born for her.

The Harmons hadn't done service. They were running before they had to. But West and Gumby had deserted by using the very same trick Keith had intended to use. Playing dead. There was no way of telling if the ruse had worked or if the Rebs were after them or not. Joe West said he'd left a bloody shirt that had his wife's picture in the pocket along with a letter from her. Gumby had been working at a field hospital that was hit, and he laid low until the Boys in Blue came by and rescued him. Once they saw his lame leg though, they'd told him they didn't need him in the Union. But Gumby sure as blazes wasn't going to head back home where he knew he'd be picked up and forced to serve for the Rebs again. The Rebs weren't nearly as particular about little defects such as a short leg as the Union seemed to be!

Keith glanced at the two cots where Clyde Jamison and Bud Riggs were sleeping. Both of them were deserters, too. It was time to wake 'em for their watch. Didn't make much sense though, trying to do a watch in this weather. A man couldn't see far enough in front of his face to tell if a gun was pointed at him or not. Keith ran his fingers through his hair. It did make him uneasy leaving the back of the hut unguarded. The only window slit was here at the front beside the door, so if the rear was to be kept under surveillance, somebody had to sit outside in the rain. Oh hell! Not even a Reb would be out in this weather.

* * *

A disgruntled Robert Green held up his hand, ordering the posse to a halt. According to the map they were still more than a quarter of a mile from the hideout. All uphill. The damned weather was turning this whole thing into a disaster. He'd been able to round up a dozen men, and with the two Conscription agents and himself that made the odds nearly two to one. But of the fifteen men he'd started with only twelve were left. Three had given up because of the rain, claiming illness, and even the agents were talking about calling it off. The South would never win the war if this kind of *laissez-faire* attitude prevailed. One of the most vexing problems Green had personally encountered was trying to convince people that the North was dead serious about destroying the Southern way of life. So many of these ignorant mountaineers thought this was nothing more than a damned clan war.

Green motioned a dismount. Horses were becoming a hazard as the terrain worsened. Frightened, they might cry out and send an alert. And there was plenty to frighten them in this vertical mud hole they were trying to climb. Of course if the weather was against them, it was against Blalock, too.

Green's original strategy had been to approach the hideout from the least expected direction which was North. Then spread out and surround the hut. This plan, however, necessitated a long and tiresome ride in order to approach from the North and the twelve who were left in the posse were wet and weary. He hoped when the shooting started they would come to life again. Naturally, the intent wasn't to kill anybody. Their task was to capture the shirkers and put them back into uniform where they belonged. Except for Blalock. He was going to jail.

Green had hoped to time their arrival around dusk when the gang might be relaxing over supper and hopefully less alert. But this maddening rain had ruined those plans. Now they would be approaching from the south and fanning out to cover both the east and west.

* * *

"Keith?" The word was scarcely more than a whisper.

Keith looked up from the cot where he had been dozing, uncertain if he'd heard Malinda call his name or if it was part of his dream. Then he read the expression on her face and adrenaline began shooting through his veins. Instantly, he was on his feet, noting that Bud Riggs was half-asleep on the floor beneath the window slit. "What is it?" he rasped.

At the sound of Keith's voice everyone in the room sprang to life.

"I'm not sure. I think I hear—sense something."

Bud rose to a crouch position and carefully pulled back one corner of the rawhide at the window slit. The rain was still a torrent. He could see nothing. Silent, he shook his head.

Nonetheless, each man reached for his firearm. Malinda picked up the Bowie from the table and looked at Keith. He pressed a finger to his lips. There was no sound outside the pound of the rain, but everyone sensed the danger was real.

"Where's Clyde?" Belatedly, Keith realized one of their gang was missing.

"He went out to take a dump about ten minutes ago," Will whispered. "He headed round back."

Keith stepped cautiously to the window slit; pulled back the other side of the rawhide covering. Nothing. "Then he should be back by now."

Bud nodded agreement.

"Okay, here's what we do." Keith formed his plan as he spoke. "Jim, you take the window. Bud, you and Will take the door. I'm going out back, real casual like, as if I'm looking for Clyde. Give me a few minutes and then Joe, you and Tom take Malinda and head for the horses. Bud and Jim will cover you. Hopefully, the Rebs will follow me, and we'll do what we've planned about heading for Tennessee. Everybody knows the route we'll be taking. If we get separated we'll meet up across the border behind Union lines. Good luck."

"Keith?"

"Do as you're told, Malinda." He handed her his musket and took the Bowie from her hand, checked his pistol and slipped the knife into his belt beside his holster. He forced a smile. "I'll catch up with you as soon as I can."

"I'm going with you."

"No."

"But I moved the horses. Not all of them. Just ours. Something. . . . something told me to do it."

"Jessuzz, Malinda! "Where?"

"Up the mountain. In back."

Keith shook his head. "Why?"

"I told you I don't know. I … I guess I thought it would be safer. Something … something told me to do it. They are about fifty yards farther up."

There was no time for questions or reprimands. Keith bent quickly and brushed his lips across her cheek. Her hair smelled sweet. Like lavender. "Okay boys, I'm counting on you to cover me as best you can." He took a deep breath, opened the door and stepped out into the rain.

The familiar snake was again coiled in his gut. Two steps … Three. *Easy…easy now. If they were going to blast you they'd have done it by now.* The pelting rain stung his face. His breath ghosted about him. There was no way to see the men he knew were hiding behind the trees. There was no way to tell how many there were, but there was little doubt about where their guns were trained. The closer he got to the corner of the hut, the louder his heart thumped. "Hey Clyde? Where the hell are you? Did you fall in it?" His voice bounced back at him from the wall of rain. He took several more steps and rounded the corner of the hut. He was now at the rear.

"Hey Clyde?" Before the words left his lips instinct told him to duck. The first shot missed his head by less than three inches. He rolled across the shallow clearing toward the nearest tree and was instantly in a crouch position. Gunfire was erupting from three directions. He dove into a rhododendron thicket, fighting his way into its piney depths. Then he forced himself to remain still. There was no way he could be seen and as long as he didn't fire back they couldn't be certain where he was. But he knew where they were by the flash of fire from their gun barrels. He counted at least seven shooters. Maybe more. *By God there sure as shit is enough of 'em!*

Shots were now being returned from inside the hut, yet above the crackle of gunfire, he heard the scream of horses. *Damn! The bastards are shooting our mounts!* The sound was coming from off to his left where the animals had originally been tied. *Thank God Malinda took ours to higher ground. I'll never question her "knowing" thing again!*

He slipped the Bowie from his belt and began hacking at the trunk of a rhododendron. When he had managed to break it enough to bend he pushed the trunk aside and crawled through the giant bush and out the other side. Shots were ringing overhead from two directions. Some were dangerously close.

There was a shriek from somewhere downhill, and a man cried out, "Help! Help! I've been hit!" *Pray God it's one of them!*

Keith began working his way up the mountain toward where Malinda said the horses would be. Bullets whizzed around him. Suddenly, he was being spun to one side and his left arm caught fire. He stifled the instinct to cry out. *Son-of-a-bitch I've taken a hit!*

Another man screamed, and there was another indistinguishable shout. Keith grabbed his upper arm in an attempt to stem the blood and lunged upward. There was a shout not far below and two more balls zinged overhead. Even though they couldn't see him they were aiming in his general direction. Ignoring the pain he continued the upward climb, letting go of his injured arm intermittently to grab for a root or limb to pull himself upward.

Gasping for breath and certain he had climbed more than fifty yards, there was still no sign or sound of horses. The rain was merciless. He wove in and out among the rocks and trees, as much from necessity to make his climb as from an attempt to dodge bullets. He heard more shots that seemed to be coming from the hut. Were they trapped inside?

Another fifteen minutes passed before panting and exhausted he fell to the ground. Gunfire was still coming in his direction. He resisted the urge to take cover and return the fire. They'd have him pinned down in minutes.

Abruptly, there was another sound above the drum of rain. It sounded like … like *PIGS! Squealing pigs!* He risked raising his head in an attempt to determine where the sound was coming from. He couldn't see anything, but the noise was coming from somewhere off to the left. It was pigs all right. If they were penned that meant there was a cabin nearby.

Crouching, he dashed across a narrow clearing in the direction of the sound, saw the sty only when he was three feet from it, grabbed the top rail and hurled himself over. He landed butt first in the mud. The animals' squeals grew louder at the unexpected intrusion. Keith elbowed his way deeper into their midst; pushing against haunches that felt like rock walls.

Several more minutes passed and now for some reason the shots seemed to be coming from farther away. He raised his head and saw a distant light. The pigs were still grunting, piglets squealing, and all were pushing hard against their intruder. Keith braced himself and pushed back, slapping one or two on the rear in order to get them to move. The light flickered. A lantern. Coming this way. Voices raised above the din of the storm. He sunk lower, making sure his back was no higher than those of the animals.

Another lantern off to the right. The pigs began moving in a circular motion around the pen. In their midst, he kept pace, feeling dizzy, but thankfully the rain was keeping him from fainting.

The pain in his arm was excruciating, and he knew he was losing a lot of blood. The sound of gunfire had almost ceased now. Only an occasional blast. No doubt they were still trying to root out somebody. Did that mean some had gotten away? How many? Who? He didn't have time now to torture himself with unanswerable questions.

Sometimes the lights drew nearer, sometimes they faded away. They must be searching the barn and outhouse. Keith kept pace with his pigs, moving round and round the sty.

A voice loomed from the dark behind one of the lantern lights. "That's my pig pen. Ain't nothin' in there 'cept pigs."

"We'll take a look." One of the lights moved closer, played over the backs of the animals, roamed about the pen. Keith sank lower.

"I'm goin' back to the house. And if'n you fellers got any sense y'all will head on back down offa this here mountain and leave these men be."

"There's a price on the head of one of them. If you find him the government will give you money."

"I ain't one fer buyin' and sellin' folks. I'm one fer leavin' people be. Now y'all can stay out here all night if'n ya want to. But I'm goin' inside where it's dry."

One of the lanterns dimmed as the farmer turned his back and headed for his cabin.

"I think he's got the right idea," someone else shouted. "I've had enough. I'm headin' back."

"But Blalock is still out here somewhere!"

"I don't give a good shit if he is!"

"Are you forgetting about the money?"

"I ain't forgettin' nothin.' I'm sayin' it ain't worth it."

"All right. All right. I can't do it alone."

The two men sloshed away through the mud, the lantern light faded and Keith fell to his knees, as weak from relief as from loss of blood. Slowly, painfully, he crawled to a corner of the pen, pulled the bandanna from his neck and wrapped it around his arm. Oh God, please take care of Malinda, he silently prayed. Then he closed his eyes and allowed the blackness to settle in.

* * *

Keith awoke to find a huge sow licking his face. He started to raise his hand to brush her away, then grimaced as a white hot pain shot up his left arm to the shoulder. With his right arm he pushed the pig away then pulled himself to his feet. He was light-headed, and his legs felt wobbly. Gingerly, he examined his wounded arm. The ball had gone clear through but had apparently missed the bone.

The rain had stopped and the sun rising over the ridge was bringing promise of a clear day. Keith surveyed his location. The cabin was higher up the mountain near the ridge. A little farther down and closer to him was the barn. Almost on a level with the pig sty was a smokehouse. The pasture off to the left housed a handful of cows. Nice little spread. Remote. Funny, he hadn't known this place was here. But then, this was the other side of The Grandfather, and somewhat unfamiliar territory.

Better get moving before the farmer comes out to feed his livestock. Keith stretched his leg over the top rail of the sty then ducked down and keeping close to the pen he headed downhill toward the woods. The clearing was narrow; the farmer hadn't cut back more than was absolutely needed. Thoughts of Malinda filled his head and determinedly he set them aside. He had to believe she was on her way to Tennessee by now, along with the others. The first thing he needed to worry about was getting the hell out of here and making sure that damned lynching party was gone.

Once he passed the pen he made a dash across the clearing, slipping and sliding on the wet earth as he ran down the hill. In the cover of the trees he took a few more steps, turned and looked back. The farmer was standing at the entrance to his barn; watching. He carried a bucket of feed in each hand. And no gun.

* * *

Bud Riggs sat astride a giant oak limb seventeen feet above the ground, his long legs dangling like two limp flour sacks, back braced against the sturdy trunk. Across his lap lay his musket.

The first rays of sun were kissing his tree top home, sparkling the raindrops left on the leaves, and warming bones he'd begun to think would never be warm again. The night had been long, and the inside of his legs were raw from his shinny up the tree. It had taken three tries on the wet trunk, but with shots coming from all directions, he was inspired to use the same technique he'd practiced since boyhood: Get out of the line of fire.

Once in the tree he was lost in the dense foliage, as invisible to the men passing below as they were to him. But he could hear them. The sons-of-bitches.

Bud was nineteen years old. He'd been forced into Confederate service much the same way Keith had been. And he hated it every bit as much. The only good thing about the army was that he was free of the war at home, a place he vowed he would never go back to.

Bud was the fifth and last son of Jim Riggs, a drunken tyrant who beat his sons with a horsewhip whenever the urge came over him. It didn't matter which one, or whether there was a reason. He just did it. Being the youngest, and slowest on his feet, Bud had taken the heaviest load.

These early experiences had made Bud a suspicious man; one who trusted few others. An exception was Keith Blalock. Bud saw in Keith a man who knew no fear, yet was intelligent enough to weigh a situation and know when to run and when to take a stand. Although he had known Keith for only two weeks now, he'd known *about* him for years. He'd heard how Keith would take on two, sometimes as many as three opponents at a time and always come out the victor. People as far away as Asheville respected Keith Blalock for his strength and fearlessness, and Bud considered it his lucky day when he'd come face-to-face with his hero.

Now, from his perspective in the tree Bud viewed the scene below, or what he could see of it through the leaves and branches. It appeared the posse had given up and headed back down the mountain. Stupid Rebs, if they'd delayed their attack until morning he more than likely wouldn't be sitting in this tree. He'd be hanging from it.

He knew the route to Tennessee; Keith had gone over it repeatedly, making sure that everyone committed it to memory before he burned the map. It was a long trek, and not one Bud was looking forward to, but maybe he would meet up with Blalock again along the way. If anybody had survived last night's attack it would be Keith.

At that moment, as if Providence were on his side, a figure moved below; cautious as a deer. Bud felt an overpowering sense of relief and for a fleeting instant believed there truly was an Almighty. He pursed his lips and whistled softly.

The man stopped in his tracks and looked up, then broke into a grin of recognition. "Bud Riggs, you polecat," Keith laughed. "What in the hell are you doing up in a tree?"

CHAPTER 17

It seemed as if everything had happened in slow motion. Struggling now toward wakefulness, sketches of the long black night crept into focus. Malinda thought it was like one of those scary stories in Ma's books. You knew it was happening to someone else, but you got scared anyway. But had it happened to someone else … or?

She remembered watching Keith walk out the door; his old wide brimmed cowhide hat drooping almost to his shoulders from the force of the rain. Then, strong as a steer, taking his time and picking at his teeth with that reed, trying to look casual, he'd walked straight into danger. It was hard to believe what was happening; Keith going out there to draw attention away from the hut so the rest of them could escape. What if he got killed? If they killed him, might as well kill her, too. There'd be no reason to go on living in a world without Keith.

After what seemed like hours but was really only minutes—maybe seconds—the gunfire from the woods started and she knew they were shooting at Keith. She'd tried to scream but couldn't make a sound. The scream was only inside her head. Then Jim Harmon opened fire from the window slit and Will threw open the door and he and Bud Riggs started firing and shouting at her and the others to, "Git damnit! *RUN!*" But everything was moving so slow. Tom Gumby standing in front of her. Stepping out the door. Taking a shot to his chest. He fell backward, arms outstretched like a bleeding Jesus. She caught him before he hit the floor, grabbed him around the waist. Dragged him out the door like a sack of potatoes.

Joe West in front of them now, firing with both hands. They ducked and ran under the window slit heading for the woods. Dragging Tom. Feet sinking in the mud. *Can't see. Sitting ducks. Hope for solid ground. "AHHH! . . . NO!"*

Slipping … sliding … losing Tom … losing her grip on him. Grasping at tree limbs. The tug of Tom's body breaking free of her hold. Falling. Screaming. Tumbling. She could hear his body bouncing down the gorge. The screaming stopped.

Joe West shouting to "Hurry! Hurry!" The shriek of horses. Shots! Shooting the horses. Joe's voice no more. Had he been shot, too? Will Harmon behind her shouting, "Go for the ridge! Go for the ridge!" Turning. Clawing her way up the mountain. Was Keith alive? Where were the horses? Where had she tied them? Lost. She was lost.

Bud Riggs beside her. Firing his musket. A man screamed. Had Bud taken a hit? Upward. On hands and knees … Clawing. For each step up sliding back two. Breath raking her chest. A figure looming before her. Gun raised. A scream. Was it her own? *"NOOOOOOO! Don't shoot! It's Malinda! Don't shoot!"* Raising her musket. Still screaming. "*Don't shoot! It's Malinda!*" Her pull of the trigger. The red orange explosion before her. The man's cry trailing away. Mud splashing on her when his body hit the ground. Gasping for breath. The pounding rain. Her pounding heart. Her chest bursting. *RUN!!! RUN!!!* Then … FALLING … falling … falling …

Now … the sun shinning down on her … letting her know it was not a dream. She had killed a man, and she had let Tom Gumby fall into the gorge. She could still hear his screams. *Where's Keith? Why isn't he here to help me? Is he dead? Can't think now. Can't think. Maybe I'm dead …*

* * *

"By God, I knew if anybody was goin' to walk away from this it would be you!" Bud Riggs grabbed the tree limb with both hands, swung his gangly legs around the trunk and slid to the ground, wincing as he went.

Keith laughed aloud at the comical sight. "Riggs, you look like one long green bean wrapped around that tree.

"Feel more like a piece of raw meat." Bud touched ground and gave his stiff limbs a stretch. "And YOU! You smell like shit!" Then seeing the blood on Keith's shirt. "God man, you've been hit!"

"Nice of you to notice."

"How bad is it?"

"Missed the bone. Tore everything else to hell!"

"Maybe we oughta find some water. Wash it out some."

"I think it needs a good shot of whiskey. Pa always says whiskey cleans out more than a man's insides." Keith rested his arm on a nearby stump as he unwrapped the bandanna and scrutinized the wound. "Tell me what you know. Did Malinda and the others get away?"

Bud shook his head. "I wish to God I could say, but the last I saw of her we were runnin' across the clearin' and fire was comin' at us from the back and from the sides. I think Joe was with her, but I ain't sure. When we reached the woods I dove into the brush for cover and called to her, but I think she kept on runnin.' After that I don't know where she went. The weather was so bad I couldn't tell. That's when I decided the smart thing to do was get up a tree."

Keith rewrapped the soiled bandanna around his arm. "So you don't know if she made it to the horses or not?"

Bud shrugged. "Sorry, but I can't say one way or the other."

Keith nodded. "I think I heard them shooting horses. Could have been yours. Sounded like it was coming from where we first tied 'em up."

"I don't reckon they killed 'em all. Sometime durin' the night, could have been early this mornin,' I heard your mule brayin.' I think they were tyin' a body to his back."

"What makes you say that?"

Bud ripped back his torn pant leg, scooped up a handful of wet mud and patted it on the inside of his thighs. "I heard 'em talkin.' I'm pretty sure the dead guy was one of theirs."

"Why's that?"

"One of 'em said they were goin' to take him back so he could be buried proper. The way I figure it, the only ones they'd care enough about to bury would be one of their own."

"Makes sense." Keith walked the few paces to the edge of the clearing, peered out and checked all directions before motioning to Bud. "It's time we take a look around."

"Whatever you say."

Keith pulled his handgun from his belt.

Bud raised his musket.

Keith looked up the mountain in the direction from which he'd come a short time before. The only thing visible was a brown rabbit scampering across the clearing, and a thin veil of steam rising from the wet grass where the sun's rays were beginning to warm it.

They were on the south side of the hut now; the clearing no more than fifteen feet wide. The tiny structure held its secrets. No smoke. No sound. No signs of life.

Keith hunched low. "Stay here and cover me." Without waiting for an answer he dashed across the clearing to the side wall of the hut and pressed his ear against the thin surface. Listening. Crouching still lower, he took two more steps and was at the front corner of the hut. He peered around it. A soft breeze was wafting from the west causing the door to move to and fro; banging gently. The only living thing in sight was a squirrel on a bare branch.

Keith rounded the corner, rising slowly to his full height, back to the wall as he edged his way toward the open door. He took a deep breath and sprang inside, handgun raised.

Young Jim Harmon's body was on the floor in a half seated position; his back against the table leg where he had been thrown by the bullet that had turned his head into a smashed watermelon. The pan of corn pone sat on the cold stove. The smell of gun powder hung heavy in the room. Malinda's dulcimer lay in the corner; her basket of berries still atop the bucket. The walls were peppered with bullet holes.

He stepped to the window slit. Strips of the shredded rawhide were blowing gently in the breeze. He surveyed the room. Near the door, the floor was damp and red. Too far away from Jim's body to be his. Someone else had taken a hit.

He walked outside, moved to the corner of the hut and motioned to Bud. Next he checked the ground beside the door. If they'd headed for the horses they would have passed in front of the hut. Plenty of muddy footprints, and a rut that could have been made by the boot of somebody being dragged.

There was a small, nearly level patch of earth surrounding the hut, but it was bordered by a network of fissures that opened into gorges, most of them hundreds of feet deep. That was one of the reasons he'd chosen this location for a hideout. But even if a person knew where these rutted traps were, amid all the shooting, and the rain it would have been easy to fall into one. That was the very thing he'd worried about when Malinda went berry picking yesterday afternoon. A hundred years ago yesterday afternoon.

"Bud! You take the south side, I'll do the north. Circle your way east toward the ridge," Keith gestured up the mountain. "There's a homestead near the top. I think the farmer's Unionist, but no sense testing it. If you get that far and don't find anything, work your way back through the woods. We'll meet back here."

Bud nodded agreement and disappeared around the corner of the hut. Keith went back inside, picked up Jim's musket and powder horn, and loaded the gun. He paused and untied the bandanna. Since I don't have whisky, I'll just have to make do. He scooped up a small handful of gunpowder and poured it into the raw wound. *"AAAHHHeeei"* He leaned against the wall for support, waiting for the black waves to pass, and the biting pain to lessen. "By God if that doesn't clean it out nothing will!" He began rewrapping the wound with the filthy bandanna, thought better of it and tossed the rag aside. The gunpowder should stop whatever bleeding there was left to do, and hopefully burn away the pig shit.

He walked out into the morning sunshine. A cardinal, his belly full and rounded was sitting on the branch where the squirrel had been. He cocked his head and looked at Keith. Off to the left a red-headed woodpecker was knocking at a poplar. Everything seemed so normal.

He followed the gutted heel track into the woods where he immediately lost it amid the pine needles and leaves. There was a fissure a few feet in. He dropped to his knees and leaned over; picked up a fallen limb and poked at the brush surrounding the mouth of the treacherous gorge. Oh God, Malinda, where are you?

A hundred feet farther into the woods he found the dead horses. Each had been shot through the head at close range. During the night some forest animal had come to feed. A wolf or wild pig most likely. It was a disgusting sight. Bud was right about the mule. It was gone.

The trail they were to take to Tennessee started farther down the mountain to the west. But would they have tried it without horses? It seemed more reasonable that whoever was left was holed up somewhere; maybe a little more cautious about coming out than he and Bud had been. He decided to start with the trail.

* * *

Bud found nothing on the south side of the clearing. As he passed the oak where he'd spent the night he patted the trunk as if it were an old friend, then headed east, up toward the ridge. What was it he'd overheard Malinda say about the horses? Yeah! That she'd tied them fifty yards straight up from the back of the hut. Maybe they were still there. This must be the direction Keith had taken last night, but it wouldn't be surprisin' if he'd missed 'em with all that was goin' on—

What was that? He froze. Breath blocked. Listening. *By God if that ain't a horse snortin'!* He took running steps upward in the direction of the sound. *There it is again! DAMN! It IS a horse!*

Two minutes later his heart leaped when he came upon the roan and pinto, tied to a tree and pawing at the mud. "Steady now, fella. Steady!" Gently, Bud stroked the neck of the roan, and in turn the horse nuzzled his chest. "That's it fella. I know you're hungry."

He untied the animal and led him down to the clearing where he might be able to find a few blades of grass among the mud. He was a good mount; well trained. He wouldn't run. At least not until his belly was full, and that would take a while.

He hurried back up the mountain for Malinda's pinto. This didn't look good. The last he'd seen of her she was headin' this way. If she'd made it wouldn't she have taken her horse? The air was fresh and clean after the rain. Branches bowing in the breeze carried with them a soft humming sound. He untied the pinto. *Wait a minute! Was that the wind or. . .?* Well by God if that was wind it was the first time he'd heard it whistle a tune!

Listen to the mocking bird
Listen to the mocking bird

The pinto neighed. The sound stopped. Bud strained to listen. By God, there it is again! Almost like a whisper.

Listen to the mocking bird
Listen to the ...

Bud stroked the pinto to keep him still. Cautious, he followed the sound, holding the pinto's reins, he walked toward a clump of scrub pine. Creeping nearer, he realized just in time that he was at the mouth of a fissure. He paused again.

"MALINDA?" He dropped to his knees. "Malinda? Malinda I can hear you, I just can't see you." He poked his head through the bottom branches of the pines and pushed himself far enough forward to peer over the edge.

Ten to twelve feet below was a narrow outcropping of rock. It couldn't be more than three to four feet wide. Someone was sitting on the ledge, back to the wall, feet stretched out so all that could be seen was a pair of boots.

"Malinda, it's Bud."

For a long moment there was nothing but silence. Then. "Bud?" The voice sounded like it was coming from the bottom of the cavern.

"I'm up here. Straight above you."

There was a rustling below. A shuffling of rock. Then Malinda's smudged, bruised face was looking up at him. There was a vacant look to her eyes. As though she didn't recognize him.

"Who?"

He leaned as far forward as he dared. "Bud Riggs."

"Bud Riggs? How … how did you find me?"

"Why your whistlin' a course!" He tightened his grip on the scrub pine. "Are you okay, Malinda?"

"I'm not sure … I … I think I'm okay." Her face brightened then and there was the trace of a smile.

"God Almighty! Keith Blalock is goin' to be one happy man!" Bud risked edging forward another inch or two, enough to get a better look at her situation.

The ledge was halfway canopied by a smaller one, but there would be no problem in dropping a rope down to her. And there was one on the pinto's saddle! "Stay where you are Malinda. I'll be right back."

Bud backed out of the underbrush, unleashed the rope from the saddle and tied one end around the saddle horn. Then he returned to the mouth of the fissure carrying the rope.

"Malinda? I'm makin' a loop at the end of this rope. When I drop it to you slip it over your head and tighten it around your waist. Then grab the rope above your head with both hands. That'll relieve the tension on your body. That ledge above your head looks kind of sharp, so kick away from it with your feet as I pull you up. Not too hard though."

Bud tossed the rope over the edge and waited while Malinda secured it around her waist. "Do you see a spot of rock that looks pretty smooth?"

Looking up. Eyes clearer now. "Yes, I think so."

"Good. Try to place the rope so that I'll be pulling you up from there. Okay now, you'll feel a pull on the line in a minute. Are you ready?"

"Yes, ready."

"I'll be on the horse so I won't be able to watch you. If you get into trouble give a shout. Loud." Bud mounted the pinto, tugged on the rope and slowly began tightening the line. "Hold tight to the rope, and kick yourself away from the ledge."

No response.

The rope tightened as he urged the pinto forward. "How are you doin'?"

"All … right."

Bud slapped the horse on its flank. "Come on, boy. Come on." He looked over his shoulder, and saw nothing but the taunt rope cutting deep into the soft, water soaked earth. "I almost gotcha Malinda."

No response.

He urged the pinto forward again. "Come on boy. Come on."

Abruptly the rope slackened and a moment later the piney bushes parted and Malinda crawled out. Her face was scratched and streaked with blood, her skirt and blouse torn and dirty.

Bud dropped the reins and ran to her. She leaned against him, and broke into sobs.

"It's all right." He patted her awkwardly. "You're all right now. It's over. You're okay."

"K … Keith? Is … is he—"

"Keith's fine. Just worried to death about you, that's all."

"He's okay? Keith's alive?" She pulled back and looked at him, needing to see the truth in his eyes.

"Malinda, I'm tellin' you he's okay. He's down the mountain right now lookin' for you." Bud loosened the rope from her waist and pulled the loop over her head. "Come on, we'll go find him."

* * *

Keith checked the Tennessee trail for signs of recent use. There weren't any. No fresh prints in the mud, no newly broken branches. It was an old Indian path that led from Watauga into Mitchell County, North Carolina and across the mountains to Greene County, Tennessee. When Austin had given him the map, he'd cautioned about the treacherous terrain. But the good thing was, not many people knew about it.

Keith stepped back into the clearing; looked up toward the hut and into the sun. It seemed unlikely the posse would have taken Malinda. They certainly didn't want to put *her* back in a uniform … Unless … they were planning to hold her hostage in order to get him to come in. Yeah. He had to accept that that was a strong possibility.

He raised his right hand to shield his eyes from the sun. *Hold on! Is somebody coming down the mountain? TWO somebodys! Could it?* He recognized the gait, the body form. *MALINDA! Dear God it is! It's Malinda! And her pinto!* He started to run, ignoring the pain in his arm. Struggling up the sharp incline. Waving with his good arm. She'd seen him now. She was waving back. Running toward him. More beautiful than ever. My God, she's safe! My wife is safe! "Malinda! Sweetheart!"

"Keith! Oh, Keith!"

There was blood on her face. "My God! Malinda!" Pulling her to him. Burying his face in her neck. He felt her body tremble. Winced as she touched his wounded arm.

"I was afraid I'd never see you again. I thought they'd killed you."

"Not quite." He held her away from him. "Tell me what happened."

"I fell. Bud found me."

Keith waved his hat at Bud. "Thank you! Thank you!"

Bud returned the wave.

"What do you mean you fell?"

"I fell into one of those fissures you were warning me about. I … landed on a ledge. I truly thought I was going to die there. I thought I would starve, and be fodder for the buzzards. I didn't think anybody would ever find me. I was afraid you were dead. There was so much shooting … "

"Malinda," Keith cupped her chin in his hand and looked at her deeply. "You forgot what I told you, now didn't you? Remember the day we got married I told you that you and me are going to grow old together. We're going to have a long life and make lots of youngins. And you'd better remember what I'm telling you now, 'cause it's the God's truth. We may have our setbacks now and then, but we'll come out on top. Always."

"I know." She managed a smile. "*Keith!* What happened to your arm?"

"It's none too serious." He started to put his good arm around her waist, then pulled back. "I'm afraid I don't smell so good. I spent the night with some pigs."

"So that's what it is!" she laughed.

He draped his arm around her shoulder and turned in the direction of the hut. "I'm powerful hungry and I'll bet you are, too. I'm thinking about those berries you picked yesterday. They're still in the basket where you left 'em." Then he remembered what else was inside the hut. "You wait outside and I'll go in and get 'em."

"Maybe I can warm up the corn pone or—

"Malinda, I want you to wait outside."

"But I need something to dress your wound."

"I've already taken care of it. And I don't want you going into the hut. Jim's in there, and it isn't pretty—"

"Oh my God! … Oh no!"

* * *

Malinda settled herself on a large rock a few yards from the hut while Keith went inside. He returned a moment later carrying the basket of berries. Bud Riggs joined them and they gorged themselves on the fruit while the horses searched for a few blades of grass.

"No sign of anybody else?" Keith's gaze turned upward toward the ridge.

"Nope." Bud rose. "I'll be takin' another look around." He tucked his musket under his arm and headed for the woods.

Of the eight, Keith could account for only four. And one of those was dead. Where the hell were the others? If they hadn't come out of hiding by this time they were either dead, badly wounded, or had been taken prisoner.

He decided that after they rested a bit he and Malinda could take another poke around, too. It was fairly certain no one had started down that Indian trail. Foolhardy without horses, and damned little chance of getting any along the way. If Pa was right, this whole area was as wild as it had ever been, and next to no settlers. Of course, the trouble with heading out now was the agents would be looking for them. God willing they didn't know about the trail. The hope was they would be laying for them at the more commonly traveled passes. One thing *was* certain, however, they would be expecting them to head for Tennessee. Was that a good enough reason to wait?

Bud called from the woods interrupting Keith's reverie. "Found Will. He's dead."

Keith rose, looked down on Malinda's bowed head. She was crying softly. "You wait here, Sweetheart." Keith started across the clearing.

* * *

Bud Riggs threw the shovel up out of the hole and climbed out. "I reckon that's big enough fer both of 'em. Don't guess they'll mind sharin' the same bed, bein' brothers."

"No, I reckon not. I'll get Jim while you fetch Will." Keith turned toward the hut. "I hope these are the only ones who need praying over."

Malinda reached out and touched Keith's sleeve. "Tom Gumby needs our prayers, too."

Keith stared at her with surprise. "What are you talking about?"

"Tom's dead."

"Well it's right nice of you to mention it Malinda. Why didn't you tell me this before?"

"I ... I dragged him as far as I could into the woods and ... then ... " Her voice trailed off and she bowed her head.

"And then what?"

"I dropped him."

"Dropped him?"

"Down ... down a gorge. I couldn't hold on and I ... I dropped him."

Keith shook his head, then put his good arm around her shoulder. "Sweetheart. There's nothing we can do about it now. You did your best, and you sure didn't mean to drop him."

"You don't understand! He screamed all the way down. Even over the rain I could hear him screaming. I'll never—"

"Now listen up, woman." Keith lifted her chin and looked hard into her tormented eyes. "You did what you could. It's over. It does no good to look back." He turned to Bud. "We need to get these boys planted."

Thirty minutes later the Harmon boys were laid to rest. Bud leaned on the handle of his shovel, Keith removed his hat, and Malinda folded her hands and lowered her head.

"Please Lord," she said softly. "Take these fine boys into your loving arms. They were good boys and didn't mean any harm. And please look after Tom Gumby, too. I'm sorry we can't give him a proper burying. May they all rest in peace. Amen."

Keith put his hat back on and gestured to Bud. "I think that farmer up on the ridge more than likely has a horse to spare, and you're going to need one. Why don't you go take a look while Malinda and I wait for you down by the trail."

"Sounds like a fine idea to me."

"Need some help?"

"No thanks!" Bud shouldered his musket and headed up the mountain.

He wasn't yet out of sight before Keith took Malinda's hand, leading her toward the woods. Once there he kissed her hungrily, at the same time lifting her skirt, and caressing her thigh and buttocks. "We've got time. It'll take him a while."

Malinda let out a soft moan as his hand touched the thick thatch between her legs. "Keith, we … we just buried those two boys—I mean, it doesn't seem right—"

He eased her back onto the soft wet pine needles. "That means they won't be watching then doesn't it?"

Another movement of Keith's fingers, and Malinda stilled her feeble protests, which they both knew had been pretense anyway.

* * *

They were waiting at the mouth of the trail when Bud returned riding a smoke colored stallion, and carrying a gunnysack over his shoulder.

"Have any trouble?" Keith called.

"Not a mite," Bud grinned. "Lordy, that farmer's older than dirt! Sort of reminded me of my Pa. Well now, when I told him I was takin' his horse, he got a trifle upset, so I told him, I'd be takin' a chicken, too." He gestured to the gunnysack. "Then I mentioned that if he was right friendly about givin' me his horse and chicken, I more than likely wouldn't be takin' one of his pigs." Bud wiped his mouth with the back of his hand. "Course while I was tellin' him all this, he was lookin' down the barrel of my musket, and his wife was on her knees prayin' for me to spare her husband."

Keith laughed. "I suppose that lady's prayers were answered?"

"You bet! And she was right happy about gettin' her husband back in exchange for a horse and a chicken. Guess she thought it was a fair trade."

Malinda said nothing, but Keith saw she was disturbed when he'd laughed about Bud stealing from the old farmer. Well … maybe it *wasn't* funny. Nothing about this damned war was funny! But if a man was going to survive he had to keep his sense of humor! Like Pa always said, "A man loses part of his humanity when he loses his sense of humor." Anyway! There were other things to think about now.

Keith pushed aside the throb in his arm and the ache in his bones as he guided the roan onto the Indian trail and headed for Tennessee.

☆

CHAPTER 18

Elizabeth Pritchard felt uneasy. It was a fleeting thing, wafting in and out of consciousness with no plausible reason as to why. As if something was hovering over her … or around her. And then it was gone.

She laid aside her dusting cloth to check the beans simmering in the kettle over the fire, then put the back of one hand to her forehead. Lord a mercy this day is hot, she thought, and brushed back an errant strand of silky black hair as she stirred the beans. The cabin door was open wide to let in light and much needed air in the hope of dispelling the habitual smell of dankness. But it wasn't enough. Her chest swelled with a deep sigh as she again took up her dusting cloth. She felt weary.

Glancing at the mantle clock she told herself there was still time enough to fix a tart for dinner. She had a bit of flour left, and there was a handful of blackberries from yesterday's picking. She disliked baking, but it would be a nice surprise for Alfred. Poor man was losing weight. He'd cut back on his eating to make sure there would be enough for her since she was still nursing Jacob. Of course he'd never own up to that being the reason. But Alfred's poorliness could be due to worry. There was enough of that to go around! Worry over Malinda, worry over this senseless war, worry over their food supply. A person didn't have to look far to find something to worry about.

She picked up the basket of berries she'd left behind the door in a cool spot, carried it to the wide plank table and began sorting them out. Her mind kept turning again and again to Alfred's welfare. He hadn't been himself since that raid by the Home Guard last week. They'd been hit twice before, right after Malinda and Keith ran off to join up with the Union. But this time was different. This time they'd taken more than chickens and vegetables. They'd taken Alfred's spirit. It was hard to tell which was worse to bear, watching those ruffians steal the very food from their mouths, or seeing the heartbreak in Alfred's eyes while they were doing it. He'd been so humiliated, not being able to defend their property. But if he'd stood up to them, no less than ten of the scum, they'd have shot them both without thinking twice. And no doubt little Jacob, too. The only thing a person *could* do was watch, helpless, while they robbed you, then cry your heart out after they'd gone. Like Alfred. Elizabeth thought her very soul was being shredded that night as she lay there in the dark, listening to her husband sob until he was too spent to sob anymore. One thing was certain about this war. It wasn't confined to the battlefields.

There it was again! That feeling of uneasiness. Almost like a chill. Maybe she was coming down with a cold.

She put the tart to bake and walked to the open door. Alfred was playing with little Jacob under the maple tree; tossing the ball and the child running pell-mell to fetch it. A soft breeze rustled the willow in the side yard and brought a gentle fragrance from the field bordering the mountain. The trees on the lower slopes were bathed in their perpetual blue haze, but rising above them, like God himself, stood The Grandfather.

"Time to bring him in yet?" Alfred looked up. "I need to go check on the mare."

"It's all right, I'll get him." Elizabeth headed out into the yard. The mare was healing from an infection in her hoof and it needed to be soaked every morning and night. Dear old thing. She was so old even the Rebs didn't want her.

Elizabeth scooped Jacob up in her strong arms and spun him around. "You come on inside now and play while Ma finishes up her dusting."

The child wrapped his arms around her neck, his spindly legs about her waist. "Top. Jacob want top."

She carried him inside to a small wooden box beneath the window slit. "Here you are, Jacob. Here's your top!" She set the toy to spinning on the puncheon floor. "See how pretty it is? See the pretty colors?"

The baby clapped his hands.

"What colors do you see Jacob? Tell Ma what the colors are."

"Wed!" Jacob squealed. "See wed!"

"Yes, that's red. That's very good!"

The child momentarily entertained, Elizabeth continued her dusting; brushed the frames of the Currier and Ives prints hanging on the wall opposite the fireplace. Alfred always said these pictures were too fancy for this house. They'd been a wedding present from Ma. Riches from another generation.

Next she reached for the daguerreotype of Malinda, dusted it carefully, then set it back in its place on the cupboard shelf. Maybe this feeling of uneasiness had something to do with Malinda. Maybe there would be more news of her soon.

News from Malinda was seldom a cause for rejoicing, she reminded herself. But no news brought apprehension as well. It had been more than six weeks since they'd received her letter telling how she and Keith had made it to Union lines after escaping a Reb posse. She'd written that Keith had joined the Union Army and was now serving under the command of Major George W. Kirk. Even that didn't feel right! It was said the men who served under Kirk were more afraid of the Major than they were of the enemy. Elizabeth clucked disapproval.

Jacob had tired of the top, and turned his attention to the dulcimer. Elizabeth smiled as she watched him pluck the strings with his little worm-like fingers. The child had a natural ear for music. In the evenings when she played, he would clap his hands and twirl about the room trying to dance.

There was a smell of rain when Elizabeth again walked to the door. Dark clouds were beginning to settle over The Grandfather, and it looked as if it might already be raining up in the high meadow.

"Come on now. Supper's near ready," she called. As she wiped her hands on her apron she watched Alfred heading toward her from the barn. Age was moving in on them all right. Funny though how sometimes her heart could still speed up when she looked at him. She chuckled to herself. After all these years!

She turned again to her duties. Still feeling a chill. She moistened a clean cloth and wiped Jacob's hands and face. After collecting bowls from the open cupboard she turned her attention to the kettle, giving the beans one final stir as she heard Alfred come through the open door. "How's the mare?" she called over her shoulder.

"She's comin' along. 'Nother day or two and she'll be—" The words died in Alfred's throat as the earth suddenly trembled with the thunder of horse's hooves. He turned to see a cloud of dust and a cluster of men on horseback riding up to the front gate. He turned again, and Elizabeth spun around to see the look of surprise on her husband's face as blood, heart and lung tissue exploded from his chest along with the bullet. The ball sailed over Jacob's head and ripped into the cupboard Elizabeth had just finished dusting. It all happened before anyone could utter a scream.

* * *

An hour's ride away in Coffey's Gap, Austin was knocking for a second time at McCaleb's front door. While he waited he smoothed his beard and mustache. Coming here was not anything he wanted to do, but his heart wouldn't let him do otherwise.

This morning, Margaret had brought him news that McCaleb's oldest son, Rufus, had been killed at the Battle of South Mountain. Since the church had burned to the ground the week before, they were holding a prayer meeting for him at McCaleb's house.

Austin was not only saddened at the news, he was angry. Rufus shouldn't have been at South Mountain. He shouldn't have been part of a Northern Virginia regiment at all! But McCaleb's boys were as fanatical about "The Rebel Cause" as their parents were about religion. Rufus and his brother had grown impatient when North Carolina drug its feet about becoming part of the Confederacy, so they'd rushed off to be a part of the already committed troops of Virginia.

Austin glanced over at the hitching post; relieved to see two mules tied there. Margaret and Zechariah's. At least he'd have someone to converse with. They were the only members of the family who still spoke to him.

Among the horses at the hitching post were two Austin recognized as belonging to William and Reuben. The parson's tired old buggy and equally tired old mare also stood waiting.

The last time Austin had seen the parson was on Mary's burying day. Which was more than he could say for McCaleb and Sally. After all their Psalm singin,' prayin' and weepin' at Mary's deathbed, they hadn't bothered to show up at her funeral. Probably didn't want to be seen in public alongside a Unionist.

Austin stomped his feet to shake off the dust. Maybe it was time to let go of it, he mused. God knows there was enough pain and misery in the world without holding grudges. If Sally and McCaleb wanted to carry on with their hatin' there was nothin' he could do about it. He had to do what his own conscience directed, which he reminded himself, was why he was here.

He knocked again. Had they seen him comin' and chosen not to answer? It was hard to figure how Sally, unstable at best, was apt to react to this tragedy, and McCaleb, poor soul, would pretty much do whatever Sally dictated. Well, if they turned him away, so be it; right was on his side, and he'd prepared himself for any sort of reception.

But no amount of mental rehearsing could have prepared Austin for what he saw when Margaret opened the door. He caught only a glimpse of his sister's anguished face before she stepped aside to reveal Sally, kneeling behind her on the floor with a bucket of water at her side. He stared first at Sally then back at Margaret. Was Sally scrubbing the floor? *Now?*

"She wants you to take off your shoes," Margaret whispered. "She insists on bathing the feet of everyone who comes to call." Margaret motioned to a milking stool placed at the side of the bucket. Austin looked again at the kneeling Sally, then back to Margaret.

"Maybe … maybe I'd better come back later."

Margaret reached for his hand. "No. No, please. It's … Sally's way. She needs to do this. It'll be all right. Truly."

It was only then that Austin noticed Margaret's bare feet and several pair of shoes and boots lined up along the entry wall.

"I bid you enter to our sanctuary." Sally looked up at her brother-in-law with eyes that held no recognition. Her red hair was a tangle about her chalk white face, her lips a strange shade of purple. It crossed Austin's mind that she resembled his darkest imaginings of what a ghost would look like.

Margaret tugged on Austin's arm, motioning him to the stool. Awkwardly, he sat down as his sister closed the door, and at her prodding, he leaned over and unlaced his brogans. Once he had removed his boots, along with his socks, he set them to one side in a line with the others. Feeling utterly foolish.

Sally lifted Austin's right foot, placed it in the bucket and began dipping water over it with her hand. She was murmuring something he couldn't understand—a chant of some kind—then, she lifted his wet foot and placed it against her breast. Next she reached up and pulled a comb from her hair, allowing the long tresses to tumble about her shoulders. She then took his wet foot, wrapped it in her hair, and dried it as gently as she would have a baby.

"This is what our Lord Jesus told his Beloved Disciples to do at the Last Supper. He directed them to bathe each other's feet and to partake of the bread and wine in remembrance of Him. This we shall do this day in remembrance of Him and of our beloved son Rufus who has gone to join Our Savior in His Mighty Kingdom."

Sally repeated the ritual with Austin's left foot, then without another word, rose and disappeared behind the curtained archway that lead to the parlor.

"You may get up now," Margaret said gently.

"For heaven's sake, Margaret, what is goin' on?"

"Sally's taken the news very badly, I'm afraid." Margaret shook her head, gently urging Austin in the direction of the parlor.

Just then McCaleb appeared from the kitchen. Austin's heart quickened as his brother walked toward him with outstretched hands.

"I'm glad you came," McCaleb said softly, placing his arm around Austin's shoulders. "It's time we put aside our differences and be a family again." He gestured toward the parlor. "Please join us now in prayer." He pulled aside the curtain to reveal a line of people seated on chairs and wooden crates placed against the far wall. All the other furniture had been pushed to one side.

William Coffey was seated alongside his wife, and beside her was Reuben. Zechariah, the parson, and two neighbors were also present. Austin was relieved to see that none of the Moores were here. This was painful enough as it was.

Austin's embarrassment over his naked feet was lessened when he saw that everyone else was barefoot, too. Most people had their feet tucked beneath their chairs, an indication they felt as uncomfortable as he did. He moved silently, to the wooden box at the end of the line. Two places down from William.

A moment later, Sally and McCaleb, chins touching their chests, stood in front of the line of mourners. "We are now goin' to ask the parson to lead us in a few moments of prayer." Sally lifted her head only enough to make eye contact with the minister. "Y'all realize that the parson here is God's messenger on Earth. He will show us the way to our Beloved Jesus to whom we commend the soul of our dear son, Rufus. We have no body to offer to our Lord Jesus. The Devil took that with him when he killed our son, leavin' only shattered fragments of his broken body." Sally's gaze turned toward heaven, and Austin thought how her eyes looked like sea green marbles as she continued her lament.

"We, the parents of this tortured child have this day vowed to slay these villainous demons from the North, these messengers from Hell. We are willin' to give our life's blood to avenge the murder of our beloved Rufus. Just as Your Beloved Son, Oh Lord God, was put to death by ..."

As the litany continued, Austin shifted his glance down the line of mourners. Not a single head turned his way. The man seated next to him was a friend of McCaleb's, a Confederate, of course. Austin leaned back, reached around the man's back and tapped William on the shoulder. His brother glanced up, gave him a dark look, and returned his attention to Sally. It was at that point the parson rose and limped forward, raising his bible and finally silencing the diatribe.

Forty minutes later, every conceivable prayer having been said, the parson hobbled back to his seat. Grasping the opportunity for escape, Austin rose and eased his way through the curtain. Reaching for his boots he sat down on the milk stool, then sensing a presence, he looked up into McCaleb's tear streaked face. "I have to go now," Austin apologized, as he tugged at the stubborn boot, "but I want you to know how sorry I am about Rufus. He was a good boy. A fine boy. Is there anythin' I can do for you?"

McCaleb placed his hand on Austin's shoulder. "I thank you for comin,' and no, there is nothin' to be done. My main concern now is Sally. I don't think she fully realizes that he's gone. One minute she's talkin' about him being dead and the next she seems to be carryin' on a conversation with him. Sally has a frail nature, and—"

Austin rose. "Yes. Yes, I understand that. Have you heard anythin' from your other boys?"

"We're not sure where Jones is, but—and I haven't told Sally this—it appears Matthew was with Rufus at South Mountain. Although we're not sure. They were together shortly before the battle, and—"

"I think you're wise in keepin' anymore bad news from her. At least for now." Austin gestured with his head toward the parlor. "Any news of Will or Reuben's boys?"

"Unfortunately, no"

Austin put his hand on the latch. "I thank you McCaleb for welcomin' me as you have."

"We are brothers, after all."

"But standin' on different sides of a line nobody can see but everyone knows is there."

"Do you have news of Keith?"

For a moment Austin studied the hat in his hands, then looked up at McCaleb. "I'm surprised at you're askin,'" he said finally.

"You know I've always considered Keith my blood nephew even if he is adopted."

Austin's throat suddenly tightened. "Just between us, he's all right."

"I understand he's in Tennessee."

Austin's eyes searched McCaleb's face. "I don't know where he is," he lied. "Just North." Opening the door. "Tell Will and Reuben I was askin' about them and their boys. I'm surprised at not seein' the Moores here."

"Carroll and Zinnia were here earlier. Cal, too. But you know Carroll, he's never been much of a one for prayin.' Cal got shot up, but he's healin.' The other two boys are off fightin' somewhere."

"I can't say I'm sorry I missed them," Austin managed a wry smile.

"I thought things had settled down some since Keith's been gone."

Austin shrugged. "Hate burns deep in some people McCaleb."

"Yes, I know. I'll tell Will and Reuben you were askin' about them."

"Austin?" Margaret appeared from the kitchen, her oversized bare feet a comical companion to her prim Sunday dress. "I just want to give my brother a hug."

Austin wrapped his arms around Margaret's bony back. Although he had been tall in his prime he was now at eye level with his gangly sister. "How are you doin' Margaret?" he asked. "I mean, *truly*, how are you doin'?"

"Zechariah and I have no sons to give to this war, so we're better off than most. All my life I've regretted being barren. But not anymore." She pulled back and looked at Austin, her face glistening with tears. "Y'all take care of yourself, you hear? I worry about you since Mary's gone."

"Don't worry about me Margaret. I'm doin' all right. Give my regards to Zechariah." Austin stepped out into the late afternoon sunlight and took a deep breath. He couldn't think of anything he needed more than fresh air.

The distance home was short, less than a quarter mile down the rutted road and around the bend. His gnarled walking stick cut impatient holes in the dust. Had McCaleb asked about Keith out of real concern, or was he digging for information? How had he known Keith was in Tennessee? How many eyes, he wondered, had seen Keith's letter before it came into his own hands; slipped under his door in the dead of night?

Dear Pa.

I'm fine, and so is Malinda. I joined the Union here in Tennessee. I'm a member of the Second North Carolina Mounted Infantry, and I've been assigned as a Scout under Major George W. Kirk. Malinda rides with me. I think of you often, and hope to see you again in the near future. I miss you.

Your devoted son … Keith

What a world we live in when a man has to be suspicious of his own brother, Austin thought bitterly. And what exactly is a Scout, anyway? No doubt it's risky or Keith wouldn't be doin' it. Austin chuckled when he thought of what Keith had written about Malinda. He could just imagine her ridin' beside him, totin' a gun, that handsome face glowin,' dark hair rustlin' in the wind. There never would be another one like Malinda!

Austin's head was bowed, watching to avoid stepping in a mound of horse or cow droppings, but still his eye caught the poster nailed to the huge oak at the bend in the road. It flitted in the soft breeze like a hummer's wing.

He told himself he would have noticed it if had been there when he'd passed by before. Someone had put it up while he was at McCaleb's. Don't people have anythin' better to do? he fumed. Although he wasn't close enough yet to read it, he knew full well what it said. The posters were everywhere.

WANTED FOR DESERTION
REWARD TO ANYBODY SUPPLYING
INFORMATION ON THE WHEREABOUTS OF
L.M. "KEITH" BLALOCK

"Lying bastards!" Austin grumbled. "My boy was discharged from your damned army! He's no deserter!" When he reached the tree, he stepped up on the lower rung of the split rail fence and with one angry sweep of his hand tore the poster free and threw it in the dirt.

He scarcely noticed the gentle warmth of the late afternoon sun, nor did he hear the rhythmic droning of the honeybees, nor feel the caress of the zephyr blowing down from The Grandfather. The glories of the day were lost to him. How many more funerals before this madness ends? Would his own son be next? Austin's step was plodding. He felt shrunken; as if his bones were decaying within him.

The Tennessee/North Carolina Border

Late Autumn, 1862

☆

CHAPTER 19

Perhaps it was destiny that led Keith Blalock to George W. Kirk. Perhaps it was that unfathomable attraction that occurs between people of like minds. Or perhaps it was, as Malinda chose to call it, "God's Will." Whatever it was, as soon as Keith led his little party of Union sympathizers through the treacherous mountains from North Carolina into Tennessee, he rode straight into the welcoming arms of Union Major George W. Kirk.

Kirk's military mission was to rescue any man wanting to escape the Confederacy and deliver him into Union hands. And he was good at his job. Kirk was a mountain man, a native of Greene County, Tennessee, he knew this area of the Blue Ridge as well as any Cherokee, and certainly better than any other white man. He was a man Malinda neither liked nor trusted, and one Keith idolized. Malinda saw Kirk as cunning and arrogant. He was about the same age as Keith, mid twenties, but he had an air about him that made him appear older. No matter the temperature, Kirk was at all times attired in full uniform complete with immaculate white gloves. Malinda wondered how he kept them that way—but wouldn't dare ask.

When it came to military strategy, even Malinda had to admit it was hard to fault George Kirk. He had set up a network of *safe houses*, places where men trying to get to Union lines could hide until someone came to lead them through the hazardous passes into Tennessee. He made certain his men were supplied with the best weaponry available, primarily Spencer repeating rifles that could carry eight rounds, one in the chamber and seven in the tubular magazine inside the stock. When Keith expressed an interest in the Sharps rifle, a weapon favored by buffalo hunters because of its tremendous stopping power, Kirk made sure he was issued a Sharps *and* a Spencer. Nothing was too good for his protégé.

That Kirk was able to supply these weapons to his men said something of how highly he was regarded at the upper levels of the Union Army. Major-General John M. Schofield at Headquarters, Department of the Ohio, was acutely aware of how invaluable Kirk's mission was to the Union cause. He brought in the one thing no army could do without; manpower. Primary among Kirk's accomplishments had been the 300 deserters from the 64th North Carolina Regiment. Kirk was given sole credit for getting these men safely into Tennessee where they were all now fighting for the Union.

Malinda gave a contented sigh as she leaned against the door frame of the cabin. The roots of her dark hair and her high Cherokee cheekbones were moist with sweat. She breathed in the cool, fragrant air like a nursing calf. The mountains were aflame with autumn and the smell of the leaves reminded her of other autumns back home in Caldwell County.

The summer had been smoldering; longer and steamier than any she could remember, and now it was November and she was still sweating. But maybe that was because of the pregnancy. Women got hotter than usual during their latter months. She remembered Ma saying that, and who should know better than Ma? Lord knows she'd been through it often enough!

Malinda's hands caressed the bulging mound at her waist. Another two months, according to her calculations, and she would bring a new life into the world. What a wonder! Although none of this was as she had once imagined it would be. Who would have thought she'd be bearing her child so far from home? And without Ma to help her ... This place wasn't even something you could call a home. Shanty was more like it.

Ever since she'd seen the Reynolds' place she'd had it in her mind they would have a big house one day, too. After the war was over and they were all fixed financially, they'd fill it up with babies. Her heart ached when she thought of their cozy cabin back in North Carolina. Not a lot of rooms, but it was a sure enough good starting place.

This poor old ruin of a cabin had no doubt been abandoned by someone fleeing the war. A prospector probably. Which way, which side, no one knew. She looked around at the dingy interior. A couple of logs were missing and in other places there were gapping holes where the chinking had fallen out. Keith would have to fix it before the baby came. No, this sure wasn't the place she would have chosen to birth her child, and she knew it wasn't what Keith wanted either.

She let the next thought in cautiously. Maybe Keith didn't even *want* the baby. He hardly ever talked about it, and when she'd told him of its coming he'd said something that would rest in her heart forever ... "This isn't a good time to be having youngins, Malinda." Then he'd sort of closed himself off and scarcely ever mentioned the baby again. Maybe it was just the man in him, not being able to love it until it was full born. But oh, how she did wish they could talk about it sometimes. Make plans and things.

This is not the time to be thinking cold thoughts, Malinda scolded herself. We'll be riding out soon, and there's no need of getting all weepy and sentimental just when being keen minded and alert is what's called for. She knew this ride would most likely be the last until after the baby was born, and the thought of being left behind made her face bead with still more sweat.

That was one thing she could thank George Kirk for—he didn't stand in the way of her riding with Keith. When Keith told him, "My wife and me, we're a team," Keith said Kirk hadn't blinked an eye, and she'd been included right from the start. And her not even military.

Within weeks Kirk had given Keith his own command and let him choose the men he wanted to ride with him. Malinda couldn't say she enjoyed the scouting parties, she was scared out of her wits most of the time. But at least she was with Keith, and not having to worry and wonder if he was laying dead or wounded somewhere. She took a step back from the door and glanced upward. Their rifles were in place, nestled on the deer antlers that served as a gun rack. Loaded and ready.

Kirk's unit was informally organized. There was a core group, but others came and went. The camp consisted of a dozen two-man tents and a mess tent. It was sequestered in a high hollow so narrow as to be little more than a cut between the impenetrable blue tinged mountains. The only way in or out was through a series of hidden mountain passes, which connected to still other passes, which eventually wound their way into North Carolina—or deeper into Tennessee, depending on the direction you were traveling. The shack that Malinda and Keith occupied was the only evidence that anything remotely resembling civilization had ever touched this spot.

Kirk's unit moved frequently to other similar settings, but always one within striking distance of North Carolina. The major boasted that these hidden locations were known only to the Cherokee, which was no doubt true, because this region of hemlock, spruce, oak and chestnut was undergrown with a tangle of mountain laurel so thick the only way to penetrate it was with an ax.

Essentially, the only Cherokee in the area were members of Colonel Thomas's Highland Legion. But Thomas was so occupied fighting other Union forces there was little time to go scouting out Kirk's hiding places.

Malinda stepped out onto the doorstone and lifted her hair with both hands, letting the breeze ripple through it. Her hair had grown like a weed during her pregnancy; it now brushed her shoulders again. Keith loved running his fingers through it, and she'd laughingly told him she'd let it grow as long as a horse's tail if it would please him.

"Sweetheart?"

Keith's voice lifted Malinda from her mental wanderings. He was coming up the hill from the camp, his lanky six-foot frame moving with the grace of a bird in flight, the sunlight turning his wheat colored hair to gold. Even from this distance she could read the glint in the gray, thunderhead eyes. That spark was always there just before a scouting party. She chuckled. Keith was like a hound dog after a rabbit. Loving the chase as much as the sniffing out of the prey.

"You'd better be packing some extra supplies," he called. "This run will be a long one."

"Where are we headed?"

He grinned mischievously. "Caldwell County, North Carolina!"

Malinda stared at him with disbelief. "We're going home?"

Keith shook his head. "Not exactly. We *are* going to Coffey Gap, but we'll be aiming for a spot down the road from our place."

A small intake of breath. "You can't mean the Moores? But why? We're not going to find any Reb deserters there!"

"Major Kirk found out that ole son-of-a-bitch Carroll has been running his own raids on Unionists, and he's stolen two dozen or more horses for the Reb Army that he's keeping pastured on his property. The major thinks we just ought to go over there and relieve him of the trouble of caring for all those animals."

Malinda stepped back into the darkness of the cabin to hide the unexpected tears that threatened her eyes. Keith had been itching for a chance to strike back at the Moores—he hated their souls. And now he had it! "Sounds more like horse stealing than a scouting party if you ask me!" she said hotly.

"Well if it's stealing, it's just stealing back what the ole son-of-a-bitch stole in the first place!"

Malinda bit her lip. Once Keith's mind was set on something the devil himself couldn't change it. And Ma always said *she* was stubborn. *Keith Blalock could out stubborn a mule!* If she challenged him Malinda knew he would only remind her that he was following orders. They'd had *THAT* conversation before! Damn George Kirk anyway! Well, at any rate, they would get to go home. Even if it was to handle dirty business.

"I guess I'd better be packing some extra jerky then and collecting a few more apples." Reaching for the earthenware jar, and forcing a smile, she tried to look as if the thought had just popped into her head, although the truth was she'd been hoping for an opportunity like this for weeks. "We won't be too far off from my folks' place now will we? It's kind of on the way, isn't it? Maybe we could stop by."

Keith's bronze face tightened with a frown. "Malinda, this is no social visit, for chrissakes, this is a military operation! Besides, if memory serves me right you said you didn't want to see your Ma again after she got so steamed about you coming along with me to Tennessee."

Another sigh escaped. "I know that's what I said, but Ma and me … we need to set things straight between us. I can't just let it go like that, knowing she's put out with me."

"Malinda?" Keith's voice had suddenly grown softer. He reached out and took her hand between his own; the look on his face was one she had never seen before. When he coughed in a quick, raspy kind of way, it was a sure sign she wasn't going to like what was coming.

"Malinda …" he began again.

She stared at him. Waiting.

"I … I've been … looking for the right way to tell you …" His words trailed off again.

Why had Keith's face suddenly gone ghost white? "Tell me what?" Abruptly she withdrew her hand from his and dropped onto the wobbly chair. The tears were threatening to spill over again, and she didn't even know why.

"The major got some news about your folks, Malinda."

"About *MY* folks? What news?" Her heart seemed to be chugging like a steam engine.

"He just told me yesterday, but I think he's known about it for some time."

"Known about *what*?"

"Your Ma's not … your Ma and Jacob … they're in Virginia."

"In *Virginia?*" For a moment she wondered if he'd lost his senses. *Ma would never leave her home and go off to Virginia! Why would she go to Virginia?* "You said Ma and Jacob. Then where's Pa?"

"There's another reason why we're making this call on the Moores—other than the horses. It's about your Pa, Malinda. I've got to find out if ole Carroll had anything to do with it."

"Anything to do with what? What about Pa?"

"He was shot Malinda. Your Pa's dead. Four, maybe five men ambushed him in his own doorway. Your Ma and the baby … they saw the whole thing."

There was a ringing inside Malinda's head. Like the blacksmith pounding horseshoes on an anvil. "Pa's dead?" she whispered. This couldn't be true! Kirk had made this up! He was lying! But why would he do that? She fought against the hysteria that was bubbling up to consume her. "When did it happen? What about Ma and Jacob? Are they all right?"

"I'm not sure just when it happened. I reckon about three weeks ago. Afterward your Ma packed up and headed for Virginia. To her family."

The sweat was now streaming down Malinda's face along with the tears. The morning sickness, which had finally disappeared, suddenly returned. She lifted her hand to her mouth, swallowing against the sour muck in her throat. This had to be some kind of mistake. Pa couldn't be dead and Ma wouldn't run off to Virginia. Ma hadn't been close to her family in years! "Who in Virginia?" she gasped. "Where did she go?"

"Galax. Seems she has a brother there. A doctor."

Malinda blinked up at him stupidly as she sifted memories of childhood, searching for a name. For her, family relationships had always been like a puzzle with some of the pieces missing. Ma was the youngest. Some of her brothers were nearly grown by the time she was born. Finally a name emerged. "I guess that would be Uncle John," she said carefully. "John Whitehead. But I didn't think Ma liked him. I didn't think they got along." Her voice sounded like an echo inside her skull.

Keith knelt before her; again took her hand and placed it between his own. "Malinda, Sweetheart, if there is anything I can do—anyway I can make this easier for you just tell me and I'll do it. The only thing I can think to do is to go after the man I believe is responsible. If Carroll wasn't involved, he sure as hell knows who was. And I'll get whoever did this, Malinda. I swear to you I'll get all the bastards. Major Kirk found out that the first plan was to go after my Pa, but because of his brothers being Rebs they decided to take your Pa out instead. It's pay back for me joining the Union." He raised her hand to his lips.

"And for me riding with you," she murmured sadly. "It's my fault Pa is dead."

"Now don't go blaming yourself Malinda, because that ain't going to do anybody any good. The best thing we can do is to saddle up and ride over there and find out for ourselves what's happened."

Malinda experienced a rush of unexpected calm. A warm blanket on a cold night settling over her. She had something to do! She didn't have to just sit and wallow. She stared at Keith a long moment, then rose and began stuffing food into the haversack. "I thank you for trying to spare my feelings," she said without looking at him. "I know this has been a worry around your heart."

Keith stood helpless. Wordless.

A gust of air swept through the open door, carrying the crisp scent of autumn woods. "It isn't real to me, yet," she said softly. "I mean, Pa being dead. My mind keeps turning to Ma and Jacob. Wondering if they're all right." She braced herself against the corner of the table. Now was not the time to faint—but the Lord be blessed if she didn't feel like she was going to. She took a deep breath, held it, let it out slowly. "If you'll be giving me a minute or so, I'll have things ready." She reached for a smile but missed it.

Keith lifted the guns from their resting place. "I'll get the horses saddled." He turned to face her. "Will you be all right, Malinda?"

"Yes, Sweetheart, I'll be all right."

* * *

Soft, filmy veils pooled the mountain passes in a mantle of blue gray mist that seemed impermeable. The morning was hushed, the only sound an occasional snort from the horses. Keith was riding ahead, although Malinda could scarcely see him through the eerie light. To her rear rode Bud Riggs, and behind them, three more trusted men. Keith was the only one wearing a uniform. The others were purposefully dressed in civilian clothes.

This was the first time they'd ventured into North Carolina farther than the bordering counties of Mitchell and Watauga, and everyone was feeling apprehensive about penetrating so deep into enemy territory. They kept to the precarious, rocky passes, some places little more than a ledge so narrow they had to ride side saddle to avoid having their legs crushed against the wall of mountain rock that towered above them. This gave the riders the unpleasant view of the gorges yawning below, their depths unfathomable due to the tangle of trees, bushes and brush. Malinda wondered if she would ever again look into a gorge without thinking of Tom Gumby. The horses picked their way carefully and she could feel her pinto's sides heaving. She knew the animal sensed her fear; poor thing had its own. She tired to keep her eyes focused on the sky rather than looking down into the endless void—but either view was dizzying.

She tried to think about what lay ahead instead of dwelling on what still seemed unimaginable—but the thoughts cascaded like a waterfall. *Pa is dead. Ma and Jacob have gone away.* The tears came intermittently, and often she didn't know they were there until she felt them drop off her chin, or tasted their saltiness on her lips. There was no wailing or crying aloud. Instead she merely let the pain seep through her, like a soft rain touching sand.

As for where they were heading, Malinda knew the only way Keith was going to get information was by taking prisoners and questioning them. But what good would that do? There was no changing what was done. He would be aiming for Carroll—and Jesse too, if he could find him.

Keith had never talked a lot about why he hated the Moores so, but she was convinced a big part of the problem sprang from jealously. The Moores were uneducated, and Jesse, in particular, was butt ugly! Even uglier after Keith got through with him! Keith, on the other hand, was a looker, even when he was a kid, and added to that, the Coffeys had some education.

Of course there was the thing about Keith being illegitimate. He never talked about it much but she knew it was a torment to him. Especially since he didn't know who his real father was. He'd said that if he just knew who he was he'd rest easier. It was hard to understand why Mary had taken that secret to her grave.

* * *

The early morning mist had burned away, and now, through the trees, Malinda caught her first glimpse of The Grandfather. Her heart began to drum a stronger rhythm. Pa was right, The Grandfather was the one thing that never changed. The trees on his lower slopes shifted from green to crimson and gold and even bared their bones before a winter cover of white—but high above it all, The Grandfather slept on. As changeless as God Almighty Himself.

Keith had chosen a route around The Globe Valley that took them far from her childhood home. When she first realized what he was doing she'd wanted to protest—but then thought better of it. He was only trying to protect her. And maybe it was better this way. What would be the use of looking at an empty house? More than likely the Rebs had burned it down anyway.

Keith's plan was to arrive at the Moore place at mid morning. This was a time when the men were most likely to be scattered about doing different tasks. Confederate friends and neighbors had been seen coming and going, presumably to help with the haying since Carroll owned several acres of good fertile land. And he did have all those horses to feed!

A mile from their destination Keith raised his hand for a halt. So far the road had been deserted, but there was no reason to press their luck. Malinda and the men gathered in a circle around Keith as he laid out his plan.

"They've got a makeshift stable in back of the house so that's sure to be the pasture where they're keeping the horses corralled." Keith glanced at his hand drawn map and pointed a finger in the exact direction. "Bud and Russell, you two leave the road here and take off through that field. That'll put you on a direct course for the stable if you head in the direction I'm pointing and keep to it. When you get near the pasture, circle around and make sure the horses are still there. You'll find enough trees around to give you cover. Our signals will be like usual. Two quick shots for Charge. One shot … pause for a count of two … then one more shot, for Abort." He pushed his hat back from his forehead and looked each man square in the face. "And if anybody says 'Abort' he'd better have a damned good reason for saying it.

"Now they aren't likely to give up those horses without a fight, but one real important thing to remember is not to shoot ole Carroll Moore. I intend on taking him prisoner."

"None of us know what he looks like," Bud Riggs said.

"That's what I know, so listen up. He looks older than dirt, but he's looked that way for the past twenty years. He's got a gray mustache and a long beard. He wears a wide brimmed straw hat, winter summer and fall, and he'll be wearing a red bandanna around his neck. He's had that for the last twenty years, too. He's about my build, with a few extra pounds around the middle. If you see anybody that fits that description, and you have to shoot, just wing him. Don't kill the old coot. Least not until I can have a little talk with him. He's the one I'll be aiming for, and I'm sure when he sees me he'll be taking a bead on me too, so just watch out and let me have him."

Confident he had made his point, Keith settled his hat back into place and continued. "When it's over we'll head the horses down the main road. Nobody is going to be fool enough to try to stop a herd of hard running horses. We'll be taking them down to Major Kirk's main headquarters in Sevier County. You all know the way. From there our forces can get them as needed. The idea is to get as many of those horses as we can. They're aimed for the Rebel Army and it's up to us to see they don't get 'em. Whatever we can't take, we shoot."

Malinda watched the faces of the men as Keith gave his instructions. She felt a particular kinship for Bud Riggs. He *had* saved her life. And something about him reminded her of a younger version of Pa. She pushed the thought aside, wondering instead if the others were as scared of what lay ahead as she was.

"Virgil, you and Frank ride on up ahead," Keith continued. "Keep it casual like, as if you've got no place in particular to go. When you get to the gate of the pasture, just stop as if you're talking something over and when Bud and Russell start shooting to herd the animals your way, you make sure that gate is open. When they come charging out of there it's your job to get them heading in the right direction. From there on I don't foresee any big problems. Unless we run into a Reb regiment, that is. Now, Malinda and I will be up front by then and we'll try to keep their attention focused on us. The hope is they won't catch on till you boys have made your move."

The men nodded and rode off in their appointed directions. Malinda waited for Keith to lead the way.

As they turned into the woods, squirrels scolded from high up in the trees. Leaves crunched under the horses' hooves. There was the smell of a cooking fire. We're so near our cabin, Malinda thought, it could be coming from there. Maybe somebody has moved in. The thought of strangers living in her home, handling her books … Ma's china plate … Oh, if only they could walk in and shut this awful war and its agony outside—but hold on! Keith was taking a roundabout route and they wouldn't come near enough to see it even if is was still there. Malinda whispered a prayer, "Dear Lord, please let our home be all right. If there's somebody living in it, finding shelter there, please let them be kind to it, and to our belongings." But there was very little faith behind the words.

Once they neared the edge of the woods Keith pulled his mount to a halt. Though still hidden, from this vantage point they could view the entire scene.

Zinnia Moore was on the front porch, a bowl of green beans in her lap. Off to the left her son Cal was pulling up cabbages from the garden. Far to the right of the house Carroll and two other men were whacking away at the grass with their scythes. And further still, horses were grazing in the fenced-in pasture.

Keith motioned Malinda to the left with one hand while he raised his handgun in the other. She pulled her own Colt from the holster at her hip. Her stomach rumbled and it seemed her bowels had turned to water.

They waited an interminable ten minutes before hearing Bud's signal to Charge. When it finally came, Keith spurred his horse and rode out into full view, firing his weapon at the sky. As expected, everyone's gaze was directed at him. On the porch, Zinnia's hands froze over her bowl of beans. Cal dropped his basket of cabbages and started running for the house. Malinda raised her own gun, her pinto responding to every pressure of her knees. Keith guided his mount into a sweeping arc and aimed for Carroll and the others with him.

From the back pasture the scream of horses could be heard as Bud and Russell prodded them in the direction of the road. Malinda heard the cry of the animals and the shout of the men at the same moment she saw a burst of red-yellow flame erupt from a second story window and she let out a wild shriek as the impact from the musket ball tore into her right shoulder. She slumped forward, grasping the saddle horn with her left hand. Shouts and gun shots were erupting all around her. Discordant. Frenzied. The bitter smell of gun smoke burned her nostrils as she struggled to stay conscious. Her horse was running blindly. Suddenly Keith was there, seizing the reins. Musket balls whizzing about them as he screamed, "Hold on, Malinda! Hold on!"

* * *

She awoke in the deep woods, cradled in Keith's arms. Her right shoulder and arm were wrapped in a blood soaked bandanna, and it seemed her entire body was burning with pain.

"We need to get you to a doctor, Sweetheart." Keith's face was grim with worry. "The bullet's still in there and we need to get it out. We'll head for your uncle's place up in Galax. I know it's a ride, but it's closer than heading back to camp." He brushed the hair back from her face and added gently, "and you'll be able to see your Ma and Jacob."

Malinda's lips moved feebly. "That's a long way, isn't it? Can't we go to your Pa's?"

"Pa's no doctor, Malinda. Besides, they'll be looking for us there." He raised her to him, brushing his dry lips against her forehead. "Everything is going to be all right, Sweetheart. Trust me now. I'll get you through this. Do you think you can ride?"

"I'm not sure. I'll try." She grabbed for his arm with her left hand. "Keith ... the baby."

"What about the baby? Are you having pains?"

"I hurt so bad all over I feel sick to my stomach. I don't truly know if it's the baby or not. How bad am I?"

Keith lifted a canteen to her lips. "I've seen you looking better." He smiled down at her. "Here, Sweetheart, drink this." She took a deep, thirsty swallow. "That's it, Malinda, take a nice long drink. That's good. You'll ride with me, I'll tether your pinto behind us."

"Did ... we get the horses?"

"Two dozen or more I'd say."

"What about Carroll?"

He smoothed the hair back from her face. "There'll be a next time for me to get Carroll. You know one thing I'm long on is patience."

"Why aren't they following us?"

Keith grinned. "Not without horses. What we didn't take, we shot." As he spoke, Keith lifted her to her feet, and as gently as possible eased her into the saddle.

The next hours passed in shattering images. Blinding sunshine ... cloistered forests with giant, sheltering arms ... dark creatures reaching out. Clutching ... terrifying ... "Water ... water," she moaned. Keith lifting the canteen to her parched lips. Her left arm looping his waist, head jostling against his back. Riding ... riding ... head spinning ... vomiting ... and the ever constant searing pain ... the ever constant prayer ... *Please God don't let my baby die!*

* * *

The portly colored man who opened the door of John Whitehead's mansion wore a white nightshirt and a white stocking cap on his head. He was holding a lantern and his black eyes were bulging so far from his head they looked like buckeyes. It was four a.m.

"Is this Doc Whitehead's place?" Keith asked, straining against the weight of the unconscious Malinda who lay across his arms.

"Yassir, this here's Doctor Whitehead's all right, but he be sleeping now. Y'all come back later." He started to shut the door.

"Damnit, let me in!" Keith stuck his boot on the threshold. "This woman is hurt bad. She needs a doctor."

"Doctor Whitehead he ain't gwoin let you in here Mister." Moving the lantern closer to Keith's face. "Do he know you?"

"This woman is his niece. Now stand back I tell you!" Keith pushed the man aside with his shoulder and stepped into the hallway.

"What's going on down there, Arthur?" A baritone voice rumbled from the top of the circular staircase.

The colored man spun around as if he'd been shot. "I sorry Massa, I didn't let him in, he jest—"

"Never mind, I'll take care of it." A few moments later a man of about forty-five, wearing a burgundy wool bathrobe and leaning heavily on a black cane, lumbered from the shadows. He was tall, dark hair streaked with gray, and an immense mustache that curled downward at the corners of his mouth.

"Sir, what is the cause for your intrusion into my home?" His stern gaze took in Keith's uniform and the unconscious woman in his arms. "I will ask you to leave immediately."

"She's your niece. Elizabeth's daughter. And she's been shot."

"I can see she's been shot. She's also pregnant."

"And heavy!" Keith snapped. "Where can I put her down?"

The doctor's dark eyes flashed with anger. He paused a long moment, the silence so heavy you could feel its weight, then abruptly he turned to his slave. "Arthur, show this man into my office."

"Yes, Massa." The colored man led the way across the foyer, holding the lantern high so Keith could follow. They walked through another room and when they came to a closed door the slave pushed it open and motioned Keith inside. "There be a 'xamin' table there, Sir," he said as he sat the lantern on a table and lit an oil lamp.

The doctor appeared in the doorway. "Get some more light in here Arthur and bring me a clean bowl of water."

"Yes, Massa."

"And wake Thomas. I may need him."

"Yes, Massa."

The doctor bent over Malinda, pulled back the bloody shawl and untied the bandanna. "How long until the baby is due?"

"About another six weeks I think," Keith answered. He found a straight back chair alongside the wall and dropped into it. His aching arms fell limp at his sides.

"When was she shot?"

"This morning ... or I guess that would be yesterday morning. Around ten o'clock."

"Why have you waited so long to get her medical attention?"

"It was a long ride."

For the first time the doctor raised his eyes and looked at Keith. "Are you telling me you put this woman on a horse?"

"She rode with me. I didn't have any other way."

"How did you know where to find me?" he asked as he checked Malinda's pulse.

Keith gave a dry chuckle, remembering the man he'd grabbed off the street at knife point. "I asked somebody," he said.

Arthur came back into the room carrying a basin and a pitcher of water. He placed it on a counter and the doctor washed his hands, returned to his patient, picked up his stethoscope and placed it first against Malinda's chest and then her belly. He listened a moment, then removed it from his ears.

"Sir," still without looking at Keith, "she has lost a good deal of blood. The baby's heart is still beating, but that can change at any time. It's amazing she hasn't lost the child already considering what she's been through. After I get her stitched up she'll need to rest. When I finish you can help me get her settled. You realize I wouldn't be doing this if it weren't for the pregnancy. A child should not be held accountable for the sins of its parents."

"But I need to take her home."

The doctor turned and gave Keith an imperious glare. "If you put this woman back on a horse before she has a chance to mend you'll kill her. Along with the baby. Good God Sir, have you no sense? She had no business being on a horse in her condition. Don't you care what happens to her?"

"Of course I care what happens to her! She's my wife!"

"Then have the good sense to listen to reason and understand that *if* she lives she is going to need rest. Complete bed rest for several days." He placed his ear on Malinda's belly and without looking at Keith, added, "I am intolerant of that uniform in my home. I will ask you to remove it if you intend to wait. I'll have Thomas bring you something suitable to wear."

A colored boy of about twelve, with the same bulging black eyes as his father, appeared in the doorway.

Keith was exasperated, but he knew he was in no position to argue. "I'll remove it if you insist."

"I do insist." The doctor continued the examination of his unconscious patient as he addressed his slave. "Thomas bring this man some clothes. You'll find something in my room."

"Yes Massa." The boy disappeared.

"You should know Sir, that I am a medical officer in the 7th Virginia Cavalry, Army of the Confederacy. The reason you caught me home is because I am myself on medical leave, having been shot in the leg by one of your comrades."

"I … we assumed you were a Unionist since Elizabeth—"

"Ah, yes, my dear sister." The doctor picked up a bottle of chloroform, poured some onto a piece of white cloth and placed it over Malinda's nose. "She was here briefly with the boy. We agreed they would be more comfortable at the home of our brother Samuel." The doctor picked up a scalpel and began cutting into Malinda's flesh.

Keith turned his head away. "And where is Samuel?"

"In Louisville."

"When did they leave?"

"Approximately three weeks ago."

"Did they arrive safely in Louisville?"

"I have no idea."

Thomas reappeared carrying a pair of denim overalls and a green flannel shirt. His hands were trembling as he handed them to Keith; his eyes fixed on Keith's face.

"Thank you," Keith murmured, and offered a tight smile.

The boy quickly disappeared into the hallway. Keith disrobed and changed into the new clothes, making sure not to watch too closely what was happening on the table. As he was buttoning the shirt he heard the clink of a bullet being dropped onto a metal tray and heaved a sigh of relief.

"Now kindly carry those clothes outside," the doctor said, still without glancing Keith's way.

Keith inhaled sharply and tightened his lips as he folded the uniform. "Is it all right if I keep my boots?"

"You may, Sir."

Keith carried the bundle outside to his waiting horse, grumbling as he went, and stuffed it into the saddlebag. When he reentered the house Malinda was just opening her eyes.

CHAPTER 20

Three days after Keith and Malinda's arrival at John Whitehead's home, the doctor was preparing to return to his post. He had delayed his departure in order to look after his patient. As was his custom, he was leaving Arthur in charge of the household.

Malinda had learned through Arthur that her uncle's wife of twenty years had died of scarlet fever and was buried the day before she and Keith arrived, which was the real reason for the doctor to be at home. But he had never mentioned it. Malinda sensed there was a soft side to John Whitehead, one he was reluctant to show, but the care he had given her, as well as the apparent well being of his slaves, bespoke far more than words.

Malinda's shoulder wound was healing, and to the total amazement of the doctor, her pregnancy was continuing. He cautioned against over exertion, and ordered complete bed rest for another ten days.

"If there is anything you need, Arthur will get it for you," he said as he pressed his stethoscope against Malinda's bare stomach. "The baby appears to be viable." He straightened and removed the instrument from his ears.

As if responding to the comment the unborn gave a strong, healthy kick which brought a laugh to the lips of both doctor and patient.

"He's telling you he's not only viable, he's wanting to get himself born!" Malinda beamed.

"The longer he stays where he is the better his chances."

"You think it's a boy too, don't you?"

John Whitehead smiled. "It's a figure of speech, Malinda. I'm the father of ten, and I guessed right on only two occasions." He patted her hand. "You've been through quite an ordeal, and you're fortunate to have come through it as well as you have, but you're young and exceptionally strong. I do recommend, however, that you take better care of yourself for the next several weeks, and I strongly recommend that you postpone your trip back to Tennessee. That's a long ride on horseback. Is there no other way?"

Malinda thought about the narrow mountain passes, and shook her head. "Not unless I could sprout wings and fly in."

"Couldn't you take a stage coach?"

Malinda stifled a giggle. "The stage doesn't run where I'm going."

"But surely you have friends in North Carolina who would let you stay with them until the baby is born. Then when you're both strong enough you could go on to Tennessee, if that's what you feel you must do."

And leave Keith? she thought. *Birth our baby without my husband being there?* Her breath shortened at the thought of it. "If we're talking safety, Uncle John, I'm a lot safer in Tennessee than I am in North Carolina."

The doctor shrugged. "Very well, Malinda. Do what you must. I've explained the risk." He stuffed his stethoscope into his black leather bag.

She raised on one elbow and touched his arm with a staying hand. "Uncle John. Please, before you go, can't you tell me anything more about Ma? An address? Anything?"

"I've told you all I know." His mood turned impatient. "I gave Elizabeth an escort to the Kentucky border, and enough food for the trip. All I know about Samuel is that he is a Unionist and runs some kind of business in Louisville. As for an address, I don't have one."

"Then how was Ma supposed to find him? Louisville is a big city, isn't it?"

"She was confident that she could. Elizabeth and I do not see eye to eye. We never did. She wanted to go as much as I wanted her to leave. Your mother is very strong willed, you know." Then added. "Apparently it's a trait she passed on to her daughter. Don't concern yourself about Elizabeth. Believe me, she'll be fine."

"What about Jacob?"

"What about him?"

"Well, is he all right? I mean—"

"He's a charming little fellow. And very bright."

Malinda slumped back on the pillow. It was obvious she wasn't going to get any further information from him—if indeed he had any.

She watched her uncle as he stood before the mirror buttoning his uniform, and thought how distinguished he looked. She knew Confederate officers had to supply their own uniforms, and since money wasn't a pressing problem, he was surely among the finest dressed in his company.

The doctor turned from the mirror and picked up his medical bag. "I'll say good-bye now, Malinda, and I wish you God Speed." As he reached for the latch the door swung wide and Keith stood in the open doorway. The two men eyed each other silently, Keith's gaze taking in the immaculate gray uniform. After a tense second, he stepped aside. The doctor left without saying another word.

Keith closed the door behind him. "How are you feeling, Sweetheart?" He knelt beside the bed and took Malinda's hand.

"Better. The laudanum Uncle John gave me helps with the pain, but he said I shouldn't take too much because it might make our baby sleepy. Sure makes his Ma happy, though."

"Maybe your uncle should take some of it himself," Keith said wryly.

"Please don't fault him, Keith. He's been good to us."

"He's been good to you, Malinda, and for that I'm grateful, but he'd shoot me in the back if he had the chance."

"I wish you wouldn't talk that way."

"How else do you want me to talk? He's a Reb, Malinda, and not to be trusted. Best you don't forget that."

Malinda turned her face toward the window. This conversation could easily escalate into a verbal battle, and she was too tired to face one. She glanced about the room. "This is the second grandest house I've ever seen. Not as big as the Reynolds' place, but awful nice. Did you notice that when Arthur brings me my meals he carries them on a silver tray? And the dishes are so beautiful. There's a china soup bowl that's so thin you can almost see through it."

"Yeah, it's rich all right," Keith agreed. "House is big enough for four families."

"Just look at that mahogany table over by the window. It shines so you can see the bowl of flowers reflected in it."

Keith rose and began pacing the room. As he walked he ran his fingers through his hair—a sure sign he had something on his mind. "Malinda, about your uncle. I've got a strong hunch he's going to turn us in."

"Now why would he do that? Why would he go to all the trouble of patching me up and then turn us in?"

"He wouldn't let his own sister take refuge in his house, so why should he let us?"

"Because I'm pregnant! I'm sure that's the reason. He has a soft spot for children—God knows he has enough of them! I guess they're all growed. But as for Ma, I think there's been trouble between them since childhood, and—"

"And I think we need to get out of here before another Conscription Party comes calling to collect my ass! What am I saying? Could just as well be a Lynching Party!"

"I don't think he'd do that! We're family!"

Keith's eyes grew wide. "Family?" he smirked. "Please Malinda, don't talk to me about family loyalty! I think that stuff he's been giving you has affected your mind, or else you've got a real short memory!" He paused at the foot of the bed and gave her a hard look. "And to be blunt, the Conscription agents aren't looking for you. It's me they're after."

"Keith, don't get mad. I'm just saying that I don't think Uncle John woul—"

"I have to trust my instincts, Malinda. That's the way I stay alive."

"Well, what is it you want to do then?"

"I want us to get out of here. If you think you're strong enough."

"But—"

"If you don't think you're ready to travel, then there's no reason why you can't stay here until the baby's born. Your uncle won't object. He won't even be here. As for me, I'm heading back to Tennessee."

The discussion continued for another several minutes, and in the end Malinda had to agree that betrayal *was* a possibility. She didn't mention what the doctor had said about ten more days of bed rest. If she told him he might leave without her. The old familiar panic took hold again, and in the end Malinda relented. No risk was too great if she could be at Keith's side. She was strong. There was no reason to worry about the baby. Her uncle was being overly precautions.

* * *

The morning was chill and washed in a dense mountain mist as Keith and Arthur packed up the horses. The wide-eyed Thomas ran back and forth from the kitchen to the stable with supplies his mother Carrie had prepared for their trip, which included a heavy woolen blanket for Malinda.

When the boy was out of hearing distance Keith turned to Arthur. "I'm thinking you won't have many more chances as good as this one. If you've got the horses, you and Carrie and your boy could come with us. Nobody will take mind of Negroes traveling with Whites. Naturally, once we get to Tennessee I'd see to it that you find passage North."

To Keith's complete surprise the huge eyes filled with fear. "Massa Blalock, Sir, I do thank y'all kindly for what y'all be offerin,' but oh, Sir, no Sir, we doin' jest fine right here in our home with Massa Whitehead. He be a good Massa, and when Mistress Whitehead, she be alive, they used ta invite us inta the parlor foe a glass a mulled wine at Christmastime. Massa Whitehead, he say this whole mess gwoin be over right soon anyways. He say sombody gwoin ta shoot Massa Lincum and then things'll be jest like they was afoe. But thank y'all kindly Massa Blalock."

"You're turning down a chance to be free?" Keith was stunned.

"Massa Blalock, Sir. From where I'm sittin' I's already free. And this here our home."

* * *

While preparations for departure were going on below, upstairs Malinda was looking around the bedroom with sad eyes. She really didn't want to leave this fine house with all its lace and shiny wood, its feather beds and crystal glasses and silver drinking cups. She knew Ma must have loved it, too.

Her movements were slow and labored as she slipped out of the nightshirt her uncle had loaned her, and into her own clothes which Carrie had laundered. She brushed at her hair awkwardly, using only one hand, then preened a moment in front of the mirror before picking up the laudanum from the bedside table and slipping it into her skirt pocket. I won't be needing this, she told herself, but it's nice to know I have it. Just in case.

Keith had decided they would take a different route back to Tennessee. It could be as much as a three or four day trip going back through Carolina, due to her inability to ride hard. He figured they could cut off some travel time by heading directly into Tennessee. It would mean crossing Iron Mountain, which could be cold and treacherous this time of year, but there was a safe house Keith had heard about where they could take shelter; a safe house set up by Daniel Ellis, another Union scout. And Malinda knew Daniel Ellis was a man Keith very much wanted to meet.

* * *

Ellis was known to both Union and Rebels as "The Old Red Fox," a nickname Keith found unusual since he was said to be no more than thirty years old. Ellis's reputation was on a par with Major Kirk. A friendly rivalry had developed between the two; a competition as to who could bring the most Confederate deserters to the Union side. Keith knew Kirk and Ellis had never met personally, and he was anxious to get a firsthand look at his major's rival with intentions of reporting back anything he might learn concerning Ellis's tactics. Although Ellis was a civilian, he seemed to operate with military expertise.

The first two days of their journey passed uneventfully. They encountered only a handful of people on the main road and two Rebel patrols on a narrower wagon road, who gave them no notice—thankfully. If they had checked Keith's saddlebag and found his uniform no doubt they would have been shot on the spot. But once they entered the mountain passes, they saw no one.

The first night was spent under a chilly, starless sky, bodies pressed close to exchange heat. Both were grateful for the warm blanket Carrie had provided. The second night they found a cave whose ceiling was so low they couldn't stand upright. They risked making a fire at the entrance, not only for warmth, but also to keep wild animals at bay.

Now on the third morning, they ate a breakfast of apples and jerky and the last of the corn pone Carrie had made for them. They were back in their saddles before sunrise.

The climb through the darkness was tedious and once again Malinda could feel her pinto reacting to her fear. As the blue light of dawn broke over the mountain, they could see dense thicket on either side of the narrow path. The briars clawed at the horses' legs and opened long bloody gashes just above their hooves.

By eight o'clock they had climbed high enough to be above the cloud layer and the sun's warming rays made the ride far more pleasant. Keith turned frequently, keeping a watchful eye on Malinda. She seemed to be bearing up well, and for the hundredth time he was thankful for her toughness. What he didn't see was that she occasionally slipped her hand in her pocket and took a sip of the laudanum.

It was early evening by the time they drew near their destination. Keith told Malinda to wait while he rode on ahead. The directions he'd committed to memory only weeks before somehow didn't seem to fit with the terrain. Shouldn't there be a rocky outcropping off to the right just about here? Had he taken the wrong trail off the pass? Fifty feet farther on he sensed he was not alone. Every muscle tensed for the unexpected.

"Halt three times or I'll shoot!"

Idiot words from out of the past! Keith pulled on his mount's reins and sat motionless as a rock. From a cliff above and to the left a figure appeared. Without moving his head Keith shifted his eyes upward, took in the mass of red hair shimmering in the fading twilight. "Lonnie Coones! I damned well don't believe it!"

"Well, if it ain't Keith Blalock!" The young boy lowered his rifle and began scrambling down the cliff. "What in the hell brings y'all here?" Shifting the gun to his left hand Lonnie reached up for a handshake. "Where's Sam?"

"Sam? Oh! Malinda's waiting back on the trail. I'll go back and fetch her but first tell me what *you're* doing here?"

Lonnie gave a quick glance around and lowered his voice. "I reckon it's all right me tellin' y'all, beingst y'alls a Unionist. I'm with Mr. Ellis now. We kinda scout out people, ifn y'all know what I mean?"

"Yes, I've heard about Mr. Ellis. That's why we came this way. We're hoping to meet him."

"Well, he'll sure enough be pleased to meet y'all, too, I reckon! He's talked 'bout The Blalock's more'n once. He was plum proud when he found out I knows y'all."

Just then another familiar figure came wagging its way through the brush. "Hey Fart! Y'all 'member Keith, now don'tcha?"

The dog looked up happily at Keith; yelped and wagged.

Keith bent down and petted the wet nose "Hi there Fart? How ya been? Like living with the Yankees, do ya?"

Lonnie was grinning so broadly his freckles were running all over each other. "I'll be goin' on ahead now and be lettin' 'em know y'all are comin.' Jest follow right along this here path. Cabin's yonder 'bout a quarter mile."

The cabin belonged to Earl and Lavinia Sheets. Lavinia, a tall, gaunt faced woman had been born in Watauga County, and Malinda commented that almost made them neighbors. Earl Sheets was a mere wisp of a man with a wiry white beard and suspicious eyes.

Ellis was not present when Malinda and Keith arrived, although he was expected sometime during the night. Besides Lavinia and Earl, there were their two boys; Monty, 10, and young Earl, 12, Lonnie, and another short, squat man called Lum, also a member of Ellis's group.

In the root cellar were seven Rebel deserters; two from Virginia, the other five from Alleghany County, North Carolina. They came up from the cellar for supper and were introduced. One of them commented he was "right privileged to meet up with The Blalocks." Keith felt embarrassed and didn't know what to say, so he merely nodded. After the meal the men returned to their hideout. Keith and Malinda were told that a tunnel ran from the root cellar under the mountain and ended in a hidden cave on the other side where horses were waiting. Escape could be swift if required.

Keith noticed how Malinda's eyes lit up as she sat on the rug before the fire. Her belly was so swollen now she couldn't bring her knees up to her chin like she used to, so she sat with her legs folded onto each other, her back arched, and looking so peaceful and serene it was a joy just to look at her. This place had the smell of home to it. That must be why she looked so satisfied.

Keith also watched Lonnie watching Malinda, and he chuckled silently. The kid looked like a hound dog who'd just found a bitch in heat. He poked inside himself for feelings of jealously, but couldn't find any. Malinda saw Lonnie as a kid brother, and to tell the truth he felt pretty much the same about him. You couldn't help but feel sorry for the kid. At Kinston he'd been the butt of countless cruel jokes because he was so slow minded.

The story unfolded as to how Lonnie had come to be part of Ellis's group. When his Confederate officers grew tired of his foul ups, they pegged him a *disposable* and shipped him off to the front lines. But Lonnie proved to be more cagey than his superiors had imagined, and he escaped from the Rebels by means that was now commonplace. Playing dead. He'd then headed for Tennessee and was picked up by Daniel Ellis himself. Ellis took a liking to the boy and gave him the task, under Lum's supervision, of guarding safe houses. Ellis had a forged Confederate discharge made up which stated that Lonnie had been released from the Confederate Army for reasons of mental incompetence, a claim not likely to be challenged. Keith had the impression the boy was content with his lot, and since Ellis was keeping him on, it was evidently mutual.

Keith and Malinda were curled into their blanket, asleep before the fire when Daniel Ellis arrived. Although he entered the house quietly Keith was instantly awake, as was Lum, who had been sleeping on a pallet next to the door.

Ellis removed his hat and leaned his Spencer against the wall as Keith rose and crossed the room, extending his hand. "Mr. Ellis, I'm Keith Blalock."

Ellis's handshake was as strong as Keith's own. "Then I reckon that would be Mrs. Blalock." Ellis nodded toward the sleeping Malinda. "I was wonderin' who the horses belonged to." He gestured to Lum. "We need to get them animals stabled where they can't be seen by visitors."

Lum grunted, "Sorry, Mr. Ellis, I thought Lonnie had tended to it." Lum picked up his gun as he nudged the sleeping Lonnie with his boot. "Git up and git. We got them horses to take care of."

Lonnie was on his feet and out the door, pausing long enough to nod sheepishly to Ellis.

"Well, Mr. Blalock, will we be disturbin' your wife if we sit a spell before this splendid fire? I feel the need to warm my chilled bones."

"I'm sure not, Mr. Ellis." As the words were leaving Keith's lips, Malinda turned on her side, her back to them, and tucked her hand under her cheek.

Keith sat down on a cane backed chair, leaning forward, arms on his knees. "My wife's about run dry. She took a hit to her shoulder last week and she's still healing."

Ellis eased himself gingerly into a chair opposite Keith, as if cautious it might give way beneath him. The firelight cast an amber glow to his thinning red hair and dense beard, reflecting little pinpoints of light in his hazel eyes. The eyes reminded Keith of Major Kirk's; never still, shifting from place to place, taking in every nuance of the surroundings, yet giving the impression they had never left your face. Keith decided immediately it was the eyes more than the hair that had earned Ellis his nickname. They were the eyes of a fox.

"I'm sure it's dangerous takin' a hit in her condition," Ellis commented.

Keith could barely hide his surprise. "You knew Malinda is pregnant?"

"Yeah, I heard about it. I heard too, that she's one remarkable woman. Took up soldierin' when you got cornswaggled into the Reb Army."

"That she did." Keith grinned.

"You know they're callin' you two The Robin Hood and Maid Marian of the Union."

"Who's they?"

"Just about everybody. Surprised you ain't heard it." Ellis pulled a draw-string pouch from his pocket, shook a handful of *kinnikinnic* into his palm, and methodically began to crumble it to manageable size. As he worked, his voice remained low, measured, as if thinking carefully before speaking each word. "As for hearin' things, I hear you got yourself a medical discharge from the Rebs." He pulled a corncob pipe from his pocket, poured the mixture from his palm into the bowl and lit it. "I learned this from the injuns. Mighty good tastin'." He peered at Keith through the rising smoke. "So what kind a medical discharge did you come up with?"

Keith tilted back in his chair and folded his arms across his chest. Evidently there were a few things Ellis didn't know. He smiled. "I knew the Army is scared of anything contagious. One good epidemic can wipe out a whole company."

Keith went on to explain about the poison oak and Malinda's release from the army for being a woman.

Ellis threw back his head and laughed. Poor ole Zeb Vance that must've give him a turn er two." He blew a perfect smoke circle into the air and poked his finger through it. "Smart idea you had there."

"It may have been smart, but I'm telling you that's the closest I want to come to dying without going through with it."

"But it worked." Ellis smiled. "That's what counts."

"Yeah, it worked all right. Trouble is when I got healed up our thoughtful Rebel neighbors decided to sic the Conscription Agents on me. They came 'round and told me I either go back in the Army or face the consequences—which meant a hanging—so we packed up and hid out on Grandfather Mountain. Until the sons-of-bitches tracked us down. We lost two men during a shoot-out and I don't know what ever happened to another two. Most likely dead."

"That would have been the Green posse," Ellis commented.

The front legs of Keith's chair struck the floor. He leaned forward, elbows on his knees and looked intently at Ellis. "Who did you say?"

Ellis studied him through the blue/gray haze of smoke. "Robert Green, the merchant from Blowing Rock. He's the one who led the posse that tracked you down."

"How do you know that?"

Ellis smiled slyly. "I have ways of findin' out things. From what I hear it was personal. What's Green got against you, anyway?"

It was Keith's turn to be coy. "Damned if I know," he said. And damned if I'd tell you, he thought.

After that the conversation took on a more general tone, Ellis commenting on the latest developments near Nashville where the Union had pushed back Confederate forces under the command of General Forrest, and how Rebels in Brownsville, Tennessee had also been routed.

Keith realized Ellis was every bit as well informed as Major Kirk. But how did he get his information?

Lonnie and Lum returned and settled wordlessly onto their respective pallets. Ellis finished his pipe, rose and flexed his tall frame, then nodded a good-night to Keith before stretching out on the floor in a far corner of the room without benefit of either blanket or pillow.

The following morning Lavinia cooked a hearty breakfast and everyone, including the men in the root cellar, had a tin plate filled with warm cornbread, chitlings, eggs, and chipped beef, washed down with pitchers of steaming black coffee. Keith assumed Ellis's "scouting," like his own, included livestock and crops as well as men. A good many people were going hungry this frosty December morning, but none of them were in this Daniel Ellis safe house.

After the meal, while Malinda was helping Lavinia clean up, Ellis told Keith of his plans. "I'll be headin' for Tennessee with the group I have now." He gestured toward the cellar. "Generally, I wait till I can get a score or more, but some of these men have been waitin' a spell and they're gettin' restless. Then, too, we'll likely be pickin' up a few more on the way. You and your wife are welcome to ride along if you like. There's safety in numbers, and we're all headin' in the same general direction."

Did that mean Ellis knew the location of Kirk's current hideout? There was a lot more Keith wanted to learn about Ellis, and what he said was right, the added protection would be appreciated. "Will you be riding hard? We've been taking it pretty slow because Malinda's not able to ride like usual. I wouldn't want to hold you back."

"We'll take our time. Can't move fast through the passes anyways. Besides, none of these boys have anythin' more important to do than save their own hides."

A few minutes later Ellis went outside and Keith watched through the window slit as he talked with Lonnie. He assumed he was reprimanding the boy for neglecting to hide the horses the previous evening, but suddenly, and to Keith's utter surprise, Ellis wrapped his arms around Lonnie and gave him an affectionate hug. The way a father would hug a son.

"That pretty much fits with what Lavinia told me," Malinda commented later when Keith repeated what he'd seen. "She said Ellis used to have a son who looked a lot like Lonnie. He came home one day and found his boy's scalp hanging from the fence post. Later on he found his wife. She'd been raped and butchered. Lavinia said Ellis lived among the injuns at one time, but now he hates them."

"I guess he's got reason," Keith said dryly.

* * *

By noon of the next day Ellis's little party was well into Tennessee and everyone breathed easier. The pass had widened to the point where they could travel two-by-two and the soon-to-be new recruits were joking among themselves and exchanging stories of their exploits.

As they neared the top of yet another ridge they were met with the unmistakable smell of fire. Ellis, riding at the front with Keith, raised his hand in a signal of alert. Malinda, midway in the group was unable to see what was happening, but a few yards farther on she saw black smoke billowing up from the valley below. It rose in huge rounded puffs that carried bits of red burning wood. Nearing the top of the ridge she heard loud shouts and men's laughter. Along with agonized screams.

Daniel Ellis waved his Spencer above his head, shouting, "Come on men, that's a Union farm!"

Malinda watched Keith spur his mount and grab his rifle. Her pinto whinnied with excitement as she urged him into a gallop.

* * *

The farmer's mistake was pride. Victimized twice before by Rebel guerrillas, he had vowed to "shoot it out" should they ever return. The outcome was preordained. The farmer and his four-year-old son went down in the first volley.

His hysterical wife then rushed from the house clutching her baby to her breast and dragging her six-year-old daughter behind her. When the leader of the eight-man Rebel band leaned down from his horse, easily lifting the woman from her feet, she dropped the baby and it was trampled under the animal's fierce hooves. Her only remaining child was grabbed by another member of the band.

The woman's hands were tied behind her and she was hung by the neck from an oak tree so that only the tips of her toes touched the ground—and questioned about Unionists activities in the area. Mad with grief she was unable to tell them anything. She was then pulled by the rope until her body dangled in the air. When her face began to turn blue she was lowered and questioned further. When no information was gained, she was hung again. Over and over and over. While the questioning was going on, other members of the band ravaged the root cellar, packing what they found into their haversacks, then picked up the few chickens that were left. After that they torched the barn.

When the woman was still unable to give them any information they dragged her daughter into the cabin, boarded up the door and set it on fire. The screams Malinda and the others heard were those of the little girl.

CHAPTER 21

"Keith? Keith can you see what's hap ... pe ... ning?" When Malinda reached the top of the ridge she saw that a barn and cabin were fully inflamed. Several riders were already engaged in gunplay with Ellis's men. Near the bottom of the steep slope she saw Keith take aim. He dropped one man. Then a second.

Malinda rode into range and lifted her own rifle, using only one arm. But just as she zeroed in on her target the rider was suddenly yanked from his horse. Roped by Daniel Ellis! Surprised, Malinda lowered her gun and reined in her mount.

Ellis was dragging his victim behind him and riding straight toward the burning cabin. When he neared the flames his horse reared. Ellis hit the ground running, still towing the bound man and heading toward the inferno. She watched horrified as he pulled in the rope and when the man lay at his feet he pushed with his boot and rolled him into the fire. Even above the shriek of the crashing timber and crackle of gunfire she could hear the man's screams as he roasted alive.

Ellis ran from the hail of flaming wood and brought another rider down with a single shot. Men and horses wove in and out of the churning black smoke making it nearly impossible to tell friend from foe.

Keith rode out of the thick haze and headed for a tree where a woman was tied. Malinda saw him dismount, cut the rope from which the woman was hanging and slice the one binding her hands. The woman collapsed at Keith's feet ... but a moment later she began crawling toward the burning cabin. Keith grabbed her attempting to drag her to safety but she was fighting him, pummeling his chest.

Malinda urged her mount down the slope, her heart beating like a war drum. She looked around for another target, then realized the slaughter was over as quickly as it had begun. Bodies of men and horses were strewn about the yard like broken toys. One horse lay crying piteously. She took aim and ended its misery. As she galloped toward Keith she saw long fingers of fire racing across the scorched earth, feasting on anything in its path. One finger touched the rail fence and found new life in a joyous burst of flame.

Keith was still wrestling with the woman, holding her tight against him as she clawed at his face. Malinda rode up, dismounted clumsily and ran to his aid. "Let me help!" she shouted, grabbing one of the woman's flailing arms. Keith took her other arm and together they wrestled her face down onto the ground.

Malinda handed Keith her bandanna and he tied the woman's hands behind her while Malinda straddled her haunches. A thick cloud of acrid smoke enveloped them and when it drifted away all three were left choking.

"Careful!" Keith cautioned. "She's a wildcat! I thought sure I was going to have to sock her!"

"Listen to me! Listen!" Malinda bellowed. "Calm down! You're all right now! It's over! It's all over!" Beneath her the woman was still struggling, then a moan escaped her lips.

"My ... babies!" Her voice was tortured, rasping. "They killed my babies!"

Malinda stared up at Keith whose face was as hard as river rock.

The strangled sounds kept coming. "Sarah! My Sarah! They put her in ... in the ... the cabin and ... they set it on fire! My Jake and ... little Bo. . they ... they shot 'em! My baby ... Oh ... my baby ..." She let out a wrenching moan and then, as if no longer able to struggle, her body went limp.

Keith nudged Malinda. "Let her up."

"But—"

He squatted down beside the woman. "If we untie you, you've got to promise you'll try to get hold of yourself. There's no sense in running into that cabin now. You can't save 'em. It's over."

The woman shuddered and nodded feebly. Keith helped Malinda to her feet, then knelt and untied the woman's hands.

For a moment she lay motionless. Then slowly, painfully, she lifted her head, pulled herself to her hands and knees and gazed through the drifting smoke to the spot where her home had been. With what seemed tremendous effort she staggered to a standing position and began wiping her hands on her apron in slow, stroking, ritualistic motions along her hips and thighs. A roll of thunder rumbled through the valley. The sky darkened.

The woman's gaze shifted to Ellis and his men gathered beneath the oak tree where they'd hung her. In front of them were two Rebel prisoners, on their knees, hands tied behind their backs. The woman started walking very slowly up the incline toward them. Stroking her sides.

Keith slipped his arm around Malinda. She leaned her head against his shoulder. She felt weak and sick to her stomach. The woman walked directly up to the prisoners. Malinda and Keith stopped a short distance away. Ellis and his men, standing in a semi circle around their captives, watched the woman silently.

She stood before the kneeling men, paused a long moment, then reached down and grabbed one man by his hair and lifted his bowed head. Stared into his face. Then she let go of him and turned to the other prisoner. Lifted his head by the hair. "That's the man who put my Sarah in the cabin and set it afire." Her voice was raw but steady as rain. She stepped back, looked around the circle of silent men and gestured to one. "Mister, can I have your gun?"

The man shot a questioning glance at Ellis. Ellis nodded. He withdrew his weapon and handed it to the woman. Without hesitation she took two steps forward, held the gun a foot from the whimpering man's face and shot him directly between the eyes. The body fell backward as the brain exploded, blood shooting like steam from a geyser. She stepped back, handed the gun to its owner then walked slowly toward the trampled body of her dead baby. The wind moaned through the trees as she scooped up her child and cradled it in her arms. Then she sat down in the dirt and began rocking. Slowly. Silently.

The men turned their backs and murmured quietly among themselves.

"I hope she has kin who'll look after her?" Keith whispered.

"I don't think it much matters," Malinda said softly.

"Why do you say that?"

"She's not going to survive this. There are some things a person can't get past. And shouldn't have to."

Not twenty minutes later, while the men dug graves for the farmer and his children, the farmer's wife lifted a knife from one of the saddlebags, knelt beside her dead baby, and without making a sound pushed the ten-inch blade into her own chest.

When the diggers saw her body topple forward they heaved a collective sigh and began shoveling out still another grave.

* * *

Sometime later, Malinda stood beside her pinto, head pressed against her folded hands resting on the saddle. She had tried to pray and couldn't find any words to say. She'd also tried to shut out the animal screams coming from the grassy knoll where Ellis and his men were questioning the remaining prisoner. But couldn't. This was something she didn't understand and wondered if there was something missing from her brain. Did other people understand it? Did Keith understand it? Would he be able to explain to her what had happened here today? Did he understand a cause so important it justified the killing of babies? Justified torture?

Suddenly, the child within her moved, and a soft cry escaped Malinda's lips. She reached down and cradled her stomach. "Oh little darling," she cooed. "I was so afraid you'd gone to sleep and wouldn't be waking up again. It's been hard here today, I know. But don't be afraid. Your Ma won't let anything hurt you." Then she remembered the dead woman and wondered if she had made the same vow to her children?

Another shriek tore the air. Malinda buried her head deeper against the saddle, inhaling the comforting aroma of the leather, trying to block out the acrid smell of burned wood; the cry of human agony.

* * *

While the grave diggers went about their work, Keith stood shoulder to shoulder with Daniel Ellis, learning firsthand how he obtained information. Before the bound man lost consciousness for the third time, an eight inch square of skin had been peeled from his chest. Crazed with pain he had told Ellis everything he knew about Rebel troop movements, proposed attack plans and strength of Confederate forces in the area.

When Ellis was satisfied he had gleaned all he could from his prisoner, who was again unconscious, he rose and wiped the bloody filleting knife on his pant leg. Slowly he looked around at the burned ruins. "I guess you can say we've had a fair day. Not one a our boys took a hit." He whistled for his horse, took a rope from the saddle and tossed it to one of the men. "Hang him from this oak, but make sure you wake him up first so's he can enjoy it."

It wasn't yet three o'clock when Ellis summoned his band to reassemble for the last leg of their journey. They had been at the farm less than two hours.

As they moved out Keith rode directly behind Malinda at the rear of the line. Their mounts were beginning to plod up the steep incline when she turned to say something to him—but the words died in her throat. From this vantage point she had a full view of the carnage below. Men and horses, stripped of all valuables, were now carrion for the hawks and crows who had already begun to feed. In the distance a wild dog howled and another answered. They had picked up the scent. Soon they would join in the feast.

From the oak tree the body of Ellis's latest victim spun leisurely, buffeted by the will of the wind. The fresh turned earth of the five graves was visible on the small hillside a few yards from the smoldering ruins. One small tree limb, broken and tied with rope to form a cross, stood as silent sentinel. The promised rain had dissipated.

* * *

Malinda would never have thought she would be happy to see their Tennessee camp and that old broken down cabin again, but exhausted beyond anything she could have imagined, she tumbled onto her bedroll beside the stove and within seconds was fast asleep. Hands curled protectively around her belly, she slept for fourteen hours.

"Sweetheart?"

Malinda opened her eyes to find Keith bending over her.

"I'm sorry to wake you, but it's been more than a day since you've had anything to eat. I boiled up some hocks and collard greens."

For a moment all she could think was how dear it was of him to do such a thing—but the next instant her eyes clouded as memory returned and she was filled with an overwhelming sadness.

Pulling herself to a sitting position she leaned her back against the wall. "Will you be serving me in bed?" she asked lightheartedly, forcing a winsome smile.

Keith gave her a teasing look. "Now let's not be taking this thing too far, Malinda." He spooned the hot greens into a wooden bowl and handed it to her. "Guess what? We've got some cider, too!"

"Wherever did you find cider?"

"Stole it off one of the men who stole it off some Reb." His eyes danced with mischief as he filled two tin cups from the jug and sat down beside her.

Malinda took a hearty bite and dabbed at her lips with her fingertips. "Ummm, that's good! You've been keeping this a secret, haven't you?"

"Keeping what a secret?"

"That you can cook."

"Don't plan on it becoming a habit." He leaned over and nuzzled her neck. "You know Sweetheart, I've been thinking about something I overheard your uncle say to you."

"You mean about Ma and Jacob?"

"Well, no, about how you should be giving some thought to what you'll be doing after the baby is born. It needing care and all. And you told him you hadn't made any plans. We haven't talked about that much, Malinda, but I'm wondering if by now you've given any thought as to how we'll be handling things?"

Malinda blinked with surprise. "Keith, I've been *wanting* to talk with you about our baby, but every time I try you—"

"Malinda, you know as well as I do that I need every hand I can get. And you're one of the best." Keith studied his tin cup. "I'm thinking we ought to get some woman to look after the youngin so you can keep on riding with me like we've been doing all along. Maybe somebody at one of the safe houses. I'll wager Lavinia Sheets would be willing to do it."

Malinda thought her heart had stopped beating. She set the bowl on her belly and stared at him in disbelief. After several seconds of heavy silence she found her voice. "You listen to me, Keith Blalock, *NOBODY* will be caring for my child except me! And that isn't even anything that needs discussing!" Had she ever been this angry at him before? Was this the kind of father he was intending to be? "So you want to pawn our child off on somebody else so it won't be an inconvenience to you? Is that it?" Tears of rage and despair broke loose.

"Malinda, for heaven's sake, calm down. You're getting yourself all upset over nothing."

"You call our child *nothing?* Maybe you wish we weren't even going to have this baby! Maybe you call those other babies that were murdered yesterday nothing, too!"

Keith leaped to his feet and glared down at her. "What is the matter with you Malinda?"

"There's nothing the matter with me! I want to know what's the matter with *YOU?* I want to know what that bastard Ellis did to that Reb prisoner! Before he hung him, that is! You were up there while it was going on and I've got a real sneaking suspicion you were helping out! Did you enjoy yourself?" Her voice was shaking so, the words began coming in short, jerky gasps between the sobs. "I … wa … want … to know … why things li … like that happen?"

Keith tossed his bowl on the table. It spun off the edge and crashed to the floor. "Goddamnit Malinda, you do have a way of spoiling things now don't you! We just can't have a peaceful minute without you trying to pick things apart!" He took two heavy steps toward the door. "You want to know why things like that happen? Well I'll tell you why, Malinda! There's a fuckin' war going on! Or maybe you didn't take notice! Cozying up to that Reb uncle of yours. Lollygaggin' over his fine house and fancy dishes and all—sometimes I honest to God think you live with your head in a bucket! And because you're so all fired curious about that Reb, let me tell you I didn't do anything to him. I just watched! I've never questioned prisoners before. I only bring in deserters. And I wanted to see how it's done. I swear to you on my Ma's grave I didn't do anything, I just watched!" He stormed out, banging the door until the walls shook, leaving her staring after him, conscious of a terrifying emptiness within.

He just WATCHED?

Gradually her sobs dissolved into whimpers and she curled herself back onto her bedroll, closing her eyes on a world she didn't want to see. Finally the whimpering subsided and she again fell into a sleep of total exhaustion.

* * *

When she awoke the room was black, empty and freezing. But it wasn't the cold that had wakened her. Her body tightened as a spasm of pain tore across her back and shot through her groin. Dear Lord it can't be! Oh my precious darling, not yet! Not yet! Rest a while longer where it's safe and warm. Was she going to be like Ma and birth her child before its time only to watch it die?

Another spasm shot through her and she felt a warm gush of fluid between her legs. As the contraction began to wane she pulled herself to her feet and groped for the door. A blast of freezing night air greeted her as she flung it open. "Keith? Keith, where are you? Come quick!"

Down the hill in the campground, a group of men were seated around a campfire. She could hear fiddle music and loud singing, and the sound of boisterous laughter. Then one man stood up and stretched his arms over his head. "Keith!" she called again. Only this time it was more of a scream.

The darkness deepened as the spasms intensified. She was alone on her bedroll. Keith had not responded. Had he heard her, or didn't he care? It didn't matter. Nothing mattered but the pain. *The laudanum! Maybe that will help! Oh no! Oh God, no, I finished the bottle!* Even though the room was near freezing, sweat was streaming from every pore of her body. Through the haze of pain one thought tormented her. My baby will surely die, if not from being born too soon, then it will freeze to death. Was there no one to help her? *Oh Keith, please, please come back. Please!!!* But the one face that danced through her mind was not Keith's, it was Ma's. Oh Ma, I need you Ma! You'd help me. You'd know what to do. How long had she been here? How much longer could this go on?

Suddenly the door flew open and a rush of icy wind whipped the room.

"Keith?"

"Malinda?" The door slammed shut. "You … you awake?" There was the sound of shuffling footsteps.

"Keith, help me," she begged, then pain gripped her again and her words turned into a soft cry … *"Ooooohhhhhaaaaahhhh!"*

A lamplight sputtered to life. Keith was bending over her, his face inches from her own. She could smell the cider on his breath, see the glaze in his eyes.

"Malinda, Sweetheart, what's wrong?" His words were so slurred they were barely comprehensible.

"The baby's coming!" she cried, grabbing his shirt with both hands. "You've got to help me. Light a fire. Get help! *PLEASE!"* She released her hold on him, reached above her head, grabbed the legs of the cold iron stove and pulled with every ounce of her strength, oblivious to the pain shooting through her shoulder. It was nothing compared to what was happening at the other end of her body.

Keith wiped the drool from his mouth with the back of his hand. "Sweetheart, you just hold on here now, and I'll light up a fire and get this place warm." He stumbled about the room gathering kindling, fumbling with matches. Moving at a snail's pace. Then, holding the oil lamp near her face, he bent over her. Grinning idiotically. "It'll be all cozy in just a minute, Sweetheart."

An eternity passed before the fire took hold. Writhing, Malinda watched him stumble about the room, running his fingers through his hair. *Oh God! He isn't going to be any earthly help at all!* "Keith, we'll need blankets. Warm blankets for the baby."

Finally, he stopped pacing and pulled a wooden box up beside her bedroll. He sat down and leaned forward, hands folded. "There now," he slobbered, "we're all set. We got a blanket and now we can have ourselves that baby." He burped. Then hiccuped. "If there's anything I can do for you Sweetheart, you just let me know."

Another contraction seized her and Malinda was sure her body had turned inside out. *If I live through this you slobbering bastard, so help me I'll stick a pole up your ass and turn you on a spit!* "Aaahhh! Get help, damnit! Get someone to help me! *PLEASE!"*

Keith attempted to focus. Pulled back and studied her for a long moment. Looking puzzled. Then *s. .l. .o. .w. .l. .y* he rose and stumbled toward the door.

"Okay! Okay! No reason to get riled. I'll go get Maureen. You know Maureen? Ben Johnson's whore?" He turned and stared at her stupidly. "You like Maureen, don'tcha, Sweetheart? Maureen's got a good heart. She means well. She just happens to be whore, that's all." The door closed behind him as Malinda pleaded with God to take away the pain.

* * *

Someone came and brought more lamps. More blankets. Someone stuffed rags and straw into the holes where the logs were missing. Warm hands prodded at Malinda's groin; bathed her with warm, soothing water. The pause between contractions grew shorter. Nonexistent. Pain was constant now. Nothing else mattered. Nothing but the brutal, unrelenting, unending, tearing, searing pain.

A kind voice. A lilting voice. Encouraging. "Push! Push Malinda! PUSH!" After what seemed like hours, Malinda's bones at last broke open and the child thrust its way into life. Malinda heard a lusty cry. Then the lilting voice was saying, "'Tis a lad. Ye have a fine son!"

Gentle hands placed a warm bundle in her arms; undid her wet blouse and put the baby's lips to her breast. Tears and sweat coursed Malinda's face as she examined the hands and fingers, stroked the thatch of dark hair, peered at the perfect, miniature features that were a mirror of Keith.

"He's so heavy." She smiled up through dazed eyes.

"'Tis the rocks I warmed and wrapped in his blanket. The wee tad needs to stay warm, ye know."

"Is he too little? Did he come too soon?"

Maureen chuckled. "Ye cay not prove it by me. I hain't done this more'n twice afore. One of the girls at the house in Knoxville birthed a babe. Pretty little lass she was. And me sister, back in the old country, but I was just a wee lass meself then." Maureen reached down and stroked the velvet cheek. "Hay ye found a name fer him?"

"Columbus," Malinda whispered. "Columbus was a great man and did great things, and my boy is going to be just like him."

Maureen's laugh trilled through the room. "Well, from what I be hearin' his father is some kind of man, too! Fearless, they be sayin.'"

Fearless? Yes, that was Keith, all right. Fearless.

Maureen moved toward the door. "Speakin' a Keith, we'd best be lettin' him in so's he can take a look at what he's spawned."

Then Keith was kneeling beside her; his eyes surprisingly moist as he touched the fuzz covered head. "Sweetheart, you did a fine job. He is one fine boy, and he'll make us proud one day. And the best part is, he'll know who his Pa is. That's real important, knowing who your Pa is." His lips brushed Malinda's forehead. "I love you, Sweetheart," he whispered.

And then he hiccuped.

Caldwell County, North Carolina

March 1863

CHAPTER 22

They take from the rich and they give to the poor,
Like Robin Hood's merry old band of yore.
They make Rebels pay for the sins they have done,
Then ride off so rich with the setting of sun.
But 'tis not Robin Hood and his Maid Marian,
No, these are Keith Blalock, Malinda, and son.
How bravely they ride through the perilous night,
She with her babe at her breast oh so tight.
They unveil Rebel plans and they raid Rebel homes,
Then off in the night with their sacks full of gold.
To feed Union hungry so the story is told ...
To feed Union hungry so the story is told ...

Nell Boyd laid her dulcimer aside and smiled up at Austin who stood warming himself by the fire. "What do you think of this latest ballad about Keith? Must make you proud that he's become such a hero for the Union."

Austin stroked his mustache as he gazed thoughtfully into the fireplace. "I guess he's doing what he feels he needs to do."

John Boyd leaned over the arm of his chair and tapped his pipe ashes into the fire. "Two weeks back when we were down at Nell's sister's place, she played us that tune on the pianoforte. Seems everybody in three states is singing it."

"I worry about Columbus," Austin said.

Nell's eyebrows headed for her hairline. "You don't actually think Malinda takes that youngin along with them, now do you? Surely, they're just makin' that up! It makes for a good song. Malinda's got better sense. I mean whoever heard of such a thing—"

"Now Nell," her husband cautioned, "it's really none of our business."

"I don't know if it's true or not," Austin answered. "All I know is my grandson's more than three months old and I haven't even laid eyes on him. I keep hearin' talk that Keith and Malinda have been seen in these parts. If that is true, I sure wish they'd stop by."

"Oh, Keith's around here all right," Boyd said. "Too many people claim to have seen him. He's thinking of your welfare, Austin; he doesn't want to put you in jeopardy. That's why he stays away."

"I know, I know. But nonetheless, I'd like to see my grandson before my time runs out."

Boyd patted Austin's arm. "Now don't go talking about time running out. You've got a lot of good years left in you. Besides," he chuckled, "we need all the Unionists we can get. Not many of us left in these parts since Keith went off to Tennessee, and Ed Pitts and his family pulled up and headed North."

"Yes, we are outnumbered, aren't we."

"Well, I'm thinking this dern thing is almost over now. We've just got to hang on a while longer." Boyd packed fresh tobacco into his pipe. "Did you hear how Captain Tucker pushed back that band of Confederates at Old River, Louisiana?"

"Yes, and I also heard how we were routed by the Rebel Third Louisiana at Lake Providence. One day we win, the next day we lose." Austin knew he sounded like a defeatist, but he was unable to help himself. He reached for his brogans drying on the hearth. "John, I hope to heaven you're right about the war being over soon, but I personally don't see any signs of it. Folks have been saying that for two years now."

As he pulled on his boots Austin looked up at Boyd. "Did you hear Carrie Seagraves died? The Home Guard raided her place again and took the last of her livestock. Folks say she starved to death. Too many people starving. On both sides." Austin shook his head. "Here these woods are spilling over with game and we've got no gunpowder to shoot 'em with. Pretty hard to hit a deer over the head with a tree branch, now isn't it?" He gave a mirthless chuckle. "Speaking of victuals, Nell, I want to thank you for a mighty fine supper. Can't recall when I've had better."

"We enjoyed havin' you, Austin. I worry about you not eatin' right. You come over anytime. So long as them rabbits we've got caged in the root cellar keep on thrivin' we can keep food on the table."

Boyd laughed. "Those little dickens multiply faster than a Reb can run."

Austin rose and shook Boyd's hand, then lifted his great coat from the peg and slipped it on. "I'll be saying good-night now." He picked up his musket resting beside the door. It wasn't loaded, but if you were carrying a gun there was always a question in the troublemaker's mind as to whether there were bullets in it or not. He opened the door and bowed his head into the chill night, giving an empty wave to his hosts.

Boyd pushed the door shut behind Austin, shot the bolt, then turned to his wife. "He never said a word about William or Reuben now did he? Come to think of it he didn't have much to say about McCaleb either. Except about his boy." Boyd eased back into his chair. "It's a blasted shame what's happened to that family."

"It's a real shame about Matthew. He was a nice young man."

Boyd shook his head. "That's two sons dead now. Sally must have gone clean out of her mind over this one."

Nell began clearing the plates from the table. "If you ask me Sally was clean out of her mind long before her boys started gettin' killed." She slid the plates into a washing tub. "Did you notice Austin's eyes? The fight's gone out of that man since Mary died."

Boyd watched the smoke from his pipe drift upward. "He's had a bad go of it for a long spell, there's no denying that."

Nell lifted the iron kettle from the fire and poured hot water over the plates. "Well, none of us can pick our kin, and heaven knows it's painful when they turn against us, but when somebody you considered a friend turns his back, that's doubly hurtful."

"You mean Carroll?"

"Of course, I mean Carroll. You know how close he and Austin used to be."

"That's going back a spell," Boyd said.

The wind whipped the chestnut in the front yard causing it's branches to make scratching noises against the roof. "I don't know what there is about those Moores." Nell wagged her head. "I know Carroll and Zinnia tried to do their best with 'em, but there just seems to be a river of meanness runnin' through those boys. It's no wonder Keith turned out to be such a scrapper. The way they used to torment him was terrible."

"Keith took heat from a lot of people. Not just the Moores."

"I suppose that's true." Nell wiped her hands on her apron. "Who do you think it was?"

"You mean who do I think sired Keith?" Boyd leaned his head back and studied the ceiling. "I always figured it was Will Coffey. He had an eye for Mary for years. Austin knew it. Everybody knew it."

"I don't believe that for one minute!"

"You mean about Will being sweet on Mary?"

"No! I mean if there was somethin' goin' on between Mary and William she wouldn't have up and married his brother."

"Well, she couldn't marry Will, he was already married."

"I'm tellin' you, John. Mary was far too decent a woman to carry on with one man then up and marry his brother. It just ain't right!" Nell took off her apron and hung it beside the fire. "Land sakes! Will you listen to that wind! Hope Austin gets home before it gets any worse." Nell gave the wick on the oil lamp another turn. "You know, I pray to heaven you're right in what you said earlier about this damned mess being over with soon. If it ain't, William and Reuben will be comin' after our own boy afore long."

John Boyd looked away so his wife couldn't read the concern in his face. Their son would be fifteen in another two months, and rumors were already spreading that he was the next apple to be picked.

* * *

It was a brilliant April morning. A Thursday. Smiling, Keith folded the map and stuffed it into the inside pocket of his uniform. His informants had outlined the route Robert Green traveled twice a week—Saturday and Tuesday—between his home and store in The Globe Valley and his other home in Blowing Rock. Green has TWO houses to spread out in, he thought bitterly. A lot of people don't even have one!

Keith was heading for Major Kirk's command tent when he spotted Bud Riggs walking across the compound toward the mess wagon. Keith gestured and immediately Bud turned in his direction.

"I want you to round up the men," Keith said. "We'll need a dozen this time, and make sure they all wear uniforms. We'll be moving out right after breakfast."

"Where we headin' this time?"

"Back to my old stomping grounds," Keith grinned.

"That's gettin' to be familiar territory," Bud laughed.

"I want to check out the safe houses, and also there's some other business that needs taking care of over there." Keith gave the grin full rein. "We'll be dropping in on Mr. Robert Green."

"Don't believe I know the gentleman."

"You remember the night the Conscription Agents came looking for us up on The Grandfather?"

"I'm not likely to forget that night. An event like that stays with a man."

"And if you remember, I spent a good deal of that night in a pig sty with a bullet through my arm while those bastards beat the bushes to find me."

"So how does Green play into this?"

"He led the posse."

Bud rolled his head back and howled. "Sweet Jesus, Keith you are a wonder! I swear you're half hound dog the way you track people down."

"Let's just say I have a good memory."

As Bud strode off toward the mess wagon, Keith again turned in the direction of the major's tent.

"Major?" Keith poked his head through the open flap.

"Come in, Keith." Kirk, impeccably groomed as always, moved from behind the battered worktable. An unusually broad smile was lighting his handsome face. "I was just about to summon you. I want to share my good news."

"Oh? Well, Major, I'm always anxious to hear good news."

The smile deepened. "That will be Colonel. Colonel Kirk." Savoring the sound. "I've just received word from Major-General Schofield of my promotion."

"Congratulations!" Keith stuck out his hand. "I can't say I'm surprised though, considering how well things have been going."

"Yes, they have been, haven't they!" Kirk beamed. "Apparently what we're doing here does not go unnoticed at the higher levels. I must add that you, Keith, play a major part in our success."

"Thank you Maj—Colonel. I do my best."

"Have you had breakfast?"

"Yes Sir, just finished."

"Too bad, I was going to ask you to join me."

"Actually Colonel, I stopped by to let you know we'll be moving out shortly. We're taking a sweep into Caldwell and Watauga Counties to check out the safe houses and see if we can round up some more men. Also, there's something else that needs looking into over there."

Kirk chuckled. "You've been stirring up quite a ruckus over there lately. So what's this 'something else thing' you're talking about?"

"It's come to my attention, Sir, that a Mr. Robert Green has been outdoing himself in providing supplies to the enemy. Another shipment of guns and ammunition arrived at his general store in The Globe a few days ago. I figure we can use them as well as the Rebs."

"Ah, yes, I've heard about Mr. Green." Kirk's expression turned grim. "I received some information about him just yesterday as a matter of fact."

"May I ask what it is, Sir?"

"Certainly. In a way it concerns you. It appears Green and your uncles, William and Reuben Coffey, are playing from the same deck when it comes to information on Reb deserters. Green gets his news directly from the Confederate military, he's arm in arm with Robert Vance, and he likes to make himself important by passing it along to others. Namely, your uncles."

"I'm ashamed to say it comes as no surprise."

"A lot of us have relatives that shame us, Keith. Especially in these times."

"Yes Sir, I suppose that's true. And I plan to look into that situation, my uncles I mean, but for now my focus is on Mr. Green, and putting his little arsenal out of business."

The two men moved out of the tent into the morning air, heavy with the scent of wood smoke and steaming coffee. Kirk slapped Keith lightly on the shoulder. "I'll be waiting to hear how things go." Pausing. "By the way if you should happen to run into Mr. Ellis or his men in your travels, feel free to share my good news."

"Yes, Colonel, I'll be happy to do that." Keith gave a sharp salute and Kirk returned the gesture before calling to his orderly to bring him some breakfast.

Malinda was bathing Columbus in a tub she'd set outside on a tree stump when Keith walked up the hill. They'd been in this location only a few days, and the living conditions were even less favorable than the previous ones. The structure they were housed in was little more than a lean-to, but as he'd pointed out, it was better than a tent. And they did have their privacy.

"Sweetheart, you'd better either get him dried off quick or leave him with Maureen. We're moving out in another ten minutes."

Malinda looked at him with an expression he couldn't read and he suddenly realized that had been happening a lot of late.

"How long will we be gone?"

"We should be back by Tuesday noon if things go the way I want."

"Oh, they will," she said wearily. "They always do."

Keith could feel himself growing testy. When was it she'd started actin' like this? Saying things that could be taken two ways? "What's it going to be?" he snapped. "Are you bringing him or not?"

"Of course, I'm bringing him. Why would you think otherwise?"

He walked past her into the hut without answering. Why had he even bothered to mention it? She'd never left the boy with anyone. Not once. The first time she'd ridden out after Columbus was born—he couldn't have been more than six weeks old—she had him tied up in that sling she'd fashioned out of cowhide and strapped to her breast. He was so tiny you couldn't even see him, but just the same he'd been concerned about what the men would say, especially Kirk. But no one mentioned it. At least not to his face.

Keith had ordered uniforms to be worn because of his feeling that uniformed men drew greater respect. Otherwise, folks referred to them as "renegades," a word he despised. He wanted it to be clear to everybody that it was the Union Army riding into The Globe, and those that didn't like it could either run and hide, or stand and fight.

* * *

A day later as they rode through Watauga County, six men literally came running toward them out of the woods. They were haggard and hungry and three were barefoot. They first asked for food, and then said they wanted to be taken to Union lines.

"Reb deserters seem to be fallin' out of the trees like acorns," Bud Riggs commented.

"Says something about Confederate morale now doesn't it?" Keith replied.

Six of Keith's men rode double with the new group until they reached the safe house. "We'll pick you up on our way back, Keith told them. "Probably sometime Sunday morning."

He had planned their arrival in The Globe for noon on Saturday. This would give them time to confiscate a wagon and do some surveillance before Green left for his house in Blowing Rock. Green was a man who kept to a rigid schedule—which made things easy for anyone who wanted to keep track of his comings and goings.

As usual, Malinda rode at Keith's side with Columbus. The baby's head bobbed rhythmically as they jostled along and when he saw Keith looking at him he reached out one small arm and gave a toothless grin.

Keith had questioned Malinda as to why she kept the youngin strapped to her front instead of her back. It seemed it would be a lot easier to carry him papoose style. She'd answered by saying if she took a hit it would more than likely come from the back. This way the baby was better protected. Left up to him the baby would've stayed in camp, but there was no fighting Malinda on this one. She didn't put her foot down often, but when it came to Columbus, that little foot came down hard.

They spent the night in a poplar grove. It had been an effortless day, and the night was one of the most peaceful Keith could recall. The air had turned unseasonably warm, but still too chilly for many of the more pesky insects, and bedding down with the sound of the mountain stream backed by the call of night birds, made it almost perfect.

He watched Malinda as she finished feeding the baby and tucked him into his blanket near the fire. When she was satisfied the child was quieted down, she turned and walked toward him where he lay stretched out with his head on his saddle. Damn! She is one good looking woman! Always was, but motherhood has blossomed her. Her breasts are fuller. Ripe, you might say. Her hips are rounder, too.

"Come sit beside me, Sweetheart." He edged over on his blanket to give her room, then again settled his head on the saddle. "Will you just take a look at that sky? Like a million diamonds all sparkling at once!"

Malinda sat beside him, hugging her knees and gazing upward. "Do you suppose there are that many jewels in the whole world?"

"I doubt it ... Oh look, Malinda!" He rose on one elbow and pointed skyward. "A shooting star! Damn!"

"Where? Where? I don't see—oh yes! Isn't it beautiful!" Suddenly, she pushed his arm aside. "No! You're not supposed to point at it. It's bad luck."

"What do you mean bad luck?"

"Don't you know if you point at a shooting star that means a friend or somebody in the family is going to die? You can look, but you're not supposed to point."

"Horse feathers, Malinda! Whoever told you that?"

"Ma did."

"Your Ma's superstitious."

"Yes, she is that. But most times when she says something it turns out true."

Keith tugged gently at her arm. "Why don't you just lay down here beside your husband and make him happy and forget about all those superstitions?"

"Keeiith!" She pulled away slightly. "Some of the men are still awake."

"Well hell Malinda it's dark as pitch here away from the fire."

"But they'll hear us."

"Not if you keep that pretty mouth of yours closed." He reached around her, easing her onto her back beside him. Then he bent over her, his lips brushing her cheek ... eyelids ... her moist lips. As he covered them he felt them pulsate beneath his own, felt the rod in his pants begin to grow. He unbuttoned himself and lifted her skirt, then opened her blouse and found the sweet, hard, raspberry nipple. He took it into his mouth. Ran his tongue around the delicious prize. Nibbled at it with his lips. Tasted her milk. A moment later, bodies wet and straining for each other, he entered her soft, throbbing, secret place. As she began to moan, he once again covered her lips with his own as they rocked in silent pleasure.

* * *

Malinda readjusted her shawl so it fell loosely over one side of her face, partially obscuring her features. She hugged Columbus tight against her as she looped the pinto's reins around the hitching post in front of Green's General Store.

The baby was awake and responding to her tension by wiggling and twisting in his sling. Arms poking from his nest he reached for her bosom. "There, there now, little one," she cooed. "Ma will feed you after bit. We're just going to go into this store for a few minutes." Reaching down she guided the baby's thumb into his mouth.

Two men walked by the entrance of the store, stopped briefly to look in the window, then moved on. Malinda glanced at the clock on the church steeple across the road. Ten minutes after one. They were right on time.

From the woods in back of the store they had watched Robert Green's slave load his flatbed wagon with goods to carry back to Blowing Rock; saw Green climb aboard and head out at precisely one o'clock. His slave shopkeeper would be tending the store until his scheduled return on Tuesday afternoon.

Again Malinda adjusted the shawl; mounted the three wooden steps and paused on the porch before the window display. Besides the Negro she could see only one other person inside; a male customer.

The baby began to fret. "Shuhh, shuhh, Columbus," she comforted. "We'll just be a few minutes."

Malinda went into the store and moved slowly about, peering into first one barrel, then another. They were all pitifully empty except for one containing a small amount of dried beans.

Gun boxes were stacked two high behind the counter on the left. She counted ten in all. Turning to check out the other side, she saw ammunition boxes lining the three shelves beneath a few jars of quince jelly and peach preserves. At the rear of the store a yellow gingham curtain covered the opening leading to the back room.

"Thank you Mr. Simpson." A bell rang as the Negro opened the cash drawer. He handed the customer his change and made a mark in a ledger.

"Y'all have a pleasant afternoon now, Mr. Simpson." He closed the ledger and turned his attention to Malinda as the man left the store.

"Yes Ma'am, can I be helpin' y'all with somethin' today?"

"Do you have any red calico?"

"Yes Ma'am, we got a mite left. How much will y'all be needin'?" The slave walked to the other side of the room, stepped up onto a stool and reached for a pile of fabrics on the top shelf.

At that moment a woman wearing a poke bonnet and carrying a large basket, came through the front door. "Land sakes," a voice grumbled from inside the bonnet, "Mr. Green told me last week he'd have some flour. He promised to save me some."

"Excuse me," Malinda murmured. "I'm feeling faint."

She hurried outside, pulled the white handkerchief from her sleeve and dabbed at her forehead.

The signal to charge rang out instantly and the few people in the street ran for cover at the sound of gunfire. Malinda fled back into the store. Startled by the sound, Columbus began to cry.

"What's goin' on?" the woman in the poke bonnet cried, as Bud and five other men walked through the yellow gingham curtain with pistols drawn. The Negro's hands, which had been wrestling with the cotton bolts, reached for the ceiling.

"Everybody stay calm and you'll be all right," Bud ordered. Then to Malinda. "Where are they?"

"Behind the counter. Ten boxes so far as I can see." Gesturing to the shelf below the preserves. "The ammunition is over there. And there's three kegs of gunpowder to the left of the front door."

The woman in the poke bonnet dropped her empty basket. "It's the Blalocks!" she screamed and turned to flee.

"If you go outside you'll be shot," Malinda said sternly. "You're safer in here."

Keith and one of his men burst through the front door. Malinda grabbed the fallen basket and began filling it with whatever food stuff she could find. Gunfire was being exchanged in the street. Columbus shrieked. The woman in the bonnet slumped to the floor. Malinda stepped over her, swept up the dried beans from the barrel and poured them into the basket.

Keith stood guard at the front as his men carried the gun boxes and ammunition out the back. The Negro, regaining his senses, teetered precariously on the stool. "Sir? Do y'all mind if I get down offa this here stool? Isa gwoin to break my neck ifn y'all don't blow my head off it first."

"Get down," Keith snapped.

Two old men ran out of the church across the street heading for the store; their guns drawn. An unarmed boy of about twelve joined them. The four men

Keith had posted at the sides of the building took them down before they were midway across the road.

"Hand me those preserves." Malinda thrust the basket at the trembling shopkeeper.

"Yes Ma'am." The slave's hands were shaking so badly he dropped one of the jars. Horror struck he looked at Malinda with pleading eyes. "Don't shoot me, Miss," he begged, eyeing the holster and gun now visible beneath her shawl. A bullet tore through the window showering the room with glass. The black man dropped to the floor behind the counter. "Please don't shoot me," he begged.

"I'm not going to shoot you," Malinda bellowed. "But get up and put the rest of the jars in the basket. And be careful."

Columbus arched his back; his shrieks were ear splitting. In his terror he strained to escape the sling. Shots were being exchanged at the rear of the building as well.

"Do you have any cornmeal, flour or sugar?" Malinda called to the trembling slave.

"No Ma'am, we wuz promised some, but it ain't come yet. What we got, Massa Green he took it wif him to Blowin' Rock."

Malinda grabbed the basket from the man's hands, hurried toward the back of the store and looked out to where two of their men were loading the ammunition boxes and two of the kegs of gunpowder onto a wagon. Another of their party stood at the front of the wagon, attempting to control the terrified horses that were hitched to it. Three others knelt beside the wagon, covering the men doing the loading, firing in both directions. Three steps outside the door Bud Riggs lay sprawled in the dust. Face down and dead. Malinda thought of the shooting star.

"Are we ready out there?" Keith shouted.

"Another minute!" Malinda yelled, hoping she could be heard above the din of gunfire and her baby's terrorized screams.

At the front Keith fired through the window as two more men ventured across the road. He shot them both, then shouted at the slave. "Bring that keg of gunpowder over here and pour it in a line from here to the back door."

"Yes Massa. Yes Sir." The Negro scurried to carry out his task.

"Malinda! Damnit! Are we ready?"

"Ready!"

Keith glanced at the slave. "Get me some matches, then drag that woman out of here through the back and get her into the woods. The two of you stay there."

Outside, the wagon thundered away, two men riding on the rear firing at anyone foolish enough to follow. Malinda and the other men were mounted and ready to go when Keith dashed out. He dropped a lighted match onto the gunpowder, leaped over Bud Riggs' body and onto his horse. At the edge of the clearing the slave hovered over the unconscious woman in the poke bonnet as Robert Green's General Store exploded.

* * *

Two miles out of The Globe, Keith called a halt. The horses were lathered and foaming at the mouth. Glancing at Malinda, he saw that Columbus had vomited all over the sling and her dress. The child's eyes were half open and his head was bobbing to one side. "There's a stream over there. Go clean yourself up," Keith directed.

Malinda slid from her mount and supporting Columbus with her arm, ran toward the rushing water.

"Frank, I want you and T.J. to come with me," Keith said. "Two of you boys hide in the woods with the wagon while the rest of you head on to the safe house. A couple of you pick up those men waiting there and take 'em back to camp. The rest of you get some mules or pack horses and bring 'em back here and unload that wagon. Malinda will go with you. If we don't catch up to you tonight, we'll see you back at camp."

"Where we going now?" Frank asked.

"We've got some more business to take care of."

Malinda returned with Columbus in her arms, the wet sling over her shoulder, and looked up at Keith. "His stomach's empty, and I'll need to dry out the sling. I'm going to rest here a spell and feed him."

"Is he all right?"

"He'll be okay."

"I guess the rest of you better take a breather, too." Keith gestured toward a grove of trees.

The others dismounted and led their horses to the stream. Malinda laid the wet sling on a rock to dry, settled herself in the deep grass under a tree and unbuttoned her blouse. Columbus grabbed hungrily for her exposed breast. "Do you mind telling me where you're heading now? She threw Keith a look of irritation.

"They shot Bud," he said flatly.

She gave him another of those unfathomable looks. "Yes, I saw that."

"I'll see you back at camp, Malinda." Keith turned and spurred his mount back in the direction from which they'd just come. Frank and T.J. were close behind.

* * *

The road between The Globe and Blowing Rock twisted around the mountain in graceful, arching curves, just wide enough for a wagon to pass easily. Robert Green was delighting in the long delayed April sunshine, and contemplating his upcoming meeting with Colonel Palmer. The sale of this latest shipment of guns and ammunition would be profitable for all concerned. The army would have what they needed, and his pocket would be lined as well. He was proud of the scheme he'd been able to pull off through his connections in Connecticut where the firearms were manufactured. Only one man, a spy who reported directly to him, knew the true destination of the shipments. Not even his close friend Robert Vance knew how he'd managed to get them.

* * *

Keith led the way through the mountain pass known as Parson's Cut. It took less than a third of the time of the main road. He estimated they would be well in place before Green's wagon rounded the final turn into Blowing Rock. His timing was accurate. They were laying in wait less than ten minutes when Green's flatbed rattled around the curve.

As it came into view Keith wiped his sweaty palms on his pants. His mouth was dry. Frank and T.J. were stationed on the uphill side of the road where they could easily ride out and stop the wagon when Keith gave the signal. He would remain concealed directly opposite on the downhill side. He didn't want his face to be the first one Green saw. He could easily have taken him out back in The Globe, but it wouldn't have been so personal there. And this was personal.

* * *

Robert Green was whistling, enjoying his thoughts as well as the day, when two men rode out of the bush with weapons drawn. The tune died in his throat at the sight of the blue uniforms.

"Halt!" Frank ordered, aiming his handgun at Green's head.

Immediately, Green pulled on the reins. He didn't recognize them, so there was a chance they didn't know who he was either. He tried to ignore the knot of fear coiled in his stomach and casually placed the reins between his legs, laying them across the rifle at his feet. He didn't consider reaching for it, he knew he would be dead before he could get his finger on the trigger. "Good afternoon, gentlemen," he said with as much amiability as he could muster. "Is there something I can do for you?"

"Yeah," Frank growled. "You can get your Rebel ass down offa that wagon and uncover whatever it is you got hidden under them blankets."

Green jumped jauntily down from the wagon seat. "And may I ask just why it is you refer to me as a Rebel? Is there a chance you have me confused with someone else?"

T.J. fired several shots into the ground a few inches from where Green was standing. Green's boots moved as if they were on fire, creating a macabre, spirited dance as T.J. and Frank howled with laughter.

"We ain't got you confused with nobody," T.J. chortled. "We know exactly what rock you crawled out from under, you Rebel scum."

Keith could restrain himself no longer. Standing tall now, he adjusted his hat to a jaunty angle and strode from the underbrush, his Sharps rifle in his right hand. Frank and T.J. halted their shoot and dance game as he approached.

"Good afternoon, Robert," Keith smiled. "Beautiful afternoon isn't it?"

"Blalock?" Robert Green's chest began heaving like a bellows.

"That's right, Robert." Keith paused and looked up and down the road, then cocked his head. "Seems to me the last time you and me met it was under similar circumstances. Remember? We were just kids then."

Green stared at him dumbly.

"You had two of your rich, snotty friends with you that time. Elmer Severt, and some other scrubby little polecat. Can't remember his name." Keith smiled broadly. "Do you remember his name, Robert?"

Green shook his head.

Keith shrugged. "Well, I guess it doesn't much matter. Things are more or less the same way now as they were then. You're alone, minding your own business just like I was. And I have two friends with me. Just like you had back then. Kind of the same—only different."

"That … was a long time ago." Around the edge of Green's hat his blond hair was turning dark from perspiration.

"You certainly are right about that Robert. It was a long time ago. But you remember it, don't you? Just like I remember another night *not* so long ago. Up on The Grandfather. You do recall that night now don't you Robert?"

"I was only doing my job. It was my duty to—"

"Don't talk to me about *DUTY!*" Keith shrieked, his face turning scarlet. "Tracking me down like an animal wasn't your duty it was your *PLEASURE!*"

"But it wasn't me! I was only following orders. It was your Uncle William. He's the one who tracked you to that hut. He's the one who sent the agents. I tell you I was only following orders! I—"

Keith lifted the Sharps to his shoulder. "Well now, Robert, since you're so good at following orders, let's see how well you carry out this one. RUN!"

Green stared at him open-mouthed.

"I said run. I'll give you to a count of seven."

"No! You can't do this!" Green sobbed.

"I can't?" Keith looked at him with mock surprise. "Well, now you just watch me."

"No! *Please!*"

"I'm giving you a chance Robert. For a count of seven. Hell, you may be lucky and get away. Like I did that night on The Grandfather."

"Please don't do this!!!"

Keith's finger wrapped around the trigger. "One."

Green dashed for the side of the road and leaped into the underbrush. Arms waving like a scarecrow he plunged downward, heading for the safety of the woods below.

"Two … three … four … five … six … SEVEN!" The enormous stopping power of the weapon found its mark just below Green's right buttock. He crumpled instantly, screaming in agony and grabbing his shattered leg.

A smile broke through Keith's tight lips. "Want a little pig shit to rub on it Robert?" he hollered. Then lowering the rifle he started down the mountainside toward where his fallen prey lay writhing in the bracken, drenched in blood.

"Finish it off you bastard!" Green screamed. "Do it! Goddamn you! Kill me and get it over with!"

Keith laid the rifle aside and squatted down beside Green. Casually, he reached for a blade of dried grass and stuck it between his teeth. "All the same to you Robert, I think I'll just stay here a while and enjoy this beautiful afternoon. Must be real tiring on you running back and forth between your two houses, carrying all that food that rightfully belongs to decent people. I guess there's just no end to the troubles a rich man like you has to contented with." He rolled the stalk of grass from one side of his mouth to the other.

"By the way, a friend of mine got killed this afternoon. A good friend. His name was Bud Riggs. Nice young man. Sorry you didn't get to meet him."

Green groveled in agony, his brain barely comprehending the words.

"*I said his name was Bud Riggs!*" Keith's voice grew shrill.

Green rolled his head from side to side.

"I want you to remember his name, Robert. And I'm going to give you something that will help you remember. This is for Bud." Keith stood up, picked up the rifle by the barrel, and using both hands raised it above his head then swung the butt square into Robert Green's crotch.

☆

CHAPTER 23

Elizabeth and Jacob's flight from Virginia to Louisville was not without incident. After their escort, a young roughneck whom Elizabeth despised because of his course language and vulgar behavior, left them at the Virginia border, they journeyed on alone, crossing the Cumberland Mountains and entire State of Kentucky. They passed through territory sometimes claimed by Union, sometimes by Confederates. They were shot at by both, forced to hide in caves, wade icy streams, and when their meager supplies ran out, forage for food. One terrifying night, Elizabeth fought off a bear who killed their horse then turned on them. She shot the beast between the eyes as he charged.

The last seventy miles were made on foot, and the only thing that kept Elizabeth going was the knowledge that if she died, Jacob would die, too. With each agonizing mile her hatred of her brother John grew stronger. She silently vowed to live so she could one day pay him back for all this suffering. He had all but thrown them out of his house, giving her no alternative but to flee to Kentucky. She couldn't let herself think about what would become of them if Samuel offered a similar welcome.

After twenty-seven days they finally reached Louisville. It took another two, to find Samuel Whitehead's home. Her brother welcomed Elizabeth with open arms, tears lighting his eyes when he looked at Jacob. If that had not been the case, Elizabeth was certain she would have died on their doorstep.

Samuel's wife, Louise, took one look at her newly found sister-in-law and promptly set about preparing a guest room. She tucked Elizabeth into bed and saw to it she remained there until she had fully recovered from exhaustion. It was the first act of kindness Elizabeth had experienced in a long, long time, and one she wasn't likely to forget.

Samuel was a prosperous business man. Before the war he'd built a small fortune as a trading agent on the outskirts of Louisville where his Indian blood proved to be an asset. When war drums grew louder he opened a branch business in the city, which he called "Whitehead's Emporium," and sold the finest handmade Indian goods to the more affluent of the city's society, along with rare books, art, and antique china. Samuel was adept at merging the conflicting segments of his heritage; a knowledge of literature and art from his mother, and an adventurous spirit from his mountain man father. After war broke out he also became involved in helping runaway slaves find safe havens in the North. Samuel was as dedicated to the Union cause as his brother John was to the Confederacy.

It was ten days before Elizabeth completely regained her strength. During her recovery period she had little else to think about other than her situation. How could she repay her brother and his wife for their kindness? Although their physical safety was no longer in danger, she was penniless, and without means of earning a living. Perhaps she could teach school? If not that then what other work might she find to support herself and Jacob? The future was not without peril.

When she discussed the situation with Louise and Samuel, it was Samuel who offered a solution. "But why must you look for work outside our home? There is plenty to be done here. In exchange for room and board, and a small salary, you can be our housekeeper."

It was an arrangement that would work for the good of all. The house had fourteen rooms, but since the war began, money was in short supply and they'd had to let most of their servants go, retaining only the cook and butler. Louise's health was poor. She had been born with a humpback, a condition she tried somewhat successfully to conceal with full cut blouses and coats, but maintaining the house, without help, had become an impossible task. Elizabeth decided to give it a try.

For the first time in her life she found herself excited about keeping a home. There was silver to polish and crystal to wash, and lavish rooms to keep tidy. And there was an added bonus. Samuel and Louise were childless and they had welcomed Jacob with loving arms. Within a relatively short period Elizabeth saw that the horrifying memories of what her son had been through were gradually beginning to fade.

Her own memories were slower to put aside. In her dreams she relived the ghoulish events of Alfred's death, and the precipitous journey from Virginia. Awake, she carried the haunted look of one who has seen too much suffering, but by early May, life had settled into new patterns and seeing her son prosper, Elizabeth determinedly set about adjusting to their new circumstances.

Life in Louisville was far easier than it had been in Caldwell County, and she realized that through this odd twist of fate, she was being given the opportunity to live the life she had once only dreamed of. The day Samuel presented her with a new dulcimer to replace the one she'd lost, she felt life was indeed taking a turn for the better. Perhaps there was cause for hope, after all.

There was little to miss from her former life other than the few books and possessions she'd had to leave behind. All else that mattered was gone. Alfred was dead and to her way of thinking Malinda might as well be.

When Samuel first heard Elizabeth's story he was not only awed by her courage, but flattered to learn he was blood kin to the famous Blalocks. He began supplying Elizabeth with reports of Malinda and Keith's activities, believing this would bring her pride and comfort. When he realized, to the contrary, news of Malinda caused only pain, he stopped mentioning his niece's name altogether.

In Samuel's judgment, Malinda and Keith, *and* Colonel Kirk, were heroes. He was surprised when his sister turned a deaf ear to all of it. But Louise, who had become very close to her sister-in-law, understood Elizabeth's feelings completely.

"She's ashamed," Louise said quietly, as she and Samuel sat on the veranda sipping tall glasses of cool tea. "Elizabeth had hopes her daughter would marry a prosperous man and have a comfortable life. Instead she rides with raiding parties and robs and plunders. And what's worse, takes Elizabeth's grandchild with her! I agree with Elizabeth totally. The entire situation is shameful."

"Louise," Samuel said gently, "we are fortunate to be so far removed from the fighting, and I think it's wrong to look down on those who are doing the best they can for the Union cause, given the circumstances they find themselves in. They are soldiers, and they're fighting a war."

"Pish posh! Keith is a soldier. Malinda is not. And there's no reason for her to be behaving in such a manner. She's a woman! Let her go work in a hospital if she wants to support the Union cause."

"Don't misunderstand me, you know I love Elizabeth, but I do think she's being too harsh on her daughter. If she'd heard the stories these poor slaves tell about what their so called Masters did to them, she would better understand how important it is to wipe out this curse of slavery. That *is* what this war is about, and I for one, admire what Keith and Malinda are doing."

A soothing breeze touched Louise's hair and she reached up to push a jeweled comb back into her chignon. "Samuel, you know I have no love for the Confederacy, I think they are a pack of fools, but how, pray tell, does robbing Confederate homes and burning Confederate fields wipe out slavery?"

"Because one way to win this war is to starve the bastards out."

Louise rose abruptly and adjusted her crinolines. "If you're going to speak in such a vulgar manner Samuel, I'm going inside. I want you to know that I stand firmly in agreement with your sister. Malinda's behavior is disgraceful, and what she is doing to her child is criminal! In my opinion she doesn't deserve to *have* a child!"

"We don't know if any of those stories are true, anymore than we know if the stories about the pillaging are true. There is so much gossip from every cor—" But Samuel's words were spoken to the empty air. Louise had gone inside.

* * *

The May breeze from the mountain brought the fragrance of lavender. It was blooming early this year. Nature's way of getting even for the hard winter,

Malinda mused. Later, when Columbus took his nap maybe she'd climb up and collect some. Keith loved the smell of lavender in her hair.

"One more tune little one, then Ma's got to do some picking up around here. This cabin is a mess." She put her hand to the baby's forehead. It was cooler, thank heavens! Then nestling him closer to her, she again strummed the dulcimer strings as she sang:

The sun shines bright on my old Kentucky home,
On my old Kentucky home far away.
Oh the sun shines bright on my old Kentucky home,
'Tis summer and the darkies are gay ...

The words brought immediate thoughts of Ma and Jacob. As Malinda continued to sing, fantasy images waltzed through her mind; Ma seated in a yard under an apple tree, Jacob romping about chasing a robin. In her vision the air was sweetened by the scent of the apple blossoms. There was no sound of gunfire, only the song of birds. Oh please Lord let it be true. Let Ma and Jacob be in a safe place. Since the Battle of Perryville, Kentucky had been in Union hands—although the state was a caldron of military intrigue and minor skirmishes. Yet, it was reasonable to assume they were safe. As safe as anyone could be in today's world!

Malinda laid the dulcimer aside and carried Columbus into the cabin. What must that be like, she mused? Safe. Had there ever been a time when she'd felt safe? An ironic smile touched her lips. Yes, there had been. Back in the days when she didn't believe in war. Back in the days when they had their own home with a window and curtains and books and a clock and ...

She tied the baby into the chair with a length of cowhide. "There's no sense in thinking about those days now is there Columbus? Those days are gone." She poured warm water into the corn mush and stirred it. "But there'll be good days again. Not to worry about that. You'll see!" She brought a spoonful of mush to the baby's lips. Instantly, he threw his head back, stiffened his body and batted his arms. The spoon went flying. "Well," Malinda sighed, "you're going to have to get used to it Columbus, because Ma's milk is drying up and there isn't much else around here to eat. I guess you don't know it, but truth is, we're lucky to have the corn meal." Again, she laid her hand on the baby's forehead. Definitely cooler.

Columbus had been sick for more than two weeks. At first Malinda had feared it was scarlet fever, but thankfully that had proved not to be the case. However, when Colonel Kirk learned of the baby's illness he'd ordered Keith to sleep in the tents with the men and not to have contact with his family until they knew whether or not the malady was contagious.

The enforced separation had been hard. Malinda felt like a leper and blamed

Kirk. Keith, however, was used to breaking rules, even those set down by Colonel Kirk, and he came to check on her late one afternoon. They sat out behind the cabin where they weren't likely to be seen and talked and held hands the way they had when they were courting. That was the nice part. But oh the ache in her heart when she'd watched him ride out of camp without her.

Malinda picked up the spoon, wiped it on her apron and offered it to the baby—with no more success. "Well just sit there then and think about it a spell," she said wearily. Seemed the child's disposition was becoming more like his Pa's every day. Sweet and loving one minute then full of hell fire the next! What is it they say? "The apple never falls far from the tree."

Heavens, she was tired. How many nights had she gone without sleep. It seemed forever. Up with the child every twenty minutes or so, and when she wasn't up with him she was lying there wide-eyed worrying about him. And Keith.

Her gaze traveled the small, dingy room. There had been a time when she'd taken pride in cleaning their home. Now it was an overwhelming chore. There were times when she saw herself as being a lot like Ma. Ma had never taken pride in keeping a home, not like Keith's Ma did ... Had. Sometimes she had trouble accepting that Mary was gone. And Pa, too.

"Columbus, please don't start fretting again. You'll wear yourself out, and your Ma as well." She untied the baby from the chair and carried him to his bedroll. "It's time now for Columbus to go to sleep. Maybe you'll be hungry when you wake up." She lay down beside him, patting him gently on the back and guiding his thumb into his mouth. "Sleep now little one. Go to sleep." She began humming softly, and within a few minutes the baby's eyes began to close.

After Malinda had gathered wildflowers and placed them in a jar on the table, she found the spirit to tidy the room. It was ready now for Keith when he came home, and the flowers did make it a bit more cheerful. She hoped they'd stay fresh. Momentarily pleased with herself, she pushed an errant lock of hair behind her ear, went outside and sat down on the doorstone.

Two cardinals were sharing a meal of seed on a tree branch, and from the top of the tree a scarlet tanager was singing his head off. If only she had a book to read, she thought. A book would help to fill the empty hours without Keith. Oh God, how she missed him! The waiting for his return was painful beyond description. Every thundering hoof beat made her head turn, her heart quiver. How, she wondered, did some women stand it for months on end? Years even! The good part was, she didn't have to go on any raids.

The sound of distant cannon fire ended the tanager's song. It was coming from the North. Seconds later another answered. The way sound danced off the mountains it was hard to tell how far away they were. She had seen Union troops, fully armed, pass by their camp only last evening. The gunfire no doubt had something to do with them. She touched the holster on her right hip to make sure her Colt was where it should be.

Keith had ridden out four days ago. He should be back in another two, if, as he said, the only place he was going was Watauga County. She prayed he'd by pass Madison County. Ever since Colonel Kirk had made his famous "Salt Raid" and stolen the whole warehouse of salt, leaving everyone to starve for lack of a way to preserve meat, anybody riding into Madison County had very little chance of riding out again. Which was probably why the place held such an attraction for Keith!

Columbus was beginning to stir. The cannon fire had awakened him. Malinda went inside, scooped up a spoonful of mush and put it in a bowl with a few drops of water. Somehow, she had to coax this child to eat. Ahhh! There was a bit of sourwood honey left in the crock. Maybe some sweetening would help.

* * *

John Boyd stood on the porch of his home and watched the two riders thunder out of his dooryard; making sure their mounts trampled the few beans that were just beginning to sprout. He couldn't remember a time when he'd felt more defeated. Or more ashamed.

Inside the house his wife was weeping. A low, moaning sound; the kind that comes when the pain is too great to bear. He watched the riders until they were out of sight, then gave a long whistle. A minute later his son Andrew emerged from the woods. Even from this distance he could see the boy's face was as white as fresh laundry.

Boyd went inside and put his hand on Nell's shoulder as she rocked to and fro. "Please don't cry," he said. "I didn't know what else to do. Promise you won't tell the boy. I don't want him to know."

Nell Boyd reached up and patted her husband's hand. "It's all right, John. You did the only thing you could do." She dabbed at her eyes with the end of her apron. "No one else will ever know."

* * *

It was just after nine o'clock but Reuben's house was dark. Too early for him to be in bed. Keith gestured to Frank. "Check the barn for horses." As Frank headed for the barn the six other shadowy figures rested motionless on their mounts. Waiting.

Frank returned quickly. "Nope. No horses."

"Shit!" Keith pulled on his reins. "We can't wait around."

"There's somethin' funny about the barn," Frank added.

"What do you mean funny?" Keith hissed, furious at not finding Reuben at home.

"It's been picked clean."

"What the hell does that mean?"

"The only thing in there is a plow. Tools are gone. So is everythin' else."

"You mean the bastard's run?" Keith dismounted and hurried toward the barn. Frank at his heels. "Where's a lantern?"

"That's what I'm sayin.'" Frank struck a match. "Ain't no lantern. Ain't nothin'."

Keith lit a match of his own. Walked quickly past the stalls and tool area. Frank was right. The barn was as clean as a fresh plucked chicken.

They broke into the house and a five minute search revealed that the bed, table and chairs were gone, along with all the clothes, pans, and dishes.

"That son-of-a-bitch!" Keith fumed, moving toward the open door. "Come on. Let's see if dear old Uncle William has run off, too. He's the real prize."

It was hard for Keith to remember a time when he hadn't hated William. It began in childhood. When Keith was five, William grabbed him one day in the barn and beat him with a horsewhip. For no reason. When he was finished, and Keith nearly unconscious, William snarled, "If anybody asks where you got them marks, you say you was in a fight. And if you tell what really happened I'll corner you and do it again. And I'll get your Ma, too."

It was a ten minute ride from Reuben's place to William's. With every hoof beat Keith's heart seemed to beat faster. Twice now he'd had it confirmed, once from Kirk and once from Robert Green. William and Reuben were working with the hated Conscription agents.

As they drew nearer their destination Keith felt a surge of relief. There was a light twinkling through the trees. He motioned his men to dismount and tie up their horses. They then began creeping toward the house, fanning out to surround it.

Abruptly, Keith's breath caged in his chest. The front door was open! Night breezes rustled the trees. He readied his Colt. Closer now, he could see William seated in a rocking chair a few feet back from the open door. Facing it. He appeared to be dozing … and there was a musket across his knees. A rectangle of yellow light spilled out onto the porch. Maybe he'd left the door open to catch the cool night air?

Keith motioned T.J. to take one side of the door while he took the other. Quiet as serpents they approached the house. Keith wiped at his dry mouth with the back of his hand, and tightened his grip on the Colt.

Chances were good the porch boards would creak. Keith held up a staying hand to T.J., took a deep breath and leaped onto the porch and into the rectangle of light. "Touch that gun and you're a dead man." He pointed his handgun directly at his uncle's head.

William's gray eyes snapped open, but otherwise he made no move. "Now pick that gun up by the barrel and put it on the floor in front of you. Real slow like." Keith took two steps forward and stood on the threshold. Quickly, he surveyed the room. "Where's Aunt Mae?"

William put the musket on the floor then straightened and looked at Keith. "She's layin' beside yer Ma. I buried her this mornin'." There was no show of emotion.

Keith called to T.J. "Get two of the boys and check the house."

"There ain't nobody here but me," William snapped.

"Didn't your boys come home for their Ma's funeral?"

"No way to tell 'em. She died sudden. Heart, I reckon."

Keith stepped farther into the room. "Is that what the Doc said?"

William Coffey's lips twitched, causing his long white beard to wiggle. "Didn't need no doctor to tell me she was dead. Besides, Doc Petersen's in the army."

Keith gave a mirthless chuckle. "I don't have to ask which one."

"Don't matter much now, does it?"

"It will to the Doc when I see him," Keith smirked.

T.J. and the others walked past Keith with guns drawn and began a search of the house. Keith booted the door shut, then kicked the musket against the far wall.

"I've been expectin' you," William said. There wasn't the slightest show of fear in his voice or his eyes.

"Well that's right kind of you Uncle Will, but I don't recall getting an invitation."

"I didn't send one. I just figured I'd be on yer list. You've robbed and burned out everybody else in the county." He laid his head back against the chair pillow and set the rocker into motion. It squeaked rhythmically.

"We stopped by Reuben's place. It seems he's run off."

A hard glint darkened William's eyes, but he said nothing.

T.J. returned to the main room. "Nobody else here. No signs of packing either."

"Well, Uncle Will, I'll give you credit for that. At least you didn't run like that polecat Reuben."

William Coffey remained silent. Rocking slowly.

"Get the others together T.J. We're leaving now." He moved his gun closer to William's head. "On your feet Uncle. We're going for a walk."

"If you plan on blowin' my head off, right here's as good a place as any."

In one swift, deliberate move, Keith yanked William out of the chair. "Get your ass moving! *NOW*!" T.J. opened the door and Keith shoved his uncle onto the porch.

"You son-of-a-bitch!" The old man swung around, facing Keith. "You'll not be tellin' me what to d—"

Before the words were out of his mouth Keith's left fist connected to his uncle's jaw. William went sprawling backwards off the porch. Blood squirted from his nose and streaked his white beard.

"Get on your feet!" Keith took hold of his arm and pulled him to a standing position. "Now walk." Nodding in the direction of the forest, he said, "We're taking him over to Jim Gragg's mill. I'll lead the way. T.J., you and Wade cover him. Frank, you get some lanterns from the house, and find some rope."

For ten minutes Keith plowed through the tangled forest, the lantern waving dimly in the pitch blackness. His uncle walked behind him, hands tied behind his back, hunched over and struggling to keep up.

Keith paused as the night symphony stilled. The forest creatures had sensed their presence. The only sound was the rush of the river. Almost there.

Keith felt certain William had a considerable amount of knowledge about Rebel activities, and his intent was to extract this information before he killed him. He also knew that William's murder, and Reuben's, if he could find him, would put Austin in peril. Twice he'd warned Austin that it was time to pack up and leave, but so far as he knew, Pa was still here. After he was finished here, he would stop by and warn him again.

The shadowy outline of the mill was now discernible. It had been abandoned for months; there was no more grain to grind. But the wheel still turned, fed by the persistent river, ghostly reminder of other times.

Keith groped his way up the creaking steps to the platform above the wheel and held the lantern so the others could see. William struggled to maintain his balance on the wobbly stairs, toppled forward and finished the climb on his knees.

Keith set the lantern on the railing as William righted himself and staggered onto the platform. He was followed by T.J. and Frank.

"Boys, my uncle here has some things he wants to tell us. Or maybe I should say, some things he *will be* wanting to tell us." Turning to Frank. "Hand me that rope."

Keith looped the round of rope over his shoulder, sat back on the railing that surrounded the small platform and looked gravely at his uncle. "Now we'll start out with the easy stuff. Real simple. Where's Uncle Reuben? And let me tell you it will be much nicer for you if you don't lie. I have a powerful respect for the truth, and there's not too many things in this world I dislike anymore than a liar." He put one foot up on the railing and rested his elbow on his knee.

William Coffey stared at Keith with a look that held all the rage of a windstorm, but his lips remained closed.

"I'll ask you one more time, Uncle. Where is that yellow-bellied brother of yours? Where's Reuben?"

"You better git on with whatever it is yer aimin' to do, 'cause I ain't tellin' you one damned thing."

The defiance in his tone sent a chill up Keith's spine, and he had to fight to keep his voice level. "Okay Frank, it appears my uncle here needs some convincing. I want you to tie him to the mill wheel. On his back. Spread-eagle."

T.J. lifted the lantern and peered over the railing. "Water's not movin' very fast."

"He's not in any hurry. He isn't going anywhere except round and around and around."

The mill wheel groaned as its balance was disrupted. While he was being tied down William's eyes never left Keith's face. The hatred of a lifetime was spoken wordlessly.

Their task completed Frank and T.J. stepped back and the wheel began to slowly turn. Keith watched, smiling, as his uncle's body crept nearer and nearer the water. He leaned over the railing holding the lantern as William's head disappeared. "See you later, Uncle Will," he called.

The wheel stopped, straining with its extra burden. Groaned. Creaked. Then slowly it began to turn again. Minutes passed before William's body gradually emerged. Convulsing. Spewing river water. As it reached its zenith Keith held the lantern near to his victim's face. "Where's Uncle Reuben?"

William's tongue remained locked, and Keith resumed his place on the railing. Waiting for another spin of the wheel.

The torture lasted for more than half an hour. At last, tested beyond endurance, William cried out ..."I'll ... tell ... you. I'll ... tell ... you."

"Give him one more turn," Keith ordered. "I want to make good and sure he means it."

Ten minutes later, coughing, broken, William Coffey lay at his nephew's feet, holding his knees to his chest. Retching. "Richmond," he finally sputtered. "Reuben's ... heading ... for Richmond."

"Now what's a mountain man like Reuben doing in a big city like Richmond? Don't toy with me Uncle. My patience is wearing thin. I might even get nasty. I know some pretty convincing ways to make a man talk. You've only had a taste."

William lifted his head. "I'm tellin' ... the ... the truth. He ... he went to Richmond. He ... knows ... people there ... who promised to ... to help him. He says ... he ... can't ... can't take any ... anymore of the fightin.' There's ... some ... church people ... Mc ... McCaleb ... put ... him ... in touch with ..."

Keith rose and began to pace the narrow platform. "What makes him think they aren't fighting in Richmond?"

"I don't ... know."

Keith turned sharply; poked at William's gut with his boot. He sensed he was lying. "There's something else. I know you've been helping the Conscription Agents, and I know you're the one who tipped off Green about where I was hiding out, but I've got some strong doubts about you doing it alone. You couldn't have tracked me down on your own. You're not smart enough. Who else was involved?"

"Nobody. Just ... me."

Keith gave him a boot to the ribs; William groaned and rolled to his other side. "Why? Goddamnit why did you do it? And what the hell did I ever do to you to make you hate me like you do?"

"Why? Be ... because ... I ... was ashamed ..."

"Ashamed? What the shit are you talking—"

"Ashamed ... 'cause you're ... a Unionist."

"I wasn't a Unionist when I was a kid and you beat the living bejesus out of me!"

"You ... always wa ... wanted to know didn't you?"

"What the fuck are you talking about?"

"You always ... wanted to ... ah ... to know ... who sired you."

Keith's stomach tightened. The rattler was back in his gut ready to strike. "So?"

"I was ... ah ... ashamed because ... you you're ... my ... s ... s ... son."

The sky closed in. A kaleidoscope shattered inside Keith's head. *Good God NO! This couldn't be true!* All these years imagining what his real Pa would be like, look like, what name he would hold ... and all the while it was *WILLIAM!!!* How could this be? How could Ma—and oh God she'd named him after his father! Several moments ticked by before Keith found his voice. "Tell me," he whispered. "Tell me everything."

William lifted his bruised head and looked up at Keith with desperate eyes. Pleading. "I ... ah ... loved Mary. I ... always did. But I was married and she ... ah ... wouldn't have me. Except ... we ... ah ... we couldn't help ourselves. We hid out ... in ah ... barns and fields ... and then ... then you were on the way ... and she ... ah ... she said she'd never tell anyone. Never tell who your Pa was. She ... WE ... didn't want to ... hurt anybody. And Austin ... Austin loved her. I ... begged her to run off with me ... but she ... wouldn't ..." A flash of lightning tore the night sky. Keith raised his eyes to the heavens, thankful for the darkness. "She said ... too many people would be ... hurt and she ... ah ... said she ... loved Austin."

"That's why you hate Pa so much? Because Ma loved him?"

"Ye ... yes."

"Is that why you hate me? Because of Pa?"

"Ah ... Yes."

The rage was cold and seething. There were no words to give it life. The years of torment, of wondering. And now it had come to this. A man he hated had sired him! Better he had gone to his grave still wondering.

He didn't want to ask what William knew about troop movements, or Confederate plans, or numbers of Union deserters. He didn't want to hear anything more from this man's lips. He'd heard enough.

William had won.

Keith drew the Colt from his holster and William cringed, whimpering, "You won't ... k ... k ... kill your own ... P ... P ... Pa, now will ya?"

Keith looked down at William with total loathing. He couldn't even die like a man. "T.J. Come over here."

T.J. Perkins moved to Keith's side.

"Finish him," he said flatly. Then Keith walked down the warped, rotting mill steps and out into the dark night.

A moment later a flash of brilliant color sparked the blackness, a murderous sound echoed through the woods followed by a roll of far away thunder, and William Coffey lay dead with a bullet through his brain.

CHAPTER 24

Malinda was thinking this was one of the happiest days they'd had in a long time. She and Keith playing like children under the waterfall, romping through the field, swinging Columbus between them like a rag doll as he squealed with delight. What could possibly be better?

As the day wore on they had finally played themselves out, and now, his belly filled, Columbus was asleep under a tree. Malinda and Keith sat on a log beside the river, Malinda's head on his shoulder, dabbling their feet in the river and watching the fish jump.

Conflict seemed very far away. They were only a mile or so from camp, but it could have been a hundred miles. No cannon fire. No sounds of war. No uniformed men.

Keith reached over, brushed her hair aside and began rubbing the nape of her neck. "Ummm that feels good," she sighed, closing her eyes.

He was silent a moment then said, "I know something that'll make you feel even better." He slid his hand down her back.

She turned to him and giggled. "And whatever might that be, Mr. Blalock?"

"Well, you see, it goes like this." He brought his wet lips to hers as his other hand gently explored her breast. Then he slowly eased her onto her back. His tongue found her ear. Prodded inward.

A lightning bolt of desire flashed through Malinda's body; a storm that only a moment ago she hadn't known was brewing. Suddenly, she was too eager for foreplay. "Oh now. Now!" she cried, nearly weeping with anticipation. She reached down and grabbed the pulsating muscle Keith had unleashed and guided it into her welcoming flesh. He took her hands and pinned them above her head. He filled her completely. His thrusts were savage. Powerful. Glorious. Her back was pressed hard against the rocky ground. Stubble and pebbles pierced her skin. She gasped with pleasure. He emitted animal-like grunts with each pounding thrust. Her breathing shortened to a pant as the quivering climax grew near. She didn't want it to end. Ever. But her body couldn't wait and too soon it erupted in a burst of exquisite joy. "Oh, Keith," she moaned. "Oh darling." She felt the fiery burst of his passion explode inside her, the flood washing through her. Running out of her. He hovered over her a moment longer. Released her arms. Leaned on her. Panting. Spent. His chest heaving. He kissed the soft hollow of her throat, then slowly pulled from her, rolled over onto his back and gazed up at the sky.

A moment later she was surprised to hear him chuckle. "Now just look at what you've gone and done, Malinda. Here I had this nice big toy to play with and you broke it."

She giggled. "Yes, and I'd do it again! I WILL do it again!"

"Not for a while you won't," he laughed, buttoning his pants. "Maybe that makes up for some of the time we've lost."

"More than makes up for it, I'd say. Dear Lord, how long has it been?"

"Too long."

"Seems so. We were both in an awful hurry."

"Some things can't wait."

Malinda rolled onto her side and propped her head on her elbow. "You were gone a week, and your dear Colonel had us locked away from each other for two weeks before that while Columbus was sick—"

"Except for that afternoon I sneaked over to see you."

"Oh yes!" And we did dally a bit that day, didn't we?" Another giggle and Malinda rose, hiked her skirt up to her hips, and waded into the water. Cupping her hand she gently washed her genitals, and unexpectedly the stimulation brought on another climax. She quickly turned her face away so he wouldn't see. *Malinda Blalock, you are a wanton woman!*

Under the shade tree, Columbus was beginning to stir. He opened his eyes and struggled to his feet. Wobbled uncertainly and looked around. Keith stood up and tucked his shirt in his pants. "Here we are, Son." Hurrying toward the baby, he scooped him up and placed him on his shoulders, then began to trot around and around in a circle. "Ride the horsy, Columbus. Ride the horsy." The baby squealed with delight.

They look so good together, Malinda thought happily. Two peas from the same pod. Keith seemed more relaxed than he had in months. On his last scouting party he'd rounded up eighteen more Reb deserters for the Union. His tally was mounting.

Something did seem odd, though. Usually after a scouting party all Keith wanted to do was relive it. Not that anyone could ever accuse him of being a big talker, but the one thing he did talk about were his missions. This time was different. He'd barely mentioned it except to give her the count. No hashing over the details. No preening about his accomplishments. You'd think since she hadn't been there he'd want to share what had happened. But she'd learned long ago not to pry. If there was something on his mind it would come out when he was ready to let it go. And not a wink sooner. Lordy, it was nice to have him home again. And the next time he went out she'd be with him. No more separations!

With reluctance Malinda began packing up the remnants of their picnic. It was a shame to call an end to this beautiful day, but Keith was getting anxious to get back to camp. She could read the signs. Playtime was over.

* * *

It was seven o'clock on Saturday evening when Austin finished his chores and went out onto the porch for a breath of air. He sat down in the rocker and lit his pipe. It had been a quiet day. No soldiers thundering down the road. No fields or cabins on fire. Then his eye moved from The Grandfather to the squalid place where his garden had once been. And no vegetables either, he thought bitterly. The mood was broken.

From the corner of his eye he caught the bare outline of a figure coming down the road. Man seemed in a hurry. A few steps more and he came into full view around the rhododendron bush. McCaleb? Austin pulled the pipe from his mouth, leaned forward and squinted. *It is McCaleb!* The next moment the gate banged open and McCaleb hurried toward him, waving his arms, and motioning Austin inside.

He hadn't seen McCaleb since that night when he'd come to tell him their brother William had been found dead and that Austin should pack up and leave. That was what Keith had been saying for weeks now. Just the night before McCaleb's visit, Keith had stopped by and tried to get him to go back with him to Tennessee. But he'd never been farther away from Coffey Gap than Lenoir. Besides, one place was as bad as another in these times, and it wasn't his fault William was dead. If the truth be known there wasn't any sorrow in his heart because of it either. He regretted feeling that way, but whatever brotherly feelings he'd had for William had died long ago.

McCaleb was panting now as he reached the porch. "Come inside," he gasped. "I've got somethin' to tell you." Austin followed his brother into the house and closed the door.

"What's this all about?"

"They're comin' for you. Tonight. You can hide out at my place. I don't think they'll look for you there. But you'd better hurry."

"How do you know this?"

"Believe me, I know!" McCaleb glanced up at the gun resting on the antlers over the door. "Do you have ammunition for that?"

Austin shook his head.

"Bring it anyway. I have some. Not much. But I'm praying we won't need it."

"I appreciate your help, McCaleb, but I don't want you to get into trouble because of me. And what about Sally? I'm sure she won't be—"

"Don't be concerned about Sally. She's … not herself. We got news this mornin' that Jones has been killed. She—"

"McCaleb, I'm sorry. My God, I'm so sorry." Austin clasped his brother's shoulder. "There's no end to it, is there?"

McCaleb's face was as gray as his beard. "It doesn't seem so—but now, you'd better hurry. I'll go on ahead. We can't take a chance of bein' seen together."

"McCaleb, I don't think—"

"Don't argue with me, Austin. They mean business. There'll be too many of them, and you can't fight with an empty gun." He turned to go. "I wish to God we'd all gone with Reuben." He shrugged miserably. "Come in the back way. I'll make sure the door is not bolted."

Austin caught his arm. "Where *is* Reuben? I saw the covered wagon. Where did he go?"

"Texas. To some people I know out there."

Ten minutes passed before Austin left the house. He wanted to give McCaleb time to get home before starting out. Purposely, he left both doors unlatched. No sense givin' them an added reason to burn the place down. It was a thin hope at best. His gaze traveled the room. Was there anythin' else he needed besides the empty musket? Somethin' he wanted to keep in case they did torch it? Sadly, he couldn't think of a thing. He left by the back door, slipped and almost fell in the soft mud, a remnant of the afternoon rain.

* * *

Less than fifteen minutes later Lieutenant James Marlow, a man awash in self importance, along with his hotheaded second-in-command, Robert Glass, rode up to Austin's house. They were accompanied by Carroll Moore, his son Jesse, home on medical leave and dressed in a makeshift Confederate uniform, and John Walker, a boy of seventeen. It was Carroll who dismounted and walked up onto the porch. "Austin, come on out. It's Carroll. We want to talk to you."

When there was no response he pushed open the door, motioned to the others, and they did a quick search of the house. Several minutes later they found Austin's mare in the barn and knew he'd escaped on foot.

"We know where he's headed," Marlow said, spurring his horse out the gate.

* * *

John Boyd was sweating and it had nothing to do with the weather. He was more frightened than he had ever been in his life, but trying desperately, and unsuccessfully, not to show it. He turned to his son Andrew, posing again the question he'd asked twice before. "You're absolutely sure it was Austin?"

"Yes, Pa. Like I said. He was cuttin' through the trees out back when I was helpin' Ma take in the wash. I seen him clear as day. I even mentioned it to Ma, but by the time she looked up he was gone. He wasn't ridin' neither. But he was walkin' so fast he was almost runnin'."

A heartbeat later the expected visitors rode into view and Boyd turned to his wife. "Take the boy down to the root cellar and don't come up until I call you."

There was no question about who they were after—or why. Boyd squared his shoulders and nervously licked his lips. He'd made a pact with the devil and the time had come to pay up. Information on Unionists and their activities, and his son would not be forced into the Rebel Army for another year. By that time, pray God, the fighting would be over. He feigned a smile and went out to meet the riders in the dooryard.

"We're lookin' for Austin," Marlow said. His tone was gruff.

"He isn't here. And my wife isn't feelin' well, I don't want her upset."

Marlow frowned down at Boyd. "Where is he?"

"I'm ... I'm not sure."

"It's your responsibility to know."

"I can't keep an eye on him twenty-four hours a day."

Marlow looked over his shoulder at the others, then turned again to Boyd. "Where's your boy?"

"You've got no business with my boy. We have an agreement." His face was crimson. "There's a chance, just a chance mind you, that he could be at McCaleb's place."

"McCaleb's?" Carroll roared.

"I saw McCaleb earlier and he looked like he was headin' toward Austin's." The sweat was now trickling down the deep grooves of Boyd's cheeks. "A little later I saw Austin in the woods, goin' in the direction of McCaleb's place."

Marlow pulled on his reins. "If he isn't there, we'll be back. For your boy."

Boyd stayed in the dooryard, watching the horse's hooves sling mud in every direction, until they rode out of sight; then he went back inside and bolted the door.

Austin's been a marked man ever since William's murder, he told himself. And everyone knew Keith was responsible. Besides that, it was Austin's fault for not havin' the good sense to run when he had the chance. Boyd pulled the jug of blackstrap from out of the woodbox where he kept it hidden. Near empty and God only knew when and where he'd find another. He wiped his face with his sleeve, lifted the jug to his lips and downed the contents in three mighty gulps.

* * *

Austin crept silently through the back door of McCaleb's house. Night was settling in and the kitchen was thick with shadows. He heard strange sounds coming from the parlor. Sally. She seemed to be ranting and moaning at the same time.

"This way!" McCaleb stepped out of the darkness. "Upstairs. And here, take this." He thrust a bag of ammunition into Austin's hand.

"What about Sally?"

"It's all right, she won't see you."

"Are you sure?"

"Austin, trust me. And hurry. Please!"

McCaleb led the way into the parlor where Sally sat hunched into her rocker, an open bible on her lap. She appeared to be talking with someone, but there was no one else in the room.

"If it pleases you, Lord, I will next read the story of Abraham and Issac."

"Who's she talkin' to?" Austin whispered.

McCaleb's face was a patchwork of anxiety. "She's not right in her head. She's been like this ever since we got the news about Jones. She … thinks she's talkin' to Jesus. She keeps sayin' he's taken refuge from the Union in our parlor. I've tried talkin' to her but she doesn't hear me. She doesn't hear anything."

Austin followed his brother toward the enclosed staircase. It was necessary to pass directly in front of Sally's chair, but she never once raised her eyes from her book. Austin followed McCaleb up the darkened stairwell, fumbling along the walls to find his way.

At the top, McCaleb entered a tiny, dark bedroom. "Get under this feather bed. It'll be hot but hopefully you won't have to stay there long."

Austin could just make out the outline of the bed.

"It's the best I can think of," McCaleb apologized.

"Thank you." Austin embraced his brother warmly. "I thank you for your kindness McCaleb. It's been a long war, and a hideous one. I know you have so much on your mind, Jones, and … taking care of Sally, but—"

"We'll talk later, Austin. Later. For God's sake, load that gun and take cover. They may not even come here, but if they do I pray to God there'll be no gun fire."

From below they heard Sally's thin voice raised in anguish:

> *Take now thy son, thine only son Isaac, whom thou lovest, and get thee into the land of Moriah and offer him there for a burnt offering upon one of the mountains which I will tell thee of.*

This was followed by a loud lament. "Oh Blessed Jesus, why did God test Abraham so mightily? Why does he test me so mightily? Doesn't he know I fear Him? Tell me, Blessed Jesus, why does our Father treat us so harshly? *WHY* my Lord?" A pause. "You say you thirst? Please allow me to bring you refreshin' water to drink."

A moment later they heard the sound of the pump handle, and Austin whispered, "You'll have to get help for her, McCaleb. The woman is suffer—"

"Shhh!" McCaleb raised a finger to his lips. "I heard somethin'!"

Clutching the empty gun, Austin dove under the bed of feathers as McCaleb groped his way back down the stairs.

The same instant McCaleb stepped into his parlor, James Marlow came walking out of his kitchen. Marlow's look was stern and his Colt was drawn. "Good evening McCaleb," he said coldly.

"James, what are you doing here?" Pretending surprise as Carroll Moore, followed by Jesse, appeared behind Marlow.

Sally pushed past the three men, carrying a tin cup of water which she placed on a small table. She gave no reaction to their presence, as if she didn't see them, and resumed her position in the rocking chair. "There you are my Lord. Pray no longer thirst." She smiled into empty space.

"We've come for Austin," Carroll said. "It'll be easier for everyone if you just bring him out now."

"I don't know what you're talkin' about. What makes you think Austin is here? Why are you lookin' for him anyway?"

"You know damned good and well why," Carroll bristled.

"Bring him out!" Jesse's voice was shrill and his hand was trembling visibly as he pointed his handgun at McCaleb. "We know he's here. Boyd saw him."

"Boyd?" McCaleb couldn't conceal his surprise, but he tried to cover it by adding, "Why would *I* be hidin' Austin?"

"Because you're a turncoat!" Marlow took a quick step forward and pressed his gun to McCaleb's jaw.

Suddenly, Sally leaped from her chair. "You're right!" she hissed. "He's gone over to the Union! It's his fault Jones is dead! Jones, my son. Oh my boy," she moaned. A beat later her green eyes grew large and wild as an expression of triumph crossed her face. "I know where the Yankee scum is. I know where he hid him. Vengeance! *Vengeance!*" She thrust her hands toward the ceiling. "Someone is goin' to pay for my baby's death! He took the Yankee bastard upstairs to my baby's room. Desecratin' it with his presence. I heard him. I seen him."

"Sally, for God's sake—" McCaleb's words were cut off as Sally, unmindful of Marlow's gun, flew at her husband.

Startled, Marlow fell back a step, but before McCaleb could defend himself Sally had torn great gashes in both his cheeks with her talon-like nails. "You did it! You did it!" she shrieked. "You killed my baby! You killed Jones!"

McCaleb wrestled Sally's arms to her sides, and looked up at the still astonished Marlow. "You can see she's not herself," hoping desperately they would accept this explanation. "We got word today that Jones has been killed, and she's been like this ever since. She's not clear in her head." He dragged his struggling wife to her chair and pushed her into it. Pressing down on her shoulders to hold her there. "I'm afraid I'll have to ask you to go now—"

Recovering, Marlow again pointed his Colt at McCaleb. "We know he's here. He was seen headin' this way, and there's footprints comin' from the woods to your backdoor."

"But, I tell you—"

"He's upstairs!" Sally shrieked. "The first room. My baby's room. I heard them. I seen them! Isn't he Jesus? Tell them Lord. Tell them. They'll believe you!"

Carroll picked up an oil lamp and headed for the stairs. Just then Robert Glass burst through the front door. "I got him!" he shouted. "I got him climbin' out a second floor window."

The silence was moribund. Even Sally's lips were stilled. A long moment passed before Carroll splintered it by saying, "I never in my life thought it would come to this, McCaleb, but by God it has. We'll be takin' Austin now, but you know we don't take kindly to them that hide Yankee scum. Brother or no brother."

* * *

Deep in the woods there was no mockery of an interrogation. There were no questions to ask. This was an eye for an eye.

They sat in a semicircle, perched on logs and boulders. Austin, hands tied behind him, sat in the middle of the circle on a stump. Light from three lanterns created eerie, twisted images that danced across the intent faces of the men. All eyes were on Austin hoping for some sign of fear, disappointed when they saw none. They waited for James Marlow to give the order. Only young John Walker seemed confused about the proceedings. A rumble of thunder rolled through the valley.

"Sounds like we'll be gettin' some more rain," Jesse said.

"That one this afternoon didn't do much to cool things off," Carroll replied.

Then everyone fell silent again.

James Marlow rolled the toothpick from one corner of his mouth to the other as his gaze passed from one man to the next. He pulled his pipe from his pocket, packed it and lit it. The smoke curled about his head while the others waited. Grim and silent.

It was several minutes before Marlow put the pipe aside. "Austin, you know why we're here."

"Of course." His voice was firm.

"You understand why we have to do this."

"I'm sure you think you have your reasons."

"Do you have anythin' to say?"

"Nothin' that comes to mind right now." Austin's eyes were on Carroll.

Marlow stood, took a few steps and paused before John Walker. "John, you've been in the Confederate Army … let's see now, I'd say goin' on forty-eight hours. I'm thinkin' it's time you get your feet wet."

"Yes Sir?" Young Walker rose and gave a salute that brought smirks from the others, but the boy paid no attention. Someone was finally talking to him like a soldier. Up to now this whole thing had seemed more like a vigilante raid.

"This is your first military order," Marlow drawled.

"Yes Sir."

"Shoot him."

The boy's face drained of color. His legs wobbled beneath him and a stain darkened his pants. "But he's an old man!" he cried. "And he ain't hurt nobody.

He's always been good to my family, even if he didn't cotton to our way of thinkin' about the Confederacy. I can't do it. I *won't* do it!"

"Are you disobeying a military order?" Marlow snarled.

"I ain't killin' him!" Walker sniffled, turning away and moving to the perimeter of the clearing.

Austin looked skyward. A filmy cloud was passing over the full moon. He thought of Mary.

"Anybody here got some guts?" Marlow's gaze fell on Carroll who immediately rose, as did Jesse. Carroll motioned his son to sit down.

"I don't suppose anybody's ever accused me of bein' gutless," Carroll said, glancing around the group, "but before we get on with it there's a couple of things I'm needin' to say to Austin. In private."

"Boys," Marlow nodded toward the woods. "Let's give 'em some room."

Jesse leveled a questioning glance at his father, frowned, then limped off after the others.

When the men were out of earshot, Carroll sat down on the ground in front of Austin, pulled his Colt from his holster and began twirling it around his finger. "I guess we both knew this day would come, we just didn't know which one of us would be holdin' the gun."

There was almost the trace of a smile on Austin's lips. "Carroll, that just goes to show how different we are; so different it's hard to believe we were ever friends. Or even why. The Lord is my witness, I never once thought of killin' you."

"Don't go gettin' holier than thou."

"I think you know me better than that, Carroll," Austin chuckled. "That's McCaleb's bailiwick. Speaking of McCaleb, I—"

"I'll be handlin' McCaleb."

"Hidin' me wasn't his idea. I forced him into it. I threatened Sally—"

"I don't want to talk about McCaleb," Carroll said harshly, his eyes as cold as the metal in his hands. "You know I have to do this, don't ya?"

"You mean kill me? Have to or want to, you're goin' to do it either way, so you're not tellin' me somethin' I don't already know."

Carroll licked his parched lips. Another roll of thunder echoed off the mountains. "There is somethin' I'm gonna tell you that you don't know, somethin' you've been wonderin' about for years." Carroll paused the twirling and rubbed his eyes with his fingers. Then he looked again at Austin; saw how the lantern light was casting flickering shadows across his face and long, white beard. "You always thought it was William."

There was a long pause.

"What do you mean I always thought it was William?"

"I used to see you watchin' him when he was around Mary, and I knew you thought it was him. William was always sweet on Mary and everybody knew it, but as far as I know he never touched her. He told me he tried to once and she grabbed a knife and said if he didn't back off one of 'em was gonna be dead. I don't think he ever suspected it was me. Nobody did. She never told. But when she started callin' him William, I guess a lot of people figured—"

"She said he looked like her father. That's why she called him William."

"Mary about drove me nuts. I can't say I loved her—but I wanted her. You … you know what I mean."

Austin's mouth opened slightly as if trying to get more air, but no sound came from his lips.

"Sometimes I thought I was gonna go plum crazy over it. She'd come over and visit with Zinnia and they'd be talkin' and sewin' and doin' woman things, and I'd …"

Austin found his voice. "The only thing Mary ever told me about it was that she was forced."

"One evening she was goin' through the field as I was comin' back. She's ah … she's right I guess, it wasn't … as if she cooperated …"

"I take back what I said a few minutes ago about not wantin' to kill you, Carroll." Austin's voice was thick with emotion.

"It wouldn't have been so bad, damnit, if you'd raised him proper, but you turned him into a damned Yankee. My son, a goddamned Yankee scum!"

"Keith's not your son."

"I sired him."

"That doesn't make you a father. Or a man."

Carroll leaped to his feet. "You noaccount bastard!"

"Get on with it, Carroll. I'm not interested in your confessions when it's *me* that's goin' now to be with Mary. But so help me if my hands weren't tied behind me I would kill you. I always swore that when I found the man who did that to her I'd kill him. But that's not to be, so I guess I'll just have to let our Maker deal with you in His own way. Remember that Carroll. Remember what you've got to face up to on the other side."

Carroll's eyes were unexpectedly moist. He turned his back to Austin, took two steps, and when he turned again, lifting his gun, Robert Glass leaped out of the bushes jammed his Colt into the back of Austin's head and pulled the trigger. Carroll stood gape-mouthed, every bit as surprised as Austin Coffey.

The old man's body bumped to the ground as gray smoke curled from the gun barrel and the sound of death ricocheted through the black night. Speechless, Carroll stared at Glass as the others emerged from the bushes—everyone except young Walker who was doubled over vomiting in the grass.

"I nabbed him," Glass said by way of explanation. "He was mine. I don't like lettin' a day go by without killin' at least one Yankee." Even as the body still trembled, Glass picked it up, threw it over his shoulder as if it were a sack of potatoes, carried it a few yards into the woods and dumped it in a grove of laurel bushes. With the toe of his boot he raised some dead leaves and kicked them over the body for cover.

Moments later as Glass rejoined the others, James Marlow pulled a harmonica from his pocket, puffed on it a few times, then broke into a lively rendition of *Dixieland.* Glass sat down on the ground next to Carroll, grinned, and joined in the singing.

* * *

"Some local people found a stray dog in the road," Kirk said. "He ... he had a man's hand in his mouth. They followed the dog and he led them back to your stepfather's body."

"Oh dear God," Malinda whimpered.

"I'm sorry Keith. I know how much he meant to you."

"Who led it?" Keith asked.

"Probably Carroll Moore. If he didn't actually lead it, there is every indication he was there. He was seen riding with a group of men around the time it happened. But a couple of them were in uniform, so he may have just been part of the gang." Kirk moved to Keith's side. Patted him on the shoulder. "We both know this is in retaliation for William. But I'm telling you as your commanding officer and as your friend, there is no reason to feel guilty over William. He got what was coming to him."

William? Malinda wondered. What about William?

"Tomorrow we'll talk about what you want to do about this." With that, the Colonel walked out of the hut and marched back across the compound, slapping his white gloves against his thigh.

"Oh darling I'm so sorry," Malinda put her arms around Keith's shoulders. He sat with his head bowed, arms hanging at his sides, as if his bones had suddenly collapsed. They remained this way for several moments until finally, he lifted his arms and brought her closer to him. She knelt beside him, felt a dampness on her hair. There were no sobs, no shudder in his body, only tears falling like rain. Silent and steady.

☆

CHAPTER 25

The lead story in the *Louisville Courier* was about a band of Confederate outlaws led by a woman named Sue Mundy. Reportedly, they were roaming Kentucky creating mayhem. But Malinda knew the true story. Colonel Kirk's informants said that Sue Mundy was not a woman, but a young man by the name of Marcellus Clark. It was Clark's slender build and youthful appearance that had earned him the mistaken role of being a woman. Many people likened "her" to a Confederate Malinda Blalock.

Malinda laid the tattered newspaper aside with a heavy sigh. She was trying to keep abreast of what was going on in the Louisville area, hoping to find news—anything—about Samuel Whitehead. In an earlier edition of *The Courier* she'd found an advertisement of Whitehead's Emporium, and Uncle John had said Samuel owned a business. Maybe that was it. At least it was somewhere to begin. Four weeks earlier, right before the news of Austin's murder, she'd written to the address in the advertisement, asking for information about Ma and Jacob. She hadn't received a response, but there was no way of knowing if her letter had been received.

She laid the paper aside and began gathering up provisions and packing them into the saddlebag. She really wasn't feeling very well this morning. There was this nagging headache ... and ... and this inexplicable feeling of ... dread. No doubt because she didn't really want to go on this raid. Keith was still calling them "scouting parties!"

It didn't take long to pack the saddlebag. There were pitiful few provisions. They would have to forage and fish along the way, and Keith hated that. Fishing took too much time. But it was either that or go hungry. She had been able to scrape together enough ingredients to make an Indian pudding for Columbus, which was carefully placed in the top of the bag. The only sweetener she could find was honey—thank heavens the bees didn't know there was a war going on. Keith finding that goat had been a stroke of good luck all right. Otherwise Columbus would be entirely without milk. She shook her head as she closed the saddlebag. There were other children who were not nearly so fortunate.

Malinda had known since they'd first heard the news about Austin that this visit to Carroll Moore was inevitable. It was also inevitable there would be bloodshed. Wasn't that the whole purpose? Together Kirk and Keith had decided a shoot-out was the best way to retaliate. Taking each man out separately was too time consuming and too risky. Kirk had a list of names of those involved in the murder, most of whom were seen going in and out of Carroll's property with a good degree of regularity.

The surprising thing was, McCaleb had supplied most of the information—which had been substantiated by Union spies. Evidently, McCaleb had tried to protect Austin after John Boyd, of all people, betrayed him, and now the Moores had turned against McCaleb! In an unprecedented move Kirk had sent three of his men to stay at McCaleb's place until they could get the Moore problem taken care of.

Knowing what was coming, Carroll had turned his farm into a miniature fortress by building a stone fence nearly four foot high around the front and side yard of the house. Word was he had it stocked with enough men and weapons to give Keith cause to think twice before dropping by. Apparently, the place had become a hub for Rebel activities in the area. Colonel Kirk suspected it was being used as a warehouse to store guns and ammunition. It raised the hair on the back of Malinda's neck to think of what they were heading into.

Keith wasn't himself and hadn't been since getting the news about Austin. At first she thought it was shock, and surely that was part of it, but far from sharing his grief, he'd withdrawn into a self imposed shell, leaving her feeling cut off and lonely. The only thing he really talked about was getting even with the Moores and John Boyd. His anger was deep, and when he mentioned their names his eyes grew cold as a February night.

When she had asked him what the Colonel meant about William, his response had been, "Uncle William is dead and to answer your next question, no, I didn't do it!" What then, she wondered, had Kirk meant when he counseled Keith not to feel guilty about William?

Malinda paused in her packing. Should she include some clean rags for the expected "curse." It should be coming around any day now. Then a thought crossed her mind that literally stunned her.

Could it be that the last time they'd made love was nearly four weeks ago? The day of their picnic! My God, what was happening to them? To their marriage? Lovemaking was just about the most important thing they had between them. Even if at times their minds went in different directions about some things, their bodies had always been in tune. *Enough of this!* Malinda gave herself a mental nudge. Time to get moving. Keith would be ready and she knew he hated to be kept waiting. She adjusted the sling and picked up the sleeping baby.

"They say this nasty old war will be over soon," she whispered against the soft, dark curls. "God saw fit to take that Reb General Jeb Stuart, and that's a good thing, because we sure didn't need him down here working against us. It won't be long now, Columbus. You'll see. Then we'll have ourselves a nice house with books in it, and china, and pictures on the wall, and real windows to let the sunshine in—"

"Malinda!" Keith's tall frame filled the open doorway, blocking the light. He was dressed in full uniform. "We're saddled and waiting," he said impatiently.

"We're ready." She picked up her shawl and the saddlebag and walked out of the dank cabin into the dry, late August sunshine—that brought not one speck of contentment to her soul.

By the time Malinda reached her pinto Keith was mounted and the party of two dozen uniformed men were already beginning to move out. As Keith galloped ahead to the front of the line she realized her headache was getting worse. Columbus began to fret. He was old enough now to realize what a ride in the sling meant. She cuddled him against her, whispering, "It'll be all right, sweet baby. It'll be all right." Softly, she began humming a tune.

* * *

The sun was white hot, the sky cloudless, when once again they rode into sight of The Grandfather. Even the breeze, which came sparingly, was hot and dry. The plod of the horses sprayed sand and dirt that covered Columbus's curls, and laid heavy in the folds of Malinda's long buckskin skirt. Her lips were parched, her eyes red and stinging from the relentless sun.

Riding half a length behind Keith, she was amazed that he could stand to wear his full uniform in this searing heat. He had to be sweltering. The other men had stripped down to their shirtsleeves. But if Keith was uncomfortable, he gave no indication. Sometimes the way he rode so tall and straight in the saddle reminded her of Kirk. Now that's a bitter thought, she humphed, and immediately cast it aside.

* * *

A mile from their destination Keith raised his hand and pulled his mount to a halt. "We'll begin to circle now. Malinda and you four men," he pointed to those nearest him, "come with me. We'll be entering from the rear. There isn't a wall there, so that means whatever fire we get will likely come from inside the house. The next ten men will come in from the front. There'll be guns aimed at you from behind the wall. Approach in a double line, charge the bastards and jump the wall. Meanwhile, you other ten will be coming in, five on each side of the house. This'll make 'em scatter and create enough confusion so they won't know which way to shoot. If anybody thinks his mount can't make it over the wall, it'll be your job to pick off the shooters who are aiming at the others who are going over. Good luck and remember we've got the element of surprise on our side. We've put the word out that I'm sick, REAL sick, so they won't likely be expecting us. You all know the signal, and I'll be giving it because it'll take us longer to circle to the rear than it will for the rest of you to get into position.

One more thing," Keith gave a wry chuckle, "everyone inside that pen is a die hard Johnny Reb. Take out as many of 'em as you can. Then we'll torch the damned place."

* * *

Thirty tense minutes passed before everyone was in place. The horses were pawing the dirt, nervous as the men. Keith gave a final look around, withdrew his pistol, winked at Malinda, and fired the signal. The listless sky erupted with color and sound. The earth trembled as two dozen horses spurred into action. Columbus shrieked as Malinda bent turtle like over the pinto, cradling him between her own body and the saddle. He clawed at her clothing, screeching in terror.

A hail of gunfire was coming from the second floor as Malinda rounded the corner of the house. She saw men and horses jumping the wall at the front. Others crouching behind it were firing at point blank range. The belly of a horse was ripped open in mid air by a Rebel sword, spilling its entrails on its killer as the rider flew overhead and crumpled to the ground. Malinda fired and the man with the bloodied sword pitched forward, arms outstretched. Screams from the wounded were coming from all directions. Men huddled against the wall, covered in blood, hands groping to stem the flow from their own wounds. She sensed Keith at her side, saw the spasm of fire from his gun. Cal Moore leaped from a laurel bush grabbing his stomach. He rolled on the ground. Screaming.

"Got the bastard!" Keith yelled triumphantly.

The farmyard was flowing with gore as men and mounts fell like match sticks. Gunfire was coming from every direction. Malinda fired at a second story window and a body toppled forward and splattered on the ground. Carroll was running across the yard, rifle blazing. A moment later he bellowed an oath and fell shrieking beside a giant maple. Off to the right one of Keith's men leaped on Cal Moore who lay prone but still firing. He buried his bayonet in Cal's heart as Malinda thundered past. Two of their men were on the porch with lighted torches. A second later the house burst into flames.

"Jesse!" Keith shouting. Jesse running ahead of them. Toppling over a dead man, legs flying in the air. Keith fired. The bullet tore into Jesse's boot as he slumped to the ground. A man leaped from the roof of the burning house and landed in front of Malinda. Her horse jumped over him.

Then amid the screams and gunfire, Malinda heard one cry above all the rest. Off to her right she saw Keith rise tall in his stirrups, blood gushing down his face. Then he collapsed over the neck of his roan like a rag doll.

"*You Yankee bastard!*" It was Jesse screaming. "*That'll teach ya!*" Crouched beside a dead horse Jesse was shrieking with pain and glee as Keith's roan leaped the wall, miraculously taking his rider with him. Malinda gripped her reins, ordering the pinto to follow. As she cleared the wall the house exploded behind her in a hailstorm of flying bodies and flaming wood.

"*KEITH! KEITH!*" Keith's horse pounded for the road. Fleeing the inferno. Malinda spurred harder, the pinto's ears flattened with fright and speed. Keith was still slumped forward, one arm around his mount's neck. Another burst of speed and Malinda was beside him, leaning, stretching, reaching for his reins. Columbus shrieked with terror as his nest began to topple.

She pulled her pinto's reins with one hand, the roan's with the other. She fought both horses for another half mile until the animals were exhausted and she was finally able to bring them under control. Mouths foaming, bodies heaving, they gradually came to a halt.

Supporting Columbus with one hand, Malinda jumped to the ground and reached up to Keith. Wordless, he looked down at her. Blood was pumping from his right eye, and forehead. His nose was so bloodied it was little more than a mass. Dizziness overwhelmed her. She grabbed the saddle for support; took a deep breath and reached up to help him dismount, but he slid through her arms and landed on his back. Moaning. To her horror she saw that blood was also streaming from his mouth and right ear. "Oh, my God, Keith, can you speak to me?"

He rolled to his side, bringing his knees to his chest, arms wrapping his face and head. "Oh God, I'm blind. Malinda, I'm blind! *I can't SEE!!!*"

Columbus clawed at Malinda's shoulders, grabbing her throat, sobbing, slobbering, struggling to escape. "There, there now sweet baby, it's all right," she cooed idiotically as she knelt beside Keith. "Darling, I know you hurt terrible, but you aren't blind. You're just all bloodied. You're so bloody I can't tell where you've been hit."

"My eye," he moaned. "My eye."

From the distance came the beat of hooves. Malinda pulled the screaming baby from his sling and placed him in the road beside Keith as she reached for her Colt. Then, squatting between them and the approaching rider, and raising her other hand to shield her eyes, she strained into the burning sunlight. The rider, immersed in a cloud of dust, drew nearer. Malinda's heart tried to jump from her chest. When he came closer and she saw it was T.J. she dropped her gun and pitched forward into the dust; giddy with relief.

T.J. dismounted and ran to her side. For a heartbeat she leaned against him. "He keeps saying he's been hit in the eye, but he's so bloody I can't tell." She picked up the hysterical baby and pressed him to her breast. "It's bad. Real bad."

"It was Jesse that done it," T.J. said. "I seen him. He got him from the side. I thought he'd shot him in the head." Gently, he rolled Keith onto his back. "Keith, can you hear me?"

No response.

"Keith, can you hear me?"

A slow nod.

T.J. yanked his bandanna from his neck and placed it in Keith's hand. "Here, press this against it to stop the bleedin'. You know better'n I do where you've been hit."

Keith's hand groped upward; covered the upper right portion of his face with the filthy rag.

T.J. looked up at Malinda. "We gotta get him to a doc."

"The only one I know is my Uncle John up in Galax. If he's there."

"If he's there?"

No need to explain about her uncle being in the Rebel Army; instead she added, "I know he has medical supplies, and if he's not there, somebody else will be who can help us." She remembered Arthur assisting her uncle when she was his patient and overhearing them discuss her condition. Arthur knew more than the average person about medicine. For now, he was the best they had.

"I don't think he can ride."

Malinda shook her head. "I don't think so either, and it's a long way."

"Hang on a minute." T.J. stood up, removed his hat and scratched his head. "At the rate people are gettin' killed around here you'd figure there'd be a spare wagon somewheres about, now wouldn't ya?"

Malinda again shielded her eyes as she looked up at him. "Let's get him out of the road and into some shade." T.J. grabbed Keith under the arms while Malinda took his feet. Together they dragged him to the side of the road and settled him in a patch of tall grass under a willow tree.

"Water," Keith muttered.

T.J. whistled for his horse, removed his canteen and brought it to Keith's lips. "If I can get a wagon do you reckon you can manage to get him to your uncle's place?"

"Yes. Yes, I can manage."

"I'll need to be gettin' back. I'm second in command ya know, and some of our boys were hurt pretty bad back there." He rose. "That damned house musta been an arsenal. It sure as shit was full of black powder. The fucker's still poppin' like firecrackers. By God we got 'em good, I'd say."

From the grass came a feeble sound. "Jesse? Did we get Jesse?"

"I dunno fer sure. I didn't, but maybe somebody else did. There wasn't nobody walkin' around there when we left, I'll tell ya that much."

"How many did we lose?"

"I'm figerin' five. Maybe six."

"Carroll? What about Carroll?" Keith mumbled.

"If he ain't dead he oughta be. The last I seen was that crazy wife of his out there hoverin' over him and screamin' her lungs out."

"There must be others who'll be needing medical attention," Malinda said.

"No doubt about that." T.J. mounted his horse and looked down at her with concern. "Will you be all right till I get back?"

"We'll be okay."

"I'll get a wagon and bring the rest of our wounded." T.J. reined in his horse and headed back down the road to where puffs of black smoke rimed with gray still billowed upward, marking the place of the maelstrom.

* * *

Keith lay on a horse blanket on the flatbed wagon between Lou Simms and Raf Wheeler. Malinda and T.J. had hidden the blue jackets under the horse blanket and with another blanket fashioned a canopy above the men's heads to protect them from the afternoon sun. They tethered the pinto and roan to the rear of the wagon and Malinda drove the team with Columbus rolled up in her lap. Her Colt was on her hip. Her rifle beneath her feet.

Although Malinda's nerves were screaming she forced herself not to give the horses full rein. She had to make the ride as smooth as possible. Keith was semiconscious, Lou was wide awake and writhing in pain. His right leg had been almost severed below the knee. Malinda and T.J. had tied up what was left of it with some of Malinda's clean rags, and pressed other clean, wet rags against Keith's bloodied face. Raf was suffering from a knife wound to his belly. She had packed a few rags into the gaping hole, but he was still losing a lot of blood.

There was very little food left in the saddlebags, but when evening came she pulled off into the woods and offered what she had to the wounded men while the horses grazed. Lou was the only one able to take a few bites. Keith sipped water from her canteen, but Raf remained unconscious. Columbus ate the last of his Indian pudding, then quickly fell asleep. Malinda's own stomach was gnawing. There were two bites of jerky left, not nearly enough to satisfy her hunger.

Blessed by the coolness of evening, they began the last leg of their journey to Galax. They had been fortunate that the two groups of Confederate soldiers they'd encountered earlier had not bothered to challenge them. Wagons loaded with wounded men were a common enough sight. Soon they were enveloped by the blackness of night with only the stars to light their way.

* * *

An orange-yellow dawn was creeping over the mountain as they entered the town; the low lying silver mist belied the sizzling temperatures waiting to claim the day. A scrawny wild turkey scurried for cover as Malinda drove her wagon through the front gate of her uncle's home. Only once during the long night had she allowed herself to think what her world would be like if Keith weren't in it, and she'd quickly pushed the thought aside. The thought that did fill her mind was that this event was somehow fated. She had always known there would come a time when she would be needed. All the whispered criticism, all the mawkish songs they sang about her, had fallen on deaf ears. She had known her mission, and she was fulfilling it. She was beside her man when he needed her. "Please God," she whispered for the thousandth time. "Please let Keith live," then as an after thought added, "And these other brave men, too."

The house was dark, its tall structure a ghostly shadow against the still gray sky. Malinda climbed down from the wagon and hoisted Columbus to her hip. She checked the rear of the wagon. Keith was holding his hand over the right side of his face, but he made no indication if he was awake or aware of what was going on. Lou Simms was still moaning in pain, but Raf lay motionless, his head at an awkward angle to his body, and she guessed he was either dead or very near it.

Picking up her shawl she draped it about her shoulders to hide the holster on her hip, and walked to the front door. She noticed how some of the bricks on the porch steps wobbled beneath her feet, and that one of the black shutters beside the door hung askew. The last time she'd been here everything had been so neat. Taking a deep breath she lifted the massive iron knocker.

Several minutes passed before the door opened, and then barely wide enough to see Arthur dressed in his white nightshirt, eyes bulging, holding an oil lamp.

"Arthur, you remember me, Mrs. Blalock? And this is my son, Columbus." She held the baby up so he could see the full sweetness of his face. "I need your help. My husband has been wounded."

Bewildered, but nodding his head vigorously, the slave replied, "Yesem, Mrs. Blalock, I remember y'all. But Massa Whitehead, he still be sleepin.'"

"You mean he's here? Oh thank God! I hadn't dared hope—I need to talk with him. It's an emergency."

Arthur leaned forward; peering into the morning mist; taking in the wagon and snorting horses. "Massa not doin' so good hisself," he said. "He done been shot up ag'in by one of dem Yankees and he leg it ain't healin' up right."

Malinda shifted Columbus to her other hip. "Arthur please this is urgent! These men may die. They need medical attention right now. *PLEASE!*"

The slave recoiled. "Missy Blalock, Massa near been killed by Damned Yankees. Ain't no way he gwoin' let y'all bring Damned Yankees into dis here house."

"Arthur! What's going on down there?" Leaning on the newel post at the head of the circular staircase, John Whitehead's voice thundered through the morning stillness.

"Uncle John, it's Malinda." She brushed past the slave and stepped into the foyer. "I ... I'm sorry to bother you but I need your help."

"Malinda?" The doctor started down the stairs, leaning heavily on the railing with one hand, on a cane with the other. He was dressed in a blue flannel bathrobe. "Arthur," he sputtered, "for heaven's sake light the lamps!"

"Yes Massa!"

"Oh, Uncle John, I'm so glad you're home! I … I mean, it's good to see you."

By the time the doctor lumbered to the foot of the staircase, the foyer and lower rooms were ablaze with light. Was it Malinda's imagination or did the blue eyes soften when he looked at Columbus?

"This is your child?" he asked, in obvious amazement.

"Yes, and he's alive because of you." She reached out to him imploringly. "Uncle John, I need your help again. I'm sorry to ask you, but there are wounded men—"

The blue eyes turned to ice. "Yankees, I'll wager."

"My husband. He's so badly injured he may die, and two others, as well."

With the tip of his cane John Whitehead pointed to a large bandage visible beneath his bathrobe. It encircled his foot and the lower half of his left leg. "This is what a Yankee did to me!" he roared. "I may lose my leg!" He began waving the cane wildly. "Get out of my house! Do you hear me? Go back where you came from! Get out!"

Columbus started to wail. Malinda pressed his head against her breast to stifle the sound. "You're not inhuman, Uncle. You won't let my husband die."

"His kind damned near killed me! Now *GET OUT*! Get out I say, right now!" The cane slashed the air threateningly as the blue eyes grew savage with hate. Arthur huddled in the corner behind the still open door, his face a full shade lighter.

Malinda's own eyes were flashing now. They had come too far. Suffered too much to be turned away. "I will *NOT* get out!" she said hotly. "And you *will* tend to these wounded men!" In one deft move she pushed the shawl aside, pulled her Colt from its holster and pointed it at John Whitehead's chest. "Tell Arthur to get some help and bring those wounded men into your office. Do it now or you won't live to give another order."

The hate filled eyes blinked with a show of surprise. "Then it's true what they say about you," he muttered. "You are a renegade."

"Get those men in here, Uncle. I mean it."

"I'm sure you do," John Whitehead growled. "And don't call me, Uncle. I'll claim no Damned Yankee as kin of mine. Breaking into innocent people's homes, robbing and murdering—"

"Don't talk to me about innocent!" Malinda snapped. "We're wasting time. Tell Arthur to get moving. I'll count to three. One …"

The cane, held frozen in mid air, slowly lowered to the floor. "Arthur, get the two stretchers from my office. Call Carrie and Thomas and have them help you bring these men inside. Put them in my office."

"And hurry!" Malinda added without once taking her eyes from her uncle's face. She thought of the rifle on the floor of the driver's seat and prayed they would not take notice.

* * *

"I have very little chloroform." Doctor Whitehead poured water over his hands into a basin, lathered them again and repeated the procedure. "You must understand that my medical supplies are extremely low." He was drying his hands on a towel when Arthur, Carrie and young Thomas labored through the door carrying the first stretcher and lifted it to the operating table. It was Lou Simms.

The three slaves stared at the Colt revolver in Malinda's hand, but only Carrie's eyes raised to meet hers.

"Thank you," Malinda murmured. "Now please bring in my husband."

"This man's leg will have to come off," John Whitehead said flatly, adjusting his pince-nez. "Hand me the bottle of chloroform and that roll of gauze." He looked at Malinda over the top of his glasses. "And for heaven's sake wash your hands. They're filthy."

Malinda dropped her shawl to the floor, laid Columbus on it and guided his thumb to his mouth. "Stay right here, Son," she said, offering him the fringe of the shawl to tickle his nose. She watched her uncle closely as she laid the Colt beside the basin and washed her hands.

There was clatter in the hallway as the slaves struggled back into the room carrying the second stretcher. Malinda looked at Keith's blood washed face as she handed the doctor the chloroform and gauze.

"Put him down on the floor," the doctor barked, but before the slaves could comply Malinda gestured with the gun toward the operating table. "You'll do my husband first."

"I decide who goes first," the doctor snapped.

"You will do my husband first." Raising the gun to eye level.

Young Thomas bounded from the room and Carrie took a step toward the door. Arthur's mouth dropped like a trap door, but he stood nailed to the spot. After a long moment he found his voice. "De ... de odder man, Massa, he ... he daid. No sense bringin' him in, is der Massa?"

Doctor Whitehead looked squarely down the gun barrel. "No Arthur, there's no need." His voice was calm. "It will be prudent, however, to do what this young woman says. You and Carrie get her husband onto the operating table, and put this other man on the floor."

"When you've done that Arthur, you go out and lead my wagon around to the back before it attracts too much attention," Malinda said firmly. Then remembering the rifle, she added, "and I said 'lead.' That mare is mighty bad tempered. She'll turn on you if you try to drive her."

"Yes, Ma'am."

"And Arthur. Don't forget to come back. Your wife and son are here."

"No Ma'am. Not likely I be forgettin' dat."

The two slaves shuffled the bodies without the help of Thomas who was still cowering outside the door.

Leaning heavily on his cane with one hand, the doctor studied the blood-ied mass on the table. "Carrie, I'm going to need some clean water in the basin. Wash this man's face and get me a saline solution from the cabinet." Moments later the slave woman returned and quickly carried out the doctor's orders. Malinda stood at a distance, watching; the Colt still pointing at the doctor's chest.

Keith moaned as the doctor prodded at his turgid flesh, then let out a raw scream when he began bathing his face with the saline.

"Give him chloroform," Malinda ordered.

"I told you I am low on chloroform. I'll need it when I cut off that other man's leg."

"Give him chloroform. *NOW!*" Malinda shifted the gun, pointing it at the black woman. Carrie stared back at her in a rich anger that held no sign of fear.

"Carrie, give him chloroform," the doctor said without looking up. "This is the thanks I get for saving your life. And your child's. I would do it differ-ently if I had it to do over again," he said angrily, still without looking at Malinda.

Carrie poured the chloroform onto a piece of gauze and placed it over Keith's nose and mouth. "Hold his head still," the doctor snapped. "I can't work on him while he's thrashing around like this." He glanced at Malinda. "Tell me what happened."

"I don't know. Only that he was shot from the side. And … and he says he can't see."

"His nose is broken and bone fragments have pierced the eye. It's flat. The optic fluid is gone. I'll have to remove it."

"You have to take out his eye?" Malinda swayed. Fought to hold the gun steady. "If you're doing this to—"

The doctor laid the probing tool aside and glared at Malinda. "He's lost the sight in his right eye. If I don't remove it he'll die. He may anyway. Now what do you want me to do?"

Malinda swallowed. "I want you to save his life. Whatever it takes. If you don't, you forfeit your own."

The doctor reached for an instrument from the operating tray and again bent over his patient. Malinda grimaced and turned her head away.

* * *

Forty minutes later Doctor Whitehead laid his instruments aside. He had removed Keith's right eye, packed the socket and wrapped the entire right side of his head with a gauze dressing. He placed a black eye patch over the bandage before looking up at Malinda. "He will need to get used to wear-ing this. Keep this bandage on for the next three to four days, and when you change it make sure you keep the area clean. He stands a good chance of get-ting an infection."

"Yes, Unc—Doctor." Malinda's lips spread into a grim smile. "But we won't be going anywhere until he's healed. However long it takes." The gun in her right hand was now pointing at the floor.

"Put this man on the settee in the parlor," the doctor said sharply to the slaves. "Then come back and get the other one on the table before he bleeds to death." John Whitehead limped to the far wall of the room where a variety of large instruments were hanging from hooks. He selected two saws and placed them on the instrument tray beside the operating table.

Malinda's eyes followed Arthur and Carrie as they carried Keith out into the foyer. "I'll stay with him," she said. "And I'll take Thomas with me in case someone in here makes the mistake of doing something foolish."

Carrie shot a quick glance at the doctor, then looked at Malinda with an expression that reached back to the dawn of time. "Y'all don't be hurtin' my chil, ya hear?"

John Whitehead flashed a glance of astonishment at his slave.

"Yes, I hear," Malinda said quietly, regretting she had to strike fear in this good woman's heart. "But keep in mind that his welfare depends on the three of you." She looked down at the trembling slave boy and tried to smile. "Come along, Thomas. You can play with the baby in the parlor for a little while."

The boy looked pleadingly at his mother. She gave an almost imperceptible nod and he turned obediently and followed Malinda into the parlor.

* * *

Lou Simms' piercing screams traumatized the children and shattered what was left of Malinda's nerves. Burying her head in a pillow, she sobbed with uncontrollable rage. She thought of Sally and McCaleb, always preaching about the torment of hell fire. Somehow hell had gotten misplaced.

When the amputation was finished and Lou Simms had regained consciousness, the doctor offered him what was left of the bottle of whisky he had used to ease the pain of the amputation.

Carrie offered a second bottle to Keith, but his intake was minimal. He was weaving in and out of consciousness, and in his delirium reliving dark memories. "It was that son-of-a-bitch Jesse, Pa!" Keith blabbered. "He was the one who burned my house down. Don't tell me he didn't do it! You don't know what that little fucker's capable of!" His arms batted the air. Malinda fought to hold them down, keep him from tearing the bandages from his face. It took the last of her strength to control him. "I'll kill him!" Keith ranted. "I'll kill Jesse ... kill ... Jesse ... kill ..."

By evening, mercifully, the raving had subsided and Keith seemed to have stabilized. Though still in pain, he was rational. Malinda's fear began to dissipate. Unable to keep an eye on everyone at once, she locked the doctor in his operating room with Lou, reminding him that others would suffer if he tried to escape, and hoping he cared enough about his slaves not to risk their lives.

The uneasy thought came to her that she probably cared more about their welfare than he did.

Arthur accompanied her on a thorough search of the house for weapons and ammunition, which produced two handguns, a rifle, half a box of ammunition, and a sword. Malinda placed the loaded guns on the floor beneath the settee, put the box of ammunition in a cupboard, locked it, and slipped the key into her skirt pocket. Carrie prepared a questionable soup for their evening meal, more water than substance, but Malinda gulped it down greedily. When she spoon fed Columbus he, too, ate hungrily but Keith turned his head away.

Under cover of darkness, and against John Whitehead's protests, Raf Wheeler was buried under an apple tree in the backyard. Arthur and Thomas did the digging; Carrie offered prayers. Malinda stood off to one side, more an observer than a participant. She knew as soon as they were gone poor Arthur would be digging him up again. The good doctor would never allow Yankee rot to poison his patch of earth. She then had Arthur stable the horses while she retrieved her rifle from the wagon.

Malinda realized she was reaching the point of complete exhaustion. Her mind was beginning to play tricks on her. She had to sleep. But she knew her uncle would have the authorities on them the moment she closed her eyes. She had Carrie make a pallet for Lou in the doctor's office then locked her in there with instructions to tend to his needs. Next, she ushered the doctor, Arthur and Thomas into a windowless pantry just off the kitchen and bolted the door while the doctor railed at being held prisoner in his own home. With Columbus curled in her arms and Keith asleep, she settled onto a pallet of cushions beside the settee, one hand resting on her Colt, her rifle at her side.

* * *

In the morning Malinda awoke surprisingly refreshed. When she released Carrie, apologizing for the necessary precautions, she was met with a glacial stare. Well, what did you expect? she mused. Certainly not gratitude! There was more of the same when she unlocked the door to the pantry.

Breakfast consisted of four tomatoes and a small pan of corn meal mush. Malinda spoon fed Keith and Columbus while Carrie did the same for Lou.

A little later, after completing an examination of his patients, the doctor offered a surprising suggestion. "I have knowledge of a prisoner transfer scheduled to take place the day after tomorrow," he said. "Wounded soldiers from both sides are being exchanged. There is a rallying point not far from here. These are men who are no longer able to bear arms. I think Private Simms falls into that category. I suggest he be allowed to join them."

"What happens once they are exchanged?" Malinda eyed her uncle for any sign of trickery.

"It's my understanding they will be supplied with means to return to their homes."

Later, Malinda passed on her uncle's suggestion to Lou, and was not surprised at how eagerly it was accepted. "I've had enough of this bloody war." The young man eyed his empty pant leg with old eyes. "I just wanna go home."

"And where is home?"

"Indiana." he answered reverently.

"I'll see what I can do."

* * *

Two days later Malinda told Arthur to hitch up the doctor's black landau. Before departing the house with Lou and the doctor she made sure Keith was comfortable, then locked Arthur and his family in the pantry. As she climbed into the driver's seat beside the doctor, she made certain he saw the handgun concealed beneath her shawl. Holding Columbus on her lap and pressing the Colt against her uncle's side, they drove out the front gate.

A tight smile crossed Malinda's lips as the doctor nodded greetings to people they passed in the road. There were curious stares aimed at her and Columbus, but nothing more. Inside the carriage, hidden from prying eyes, Lou lay on the plush, blue velvet upholstery. Unnoticed, his fresh wound was leaving a growing, dark stain that would take all of Arthur's skill, and many hours of labor, to remove.

It wasn't far to the rallying point, and the last Malinda saw of Lou Simms he was huddled in a wagon with a score of other wounded. All amputees. Surprisingly, there was a handful of civilians present, some of whom were seeing to the comfort of the prisoners with pillows and blankets, along with pathetic offerings of food and jugs of water. It was a show of kindness Malinda could not have imagined. Was it done, she wondered, in the hope that those on the other side would be doing the same for their loved ones? Since John Whitehead seemed to know so much about the movement of these prisoners Malinda assumed he had been responsible for at least some of their medical care, and she wondered how many of them had been made amputees by his saw? She wondered, too, how many of them would live to see their homes?

Upon their return to the house the doctor climbed down from the driver's seat, and to Malinda's complete surprise, hobbled to her side of the carriage and extended a helping hand. The gesture released an unexpected flow of emotion. Malinda's eyes misted and she quickly averted her head so he wouldn't see the tears. She knew he hated her, and she couldn't blame him, yet he was treating her as he would treat a real lady. She also knew that the memory of this, her first carriage ride, would be with her for a long time to come.

* * *

Malinda and Keith remained guests in John Whitehead's home for nearly a week. On the sixth evening Keith announced he felt strong enough to travel. The news was met with a great sense of relief. Especially by members of the household.

Early the following morning they began their journey back to Tennessee. Arthur drove the wagon, the roan and pinto were tethered at the rear. Prior to leaving, Malinda apologized to her uncle for having to again confine him and the others in the tiny pantry. Her remarks were met with a villainous stare. "Don't darken my door again," he said harshly.

"I hope that won't be necessary," she answered. "And I hope your leg gets better."

"It's gangrenous," he said flatly. "It will have to come off."

"I'm sorry." Malinda closed the door and bolted it, awed by the man's bravery. These last few days must have been torturous for him, but he'd never once complained of any physical discomfort.

* * *

It was high noon when they reached the border, a pitted stone marker at the side of the road read simply: Tennessee Territory. Yellow, purple and white wild flowers blanketed the green meadow. Ahead, through the shimmering waves of summer heat, the rolling mountains guarded their secrets of war and turmoil. Only the rattle of wagon wheels and the clop of horses' hooves could be heard here. There were no sounds of gunfire.

Keith and Malinda bid good-bye to Arthur and were surprised when he wished them a safe journey. They mounted their horses and waited while Arthur turned the wagon around and urged the team into a gallop. Malinda was struck by the irony of the slave riding with such fervent haste to return and free his Massa.

They rode to a nearby stream to allow the horses to drink. Malinda dismounted and replenished their canteens, then hastily undressed Columbus and dipped him in the cooling water. After a few minutes she sensed Keith's growing impatience. "I'll be finished in a minute," she said.

"I'm anxious to get moving, Malinda."

"We're ready now." She dried the baby with her shawl, strapped him into his sling, and quickly mounted up. Far from being irritated by Keith's brusque manner, she felt relieved. He was taking charge again. This nightmare was nearly over. Without voicing a reason why, Malinda guided her pinto onto Keith's right side and rode abreast of him. A few moments later he turned toward her and gave a knowing smile. It didn't need to be said. They both knew she would now be his missing eye. They'd been given another chance.

* * *

"We'll stop tonight at Earl Sheets place," Keith said. "Not much farther so we should be there about supper time."

"That suits me fine," Malinda said happily and kissed Columbus's warm curls. "If there's food to be had little baby, Lavinia is the one who'll have it." She ran her hand through her own thick hair, lifting it from her neck and allowing the early evening breeze to caress it.

Soon they reached the turnoff from the main trail and took the narrow, overgrown path leading to the homestead. As they neared the rocky overhang that served as a lookout post, they glanced up, hoping to see Lonnie's freckled face, but the one that peered down at them was Lum's.

"Good to see you again, Lum." Keith called. Malinda continued to search the ridge for Lonnie, but no other face appeared.

"Howdy, Mr. Blalock, Mrs. Blalock. Good to see ya ag'in." Lum climbed down and started walking ahead of them, rifle dangling from a shoulder strap. Malinda thought how much thinner he looked. You could see the outline of his shoulder bones beneath his shirt. "Hey Lum, did you notice we've got someone else with us?" Malinda called.

He turned around, walking backward a few paces. "We heard about yer youngin. Boy ain't it?"

"That's right! Say, where's Lonnie?"

Lum turned around again and called over his shoulder. "Lonnie ... he ain't here."

The reception by the Sheets family was not what they had anticipated. An invisible shroud had settled over the place. They were told Daniel Ellis had left earlier in the day with some new recruits.

Keith had been right about the supper hour, but that too, proved not to be what they had hoped for; boiled mush with no flavoring. No meat. No apologies. It could no longer be said that no one went hungry at a Daniel Ellis safe house.

Something was woefully wrong, but neither their hosts nor Lum offered any clue to the problem. Lavinia's large frame was skeletal. The price of the war was cut into every deep line of her face. Earl was shrunken even more than before. And nearly mute. Their boys, Monty and Earl, Jr., were nowhere to be seen, and when Malinda asked about them, Lavinia gave a kind of hopeless shrug and turned her face away.

Over the supper table Malinda and Keith exchanged looks of concern, astounded by the mantle of secrecy and sorrow that permeated the house. Malinda spooned mush into Columbus' mouth. He took it without complaint.

Lum was the only one to mention Keith's recent injury and asked if it was painful.

"Only hurts when I wink," Keith said lightly, making a lame attempt to interject humor. But no one smiled.

After the meal Malinda offered to help Lavinia with the cleanup but was turned away. "I'll handle it. You best make your pallets there in front of the fireplace. We bed down early these days."

As shadows deepened Keith went outside to get their bedrolls from the horses and Malinda peered through the window slit and looked out at what used to be the garden. The earth was scorched and the barn had been reduced to charred timbers.

While Keith prepared the bedrolls Malinda washed Columbus's face and hands and made him ready for bed. Lavinia and Earl had said little about the baby, in fact, she had the feeling Lavinia was avoiding looking at him.

It was only after Earl grunted a good-night and went off to bed that an explanation for the strange circumstances of the household was finally offered. It came from Lavinia.

"We've had some trouble here," she began quietly. "Injun trouble."

"What?" Malinda and Keith cried in unison.

"I'm amazed injuns are still bothering people," Keith exclaimed. "Since the war—"

"They wuz army injuns."

"Thomas's Highland Legion!" Malinda cried. "We know about them!"

"They come up on us when Earl and Daniel wuz away. Weren't nobody else here 'cept the boys and me, and Lonnie and Lum. They wuz quiet like. Real sneaky. They got Lonnie first, scalped him and threw his bloody hair on the porch. My Monty, he went out, not knowin' anythin' was goin' on, and he picked it up before he knew what it was. Then he started yellin,' and about that time them injuns started war hoopin' and one of 'em shot my boy clean through the chest. I grabbed my rifle and fought off the ones what was comin' through the front door, and Earl, Jr., and Lum was shootin' at them that was burnin' the barn and garden. And just when I was sure they had us Earl and Daniel and twenty or so Reb deserters come ridin' up and fought 'em off afore they could torch the house."

Lavinia, almost swallowed up by her gray muslin dress, sat on a three legged stool as she told her story, her gnarled hands working furiously at her kneecaps. Malinda reached out and covered the older woman's hand with her own. "Lavinia, I'm so sorry. I ... we knew something was wrong the minute we came in. When ... did this happen?"

"Sunday last." Lavinia wiped sweat from her forehead, but her eyes were strangely dry. "Earl, Jr., he got shot in the head. Lum was lucky, just got nicked in the knee. Earl, Sr. ain't been the same since we buried our boys. Takes time, I guess. Daniel ... I ain't never seen Daniel cry afore, but when he held that little ole Lonnie in his arms with the top of his head missin' he dern near bawled his eyes out. I ain't never seen a man suffer like that."

Horrorstruck, Malinda stared at Keith. What could they do? What could be said? Keith gave a helpless shake of his head. They fell into heavy silence. No further glances were exchanged. Everyone sought his own private space to stare into.

After several minutes, with no parting words, Lavinia braced her palms on her knees, heaved her lank frame upright, and went off to bed. Malinda continued to sit quietly, knees tucked to her chin. Sometime later, beside her on the bedroll, Keith started to snore.

Lavinia hadn't once mentioned her own pain. Hadn't touched on it. She'd spoken only of the suffering of others. Maybe it wasn't real yet, Malinda thought. Both her children dead. How could it be real? She remembered the farm woman who had run a knife through her heart after her family was murdered. Somehow that woman was never far from Malinda's thoughts. It seemed so long ago, yet how many nights had that woman haunted her dreams? Still did.

And Daniel Ellis, the brutal marauder; two sons; his own, and now Lonnie, butchered. "He who lives by the sword ..." Oh dear God, Lonnie ... Lonnie ... The funny little crinkled face, the carrot nose ... the poor feet that couldn't find their way into boots ...

Malinda was amazed that she had no tears. No tears for Lonnie. She had so loved the little fella. Now as she listened to the sounds of darkness she became aware of something strange coming over her. A creeping numbness settling in around her heart. It didn't hurt. It just felt cold. As icy as a winter's wind. Was this what had happened to Lavinia, she wondered? This nothingness? Was this what allowed her to go on living?

Dear God how much longer could this hell last?

PART FOUR

THE GLEANING

1865–1867

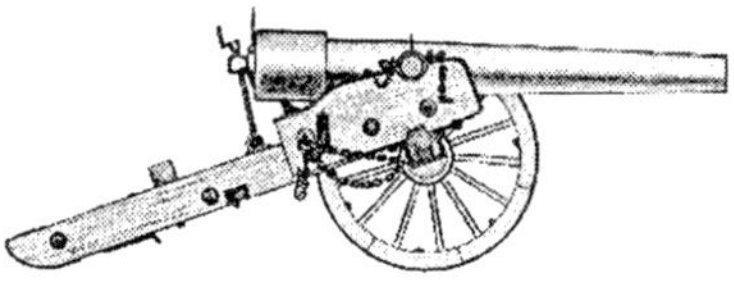

☆

CHAPTER 26

The hell lasted well into the following year; the death knell sounding with the fall of Richmond and Lee's surrender to Grant on April 9th. A few weeks later, in North Carolina, Johnston surrendered to Sherman. The war was over. The North had won. Keith was dumbfounded. How could it be over? There was so much left unresolved. He felt like a gyroscope halted in mid spin.

He knew he shouldn't have been surprised by Malinda's reaction to the news. But he was. Couldn't she see that nothing had really changed? Just because a bunch of know-it-alls were flourishing their quill pens over papers most people couldn't even read, didn't mean a damned thing! What in the hell was the matter with people? Including Malinda! The way to win this war was to grind the Rebels so far into the dust they *couldn't* fight anymore. And there was plenty of fight left in 'em, and he had a letter to prove it—*if he could ever get his hands on it again!* For the third time Keith shuffled through the pile of assorted items stacked in the corner, most of which were old copies of that stupid *Louisville Courier* Malinda was forever pouring over. Where in the shit was that letter? He scowled at Malinda as she sat cross-legged on her bedroll, strumming away on her dulcimer as if nothing else in the world mattered besides that dumb song. *My Old Kentucky Home.* Jesus! All she could talk about was finding a home and settling down, even in her music! How many times had she mentioned Louisville where her Ma and Jacob were living—as far as anybody knew. And that wasn't a sure thing either. She was forever writing letters to 'em and nobody ever wrote back! And what was it she'd said last night? Oh yeah! "Maybe we can find a house something like the Reynolds' place. Remember Keith? Only smaller, of course." She always threw in that "smaller, of course." Sometimes she just didn't act as if she had good sense. Where in the hell did she think they were going to get enough money for a house like that? And all this because some damned fool politician was proclaiming, "The wounds are now healed," everything was supposed to change. Well, bullshit! Wounds were not healed and the scales were not balanced, and anybody who thought otherwise was a sure enough moron!

Keith's eye roved the cabin; an animal looking for prey. Finally, he turned to Malinda. "Where'd you put that letter the Colonel gave me?"

She looked up from her dulcimer. "*I* didn't put it anywhere. The Colonel gave it to you."

"Goddamnit you know how important it is! If you left it laying around for the youngin to—"

"I told you I don't have the letter, and Columbus hasn't touched it."

Keith rose, ran his fingers through his hair and strode to the door. His insides were quivering like jelly. A part of him knew he was taking it out on Malinda when it really wasn't her fault, and somehow knowing that made him even madder! It wasn't just the mess about the war. He was going through another of what he had come to call his "William" periods.

There were times when he could go for days without thinking about it, but then it would come roaring back like cannon fire, and for days on end he wouldn't be able to think of anything else. He had to go through the rest of his life knowing he came from the cock of William Coffey! How in the hell Ma could ever have ...

At least his secret was safe. T.J. was the only other person who knew, and it wouldn't cross T.J.'s lips even under torture. T.J. was loyal. He'd toyed with telling Malinda; somehow it seemed she had a right to know ... but on the two occasions when he'd tried, he'd found it too humiliating to discuss. Even with her.

Why in the hell hadn't the old bastard taken his secret to the grave with him? Ma was sure right when she said a lot of people would get hurt if the truth ever came out. Maybe she should have thought of that before she bedded the old buck! A wave of revulsion washed through him at the mental image of his mother in the arms of William Coffey.

However, there were things he *could* do something about. He lumbered to the door, reached down and pulled a dead reed from among the weeds and stuck it between his teeth. There was the matter of Pa's murder. John Boyd—now that was a piece of human garbage if there ever was one—was still alive and kicking. Robert Glass had done the actual shooting but he was dead now. They all were except Boyd and Jesse.

Jesse! That little weasel had escaped the slaughter at his Pa's place. Carroll and the older two boys were dead. Zinnia had survived. They said she'd tried to save her old reprobate of a husband, and he'd lasted a couple of days before he died. Good! Gave him time to suffer.

Keith's gaze fell on the saddlebag draped across the fence. And then he remembered. He'd put the letter in the saddlebag intending to read it again when it got bright enough to see. They'd been without oil for the lamp for weeks now, and the last of the candles ran out three days ago. Any reading had to wait for sunlight.

Feeling sheepish over having stormed at Malinda about it, he ambled over to the fence and withdrew the folded letter:

> *... the confrontation between our Union forces led by that inexperienced and inept imbecile, Colonel Theodore H. Barrett, has resulted in a Confederate victory at the hands of the Rebel Colonel John S. "Rip" Ford. If we are to continue the struggle we must have adequately trained men, men who have seen combat to ...*

Keith wet his lips. Confederate victory! The letter, addressed to Colonel Kirk was from a friend of his, a fellow officer who was serving with Union forces in the far South of Texas at a place called Brazos Santiago Post. The battle had occurred in early May. That meant not everybody agreed the war was over like those big shot idiots were saying it was. If the North had won the war how come the Rebs were still winning battles?

Kirk had passed the letter on to Keith, knowing how he, and some of the other men, were looking for a place where there was still fighting going on. He understood Keith's urgency in getting relocated into another area of conflict, and promised he would make the transfer if that was what he wanted.

Funny thing about Kirk. If Keith hadn't seen it he wouldn't have believed it. Other than himself, there had been three officers, a sergeant and a corporal present, when Kirk's orderly came rushing in with the news of President Lincoln's assassination. Everyone was stunned, but Kirk's face had turned the color of cotton. He dropped like a tree into his chair, buried his head in his hands and began crying like a baby. Despite Keith's own shock at the news, he was more shocked at Kirk's reaction to it. It had been several minutes before the Colonel was able to compose himself, and when he looked up at those who remained most had slunk away in embarrassment—he wiped his eyes with his folded, white handkerchief and said, "Gentlemen, victory is ours, but at far too great a price." Then he'd gotten up and literally stumbled out of the tent. If he hadn't caught hold of the post, Colonel George W. Kirk would have landed flat on his face in the mud.

"I see you found your letter." Malinda was standing in the doorway with her hands on her hips, but before Keith could respond, a rider came thundering out of the woods toward them, drumming dust and spraying rock.

"Hey! What the hell's your hurry?" Keith tucked the letter back into the saddlebag as the rider reined in his mount.

Malinda was heading toward them, Columbus at her heels. The messenger was Corporal Glover, a fuzz-faced kid who hadn't yet learned how to grow a beard. Sweat was pouring off him so fast it was almost washing away the grin spreading across the bottom half of his face.

"It's official!" the corporal whooped. "It's over! The war's over!"

"And who says so this time?" Keith shouted above the neighing of the nervous horse.

"The Rebel Kirby-Smith in the trans-Mississippi area surrendered to Union forces! The war is *OVER*! It's *OFFICIAL!* President Johnson signed a Proclamation of Amnesty for the Rebs. 'Cept for Lee and some a the generals. Ain't no more fightin'! Y'all are goin' home. We're all goin' home! *Hallelujah!"*

Lost in numbing confusion Keith muttered, "When did this happen?"

"Kirby-Smith surrendered on the 26th, and Johnson signed the Proclamation two days after that. *Hallelujah!"* The corporal's horse reared. "I gotta spread the word!" He spurred and headed across the compound shouting, "*Hallelujah*" at the top of his lungs.

Keith turned to Malinda. She was grinning like a mountain lion with a fresh kill. "The war's over darling! The President says so! You'll have to believe it now." She picked up Columbus and waltzed her way back into the cabin, spinning round and round, and laughing like a fool.

Keith made his way to a nearby tree; leaned against it. What the hell was the matter, anyway? He felt dizzy. Couldn't be the heat. Wasn't that hot. Everything looked like a mountain stream. Kind of ripply. What was it he'd been thinking a minute ago? Oh yeah, about Malinda. No, before that.

Images of burning cabins twisted through his mind. He should've seen this coming. He was a smart man. Why hadn't he known the war would end one day? Why hadn't he made plans? He was a good planner. "Expert strategist," Kirk always said. What in the name of God was he going to do if it really was over? Settle down and start farming again? That was what Malinda wanted. Could he do it again? Build another house? Plant another crop? Harvest it? At one time that had been all in this world he wanted. Now it seemed so meaningless! So useless! Was farming all that was left for him to do with his life?

"Keith?" Malinda called from inside the house. "We'll be eating in a few minutes."

He straightened and looked toward the cabin. It was weaving like a willow in the wind.

"Darling? Are you all right?" She began heading in his direction, but he didn't want her near him. He needed room.

"I'm fine," he called. "I'll be there in a minute. Go on back inside." This dizzy feeling had happened before. Maybe it was his eye that was causing him to feel this way. A while back another man, "Mule," they called him because he wore a thing that looked like a blinder over his right eye. Mule said this sometimes happens. Mule had lost his eye when he was a kid, and he said how sometimes things would get all wavy like, and he'd come close to passing out. Then it would go away and he'd be okay again. Said a Doc told him it had something to do with the balance inside his head.

Malinda was spooning rabbit stew onto his plate when Keith entered the cabin. It was the first meat they'd had in over a week. Smelled good. His head was beginning to clear now. The dizziness was almost gone. Thoughts weren't so jumbled.

"I'm glad you found your letter," Malinda said. It was a genuine smile. No hint of sarcasm.

Finally, he felt strong enough to trust his voice. "Doesn't mean much now."

"Oh?"

He dropped heavily into the chair, reached for Columbus as the baby toddled by and pulled him onto his lap. "Like you say, the war's over." The words felt bitter on his lips.

"Oh, Keith!" Malinda set the stew pot back on the fire, wiped the sweat from her forehead with the back of her hand and wrapped her arms around his neck, nestling her cheek next to his. "I'm sorry I was so mad at you last night, Sweetheart. I said such angry things. We're both out of sorts. Things are changing so fast and … and it's hard to believe, isn't it? It is for me. I mean, hard to believe we won't have to go on scouting parties anymore. The fighting, the robbing and killing, it's all over! And we can have a home again. And—"

"I guess that's right, Malinda." He brushed his lips across her cheek. "I reckon we've got some planning to do."

She turned her head and kissed him full on the lips. "Let's talk about it over the meal."

* * *

That night after the lovemaking, they lay on their bedrolls, the fragrance of the night wafting in through the open door. Keith listened to her steady breathing, envying her ability to let go of everything and fall asleep. Maybe for her it was simple. Like she'd said, they were still young and strong and they could begin again.

During supper she'd talked more about Kentucky and finding her Ma and Jacob and maybe all of them starting over together. That was one sorry thought. There wasn't a roof big enough for him and Elizabeth Pritchard to share. He hadn't said much. Just let her talk it out. Maybe talking the dreams through would get them out of her system. Then maybe they could get down to some serious planning.

* * *

They awakened to the smell of a breakfast fire and the sound of men mulling around. Packing up. Boisterous laughter. Horses whinnied as they caught the excitement. "Goin' home." Over and over the phrase drifted through the open door, bandied on the cool mountain wind.

Malinda lay for a few moments without opening her eyes. Could it be real? Could it all be behind them? The words had been spoken, but somehow she didn't feel it yet. She hadn't really felt anything for a long time. She'd gone through the motions. Pretended. Pretended even during lovemaking. But now, it seemed as if there was a little something inside her that was stirring. Waking up. Maybe it was called hope.

She sighed, opened her eyes and stretched cat-like, arms above her head.

Then rolling on to her side she pillowed her head on her palm. Keith was lying, hands behind his head, staring up at the slits in the roof. "One good thing about this place," he said. "We've got plenty of openings for the air to come through."

"And the rain. And the snow!" She rose on one elbow and motioned to Columbus. The baby struggled uncertainly to his feet, rubbed at one eye while clutching a piece of threadbare blanket in his other hand. He toddled over and sat down beside her with a resounding "Splatt!"

"Sounds pretty wet to me," Malinda commented as she brushed back the curls from his forehead. "When are you going to stop doing that, Columbus? You'll be two years old before long, way past the age where you're supposed to be wee-weeing in your didee."

She turned her attention back to Keith; picked up the edge of the baby's blanket and began poking it into his left ear. "We won't have to be worrying about the snow coming in anymore though, will we? We'll be long gone from here before that time."

Impatient, he batted at her hand. "Malinda, I've been thinking."

"Oh, I'm sure of that," she said lightly, but recognized the edginess in his tone.

"We've got some serious talking to do. Serious planning. Spinning webs is one thing, but we've got to start talking practical here."

"I thought we were talking practical." She tried to keep her breathing steady even though her stomach had just done a flip flop.

"We don't have any money. I'm not ashamed of that because nobody else has any either, but what we do have is land."

Malinda sat straight up. "We *had* land. In Coffey's Gap."

"We still have it. The land's there. Houses are gone, but the land is ours. All of it. We own more land now than when we got married because we've got our piece and Pa's, too."

Malinda shook her head, trying to clear it. Trying to grasp what he was saying. "You're not thinking of going back there?"

"Why not? It's ours."

She cocked her head and looked at him; straining to stifle the nervous laughter rising in her throat. "Keith, are you feeling all right?"

"I feel fine."

"Then why are you talking so crazy? We can't go back to Coffey's Gap after what we've ... after what's happened there." Her stomach gave another turn. "I've got a pretty strong hunch that people over there don't think too highly of us. For that matter most of Western North Carolina and parts of Virginia, don't either. Seems to me you'd have reasoned that out by now." She rose and picked up the soaking baby; carried him to his bedroll and began removing his wet clothes.

"It's our land, Malinda, and nobody's going to take it away from us. It's all we own in this world."

"And what is it? Eleven, maybe twelve acres of scorched earth? I find it highly unlikely that the folks around there would have left even a tree stump standing on our land! Not after we burned their homes down! I … I honestly don't understand you, Keith. I'm trying to. Really I am. But … but I just don't understand how you can even think …" Her voice trailed off. *My God, has he gone and lost his mind?*

"If like they say, the war is actually over, then we won't be the only ones wanting to rebuild. Everybody else will be rebuilding, too." He propped himself on his elbow, hand cupping his head. "And remember Malinda, *WE* won the war."

"Just because the fighting is finished doesn't mean people are going to forget what happened."

"Do you want to have a home again, or don't you?"

"What kind of a crazy question is that? Of course I want us to have a home again. But why not go up to Louisville where Ma and—"

"Because we don't own land in Louisville. We own land in Coffey's Gap, North Carolina," he snorted. "And if you're afraid of what some of those fool people might do, let me remind you that most of 'em are dead. And the ones that are left are afraid of Keith Blalock. Scared shit of him, in fact! Nobody will try to bother us, Malinda," he smiled darkly. "We're the victors!" He came to his feet and walked outside to relieve himself.

Malinda stood motionless as he walked out the door. Buried feelings were rushing back like water over rapids. She didn't want them. She didn't want to feel them. She didn't want to hurt anymore. Oh God, it had been merciful not to hurt. And now, just when hope had come alive again, Keith was destroying it. Would there never be a moment again when they could feel safe? But that's what Keith wanted. He *wanted* the danger! Maybe he needed it.

The kindling was green and Malinda was having trouble getting the breakfast fire started. When Keith returned, he paused in the open doorway, his eye traveling the tiny room. "After we eat you can begin packing up. I'll go see the Colonel and make sure we have all the ammunition we need and find out what the formalities are about getting out of the army. I'll want to say good-bye to T.J. and the others. If you can be ready I'd like to move out before noon."

Malinda's eyes were shining with unshed tears. She poked at the stubborn fire, venting her exasperation. So that was it. The decision had been made and she'd had no part in the making. Finally she turned to him. "It isn't over, is it?" she said in a quiet voice.

"What isn't over?"

"The killing."

"Malinda—"

"I don't think it's ever going to be over. Not for you. I think you'll be at war until the day you die." She picked up the cloth sack and began spooning corn meal into a pan of water. "If we go back, there will be more killing. You're going back after Jesse and John Boyd. I know it as well as you do. But maybe it'll be us this time who gets killed. You, me, Columbus." She stirred the mush with a wooden spoon. "I don't know how much longer I can hold on, Keith. I don't know how much more killing I can handle."

There was a long, heavy pause before he answered, and when he did his voice was as empty as a cave. "Are you coming with me, Malinda?"

A sigh, born in her entrails, escaped her lips. Or was it the song of resignation? "There doesn't appear to be much else I can do, now does there?" She wiped her hands on her apron. "But I want you to know something, Keith. It's important that you know. I'm near my limit on killing."

"Malinda, if you want a home, this is the only way."

"No," she answered sadly, "not the only way. But it's *your* way."

* * *

The trip back to Caldwell County was made through familiar trails and passes, the route so well known the horses scarcely had to be directed. Malinda thought about all the years when she had longed for home. Now that they were actually going there, she was filled with dread.

They arrived early on a Sunday morning, soaked and exhausted after being caught the night before in a driving rain. They'd finally found shelter in a dank cave and when a red sun began to steal over the mountain, promising only temporary relief, Malinda hoped it would shine long enough to dry them out.

As her pinto plodded down the muddy road, two paces behind Keith's roan, she strained through the first fingers of light to see The Grandfather. It was still only a giant, hulking shadow. "God's Sentinel. Put there to watch over the valley and keep it safe." She could almost hear Pa's voice. But I can't remember how it feels to be safe, she thought. I'm not sure I ever did. In a reflex motion she checked the Colt on her hip.

Columbus shuddered against her breast, clutching at her although her milk had dried up months ago. He's looking for safety, too, she thought. Poor little fella, I wish I could tell him there was some.

As they passed one ruin after another, it seemed she was seeing it for the first time. Strange. They'd thundered down this road countless times, flames blazing behind them, yet she'd never looked at the devastation. Never really saw it. Now, there was nothing else to see. Nothing had survived except the meadows on the mountainside. They were still vibrant and green and sprinkled with a patchwork of wildflowers. But there was no livestock to feed on the rich grass. No crops to grace the highland slopes. Tumbling chimneys stood like wounded warriors marking the spots people had called home. The earth was tortured. Desolate. Blackened trees lay toppled one on another and she saw evidence of where someone had taken shelter beneath the rubble; a shirt and a pair of pants lay atop the pile to dry.

That was where the Phelps' place used to be, she thought, listlessly. That one had been the Hodges. Keith had been sweet on Betty Hodges when he was a boy, but her Pa put a nail in it because Keith was a bastard. And over there was the Patterson's. She remembered that one well. Seven dead at the Patterson's.

Mile after mile of nothingness, with only an occasional glimpse of wildlife. A red fox. Two hungry deer. A haunting stillness lay over the land. No rifle shots slicing the air. No crack of pistol fire. But there was no peace in the stillness, only heavy expectation. The wake of war. She had never felt more like a stranger than she did now, and in a land that had once been home.

"I want to take a look around," Keith called from his place a few paces ahead.

Malinda, merely nodded. What, she wondered, did he think there was left to see?

"We'll ride by Pa's place. And I want to check out McCaleb's, too."

Malinda found her voice. "That means we'll pass by our place. It's on the way."

Keith looked back over his shoulder. "I don't think we should expect much."

Malinda gave a dry chuckle. "I'm not expecting anything."

And that was precisely what they found. Even the towering trees were gone, their corpses rotting on the ground, felled by fire or wind or saw. Of course the house was gone. Only the chimney and the stone steps leading to the root cellar remained. There had been books on the shelves and that fine china plate of Ma's. And the pine table Keith had made. They plodded by without stopping.

Further down around the bend and across the road lay the tumbled remains of Carroll Moore's stone fence. It was nothing more now than a few rocks piled one on another, most scattered around the useless earth that had once been a yard. The house had been taken to the ground, not even the chimney remained, the explosion had blown it apart, but a few yards away stood a small shack. The pathetic structure had been pieced together from dead trees and old barrels and was held together with mud. As their horses plodded slowly by Malinda sensed eyes peering at them. Zinnia, no doubt. Most likely she had a gun. The hope was she didn't have powder to load it.

The sun was higher now. Malinda looked up again at The Grandfather. Maybe there was some comfort to be gained from him after all. In the midst of all this, he *was* the single thing that looked the same.

Austin's house was gone, along with the barn and smokehouse. Even the rail fence had been torn down. If they were going to build here they had their work cut out for them. The nearest trees were several hundred feet up the mountain. The thought was wearying. Malinda was so filled with fatigue the tiniest effort seemed too much to deal with.

Down the road from Austin's place, another black patch of earth marked the spot where John Boyd's home had stood. That one could have been torched by either side.

Fate had one small miracle in store for them. McCaleb's house was still there. It was beyond understanding as to why. Maybe he and Sally prayed for it, Malinda thought somewhat bitterly. They rode by at a leisurely pace, but it was apparent no one was at home. Fresh hoof prints in the mud indicated a recent rider had left in a hurry.

"I guess we've seen enough" Keith said finally. "I'm thinking we can hole up in that cave on the slope behind our place until I get some kind of shelter built for us."

Malinda pulled on her reins. "What are you going to build a shelter out of? The trees are all burned—"

"Malinda, just shut up with your we can't attitude! You're the one wanting a home, and I'm the one who's willing to build it for you, so please quit telling me how I can't do it!"

He was right, of course. She wasn't holding up her end. She wasn't thinking positively about anything. And immediately the thought came to mind that there wasn't anything to be positive about. If this was victory, she couldn't begin to imagine what defeat must feel like.

As they headed back, Keith's words played again through her mind. Maybe they had slipped out unnoticed, unaware of their telling importance … "You're the one wanting a home." What did *he* want? There was within her heart the slim hope that once they had a home again, Keith would change—put all this need for adventure aside ? Adventure? Good Lord! She'd had enough adventure to last twelve lifetimes! Peace. Ah, now that was a word a body could get their arms around—"

"For heaven's sake what's that?" Malinda's mental wanderings were interrupted by a foreign noise. Keith held up his hand to signal a halt. Listening. It sounded like the distant clang of a bell! There it was again. This time there was no mistaking it. It *was* a bell. A big one.

Keith looked at her quizzically. "Now what the blazes do you make of that?"

"I'm sure it's a church bell," Malinda said, raising a finger to her lips as it sounded again. When it had finished, she nodded vigorously. "I'd stake my life that it's the old Baptist Church bell."

"By golly, I think you're right. I heard that sucker ring every Sunday morning of my life. Now where do you suppose?" He shook his head. Puzzled. "The church burned down years ago."

"I think it's coming from farther up the road. Up where the church used to be."

"Let's go have a look. Sure won't get any peace till we find out, now will we?"

They followed the sound for another few minutes before it ceased altogether and another took it's place. The rattle of wagon wheels. Keith motioned toward a thicket, and they barely had time to take cover before a buckboard, it's driver in an obvious hurry, came careening down the road and dashed by in a shower of flying mud.

They waited until he had passed from sight, then ventured out onto the road again and followed.

Less than a quarter mile farther on, where the land sloped sharply downward, they spied a large clearing off to the right. It was the former site of the church. There were a half dozen wagons gathered at the side of the road, including the one they'd been following. There were also two buggies, and several mules and horses. Malinda recognized one of the buggies as belonging to the parson. My God, is he still alive? Deeper into the clearing stood a scaffolding. The now silent bell was attached to the overhead cross beam.

They took cover behind a clump of rhododendron and peered down on the gathering below. There were twenty-five to thirty people, all with their backs turned, directing their attention toward the scaffolding where the crippled parson was laboriously climbing the steps assisted by two men. His bible clutched tightly in one hand.

"They must be going to hold Sunday service," Malinda whispered.

"And from the hanging scaffold, no less," Keith scoffed. "Colonel Kirk told me they caught three of our men and hung 'em right here. Left 'em to rot, too. When our boys found what was left of 'em, they buried 'em right behind it. Now they've turned it into a damned church."

Columbus stirred and started to fret. Malinda bent over and kissed him on the lips to still the sound. "He's waking up, we'd better get out of here," she whispered.

"Try to keep him still another minute or two." Keith's eye was traveling the small crowd. "Look, there's McCaleb! See? He's kneeling down there near the front. And by damn if that isn't Sally beside him. No mistaking that mane of red hair. Look at her! Laying face down in the grass with her arms stretched out like a crucifying Jesus."

"Oh Keith, please let's go," Malinda pleaded. "What if they find us here?"

"Hold on a minute!" he rasped, his eyes still probing the crowd. "I've spotted three Unionists. And there's two or three others who may be; used to be Union, anyway." He glanced at her quickly. "Now what do you think of that? The lion shall lay down with the lamb," he chuckled.

Below the parson was raising his bible. "Brothers and Sisters, let us have a moment of silence before we begin. A moment to remember all those brave souls who have gone before us to their glory, giving their lives for a cause they believed to be just." The parson then raised his other hand as he lowered his head and closed his eyes. "Oh, God," he continued, "we are here today in a spirit of reconciliation. We come before You as innocent sheep wandering and lost in the wilderness …"

Suddenly Keith stood tall, adjusted his rifle strap and moved to the edge of the thicket. Pausing, he looked back at a bewildered Malinda as he removed his hat. "Cover me, Sweetheart," he said, grinning broadly. "I'm going to church."

☆

CHAPTER 27

Elizabeth opened the drawer of her Queen Anne writing desk and withdrew Malinda's latest letter. It was dated June 2, 1866, one week ago. Beneath it lay two other letters she'd received months earlier. She had not responded to the others, and wasn't sure she would this time either—although there were issues she longed to address. But what good would come of it? Her words had fallen short of their mark in the past, why was there reason to think it would be any different now? And yet …

Elizabeth unfolded the letter and began reading it for the third time:

Dearest Ma,

I hope this letter reaches you safely. I pray each night for your well being and for the well being of my dear little brother, Jacob. I wonder if you can understand how my heart aches for both of you? I can only trust that you received my earlier letters. I got your address from Uncle Samuel's business place. Some nice person there sent it to me. But perhaps the person was mistaken and gave me the wrong address. Or perhaps your letters in response have been lost.

It is painful being separated by so many miles.

As I explained in my earlier letters, we came back to Caldwell County at the end of the war. It's desperately impoverished here. Both Rebel and Unionist suffered mightily in this area and things are still not what you could call good, but they are improving. Many of our former neighbors were killed in the war and several members of Keith's family as well; his stepfather, Uncle William and several nephews. (Again, I wrote you about all that in my previous letters.) I can't truthfully say what neighbors we have are friendly, but at least they're not hostile. Everyone is war weary, sick to death of the killing and so busy trying to find enough to eat they aren't so interested in what their neighbors are up to. Not like before, anyway. Keith built us a new cabin, not as big as our old one was, but it'll do for now. We attend church services every Sunday, and folks there are beginning to warm up a bit. Last Sunday the parson patted Columbus on the head and asked him how he was doing.

When we first returned, Keith (you know how bold he is!) walked right into the Sunday service, and truth be known, my heart was beating like an injun's drum I was so scared that folks would be unkind, but they just sort of ignored him. At first, that is. Then when he lent a hand in helping to rebuild the church—it was burnt down—things got a little better.

Columbus is doing just fine, growing like a weed. His mouth goes continually. Doesn't seem possible he'll be four come this fall. He truly idolizes his Pa and he sure enough is the spitting image of him. But much more talkative! You know Keith never has been known for his lengthy conversations. Speaking of Keith, he's in Raleigh right now and poor little Columbus is missing him terribly. But we're expecting he'll be home soon …

Elizabeth's hand dropped to her lap. She paused, pulled her lace handkerchief from the sleeve of her dress and wiped at her eyes. After all these years, it was unnerving how Malinda's naïveté could still invoke such remorse within her. Was it truly her fault that her daughter had grown to womanhood wearing blinders? If she had been more firm with her when she was a child, not spoiled her so … would she have—*Oh God! Malinda open your eyes! Even in a letter you won't face the truth! Is it me you are trying to deceive, or yourself?*

Elizabeth wiped her nose and tucked the handkerchief back in her sleeve. She picked up the pages and continued to read:

Oh, yes, one thing I forgot to mention in my last letter. I met Uncle John. Twice to be exact. He was kind to me when I had a problem with my shoulder, and when Keith had some trouble with his eye he fixed him up real well.

One bad thing. My pinto stepped in a groundhog hole and broke his leg. I had to shoot him and it nearly broke my heart. When I think of all the miles we rode together, over all types of rocky terrain, only to have him die in his own yard. It's sad.

I've been thinking about taking a little vacation, and I was planning on maybe heading up toward Louisville, so I was wondering if it would be convenient for us to maybe stop by and pay you a small visit? I'd like very much to meet Uncle Samuel and his wife, and I so ache to see you and Jacob.

Well, that's all I have to write about. Oh yes, I must add, that if you should see some of those made up stories in the newspapers about Keith, just disregard them. They've gotten just about everything wrong and what did have an element of truth, got twisted.

I love you Ma, and I miss you, and please give Jacob a big kiss for me, and keep one for yourself.

Your loving daughter, Malinda

Elizabeth folded the letter and slipped it back into its envelope. When she again opened the drawer of the writing desk, her fingers skimmed lightly over the small stack of clippings from the *Louisville Courier*, all bearing Keith's photograph. The headline of the one on top read:

Infamous Outlaw Keith Blalock Accused of
Murdering Prominent North Carolina Citizen

The article went on to tell how Keith had lain in wait for John Boyd, a man he suspected of being instrumental in the death of his stepfather, and shot Boyd dead in the middle of the street in broad daylight.

The headline in the next clipping proclaimed:

Blalock Trial Set for Early May

The third read:

Keith Blalock Found Guilty of Murder

And the last told what appeared to be the final chapter:

Blalock Sentenced to Hang June 24

And on June 2nd Malinda writes about Keith coming home soon! Perhaps she's lost her mind. Can there be any other explanation? Elizabeth paused for a long moment before her gnarled hand pulled a sheet of paper from the drawer, dipped the pen into the ink well and began to write:

Malinda,

I am in receipt of your letters. All here is well. It seems impossible that it has been more than a year since the end of the war. We are beginning to settle down some. Finally.

I am quite comfortable here. Samuel and his wife, Louise, have been very gracious to both Jacob and me.

I am pleased to know that you and Columbus are doing well, but if you should write again please do not include any mention of your husband. Yes, I do read the newspapers, but my eyes, unlike yours, are open to the truth. You write as though he is away on a business trip and will be home in a few days. He is in prison and sentenced to hang for murdering John Boyd. It is my continual prayer that you will one day wake up and face facts. As for coming for a visit, that is inadvisable for a number of reasons. One, I have responsibilities here which cannot go unfulfilled, and Two, Louise is not in good health. You mentioned my brother John. We have learned that he is alive, survived having three horses shot out from under him, but lost a leg. I find it difficult, however, to forgive him for the suffering Jacob and I endured during our trip from Virginia to Louisville. Surely, he must have known how hazardous it would be. But God has a ledger. John will pay for his sins, as will all those who have caused suffering to others, will ultimately pay.

Ma

Elizabeth was blotting her letter when a knock sounded at the door. She quickly slipped the letters and clippings back into the desk drawer before calling, "Yes, come in."

"Elizabeth, dear, I hope I'm not disturbing you." Samuel stood on the threshold shuffling his feet like a schoolboy.

Elizabeth noted his nervousness and immediately tensed. "Not at all, Samuel," she said, "I was just going over some correspondence—"

"Am I wrong in assuming it's from Malinda?"

Elizabeth raised her eyebrows.

"When the post arrived yesterday I saw a North Carolina postmark, and I assumed it was from Malinda."

"Yes, someone at your shop gave her this address."

"That someone was me, Elizabeth." Still shuffling his feet. "I know how distasteful it is for you to discuss your family, but—"

"Is something wrong, Samuel?"

"May I sit down?"

"Of course." Elizabeth gestured to the Sheraton wing chair. "Whatever has happened? You're as pale as a ghost."

"Elizabeth, I see no reason to beat around the bush about this. I have news of Keith that you should know about."

"You can save your breath, Samuel. I know that he murdered a man and he's going to hang for it. And I'm not the least bit surprised."

"Keith's been granted a pardon."

Elizabeth's eyelids fluttered and her grip on the edge of the writing table tightened. "I'm not sure I understood you clearly."

"Governor Holden, the Provisional Governor of North Carolina, granted Keith a pardon. It's in today's paper. I assumed you knew about his arrest, it would be hard not to know since it seems to be on everyone's lips."

"But how could he be pardoned? On what grounds?"

"On the grounds that there is reasonable cause to presume he acted in self defense," Samuel said gently. "Evidently, an eyewitness belatedly came forward and stated that Boyd struck the first blow, attacking Keith with his walking cane. A scuffle ensued and Keith's gun discharged. It's all in today's newspaper. Personally, I suspect the true reason for the pardon is due to Keith's military service. He did exhibit bravery on the part of the Union during the war."

"Bravery!" Elizabeth scoffed. "Keith Blalock is nothing more than a bully, a scoundrel, and a murderer. The fact that he wore a uniform doesn't change that. It only gave him license."

The color, which had drained from Samuel's face, began returning. "But—"

"You're right, of course, I have known about it all along. When he was found guilty and sentenced to hang, I had actually begun to hope that at last my daughter would be free. And now—" Elizabeth turned her head away when she felt her eyes filling with tears. What was happening to her in her old age, anyway? All this damned blubbering!

"Louise and I were discussing the situation, and we thought that perhaps if Malinda would come for a visit the two of you might be able to—"

"I appreciate your thoughtfulness in trying to warn me of any unpleasantness." Elizabeth rose and moved toward the casement window, pulled back the curtain and gazed out at the wet street. The summer shower was abating and two small boys were taking advantage of the puddles by jumping up and down in them, squealing joyously. "I don't really feel I'm up to a visit from Malinda, just now." Elizabeth lifted her chin and when she turned from the window, her face was as gray as the sky. "Naturally, I'm not in any position to dictate who you should or should not invite into your home, but as for myself, I have no interest in seeing my daughter at this time. She has chosen a way of life that I am not in agreement with."

Samuel rose with a heavy sigh. "Bitterness does not become you, Elizabeth," he said sadly, making his way toward the door.

"No, I suppose not. But neither does pain and humiliation, and I've had enough of that for one lifetime. I'll not open myself up to more."

After Samuel had gone, Elizabeth opened the drawer of the writing desk and withdrew the letter she had penned to Malinda. Slowly and deliberately she tore it into tiny pieces and dropped it into the wastebasket.

* * *

Malinda was seated at the long pine table, a sheet of paper before her. She stared at the blank page for several minutes, then placed the plume back in the inkwell. What good would another letter do? There had been no answer to the others. And what more was there to say that hadn't been said before, other than that she was pregnant and the baby was due in late November? She hadn't mentioned it previously because she feared Ma might take her pregnancy as an excuse for her not to travel. But, on the other hand could the news sway her in the other direction?

Across the room, Keith was sitting in the rocker, his long legs stretched out before him, boots resting on the milk stool she'd padded with burlap and covered with bright calico to match the window curtain. He was staring up at the ceiling, the smoke from a long stemmed pipe he'd picked up in Raleigh, wafting around his head.

Malinda was finding it hard to believe he was as relaxed as he tried to appear. The last weeks had been so filled with turmoil there had been times when she'd feared they would both split wide open. The ordeal of the trial had taken its toll. Keith had been vilified unmercifully both by the prosecutor and the newspapers. Painted as a ruthless killer.

Seated in the courtroom with Columbus at her side she'd listened to the accusations being hurled at him and her spirit rose in defense. It was the war that made Keith a killer. Couldn't they see that? If he couldn't stop killing it was because of the war! Before he went in the army he was a scrapper, a hot head maybe, but not a killer. The irony was if he'd shot Boyd while he was wearing a uniform it would have been justified, out of uniform it wasn't.

The day they'd found him guilty and sentence was pronounced, the familiar numbness had settled in again around Malinda's heart. Her brain recognized that her husband had been sentenced to hang, but she couldn't feel it. The killing was over. Jesse, the next on Keith's list, had been saved. Now it was Keith's turn. She'd always known it would happen one day. But oh, not like this! Keith was a warrior, he deserved to die in battle, not hanging from a gallows.

He had stood stoic before the judge as the sentence was read. He hadn't shown the slightest sign of fear. But then, she'd never seen fear in him. Pain. Anger. But never fear. Oh how she envied that. She lived in fear. She breathed it. But never so for Keith.

She had been at home when McCaleb brought her the news of Keith's pardon. In still another of the incomprehensible twists of fate, it was McCaleb who had stood by Keith, testified on his behalf, and loaned Malinda a horse to ride so she could travel to Raleigh for the trial. Now, six weeks later she was still finding it hard to believe the governor had intervened. Why? His reasons for doing so remained a mystery.

"What are you doing?" Keith lowered the pipe and sent her a curious look.

"I was intending to write a letter," she said wearily, rubbing at her lower back, "but I couldn't think of anything to say."

"I guess I don't have to ask who it's to." He studied her a moment. "Why don't you come over here, Sweetheart, and I'll give your back a rub. You look tired."

Heartened by the sudden show of concern, Malinda put her hands on the table and pushed herself to a standing position. As she walked across the room, she held her back with both hands, then dropped heavily onto the stool as Keith moved his feet to give her room. "I suppose I am a little tired," she admitted.

Keith leaned forward, positioning his hands on the place where her waist used to be, then moving them gently toward her spine. "Tell me if I press too hard."

"Ummmm."

"Why do you waste time writing to her? You must know by now she isn't going to answer."

"She may. When the spirit moves her. Besides, how can I be sure she even gets my letters?"

"She gets 'em, all right." His hands moved upward toward her shoulders.

"I miss her. And Jacob. Do you realize my little brother is growing up and I wouldn't recognize him if I fell over him?"

Keith leaned forward and kissed her ear. "You're prettier when you're pregnant, you know. There's something in your face. As if you're holding a secret."

"One look at my belly and it's no secret anymore," she tittered. "I will say one thing though, not having to bear our child in a drafty old shack with cannons booming all around makes things a lot easier."

"I realize how hard that must have been for you. But ..."

"But?"

"Don't you ever miss it, Malinda?"

She turned and shot him a glance over her shoulder. "Miss what, for heaven sakes?"

"The excitement."

"Not the tiniest bit."

"I do."

"I know you do." Her body stiffened. "It's written in your face. Dear Lord, how can you even talk this way after what we've just been through—the trial and all?"

"I'm a man who needs a cause, Malinda. I can't just farm and—"

"A cause?"

"There's got to be a meaning to life. A reason for living."

Malinda heaved herself up from the stool. "And your family isn't enough? Is that what I'm hearing?"

He looked up at her pleadingly. "I think you know that's not what I'm saying. But I wish to God you'd try to understand. I've got to be doing something. I miss—"

"You miss being Robin Hood," she said disparagingly, lumbering back to the table.

His lips tightened, but he slowly nodded his head. "Maybe that's it. I miss helping people."

"Oh, my God, Keith, is that what you think we did? Helped people?"

He reached out to her, palms turned upward like a beggar. "Malinda, we did help people. We rescued men from the Rebels. We brought food to Unionists who would have otherwise starved."

"That's true! And the people we took that food from *did* starve!"

"But they were on the wrong side! They were trying to make other people their slaves!"

"Oh really? Well how about the Pattersons? They never had any slaves. All they had was a house full of kids who needed food as much as any Unionist child ever did. They had seven kids and they all starved!"

"Are you telling me that you didn't believe in what we were doing back then?"

"*Believe in it*? You've got to be joking!"

Keith stood up. "Why did you do it then? Why did you ride beside me and—"

Malinda's face twisted in pain. "Because it was the only way I could be with you. And that was all that mattered, being at your side. I wanted to be there when you got killed. And I was terrified you would be."

There was a hollow look on Keith's face, but he gave no reply. Only a tired shrug.

"I thought you knew that." Her voice was scarcely more than a whisper.

"Yes," he said softly. "I suppose I did."

Malinda looked toward the open door. Late afternoon sunlight was trembling through the grape arbor and dappling the walkway beneath. She raised her chin. "Would you like some cold tea? I found a bit of mint in the wood—"

"I'm concerned about money, Malinda, what with another youngin to feed and all."

"Youngins don't eat much. Not at first anyway. And I'll be able to nurse this one longer because I'm better nourished myself." She felt relieved they had found safe ground.

"I've figured out a way I can maybe make some money. When I was up in Raleigh last week, Will mentioned something that sort of appeals to me."

"Will?"

"Will Holden."

"You call the governor, *Will?*"

"Why not? It's his name."

"Keith, excuse me for asking, but how come you are on first names with the governor?"

"Because he likes me. After all, he saved my neck." He took another hard pull on the long stemmed pipe. "As a matter of fact he gave me this." He removed the pipe from his mouth and studied it.

"The *governor* gave you that pipe?"

"That's right."

"Why, for heaven sake? And you told me you got it in Raleigh."

"I did get it in Raleigh. In the governor's office. In Raleigh."

Malinda picked up the sheet of paper, plume and inkwell and set them back on the shelf. Then she again sat down on the wooden bench at the table. She could feel herself growing angry and wasn't sure why.

"Will was saying how he needs some good men, men he can trust, to be on his side."

"He scarcely knows you," Malinda scowled. "There's something about this whole thing I don't understand, and for some reason you're not telling me the whole truth. Frankly, I think I have a right to know."

"What is it you want to know, Malinda?"

"Why did the governor grant you a pardon? And why all of a sudden does he have such undying trust in you?"

"He knows I was framed in the Boyd case—"

"*FRAMED?*"

A sardonic smile crossed Keith's face. "Well, let's say he knows there were people on that jury who wanted to see me hang whether I did it or not. Holden has a similar problem. There are people in this state who are not happy about President Johnson appointing him provisional governor. He's got ideas on how to put North Carolina back on her feet, but he needs people in office at the local level who'll support him. And if I agree to do that I'd be getting a salary, and we sure enough can use the money. I'll still have plenty of time to take care of things around here."

Malinda looked at him helplessly. "If you agree to do what? I don't understand what you're saying. What's this about holding office?"

"The governor wants me to run for County Sheriff."

Before she could stem it, laughter bubbled up and Malinda rolled her head back and cackled. "The governor wants *you* to run for Sheriff of Caldwell County?"

"I don't think it's a laughing matter, and if that's the way you're going to take it, then I won't be discussing it with you again. I expected you to stand behind your husband. To support me. Evidently, that's too much to ask!" Keith strode through the door and slammed it shut behind him for emphasis.

Malinda stared at the closed door. She didn't know if she was going to laugh or cry. Evidently it's too much to ask that you stand by your husband? Where the hell did he think I was during the war? "That man's arrogance knows no limits!" She hurled the words into the empty room. Maybe the anguish of the trial and coming so close to hanging had really unsettled his mind. One thing seemed certain. He was hell bent on getting himself shot. Or more likely, hell bent on having an excuse for shooting somebody else! And who in the name of God would vote for Keith Blalock for Sheriff of Caldwell County?

CHAPTER 28

William Woods Holden was a man on a political tightrope. He had first been a Whig, then during his twenty-five year reign as editor of *The Raleigh Standard*, he had become a prominent leader of the Democratic Party in North Carolina. During the war, however, in a move, which proved to be politically prudent at the time, he switched allegiance to the Republicans and worked tirelessly as a peacemaker, gaining the reputation of being a man with strong sympathies for the Union cause.

When Andrew Johnson, a native of Raleigh, became president he began looking for men to serve under him who would support his, and his predecessor's, goal of guiding the seceded states back into the Union. With this thought in mind, on May 29, 1865, the new president appointed flush-faced, corpulent, William W. Holden to the post of provisional governor of the State of North Carolina.

It then became Holden's turn to begin looking for men who would help him bring these goals to fruition, and he needed people at the local level to do it. Almost immediately his search produced the name of Keith Blalock.

Keith was a likely candidate for a number of reasons. He was undeniably loyal to the Union, and a man apparently fearless in the face of danger. As Holden well knew, the political arena was not one for the weak-hearted, and apparently adversity did not deter Keith Blalock. His conduct during his murder trial spoke clearly of his ability to stand up to extreme emotional pressure. He had remained unflappable in the face of the punishing attack waged on him by the prosecutor and by Edward J. Hale, editor of the *Fayetteville Observer.* Hale called for Keith's blood, and even drudged up his illegitimate past. The attack automatically placed Keith in Holden's court. Hale and Holden had been bitter enemies for years and the war between them was anything but private. Both had unscrupulously used the printed page to malign the other.

When Keith's name was offered as a possible candidate for local office, the governor, already familiar with Keith's reputation and military background, agreed he would be an asset in obtaining their goals. The only problem being, he was currently awaiting his appointment with the gallows for the murder of that turncoat John Boyd. This, however, was a simple enough problem for a governor to handle.

Once the pardon had been signed, Holden invited Keith to his office for a private conference and was pleased with what he saw. Apart from Keith's physical appearance, which he found impressive, roguishly enhanced by the pirate patch over his eye, he was delighted to learn he possessed the razor sharp mind of a strategist. Although he was a mountain man, naïve in some respects, and overly simplistic in his views, his dominant personality and apparent fearlessness tipped the scales heavily in favor of bringing him under Holden's mantle.

The governor was also impressed with Keith's glowing reports of Colonel George W. Kirk, and filed Kirk's name away for future reference should an educated military mind be required—which he intuitively knew was inevitable.

Attempts to bring North Carolina back into the Union were not the only things pressing on Holden's mind. The very day he was appointed provisional governor he began planning for the day when he would become the state's *elected* top official. And he would need grassroots support to accomplish it.

* * *

Summer had burned itself out. Malinda opened the door to the pungent scent of autumn, inhaling it hungrily. Nature's last hurrah before the big sleep. Yet, there were times when she still expected to be greeted by the acrid smell of gun powder when she opened a door. How long, she wondered, before you could put the past behind; lock it away so tightly it could no longer haunt you? Evidently, eighteen months wasn't long enough.

She rested her back against the door frame, observing Keith as he collected the last harvest from their scraggly garden. It sure hadn't produced much. Next year would be better. But she needed its fruits this year to feed the coming child.

A lavender scented tress swirled across her cheek. She pulled the comb from her hair setting it free to the caress of the wind. She'd gained far less with this pregnancy than she had with Columbus, which surprised her since their living conditions were certainly better, and there was no longer the stress of the war. But then, other stresses had come to take their place.

Her ear picked up the sound of an approaching rider and she saw that Keith had heard it, too. She watched him lay the harvesting basket aside and head out toward the road.

A messenger pounded round the bend, saw Keith and reined in his mount. He leaned down and handed Keith an envelope, spoke a few words Malinda couldn't hear and galloped back the way he'd come.

Malinda felt an urgency to see the letter, dimly hoping it might be from Ma, but when she saw Keith open it she knew it wasn't for her. Another small disappointment to be tucked away.

Keith read the single page quickly, glanced her way, then stuffed it into the pocket of his blue overalls, picked up the basket, and headed up the hill toward her. When he was within hearing distance he called, "Gotta go to Raleigh. The governor wants to see me."

A tug of discontent. The unborn gave a gentle nudge. "What's happened? What does he want to see you about?"

"He doesn't say. Just says, a matter of utmost importance." He was grinning as he took off his hat and brushed past her. "You look good with your hair down."

"The breeze feels wonderful. I'll have to pin it up again though; your son thinks it's made for him to swing on. He'll have me bald if I'm not careful."

"I'll wash up before I start packing."

"How long will you be gone?"

"Can't say since I don't know what it's about. But I've got a hunch he wants to know how the race for sheriff is going. Can't think of any other reason why he'd want to see me." He began unbuttoning his shirt.

"What are you going to tell him?"

"Not much I can tell him before the votes are in."

Malinda twisted her hair into a long strand and secured it with the comb before hauling the knapsack from the bottom of the cupboard. "So you're still thinking you have a chance to win? I mean ..."

An exaggerated shrug. "Well dang it, I've been going around to the right places and saying the right things. Things I feel ought to be said. I think we should become a state again as soon as possible, and I think we ought to put aside the reasons for the war and get on with living. And I think we need a new jail. Now I can't see there's much in that for folks to find fault with. And to tell the truth I don't give a damn if they like what I'm saying or not! If I'd been *appointed* sheriff, that would be one thing; there isn't any doubt about my being able to do the job, but this going around begging for votes from people I don't respect or hardly even know, galls me no end."

"I'm sure it's not easy on the pride." Malinda winced as she straightened.

"Pride's got nothing to do with it." Keith looked at her sharply. "Are you okay?"

She gave him a look of mild exasperation. "I'm about ready to have your baby. But other than that, I'm okay."

"Are you troubled about me going? I sure as hell am not looking forward to it, I can tell you. It'll still be hot as a poker in Raleigh. The train's running again, maybe I should take it. I could be back sooner."

"And where are we going to get the money for the fare?" she said irritably. "All we have in this world is what we got from selling that lawyer from Lenoir the best six acres of your Pa's land." Malinda was still bristling at the thought of how they'd been hoodwinked. Although she'd blamed Keith, the truth was the man was a smooth talker and he'd taken her in, too. "And you can tell your friend *Will* for me, I don't think it's very considerate of him to call you away just when I'm about to birth our child."

"I doubt he knows it."

"Well, maybe you should have told him!"

Keith ran his fingers through his hair. "To tell the truth, Malinda, it wasn't a subject that came up. My meetings with the governor have been to discuss business. As a matter of fact the only time he mentioned you was to ask if I was happily married."

Malinda kept her gaze directed on the knapsack. "What kind of business? And what did you tell him about … about our marriage?"

"The business was politics. He wanted to talk about what's going on in the state at the local level. As for the other, I told him I'm happily married. What else would I tell him?"

"I was just wondering, that's all."

"Sweetheart!" He wrapped her to him in a giant bear hug. "I know when a woman is expecting a youngin she can get some crazy ideas, but that's one of your craziest."

Her voice was muffled against his flannel shirt and she was grateful he couldn't see how her chin was quivering. She felt bloated and unattractive and he hadn't touched her in over three weeks. "You never tell me how you feel," she said softly.

"I'm not a man who sweet talks much, Malinda. You should know that about me by now."

Her jaw tightened as she raised her head and looked up at him. "I guess I don't say it much either, do I?"

He bent and kissed the tip of her nose. "Well, then, let's say it together. One … two … three …"

"I love you," they chorused, then both erupted into a spasm of giggles.

* * *

Governor Holden, born scathingly poor in a log cabin outside Hillsboro, had pulled himself up by the proverbial bootstraps. He'd read the right books, found the right mentors, and learned to adapt the gracious, unhurried manners of a Southern gentleman. But Holden's nature was the abrupt, pragmatic approach of a Northerner. He did not enjoy mincing words—which was why he liked doing business with Keith Blalock. They understood each other.

"Keith, there's something leaking out of Tennessee that smells, and I don't like it. Right now it's not a threat to North Carolina, but I've got a sixth sense about this kind of thing, and given time it could be big trouble."

"I guess I don't understand what you're—"

"No. Of course you don't. Few people are even aware of the problem. That's why I want it cut down before it has a chance to grow. I recall you telling me about this man Kirk. I'd already heard of him of course, he has quite a reputation, but you told me some things that makes me think the two of you working as a team are the men for this job."

Kirk and me together again? This was almost too much to hope for! But still, Keith was puzzled by Holden's remarks.

The governor read his expression and smiled. "There's a new organization that took root in Pulaski, Tennessee. They're calling themselves by a variety of names, I suppose the loudest one is the Ku Klux Klan, named after some Greek word meaning 'circle', or something like that. Well, that circle seems to be spreading. It's overlapping into our state. Have you heard about it?"

Keith shook his head.

"They're a bunch of disgruntled Rebs who've decided to dress up in bed sheets and cover their faces with masks and go out and frighten the Neggres. In some instances they've done more than frighten them; they've hung 'em. The timing couldn't be worse. I'm in the process of putting together an organization we're calling The Union League, which is made up almost entirely of Neggres. These people are going to be voting and we need them on our side."

"Yes Sir, but there aren't that many niggers-er-Neggres in my district."

"I'm not speaking of your campaign for sheriff, Keith, I'm talking at a state level now. These Neggre haters from across the state line are infringing on our territory and I want it stopped before it has a chance to grow and scarce *our* Neggres out of voting. Do you follow me?"

"Yes Sir, I do."

"Now, what I need is someone with the skills to investigate what this Klan thing is all about, whether it has any kind of backing, or if it's just a case of half-assed malcontents with too much time on their hands. I want a report on who's behind it, and what can be done to either appease these folks or run them back into the hole they crawled out of."

The governor leaned forward over the desk, his pudgy fingers wrapping themselves about each other. "I'm thinking about you for the first part. The investigating. I know mountain people have a way of finding out what's going on. You certainly proved to be a master at that during the war. I'm not suggesting you personally infiltrate this group, that wouldn't be possible because you're too well known, but I want you to head it up. Get men to scout it out for you, then you report back to me what's going on. Naturally, you'll be compensated. Will you take on this assignment?"

"Of course," Keith blurted, dollar signs dancing in his head along with the names of half a dozen men who could do the scouting. Naturally, there was no reason to say so, but he would have taken on this assignment for nothing just to please this man who had saved his neck from being stretched. He believed in paying his debts, and actually that was the only reason he'd agreed to run for Sheriff of Caldwell County. To please Holden.

As the governor continued outlining his plans, Keith's mind raced. He was having some inner doubts. Was Holden making too much out of nothing? More than likely this was the same group Tom Hawkins had told him about, the bunch calling themselves The Knights of the White Camellia. The way Tom had explained it, these guys were nothing more than ignorant loafers who'd gotten hold of too much moonshine and wanted to pretend every night was Halloween.

"If this group is well organized, and if their intent is as dangerous as I suspect it to be," the governor continued, "that's the point where I think the services of Colonel Kirk may become necessary." Holden pulled a folded, white handkerchief from his breast pocket and dabbed at his glistening forehead.

Keith was also experiencing discomfort from the heat and raw humidity, and a drummer boy seemed to have taken up residence at the base of his skull.

"Now what I envision is a secret militia similar to what I suspect these Klan people have. I'm betting that with your experience in mountain warfare, combined with Kirk's, the two of you will be able to show these misdirected folk the error of their ways without making a big ruckus about it. Changing the minds—or life expectancies—of some of the top people might be necessary. If you follow what I'm saying."

Keith could feel the color rising in his face and it wasn't from the heat or headache. *Working with the colonel again! A command position! Something a man could be proud of doing! No ass licking for votes!*

"I'll have to give some thought as to how we'll go about getting you compensated, this being a secret operation. But leave that part to me. I'll see to it that you and the men you bring in are duly taken care of financially. And Colonel Kirk, too, of course, should we need him."

"Yes, Sir." Keith cleared his throat. "Can you give me any information as to how and where these people have been operating? Any ideas about their leaders?"

The governor withdrew a rolled up scroll from the top drawer of his desk and handed it to Keith. "This is not to leave your sight at any time. I want you to sleep with it." Holden again folded his hands on the desktop. "The names of some of the organizers and their next in command are here in this paper. We don't know them all, but these are the ones we do know about. You can see why it's important that no other eyes see this report."

"Yes Sir."

"If after your investigation you feel a military type approach is required I'll leave it up to you to get in touch with Colonel Kirk. Any contact between the colonel and myself will of necessity be made through you. I'll expect a weekly written report from you regarding the status of your investigation." Holden rose, still dabbing at his forehead.

Keith tucked the scroll under his arm and accepted the sweaty, outstretched hand. "Thank you Governor for the confidence you've placed in me."

"Will. Remember, in private you can call me, Will."

"Yes, Will, and … thank you again."

"I'm sure my confidence in you is well placed." As Keith neared the door Holden added, apparently as an after thought. "By the way, how is your campaign for sheriff going?"

Keith paused. "I really can't say until the votes are in, which is the day after tomorrow, so I guess by the time I get back home we'll both know. You'll no doubt hear before I do."

"Keith, I don't want you to concern yourself too much if it doesn't come out as we'd hoped. At least you've made a name in the community."

Chuckling. "Actually Will, I already had a name in the community."

W. W. Holden grinned. "But this one is somewhat more respectable."

They both laughed.

By the time Keith left the building the headache felt as if it had taken root in his brain. Wincing, he lifted his hand to protect his eye as he stepped out into the late afternoon sunshine. The trees that bordered the mall leading to the building had come alive, bending and weaving like ribbons in a wind. The carriages passing in the street were riding on waves.

Nausea overcame him and he reached for one of the building's stone pillars for support; leaned against it. The coolness of the stone brought a slight sense of relief to his throbbing head. It will go away, he told himself firmly. Any minute now it will go away. Just like before.

A man and a woman entering the building stopped and stared at him. The man whispered something to his companion then approached Keith. "May I be of help to you, Sir? You appear to be ill." He had the rich, cultivated drawl of a city gentleman.

Keith tried unsuccessfully to focus on his benefactor. "I'll ... be all right in a minute."

"Would you care to sit down? There's a bench over there. Perhaps a brief rest, or something cool to drink?"

"Yes ... something to drink ..."

"There is a tavern in the next block, Sir. I'll send someone to fetch—"

Straightening. "No. No thank you, I can make it." Without looking back Keith staggered down the flight of stone steps, wove his way down the long mall beneath the dancing trees, and once outside the iron gate turned in the direction the man had indicated. If only he could get relief from the merciless sun. These damned plains were so blistering hot. Dear Lord how he longed for the gentle breezes of home. Home! He would have to rest before starting back. Wait for the coolness of evening.

He looked up at the words floating above the door: TAVERN. *Thank God!*

Inside the dim interior Keith was immediately grateful for the muted light, although his other senses were assailed by the stench of stale beer, sweating bodies, and the tinny sound of a banjo picking out *Oh, Susanna.*

Still uncertain on his feet, he headed across the sawdust-strewn floor toward the bar. He grabbed the brass rail for support as he tried to pull the round-faced bartender into focus.

"What y'all havin'?" The bartender slapped a damp bar towel over his shoulder as he stared at Keith suspiciously.

"Apple jack. No. Wait." Feeling for the leather money pouch in his pants pocket. "Got any blackstrap?" That would probably be cheaper.

"Glass or tankard?"

"Glass. Glass'll do."

"That'll be thirteen cents."

Keith pulled the leather pouch from his pocket, fumbled opening it and spilled its contents onto the bar: five one-dollar bills bearing the portrait of Salmon Chase, Secretary of Treasury; two quarter eagles; three silver dollars and a fifty-dollar gold piece. He offered the bartender one of the paper dollars.

"If it's all the same," the man said, "I'll take the silver."

Keith slid one of the silver dollars across the bar and began putting the remaining money back in the pouch. Paper money was probably being devalued again. He tried to remember how much paper he'd left at home. He'd taken more money than he needed to, just for spite. Malinda's remark about how they'd lost so much on the land deal had pissed him off. That damned lawyer had made a fool out of him and he sure didn't need her to remind him of it.

On the subject of Malinda, he wondered what she would have to say about this latest development? Probably wouldn't like it; she had no use for Kirk. She didn't seem much impressed about his relationship with the governor either. He took the scroll from under his arm and laid it on the bar. Women didn't understand about these things.

The first swallow burned all the way down. Keith bent his head, waiting for the fire to settle. When it finally did he took another long pull, emptying the glass. Whew! Well now, that was better! The bartender returned and placed three twenty-five cent pieces, two nickels and two pennies on the bar in front of him. Five minutes more and the locomotive inside Keith's head began slowing down. Finally, he was able to focus on his surroundings.

The place was half filled. There were maybe five other men standing at the bar and approximately half of the dozen or so tables were occupied. The walls were rough hewn wood and covered with pictures of women in varying degrees of undress. At the other end of the bar the pumpkin-faced bartender was talking with a customer who'd no doubt told him a funny story. The bottom half of the pumpkin opened, showing a row of scraggly teeth that for all the world resembled a Halloween jack-o'-lantern.

A mirror ran the entire length of the back bar and was footed by a variety of half filled bottles. Keith leaned forward, hands cupping his head.

"Ready for another?"

Without looking up he replied, "Yes, I'll have another."

"Sure you don't want a tankard?"

Then another softer voice answered. "I think that would be a fine idea."

Keith raised his head from his hands. The empty mirror was now filled by an unbelievably beautiful young woman with yellow hair out of which protruded a foot long red feather that would make any injun squirm with envy. Without looking at her directly, Keith watched her reflected image as she lightly touched his arm. Slowly, he turned to face her.

"You don't mind buying a thirsty girl a drink now do you, Handsome?" Her lips reminded him of a rose, curled and pink and damp with dew. Her tight fitting pink dress, fringed with black lace, hugged a body straight out of every man's fantasy. She leaned nearer, her delicious breast brushing against his chest as she put her other hand on his arm and squeezed ever so slightly. Her scent was sweet and made him think of night blooming flowers.

Unconsciously, Keith wet his lips. "I wouldn't want to see a lady go thirsty," he said gallantly. He had wanted to say "pretty lady" but hadn't summoned the courage. He glanced at the bartender. "Bring us a tankard."

"I like the way you said that," she purred.

"Said what?" His hand moved stealthy to his pocket holding the pouch. How much would a tankard cost, he wondered.

"Us." She looked up at him, tightening the pressure on his arm. "You know, kind of sounds like we belong together or somethin'."

The bartender put the tankard and another glass on the bar before him. "That'll be a dollar twenty-five."

Keith reached in his pocket for the pouch, picked through it and laid the coins on the bar. Then put the pouch back in his pocket and filled the glasses.

"You look kind of familiar," she said sweetly. "Do I know you from somewhere?" Lifting the glass to her dewy lips.

"I'm not from around here."

"Travelin' man?"

"Yes."

"Travelin' alone?"

"Yes."

"That seems a pity. Being alone, I mean." She was studying him intently. "I sure enough think I know you from somewhere."

"Don't think so."

"You wouldn't be one of them carpetbaggers, now would you? You don't talk like 'em."

Keith chuckled. "Nope. I'm sure enough no carpetbagger."

She let go of his arm, reached out and lightly fingered the scroll. "That looks important."

He smiled, picked up the scroll and stuffed it into his shirt pocket. "Just some business papers. Nothing important." The governor's voice whispered in his ear. "*Don't let this out of your sight.*"

"What do people call you ... when you're not alone."

My wife calls me Keith, he thought, but aloud he said, "Sam. People call me Sam." Why had he lied? Malinda's image twirled before him, for a moment overshadowing the girl's face. Then faded. The pain was gone along with the dizziness. But now there was another kind of dizziness. Giddy. Enjoyable. He lifted his glass, drained it and filled it again. "What do people call you ... when you're not alone."

"Rose. They call me Rose."

He looked down into the inviting, limpid eyes; so blue, a man could hardly tell them from a summer sky.

"That's a pretty name, Rose. It suits you."

"Thank you. Would you care to dance?" She rolled the blue eyes toward a small empty space in front of the boy picking the banjo.

"I'm not much for dancing."

Then suddenly he *was* dancing, and the room was spinning, and the music was filling his head ... then fading away ...

* * *

Keith stumbled on the threshold as he followed Rose into the room. The air was heavy with the smell of incense. The walls were painted a bright red. He couldn't remember how he'd gotten here. Where was here? There was a beaded lamp beside a moth-eaten chair, and an iron bed draped with a cover that made him think of the lace scarf Ma used to wear on Sundays.

Suddenly Rose was reaching up to him, her feather-like fingers touching his hair, offering her wet lips. He bent over her as her other hand reached for the immense hardness between his legs. There was a moment of exquisite anticipation, then a sudden crushing pain in the back of his head. The walls dipped. The room exploded. He slumped at the girl's feet, groaning; rolled onto his back and blinked up at the now solemn face of the jack-o'-lantern. He pawed the air for a moment then slipped into oblivion.

* * *

He awoke in an alleyway. Night was settling in. A drizzling rain was washing his face. He groped his way to his knees, reached for the iron fence beside him and staggered to his feet. The alley was empty. The dewy-lipped girl and the jack-o'-lantern were gone. He was weaving back and forth trying to find his balance. The clanging inside his head sounded like the loud supper bell Malinda rang to call him in from the field. Where in the hell was he? Why couldn't he remember what had happened? Using the iron pickets for support he began moving toward a gaslight at the end of the cobblestone alley. The last thing he remembered was ... the ... girl ... Rose. Yes, Rose. And a red room. The ... the jack-o'-lantern bartender ... He reached in his pocket. The leather money pouch was gone! And so was his Colt! Reality hit him in the stomach like a sucker punch and he doubled over. *MY GOD! Keith Blalock you ignorant son-of-a-bitch you've been robbed by a cheap whore and her fuckin' pimp! Jessusss KEYrist!* Then he remembered the scroll. He touched his shirt pocket. It was still there. *Thank God for that!*

Nearing the gaslight, he looked around. The iron fence bordered a graveyard. A sign at the corner read: City Cemetery. He peered through the fence. The cold gray slabs of stone, the tall crosses reaching toward heaven were mere shadowy images bathed by the rain. It was coming down harder now. He glanced up at the street sign: East Street. That was the street where he'd stabled his horse. He couldn't be too far from the tavern. He'd go back there and claim his money! Those cheap bastards didn't know who they were messing with! But wait a minute! Was he in any condition for a fight? He could barely stand. And he had no weapon. Think about this, his brain rattled. Get your head straight. A confrontation will attract attention. Maybe get back to the governor. Then what? Keith pondered his situation for several minutes. Bringing attention to what had happened could only work against him. The governor and maybe Malinda would find out! His stomach dropped to his boots. Much as he hated to admit it, this was a score that would have to be settled later. He would come back when he was in better shape. He knew the meaning of patience. They would still be here, robbing other suckers. His best course of action now was to get his horse and head for home. Thank God he'd paid for the stabling in advance. On the way back he could forage for food. Kind of a replay of the old days. The real problem was, what would he tell Malinda about the loss of the money? *Son-of-a-bitch what a shitting mess!*

He scarcely heard the crash of thunder, or saw the fingers of lightning slice across the sky. Nor did he feel the chill of the drenching rain, as dejected and repentant he plodded homeward, aching to be there, yet dreading to arrive.

* * *

By the time Keith reached Salisbury the newspapers were filled with his stunning defeat, gloating that the "Union Scoundrel" had been taught his lesson. But when he arrived home, that loss, as well as the loss of the money, seemed meaningless.

In his absence, Malinda had lost her fight to deliver a healthy baby. Their little girl lived less than an hour; tiny arms waving, gasping to find air her underdeveloped lungs could not process.

The labor had begun the night of Keith's departure and lasted until early morning. Malinda had delivered the child alone while Columbus slept in the loft overhead. At the cemetery, she stood at the graveside beside McCaleb, clutching her son's small hand as he struggled to understand his mother's tears. A neighbor, Leona Miller, who happened by, joined them two-thirds of the way through the final prayer.

After the parson limped away Malinda and McCaleb picked up shovels and covered the tiny wooden box with the fresh turned earth. "You're the lucky one," Malinda intoned, the words lilting as in a lullaby. "Lucky one, oh, lucky one … You're now in the arms of Jesus. Your Pa will be sorry he missed you … so … so sorry he missed you."

Then Malinda took Columbus's hand and walked back down the hill. Her boots touched the rocky, uneven earth, but her mind was floating. Off somewhere else … anywhere else.

☆

CHAPTER 29

By Christmas Malinda had regained her physical strength, but emotionally she was trapped behind a high wall. She had a vague awareness of what was going on around her, but no involvement. She was locked inside a dream. At times she sensed she was somewhere up around the ceiling, viewing everything from a different perspective. She could watch scenes being played out below; Keith coming in the door, Columbus playing before the fire, see herself going about household tasks, eating, even sleeping. She did not find this upsetting.

Since the day little Elizabeth had been laid to rest, Malinda had not wept, but at times she was aware of a tightness in her chest that weighed her down and blocked all but the barest of communication. "Supper's ready." ... "Time for bed, Columbus." And always the ready, unreasoned reply to any question ... "Yes, that's fine."

When Keith first returned from Raleigh she realized, from a distance, that he was trying to comfort her. But what was there to say? Words were meaningless. Life was meaningless. Keith's tears were meaningless. Why was he crying? It wasn't like Keith to cry. Oh, yes, the baby had died. At times she knew he was talking to her, but his voice was so far away, the effort required to hear him seemed too great—so she didn't bother.

As time went on, Keith didn't seem to be around very much. Off somewhere. Had he said where he was going? She couldn't remember. Whenever he did reappear he always seemed to have a strained look on his face.

Sometimes she saw her son's troubled eyes when he warily approached her for comfort, and although she wanted to reach out to him, the wall got in the way. The wall she couldn't climb. Didn't want to climb. She knew that beyond the wall was pain. And there was no place left inside her for pain. It was full up. She chuckled to herself as she imagined hanging a sign around her heart: Out of Order. Could anyone but her see it? she wondered.

Thoughts were random. Usually drifting back to childhood; Ma reading her stories before the fire, pouring over her slate trying to add or subtract the numbers Ma had written there, riding through the woods on Pa's shoulders looking for mushrooms.

Occasionally she heard a distant war drum, the thunder of cannon fire, the wail of a bugle. Sometimes she head the crackle of a burning field, smelled its biting odor; saw a woman rocking the body of a dead baby. But for the most part she moved in a world of nothingness.

"Malinda. Sweetheart. You can't go on like this. *We* can't go on like this." Keith's voice. "You've got to come back to me. *Please Malinda. TRY!*"

There were times when she considered it. But then her refuge in her hiding place was so comfortable. No cannon fire here. No bullets whizzing overhead. No dead babies. And it was all her own. No visitors allowed.

There were other times when she was conscious of McCaleb's presence; seated across the table from Keith. They spoke in hushed tones. Occasionally they would look at her, study her, then speak again in whispers she could not hear. Didn't *want* to hear.

At other times Colonel Kirk was there. Talking with Keith. Planning strategy. But why? Wasn't the war over? Maybe she'd only wanted it to be.

* * *

Then one day in early Spring Malinda awoke from her dream. She opened the cabin door and saw that the stubborn earth had produced a tiny, blue crocus. She stepped out into the sunshine, knelt beside it and touched it gently.

Behind her a faint, timid voice called, "Ma?"

Malinda turned and saw her child, eyes resembling those of a stray animal, uncertain if he would be kicked or fed.

"Yes, Baby, what is it?" she answered, opening her arms. Without hesitation Columbus ran to her, burying his face in her breasts.

"Columbus," Keith appeared in the open doorway. "Leave your Ma be now."

"It's all right, Keith," she said brightly. "He just wants a hug." Looking up at the sky. "It certainly is a beautiful morning, isn't it?"

The color drained from Keith's face. He moved toward her haltingly. "Malinda?"

Smiling. "Yes?"

"Are ... are you feeling better?"

"I feel fine."

"Play with me, Ma?" Columbus implored.

"Well, let's go see if we can find some toys. Or would you like me to tell you a story?" She took the child's hand and moving with a steady step, walked back into the cabin.

Keith sagged. Dropped to the chopping stump, put his elbows on his knees, face in his hands, and wept.

* * *

"It's like a resurrection." Keith spoke in lowered tones as McCaleb poured two glasses of cider and handed one to him. "She doesn't seem to remember much of what's happened over the last few months. It's like she walked back in the door after a long journey. I'm not a man who believes in miracles, but if I was, I'd sure call this one."

McCaleb nodded, his long hair, now totally white, falling forward as he hunched his shoulders over the glass. "I'm happy for you, Keith. And for Malinda." He covered his nephew's hand with his own. "Apparently she has been able to put the past to rest." He smiled. "And I guess we have, too. I'm thankful for that. There's not many of us Coffeys left anymore. Just Margaret and Reuben and you and me."

"My name's not Coffey, Uncle." Keith's senses jumped to alert.

"May as well be. You're as much a Coffey as the rest of us."

Keith struggled to mask the panic. My God! How much did McCaleb know? Did he know that in truth he *was* a Coffey? In spite of his efforts at control he could feel his face turning red with shame. He took a deep pull of the cider, wiped his mouth with his sleeve, and turned the conversation back to safer ground. "Uncle, if Malinda can heal—if she can come back from ..."

"Madness," McCaleb said gently.

"If Malinda can come back, then maybe Sally—"

"No, I think not." McCaleb leaned back in his chair. "Malinda is a stronger woman than Sally. My wife has always had a fragile nature. She's ... forgive me Lord ... but she's happier where she is. As she is. Somethin' happens to a woman when she loses a child. Somethin' we men can't understand. Sally's not comin' back. And I've accepted that as being God's will." He swept a tired hand over his eyes. "She spends her life with Jesus now, and that's what makes her happy."

"I almost feel guilty."

"Don't. You have no control over it. It was God's will that Malinda recover. He has other plans for Sally."

Keith finished his glass and stood up. "I admire your faith, McCaleb. There are times when I wish I had it."

"The Lord moves in mysterious ways, Keith."

"Will Sally know I've been here? Maybe I should go in the parlor and—"

McCaleb shook his head. "She won't know. She knows nothin' of what goes on around her."

The two men moved toward the door. "I'm going to be away again next week," Keith said. "Would you mind checking in on Malinda and Columbus like you did before?"

"You know I will." Slapping Keith fondly on the back. "I will say though I can't help wonderin' what you do on all these trips you take."

Keith shrugged. "Just taking care of some things for the governor. Little jobs here and there. Nothing important. He likes to get a report now and then as to what's happening up here in the mountains, so I go out and sniff around, and let him know." And with what he's paying me, he thought, I've almost been able to replace the money before Malinda goes looking for it. That was the one good thing that had come out of Malinda's illness. She'd never questioned him about what had happened in Raleigh. And he'd sure never volunteered information.

Six weeks ago he'd traveled back to Raleigh for another meeting with the governor, and afterward he'd paid a visit to the tavern in search of Rose and the jack-o'-lantern. He was disappointed to learn the jack-o'-lantern had been killed in a bar room brawl. Of course it didn't take too much figuring to understand why. Shortly after that Rose had moved on. Looking for another partner, Keith thought ruefully. It seemed this was one debt that wouldn't be paid. It galled him no end, but there was no sense in losing sleep over it. At least jack-o'-lantern had gotten his and with any luck Rose would get hers, too. He just wished he could be around to watch it happen.

* * *

Willy Jackson's pathetic moans were now subsiding into whimpers and occasional grunts. The light from the flaming cross cast macabre shadows across the circle of masked men. There were fifteen in all. Most of them stood with arms folded across their chests. Watching. Others fingered the clubs tucked into the ropes that were tied about their waists. Their work was done but their hands still itched for further action.

From the cabin on the hill the terrorized screams of their victim's wife still tore at the night. There were five more of their group guarding her. Keeping her out of the way. She'd watched, helpless, as they'd dragged her husband from the house and tied him to a tree, while her children, paralyzed by fear, clung to her skirts. She'd seen Willy lose consciousness after the beating with the bullwhip that had laid his back open to the bone, then watched him come back to full shrieking awareness when they poured the bubbling tar over his wounded body. It was then that Willy had pleaded with God to let him die.

"Get me them chicken feathers," the leader of the masked gang called. "This here chicken fucker ought to be wearin' the suit the devil made fer him when he sired him."

Another masked man handed the leader a bag of feathers while three others gathered around the writhing form gleefully dumping other bags of feathers onto the sticky, smoldering tar. In seconds all traces of humanity were lost. Willy resembled a huge gray chicken.

"Now cackle," the leader goaded. And when the response was only more whimpering, he took his club and poked Willy in the groin. "Cackle, you black bastard! Cackle or so help me I'll cut yer balls off and stick 'em down yer throat!"

"Cluck ... cluck ... cluck ..."

"Louder! Cackle louder!" Another sharp poke to the groin.

"CLUCK ... CLUCK ..."

"That's better! Now get on yer knees and crawl back up to that chicken coop y'all call a home."

The circle opened as Willy clawed his way to his hands and knees, struggling to move forward. The tar was beginning to harden. Movement was almost impossible. He placed one knee forward and collapsed.

"Get up you fuckin' black bastard!" the enraged leader screamed. "And let this be a lesson to ya. Don't ya never try registerin' to vote again. Ya hear me?"

A grunt.

A slap of the stick across the back. "And y'all tell them other black bastards what'll happen to 'em if they ever try actin' like a white man!" *WHACK! WHACK!*

"Jesse, that's enough!"

The leader whirled, nearly tripping over his long bed sheet. "You ass-hole! Don't be callin' nobody by name! What the shit's the matter with ya?"

"I'm sorry. But he's had enough. Yer gonna kill him."

"So what if I do? What's one more nigger?" Turning to the prone man he kicked him hard in the side. "Crawl, you bastard!" As he watched Willy's pitiful attempts to move, Jesse noticed that the flames on the cross had nearly burned themselves out. Regrettably, the party was over. He shifted his attention to the men in the circle and waved his arm. "All right boys, fun's over. Let's call it a night." He gave one last look at his victim, spit on the ground and as he reached for his horse's reins a shot rang out.

The men in bed sheets grappled for their horses. A flurry of bright gunfire sparked the night. Jesse's frightened horse reared, wrenched itself free of his grasp and galloped away after the fleeing riders.

Jesse dropped to the ground, rolling over and over until he positioned himself beside the crumpled Willy. Using his victim's body as a shield he pawed at the folds of the sheet in an effort to get to his gun. Those of his men who hadn't fled were taking cover and returning the fire. Who in the hell were these bastards? Where in the shit did *they* come from?

A rider headed for the wounded Willy, and Jesse opened fire hitting the man in the shoulder and knocking him from his horse. Jesse sprinted toward the fallen man's steed, grasped the reins and jumped into the saddle. He raced away into the blackness, bullets whizzing about his head, not knowing how many of his men were left behind.

* * *

It was morning before Willy regained consciousness. Keith bent over him, the scraps of hardened tar and feathers were piled on the floor on both sides of the cot. It had taken hours for Keith and Willy's wife, Mandy, to pull and chisel the solidified mass from his body, and when they did, much of Willy's burned skin came with it leaving a ghastly display of throbbing raw meat.

Now, on the other side of the cot, Mandy was gently bathing Willy's wounds with soothing tannin. The fact that Willy was still breathing was a source of amazement to Keith. And moments ago when he'd tried to mouth a few words, Keith could scarcely believe it. He had seen tortured bodies before, but this put Daniel Ellis to shame. "I'll get you some Unguentine," Keith said to Mandy. "It'll help with the healing."

"Thank you, Massa," she murmured. "I sho nuff don't know what I'da done wiffout y'alls help. Dem men near killed my Willy. Dat's what they done. Dey near killed 'im."

"They came close," Keith agreed. "I'm just sorry we didn't get here sooner. We didn't get word in time."

On the cot, Willy's lips were moving again and Keith bent nearer, straining to hear.

"Myyy chillllin'?"

"Dey's fine," Mandy answered, glancing toward the corner of the room where three small black faces, huddled together, stared back with varying degrees of fear.

Keith looked toward the open door. Kirk and Wade Hopkins were seated on the doorstone. Before them, on the ground, lay two bodies. One was Booth Wallace, a member of their own band. His shoulder wound wasn't serious, he would survive. The other man was not so fortunate. He was a Klan member, and the only prisoner taken alive. Two other Klansmen had been buried in the yard; the town drunk and his fourteen-year-old son.

Kirk and Hopkins had questioned their prisoner throughout the long night, and long before dawn streamed over the ridge he had told them everything they wanted to know.

Keith turned his attention back to Willy, placing his lips close to Willy's ear. The man wasn't likely to be conscious for long and he needed to get what information he could. It was a thin hope, but he had to try. "Willy," he said gently. "Did you recognize any of the men who hurt you? Do you know who any of them were?"

There was a along pause in which Keith thought Willy had again slipped into unconsciousness, but then the wounded man whispered, "Waatter."

Keith placed one hand beneath the pillow under Willy's head and held a tin cup of water to his lips. Willy managed a swallow. Then took a second sip before his head rolled to one side and Keith eased him back to a prone position.

"I know they were wearing masks, Willy," Keith continued, "but was there anything about any of them, a voice maybe, that you could recognize?"

Mandy leaned across the cot. "Dey come up so fass we neber got to see nothin.' Willy, he don't know nothin." 'Cept dey be devils, dat's all."

Keith understood the woman's fear. Even if she did know something she wasn't going to tell it. The same could very well be true of Willy. And who could blame them? But this gang of cutthroats was growing and Holden's hope of keeping the Klan out of North Carolina had been in vain. Even here in Caldwell County they were cropping up like desert flowers after a rain.

Willy's mouth trembled and his eyes opened a little wider. "Nnneeever seen day ffaces, bbut IIII heerd one cccalll nnnotherr ooonne, JJJesseee."

Keith straightened and ran his fingers through his hair, his tongue over dry lips. Could it be *his* Jesse? The thought brought no real surprise. He'd been tracking Jesse's movements for some time. He knew he was active in the Klan in Tennessee, his name had been near the top of the list on the scroll the governor had given him, which explained Jesse's prolonged absence from Caldwell County. But could he have come back to home ground? Keith also knew about Jesse's marriage to Wanda Lucas, a Tennessee mountain girl who came from a family of diehard Rebels.

Again Keith bent over the cot and put his lips next to Willy's ear. "Did you pick up anything else? Hear anything else?"

Willy shook his head feebly, and his tortured eyelids closed.

Keith straightened again and looked at Mandy. "We'll be leaving now, but I'll see you get some Unguentine for his burns. Be sure to give him plenty of water."

Keith walked to the doorway, breathed in the chill morning air, and looked down at the two bodies in the yard. Booth was wrapped in a blanket, another blanket pillowed his head. He appeared to be sleeping. The Klansman was stretched naked on the cold ground, his body bearing the scars of Kirk's information gathering—which was not too far removed from the information gathering technique of Daniel Ellis. The man was either unconscious or dead. "Colonel, I think we've done everything we can in here," Keith said.

Kirk peered up at him. "How is he?"

"He's alive. Barely. I promised his wife I'd get her some Unguentine. She's going to need some sweet oil, too. How's Booth?"

"He'll be okay." Kirk rose, dusted off his pants and stretched his arms high over his head. "We got some information from that one." He gestured with his head toward the hapless Klansman. "I'll tell you about it on the ride back." He turned to Hopkins. "Drag him off into the woods and shoot him. No need to bury him, the animals will take care of it."

* * *

The following day, seated at the table in his kitchen, Keith penned his report to Governor Holden. He was able to fill in some gaps that had been missing up to now. He wrote that through an informant they had confirmed what was earlier suspected. The man behind the Ku Klux Klan was ex-Confederate General Nathan Bedford Forrest. He called himself "The Grand Wizard." As they already knew, the intent of the organization was to stop freed slaves from voting, and also from working for pay.

What they hadn't known before was that the Klan was opposing all attempts by the seceded states to rejoin the Union, and they were working behind the political scene in North Carolina to see that it didn't happen. It was suspected they had infiltrated into high places. Perhaps even close to the governor's office. Once we get our hands on one of the top men we'll be able to supply you with names, Keith wrote determinedly, hoping in his heart that one of those men would be Jesse Moore.

Alamance and Caswell Counties, especially around Hillsboro, had been targeted as areas of greatest Klan concentration because of the high Negro population. Activities in the mountain counties, while gaining in momentum, were less intense than other areas, due to the smaller number of former slaves living there.

Keith made it a point to let the governor know that he and Kirk could handle the mountain region, and that a number of the malcontents had "disappeared"—he knew his message would be correctly interpreted. He then passed on Kirk's urgent request that stronger military type action be initiated in Alamance and Caswell Counties. A lot more men would need to be recruited, and Kirk was requesting a secret meeting, between himself, the governor, and Keith, at a time and place convenient to the governor, to discuss plans for containment.

Keith finished his report, stuffed it into an envelope and sealed it with candle wax. When he looked up he realized Malinda had stopped playing her dulcimer and was watching him intently.

Suddenly uncomfortable, he said, "You look as if you have something on your mind, Sweetheart."

"I was just thinking."

"About what?"

"You."

"What about me?"

"About something I remember you saying a while back."

"I guess you're going to have to be more specific."

She laid the dulcimer aside. "You said you're a man who needs a cause."

Keith shifted uncomfortably. "That's true, Malinda. I need something important to do with my life."

"And we've already determined that farming and raising a family isn't important enough."

"Don't put words in my mouth. And it seems to me we've had this little discussion before." He flipped the envelope across the table with his finger, needing to strike out at something. "You've got your home, and I *am* farming, so what more do you want of me?"

There was an almost imperceptible shake of her head. "They are *your* words, Keith."

"Oh, please, Malinda. I don't want to—"

"I'm pregnant again."

"Oh? Are you sure?"

"Very." Then added sadly, "I'm not sure you want another child."

"What makes you say that?"

Pushing the question aside. "Will you be staying home this time?"

Exasperated, he rose. "Malinda you know how bad I feel about being in Raleigh when Elizabeth was born and—"

"Died. Our baby died." She focused her gaze on the dulcimer, stroking the wood as if it were a child. "This new cause—whatever it is—has … how can I say it? Consumed you. When you're here, you're not really here. It's just like it was during the war. Except I'm not a part of it."

"Malinda—"

"You come back from these secret trips and there's blood on your clothing." She raised her eyes and looked at him steadily. "The killing's not over, and I don't think it ever will be. Keith, I know in my heart that something bad is going to happen."

He weighed her peace of mind against another lie and said. "Malinda, if you want to know what I'm doing, I'll be happy to tell you." Months before he'd concocted a story about his activities and it appeared this was the time to tell it, but she surprised him by saying …

"Please don't tell me. I don't want to know. And I don't think I want this child either."

He looked at her in astonishment.

"I'm afraid what happened to little Elizabeth will happen again. I don't know how Ma survived losing all those babies. I got a letter from her."

"You did? When?"

"While you were away."

"What did she have to say? Where is she?"

"Where we thought she was. In Louisville with Uncle Samuel. She says Jacob is growing like a weed and plays the dulcimer right well and knows all his letters and goes to a real school."

"Well, I'm glad to hear that, Malinda. I know it eases your mind." Keith ran his fingers through his hair, then carried the ink well and plume to the cupboard and put them away. Returning to the table he picked up his report to the governor and slipped it into his shirt pocket. "Malinda, after this youngin is born, and it *will* be born, and it'll be healthy—we'll see to that—then when you're back feeling good again, we can take a trip up to Louisville to visit your Ma and Jacob. Get reacquainted. That'll make you happy, now won't it Malinda?"

"I already wrote and told her I'd come after the baby is born."

Disbelieving. "Are you telling me you told your Ma you're pregnant before you told *me?*"

"You weren't here when I wrote the letter."

"Well couldn't you have waited? Doesn't seem right me being the last to know. If you're trying to rile me, Malinda, it's working real well."

"That wasn't my intention. I just thought we needed to talk. We haven't for awhile." She picked up a sock from the darning basket and focused her attention on it.

* * *

Later, after Keith had gone to bed, Malinda sat alone before the embers of the supper fire, pondering the events of the day. There hadn't seemed any reason to tell Keith anymore of what Ma had said in her letter. Hurtful things that would only tend to rile him more. She removed the letter from her apron pocket. Four years of waiting, and now this bitter disappointment. Slowly, she unfolded the page and read it for what must have been the tenth time.

Malinda,

It has taken me a long while to reach the decision to write to you, and it is only due to your Uncle Samuel's urging that I do so now. He would have me say that "All is forgiven and forgotten," but I cannot. It will never be.

However, you are still my child, and should you decide to come to Louisville, as you have so stated is your desire, your Uncle and his wife, Louise, will welcome you into their home. As will I.

I must make it clear that it is my opinion that your husband has destroyed your life, and no doubt the life of your son, as well. He has blood on his hands that will never be washed clean. As have you. What you did in the name of the Union were not acts of patriotism, they were acts of plunder and murder. You are not the girl I raised, but you are the one I spoiled so miserably, and for that I share responsibility for the deeds you have done. It is a burden I will carry to my grave. It is important for you to know that should you decide to come to Louisville, do NOT bring your husband. I will not receive him, nor do I permit his name to be spoken in my presence.

As for your brother, Jacob is thriving. He attends a real school, knows his letters and arithmetic very well, has mastered the dulcimer and is beginning on the pianoforte. He is a talented young boy, and I am very proud of him.

—Ma

Malinda's hand dropped into her lap as she stared listlessly into the fire. Well Ma, at least you have one child of whom you can be proud.

☆

CHAPTER 30

The night was endless for McCaleb. He lay rigid on his bed listening to his wife carry on her mad lament in the parlor; his eyes filling with tears. Some nights were worse than others. Some nights she merely sang a few hymns and fell asleep on the settee. But tonight had been laced with more lunacy than usual. Ravings about Satan's legions consuming the earth. He sometimes wondered if Sally's torment was because their sons had died, or because she needed an excuse to escape from reality. He knew that in the morning he would find the parlor strewn with plates of uneaten food, food they could ill afford to squander, food Sally insisted he prepare for Jesus.

He rose before daybreak and went downstairs to find her curled up on the rug before the burned out fire. Her thumb was in her mouth. At least in sleep she was peaceful. And he didn't have to look at those wild, staring eyes that brought such misery to his heart.

He set about clearing away the still filled plates, aware he was playing into her mad game by preparing and disposing of the food. So be it. He put whatever could be saved back in the cupboard and dumped the remainder into the bucket for the sow and stray cats. Next he made a fire and gently tucked the quilt up around Sally's shoulders as he bent to kiss her forehead. He knew she would sleep until noon. Then with grim determination he grabbed his hat from the peg and slipped quietly out of the house.

Standing on the doorstone of Keith's cabin McCaleb turned to watch the road. Glancing first to the left then to right. When Malinda opened the door the fragrant aroma of coffee escaped into the frosty morning air.

"Why McCaleb! What brings you out so early this fine morning? Come have some breakfast with us."

"No, thank you, Malinda. I have to get back to Sally. I … I just need to talk with Keith for a minute."

"He's out back collecting eggs."

He could tell from her expression that Malinda sensed trouble, but without another word he hurried through the house to the back door. What he had to say to Keith was not for Malinda's ears.

* * *

Keith was heading back from the barn when he saw McCaleb standing outside the back door waiting for him. "Good morning, Uncle. What brings you out so early?"

"We need to talk."

The urgency in McCaleb's voice sparked warning signals. Keith tensed as he set the basket of eggs on the doorstone. "What's happened?"

McCaleb shook his head. "Nothin' yet. But it's goin' to." He gestured for them to move away from the door. "I've got some news and it's best that Malinda not hear it. I thought I should tell—warn you."

Keith sauntered after him, stopping when they were a safe distance from the house. "Warn me, Uncle?"

"Saturday night. They're comin' for you Saturday night."

"They?"

"A gang of no goods. They call themselves the KKK or some such foolishness."

Keith grabbed for his hat as the wind tried to whip it from his head, adrenaline spinning through his veins. The Klan was coming for *HIM*? Were they really stupid enough to play right into his hands? But perhaps it wasn't stupidity. Perhaps it was arrogance. He made a Herculean effort to mask his excitement as he replied, "I thought the Klan only went after niggers."

"Never mind what color you are. If they've got somethin' against you that's enough of an excuse for them. These men are ornery, Keith. Not anybody to mess with."

"Yes, I've heard about their orneriness," Keith said dryly. "But tell me, how'd you find out about this Saturday night visit?"

"Never mind how I know. I just know."

"Reliable information is it?"

McCaleb averted his gaze and stared up at The Grandfather. "Well, I guess it's all right if I tell you. You know I'm not privy to Confederate gossip anymore, but I overheard talk down at the general store. I was in the back room hagglin' with Earl Eller over the price of some feed, and two of them were standin' on the other side of the curtain. I heard one of them say that The Brotherhood would be makin' a call on Blalock, Saturday night, and to pass the word because they wanted a good turnout. The Brotherhood is another name for this KKK bunch."

"Did anybody know you were there?" There was always the possibility of a set up.

"Nobody but Earl, and I don't think he heard it. He was rummagin' through some barrels over by the far wall. Hell, who knows, he may be one of 'em."

Keith let out a sigh. If the Klan was coming for him, it was a sure bet Jesse would be among 'em. Maybe even heading it up. Had the hourglass at last run dry? Had the day he'd longed for finally arrived? Jesse riding straight into his hands! It was almost too much to hope for.

Keith wet his lips as phantom images floated through his mind. His near drowning at the hands of Jesse and his brothers. Childhood years filled with taunts of "Bastard Blalock." The burning of his cabin. The raid that went wrong when Jesse shot out his eye ... And Pa. Dear God how much he wanted to get his hands on Jesse.

"I figured you'd want to get your family to safety," McCaleb said. "Maybe yourself as well."

Keith stared at him dumbly, then rolled his head back and howled. "You mean you thought I'd run? Uncle! How little you know me!"

"Keith, be reasonable. This ain't a fist fight. These men are armed. And you'll be outnumbered by maybe twenty to one. There's a lot of people around here who won't stand up to you face-to-face, but they sure as hell will shoot you in the back if they get the chance. Remember how you got pummeled in that election? You've made enemies Keith, and people have long memories. They've just been waitin' to get back at you. If you ain't thinkin' about yourself, then think of Malinda and Columbus."

Keith's eyes glinted. "You want me to run and let them burn my house down? Destroy everything I've worked so hard to rebuild? Not hardly!"

"What will you do?"

"First thing I'll do is thank you for the warning."

"Don't tell me you're goin' to fight 'em!"

"Did you expect I'd do otherwise?"

Sweat was glistening on McCaleb's forehead. "I'm warnin' you so you'll have a chance to get away. I'd hoped you wouldn't be so stubborn."

"Stubbornness has nothing to do with it, Uncle. This day has been a long time in coming."

McCaleb's hat went back on his head with a loud plop. "I'll stand with you. I won't leave you to handle this alone. But get Malinda and Columbus out of the—"

"Don't you worry about my family." He clasped McCaleb's shoulder. "I guess I understand what it took for you to tell me this, Uncle. I'm obliged. But I'm not going to let a God fearing man like you handle a gun for me."

McCaleb's eyes grew misty. "I'm not tryin' to second guess the Lord, but I reckon He wouldn't have allowed me to come over here, if He hadn't intended for me to be of some use."

"Let's go inside and get some breakfast." Keith started back toward the house. "I've got the last of the harvesting to do today and my bones are tired before I start. I need some nourishment." He winked at McCaleb. "Or maybe what I really need is a good nigger slave." He immediately saw that his stab at humor had fallen on deaf ears.

* * *

It had been a long time since McCaleb had had a meal that was prepared by a woman's hand and he was easily persuaded to stay for breakfast. Although Keith forced himself to remain calm and keep up his end of the casual conversation, his mind was speeding like a bullet. He could round up a half dozen men on short notice. Luckily Kirk was still in the area and he could bring in some of his men, too. McCaleb had said they wanted a good turnout. How many would that mean? Twenty-five? Thirty? Even if they were outnumbered, they would have the element of surprise, and from what he'd seen at Willy Jackson's place, they all high tailed it at the sound of the first gunshot. These weren't honest men willing to stand and fight, these were cowards hiding behind bed sheets. Keith was so happy he felt like dancing!

Malinda and Columbus would have to be sent off somewhere. His first thought was to use some excuse to get her over to McCaleb's—but she would hear the gunshots from there. It was best she didn't know about this until it was over. Good and over. Suddenly, he put down his fork and fixed her with his most compelling smile. "Sweetheart, I guess the time has come to tell you. I've got a surprise."

"You have?" Malinda looked across the table at him and returned the smile.

"Yes. That's why McCaleb's here." He shot a quick glance at McCaleb. "He's come to drive you to the train station in Morganton. You and Columbus are going to pay a visit to your Ma."

Malinda looked at him as if he'd lost his mind. "Wh ... what are you talking about?" she stammered.

Keith kept his smile in place. "There's an afternoon train out of Morganton and you and Columbus are going to be on it."

"I'm gonna ride on a train?" Columbus's face lit up like the Fourth of July.

"Yes, Son, you and your Ma are going to take a little trip and go visit your Grandma up in Louisville."

"Keith, for heaven's sakes, be reasonable. I can't just up and leave. I don't have anything packed—and ... and I thought we'd talked about going to Louisville after the baby is born."

McCaleb was having a hard time masking his astonishment.

"*I'm* not going," Keith said, still smiling. "This is a surprise for you and Columbus, and I'm sure your Ma won't lose any sleep over me not being there. Now today's Thursday. With any luck you should be in Louisville by Saturday afternoon."

"I have things I need to tend to," Malinda argued. "And besides, I—"

"Besides, nothing. I've been planning this ever since you told me you'd heard from your Ma. I can't believe you'll go spoiling my surprise by being ungrateful."

He read the look of wariness in Malinda's eye. "I'm not being ungrateful," she snapped. "I'm merely saying I can't get ready by this afternoon."

Keith shot a glance at McCaleb. "I've seen you pack for a six day trip in ten minutes, Malinda. Now Uncle has volunteered to drive you to the station. We've got it all planned. The governor's asked me to come to Raleigh for at least a week, so this is the perfect time for you to go."

"Oh can we Ma?" Columbus begged. "Can we please?"

Keith could see Malinda was weakening, but she offered her last volley. "I don't see how we can go unannounced."

"Nonsense! It isn't as if you're going to visit a stranger. This is your Ma. Didn't you say she invited you?"

"Well, yes. I guess you could say that."

"You can send her a telegram from Morganton to let her know you're on your way."

Columbus jumped down from his chair and rounded the table to his mother's side. Hugging her about the waist, he gazed up at her with pleading eyes. "I'll be a real good boy, Ma. Oh please can we go?"

Keith felt a burden lifting when he read her surrender. Now he could concentrate on laying his trap. The first hurdle was crossed. Things couldn't be working out better if he'd planned it this way. They could wipe out a whole band of these lunatics without making a big fuss about it. Just the way the governor wanted. Holden would be happy, Kirk would be happy, and by God, he would be *more* than happy! He could almost taste victory on his tongue. And my oh my, wasn't it sweet!

* * *

At the first hint of dawn someone in the seat just ahead of Malinda and Columbus opened the window for some much needed fresh air, but along with it came smoke, ashes, cinders, and a near freezing wind. Malinda took off her cape and draped it around Columbus as he lay sleeping with his head in her lap.

Her thoughts had gone back to her last train ride, that hellish one back from Kinston when they'd been released from the Rebel Army. Unfortunately, this one was only slightly more comfortable. Strange how long ago that all seemed. It could have happened in another lifetime. The conductor was weaving his way down the narrow aisle toward them and Malinda stopped him to ask the correct time. The spectacled old man removed a round watch from his vest pocket and said stiffly, "6:41." Then he slipped it back in his pocket and continued his way down the aisle.

Malinda was exhausted. The night ride through the mountains had been unnerving. She'd rolled in the unforgiving wooden seat at every sharp curve as the locomotive plunged headlong down its preordained path. Once the sun went down Columbus had quickly fallen asleep, wrung out from excitement and lulled by the motion of the swaying car. She bent over and lightly kissed his forehead.

She knew it wasn't only the rolling of the train that had kept her awake, it was worry. The moment McCaleb had arrived at their door, she'd known there was trouble brewing. Did Keith think she was such an utter fool she couldn't see through his lies? Why had she relented? Why had she given in so easy when she knew the whole idea of this trip was to get her out of the way? She probed deep inside herself. The answer was simple. Because she *wanted* to get away. She didn't want to be a part of whatever was going on. This was a new feeling, and somewhat frightening. In the past she'd always wanted to be with Keith in times of danger. And this whole thing, whatever it was, *reeked* of danger. Why didn't she want to be with him now? She gently stroked her son's hair. Because there were others who needed protecting ... her children.

Her thoughts rushed forward. What would be waiting for them at the end of this trip? Would Ma welcome them? Would Uncle Samuel and his wife? Would she find the city as exciting as she had always imagined it would be?

The first full day of travel passed uneventfully. The car was sometimes packed with passengers, and other times nearly empty, which made it far more comfortable. They ate the food Malinda had packed, sharing some with a little girl of about ten who was traveling alone and said she was hungry. To show her gratitude the little girl kept Columbus occupied most of the afternoon by lending him her slate and chalk to draw with. The train made frequent stops, and whenever there was enough time, they disembarked and walked along the platform to stretch their legs.

* * *

"McCaleb, I'll ask you one last time. Are you absolutely certain you want to be part of this?" Keith looked levelly at his uncle as a bitter afternoon wind whipped at his hair.

"Keith, I told you, I believe in my heart I am doin' the Lord's work. He wouldn't want me to stand idly by and be a witness to murder. And make no mistake about it, their intent *is* to kill you. From what I've heard they take their time about it, too."

"Nobody's going to kill me, Uncle. I have a plan."

"It had better be a good one. There'll be a gang of 'em, and with just the two of us to hold 'em off—besides, I've never shot a man before. I don't even know if I can."

"You won't have to, Uncle. I told you I wouldn't ask you to hold a gun. But there is another way you can help. Here, let's sit a spell while I explain what I want you to do."

* * *

By the time the train was slowing down for the stop in Lexington where they were to change trains for the final leg of their journey, Malinda had finished reading the last chapters of *A Tale of Two Cities.* Keith had given her the book the Christmas after little Elizabeth died, but she'd had no interest in reading then.

Columbus was growing restless, although trying his best to keep his promise to "be good." He'd struck up a friendship with a man a few seats ahead, who seemed to appreciate his company. Occasionally, the man would turn and offer Malinda a reassuring smile. Apparently, they were both enjoying themselves, and it was certainly a relief for her to have Columbus occupied.

She glanced at the empty seat across the aisle. The well dressed lady who'd gotten off at the last stop had left a copy of *Harper's Bazaar, A Repository of Fashion, Pleasure and Instruction.* There didn't seem to be any reason not to take a look, the owner had either forgotten it or left it behind on purpose. Malinda picked up the magazine and began thumbing the pages. There were pictures of ladies in bustled dresses and handsome gentlemen in bowler hats playing a game called croquet. Other ladies were pictured strolling beneath stiff lace umbrellas. Again wearing bustles. Evidently, bustles were all the rage. People really do live like that, she thought wistfully. They dress up nice and go to parties, and play games on beautiful lawns. And they probably eat off china plates and drink from silver goblets, too! She felt a strong tug of envy.

The most amazing thing in the pictures were the tiny pointed shoes peeping out beneath the beautiful dresses. She looked down at her own dark brown bodice with its pointed waist and the rust colored homespun skirt that just brushed the tips of her heavy, black boots. There wasn't one picture that resembled anything *she* was wearing. But then she found an advertisement of a lady dressed in a short cape with a hood attached that did look something like hers. The text referred to it as a burnouse. Well! At least she had a burnouse, even if she didn't own a bustle!

The Lexington station was bigger than anything Malinda could have imagined. And nosier. How was she ever going to find the train to Louisville amid all this confusion? Nervous, she moved with the crowd toward the station house, gripping her carpetbag in one hand and clutching Columbus's hand with the other.

"Ma, you're squeezing me," Columbus complained. "Don't hold so tight."

"I don't want to lose you. If we get separated here we'll never find each other again."

Inside the station house Malinda wound her way through the throng and headed for the ticket desk. The line was long and while they waited Columbus began picking his nose. "Don't do that!" Malinda chided. "That's not polite."

Columbus looked at her with genuine surprise, but quickly stuffed his hand in his pocket.

When it was at last their turn, Malinda leaned forward over the counter and asked the harried agent, "Where will I find the train for Louisville?"

"Track #2. Right out that door." He nodded brusquely to the right. "Runnin' late. Won't be here for another hour."

"Thank you."

Turning, she spied a large sign on the far side of the bustling station. It read: "Refreshment Saloon." That was a term she had become familiar with during the trip. As each mealtime rolled around passengers were jolted by the scream of the steam whistle and the sudden slowing of the train. Then as the car approached the station, the conductor would open the door and shout at the top of his lungs, "Meal stop. Fifteen minutes." From the window she could see a long counter on the platform with a sign reading: "Refreshment Saloon."

Before the train had even come to a full stop people were jumping onto the platform and jostling for priority. Then they would grab their prize and rush back onto the train to eat it. She was surprised so few people had thought enough to pack some food. However, they had now finished off the last of what she'd brought, and they were both suffering pangs of hunger. Surely, it wouldn't cost that much to get just a bite or two.

Malinda pressed through the milling throng and found a small table where she settled Columbus and cautioned him to guard the carpetbag. Then she made her way to the counter, purse clutched tightly in her hand.

"What's your pleasure, Miss?" The tall man behind the counter sported a small black mustache that looked like it had been painted on with shoe black, and he looked at Malinda with what Ma would have called, "an unholy look."

"I ... I'm not certain," she stammered, feeling her face redden. "Just a little something. For my boy and me."

"How about a couple of beef dodgers?"

"Yes, that's fine." Whatever that is, she thought. But asking would make her look even more like a country bumpkin.

"How about some cherry pie?"

"Well ... uh ... just one serving, please."

"Coffee?"

"Do you have milk?"

"All outta milk."

"Well, water then. Two cups please."

"Only have glasses," he gave her a mischievous wink and piled everything onto a small wooden tray then pushed it toward her across the counter. "That'll be three dollars, five."

Malinda dove into her purse, withdrew three silver dollars and a five cent piece and laid the coins on the counter. Then grabbing the tray with trembling hands she hurried back to Columbus, deciding that Kentucky seemed more like a foreign land than another state.

* * *

When McCaleb arrived at Keith's place everything was hushed except the wind. It was gaining in intensity and it appeared they were in for a storm. Would that deter the Klan's visit? Keith wondered. He certainly hoped it wouldn't!

As McCaleb strode across the yard his gaze darted back and forth from the barn, to the house, to the clump of wild rhododendron that had sprung up at the base of the hill. "Are you sure they're here?" he asked anxiously. "I don't see a livin' soul."

"You're not supposed to," Keith smiled. "Now come on inside. We'll have us a wait. Polecats don't come out till after dark." He pushed open the door and went inside. McCaleb followed, pausing to give one final look around before closing it behind them.

Colonel George W. Kirk was seated at the long table. Keith made the introductions. Kirk's men, all civilians, had been arriving in pairs and threesomes throughout the day, spacing themselves a few hours apart so as not to attract attention. Some were already staked out in the barn, three were upstairs in the loft stationed beside the window slits. When they were assembled, there would be fifteen not counting Kirk, McCaleb, and Keith. More than enough for an ambush.

Keith motioned for McCaleb to take a seat at the table opposite Kirk, then he pulled a chair up at the end between the two and leaned forward, his hands folded on the table. "Now listen carefully, Uncle," he said. "This is how we're going to time this thing."

* * *

Columbus's juices of adventure were flowing again. The train ride, which had been exciting at first, had quickly turned boring, but now, riding in what was called a barouche, he was more excited than ever. Malinda was hoping that by the time they reached Uncle Samuel's home, he would be spun out. She understood her son's excitement. She was feeling it herself. Or was it nervous anticipation? Whatever it was, in a short while she would see Ma again. And Jacob.

So this is what a real city looks like, she mused. It seemed a lot bigger than Raleigh. But then, she hadn't seen much of Raleigh other than the jail and the courthouse. Here, huge gnarled oak trees dressed in splendid Autumn colors shaded the cobblestone avenues. On the narrower side streets their branches formed a giant colored archway. There were raised walkways bordered by iron fences that surrounded lush verdant lawns, and it seemed as if there was a church on every corner, most with tall spires reaching naked to the sky. Everything seemed so peaceful. So … refined. "Oh, Columbus, look at that building! Did you ever see anything so grand? Why, I think it's made out of marble! And look at all that carved work up there around the top."

"What's the building for, Ma? What do they do in there?"

"I don't know, but it must be something terribly important."

A short while later the carriage came to a halt in front of a tall, black wrought iron gate set into an even taller red brick wall. Peering through the gate and the cover of dense trees, Malinda could see the corner of a large house with white pillars. It looked for all the world like a mansion. She was wondering why they were stopping here when their carriage driver turned to her and said, "We have arrived, Ma'am."

"Are you sure this is the correct address?"

"It's the address you gave me, Ma'am. Shall I ring the bell?"

"Ah ... ah ... yes, yes I suppose."

The driver climbed down, walked up to the gate and pulled the rope on a huge bell fastened to the brick wall. Malinda waited. Holding her breath. Dear Lord if this didn't look for all the world like the Reynold's place! Can Ma really be living in a house like this? Who would answer the bell? Ma? Uncle Samuel? Oh she wasn't ready for this. It had been so long since she'd seen Ma. She had changed. She wasn't a girl anymore. But what about Ma? And most important, would they be welcome? Had Ma received the telegram?

An elderly colored man with snow white hair, dressed in a silver gray coat with funny balloon kind of matching pants, came walking toward them down the carriageway. When he reached the gate he peered out through the iron pales. "May I ask who is callin'?" he said.

The driver turned to Malinda. "He wants your name, Ma'am."

"Oh? Oh! It's Malinda Blalock and my son Columbus. I'm Mrs. Pritchard's daughter."

Immediately the gate swung open. "Yes, Ma'am, she's been expectin' you." The man proceeded them up the short carriageway to the house and a portico. Land sakes, it *does* smack of that Reynold's place! Malinda's heart began beating double time. The driver again disembarked and this time offered his hand to Malinda to help her from the carriage. Memories of her only other carriage ride—with Uncle John—flashed through her mind. As she bent over her purse in search of the fare, the colored man disappeared into the house, and when she looked up again, Ma was standing in the open doorway.

"Malinda?" Elizabeth, dressed in a sweeping, salmon-colored velvet gown, stepped out onto the porch. There was a strained smile of disbelief on her ruggedly lined face. Far deeper lined than Malinda had remembered.

"Yes, Ma, it's me. And Columbus." She thrust the boy forward; needing a barrier.

"Come on up here Columbus and let your Grandma take a look at you." Elizabeth moved down the steps and reached out her hand to the boy.

Malinda nudged him forward again. "Say hello to your Grandma, Columbus."

Shyly. "Hello Grandma."

"I hope we didn't arrive at an inconvenient time, but I had no idea how long the train woul—"

"We received your telegram, but you didn't say what time you'd be arriving, otherwise we would have sent a carriage to the station. Cook has prepared two extra plates." Turning to the driver. "Have you been paid, Sir?"

"Yes, Ma'am."

"Then shall we go inside?" Elizabeth signaled to the servant who had reappeared in the doorway. "James, please get Mrs. Blalock's bags."

The driver handed the small carpetbag to the colored man, and bowed to Malinda. "Thank you Ma'am," he said, tipping his hat. Then he climbed back onto the driver's seat and turned the horse and carriage around.

Malinda watched with a sinking heart as Elizabeth took Columbus's hand and led him into the house. She followed, wishing for all the world she had never gotten on that train. Could this woman who was dressed in such fine clothes and living in this elegant house really be Ma? And she hadn't even touched her hand. Much less hugged her.

* * *

Malinda could barely take her eyes off the blazing chandelier, nor off the elaborate candelabra which stood in the center of the long table that was draped in snow white linen. Seated beside her, Columbus's mouth hadn't closed on a single bite of food, and she knew he was hungry. He was too busy gapping and twisting in his chair, trying to take in all of the elegant surroundings.

Elizabeth and Jacob were seated directly across from them, and although Elizabeth's eyes seldom turned in their direction, Jacob's scarcely left their faces. He was studying them with an expression of delight tinged with curiosity. Malinda could see in his face a reflection of her own. But this was no longer the adoring baby brother who had begged for her attention. This child was a stranger, and his interest seemed more directed to Columbus than at her. He kept sending Columbus little smile covered winks that were obviously intended for support.

Uncle Samuel and Aunt Louise sat at opposite ends of the table and were far more courteous in their acceptance of their visitors than Ma had been. Indeed they had both welcomed them with warm embraces and kind words, although Malinda sensed that Louise was somewhat reserved, and was surprised at how she kept glancing at her with what could only be called curiosity. Louise's face held the effects of years of pain, but her smile was brave.

As for Samuel, he bore a striking resemblance to his brother John, but his manner was much less stiff and formal. He exuded warmth and seemed sincere when he said he had been looking forward to meeting her. For the life of her Malinda couldn't imagine why. What could Ma have told him about her?

"You're not eating your dinner, Columbus." Elizabeth's tone was judgmental as she looked at her Grandson. "Don't you care for the food?"

Columbus looked at his plate. "Yes, Ma'am, I guess I like it."

"But you haven't tasted it."

Columbus shoveled in a forkful of boiled potatoes, then with cheeks bulging, smiled. "Yes Ma'am, I like it a lot better than beef dodger."

"Beef what?"

"That's something we ate at a Refreshment Saloon in Lexington," Malinda explained.

"Well, whatever is it?" Louise asked. "I don't believe I've ever heard of it."

"It's a corn cake filled with minced beef. I think it would have tasted a lot better if it had been seasoned with a bit of salt."

"Salt is still in short supply in Kentucky," Elizabeth said dryly.

"So tell us, Malinda," Samuel intervened, "how was your trip? Was the train comfortable?"

"Not truly, Uncle Samuel. It's noisy and dirty when someone opens a window and stifling when the windows are closed. And it's hard to sit for that long without getting stiff."

Samuel chuckled and touched his lips with his white linen napkin. "I should think at your young age that would not be a problem."

"Oh yes, Uncle Samuel," Malinda said hastily. "Bone aches are part of a mountain woman's life. Aren't they Ma?"

Elizabeth looked at her sharply. "I never had that problem when I lived in the mountains," she lied.

"Tell me Columbus," Louise said, covering the awkward silence following Elizabeth's crisp remark, "How did you find the journey?"

"Ma'am?"

"Did you enjoy the train ride?"

"Yes, Ma'am. For a little while. But it was awful long."

"I've never ridden on a train," Jacob said. "What's it like?"

"Well, there's this long car with a teenie weenie walk place down the middle and it's hooked up to a whole lot of other cars, and sometimes it stops at one of those Refreshment Saloons so you can get out and pee, and then you get back on again and wait for the next stop when you can pee again."

Elizabeth shot Columbus a stern look, while Louise's face turned rose red, but Samuel laughed and said, "Yes, I suppose there are some inconveniences to modern travel."

"You wouldn't believe the changes that have taken place in Caldwell and Watauga Counties, Ma," Malinda broke in, reaching for a more agreeable topic of conversation. "When you left everything was pretty much burned out, but people are beginning to rebuild again, and before long it'll be just as pretty as it ever was."

Elizabeth nodded, but made no comment. However, Malinda didn't miss the frown of disapproval Uncle Samuel directed at his sister. Maybe things between Ma and Uncle Samuel weren't running all that smooth, and she wondered if the tension between them had anything to do with her being here ... Somehow she felt it did.

CHAPTER 31

There was hushed murmuring among the men as they wrapped their white sheets around them and adjusted their pillowcase masks. The horses, sensing danger, snorted nervously. Jesse mounted his steed and stuffed his pillowcase into the rope tied around his waist. "Ready boys?"

There were nods and grunts of agreement from the three dozen or so men.

"Y'all know the target." Jesse shouted in order to be heard by those at the rear. "It's one we've been waitin' fer, and we don't wanna be in no hurry about it and get it all messed up. We wanna do it right." Jesse's sheet billowed about him in the night wind. "I jest want to remind y'all that what we're doin' tonight is standin' up fer our rights as white men. We're protectin' our land. Protectin' it from Yankees who got the mistaken idee that they won the goddamned war. Well, they didn't win! We white men got a right to our way a life, and this here's our land! And no Damned Yankee is gonna take it away from us!" The men cheered approval. "And we ain't gonna let any niggers er nigger lovers take our rights away from us, are we?"

"*NEVER! NEVER!*"

"Y'all know there's a bunch a nigger lovin' Yankees out there who are tryin' to trample us into the dirt. But we ain't gonna hold still fer it! Them bastards don't know who they're up against! We're Sons a the South, and proud to be so!" The cries were reaching fever pitch. "Now Danny will be leadin' a squad comin' in from the rear down the hillside jest in case—"

"Danny ain't here," a voice from the rear shouted.

Jesse paused, his pock-marked face twisting with anger. "Well, where the hell is he?"

"Don't know. Ain't seen him since Wednesday."

Jesse moved his horse slowly through the gathering. His hawk eyes darting from one hooded rider to another. "Anybody know somethin' 'bout Danny?"

Several men shook their heads. At that moment the sound of drumming hooves caused all heads to turn toward the road as a horseman, riding hard, emerged out of the pitch black night and into the circle of light surrounding the campfire. The men parted, making a path as he rode straight toward Jesse.

"Where the hell you been, Danny?" Jesse screeched. "We're near ready to head out and yer supposed to be leadin' a squad!"

"I need water," Danny panted. "I jest rode all the way from Morganton." He dismounted and reached for the long handle of the tin drinking cup beside the rain barrel.

"Well, hurry it up, we need to get movin.' And what the hell were ya doin' in Morganton, anyways?"

"My cousin Tim died on Wednesday," Danny gasped, "and I had to stick around fer the buryin' or my Pa woulda skinned me alive." He took a long, thirsty gulp of water, wiped his mouth on his sleeve, then added glumly. "Pa always thought the sun rose and set in Tim's ass."

"Well, git back on yer damned horse and let's git goin.'"

"Somethin' I reckon I oughta tell ya, don't know if it's important er not, but Uncle Sy—you know, he's the stationmaster in Morganton—well he told me he saw Malinda Blalock and her kid boardin' a train on Thursday." He picked up a watering bucket and offered it to his horse.

Jesse, who had already turned away, turned again to face Danny, his face the color of the sheet that wrapped him. "Tell me that ag'in."

Danny climbed back on his horse. "Tim's Pa, Uncle Sy, says he saw Malinda Blalock and her kid boardin' a train late Thursday afternoon."

"A train fer where?"

"Didn't ask him."

"I don't know what the hell you got fer brains, Danny!" Jesse snarled. "Ya weren't sure ifn it was important? Ya don't ask where the hellcat was runnin' off to? Jessez, are you stupid!"

Danny ducked his head so he wouldn't have to look at Jesse's flaming eyes; wishing he had kept his mouth shut and let Jesse find out for himself when they got to the Blalock's place.

Jesse turned to face the gang. "Well, this puts a different slant on things, now don't it? Could be coincidence that hellcat leavin' town, but on t'other hand, it could mean she's high tailin' it 'cause somebody spilled the beans!" He pulled on his reins until the horse reared, then shrieked above the animal's nervous cry. "Now who the shit's been shootin' his mouth off?"

Dead silence.

Jesse's face turned from white to crimson. He let the silence build. "This ain't gonna change nothin'!" He rode slowly through the gathering. "We'll jest haveta be more on our toes 'cause Blalock may a been tipped off we're a comin.' Could be he's set hisself a trap." He paused, giving time for the words to sink in. "But that's all right. There ain't nothin' gonna stop this operation! This here only means y'all gotta be more alert." He paused again, weaving in an out among the men while his brain searched for a plan. "He coulda brung in some a them bastards who've been houndin' us to help him out." Then a cold smile began to spread across Jesse's thin lips. "Now gather 'round boys, and listen up close. This here's what we're gonna do."

* * *

Malinda set the tray of dishes on the soapstone sink as Elizabeth entered from the dining room carrying another.

"Beulah, our cook, usually takes care of this," Elizabeth explained, "but I gave her the rest of the night off. She's got some kind of stomach problem. I told her you would help me with the cleanup."

"Of course, Ma. Just like we used to do." Malinda looked for any sign of softening.

"I'll get you something to put on." Elizabeth gave her daughter a disdainful glance. "Although it doesn't look as if that blouse needs much protecting." She walked into the pantry and pulled two aprons from a peg as Malinda looked down at her soiled clothing, feeling embarrassed.

"The train window was open … the ashes kept blowing in …" Ever since their arrival she'd been acutely aware of her dowdy appearance compared to Ma and Aunt Louise's finery. "Maybe I should see to Columbus before we get started. I don't want him being any trouble."

"I had James make a fire in the music room. The boys will be all right. But if you're concerned, we'll take a look." Elizabeth gestured for Malinda to follow and led the way down the hall to a large room with a high ceiling and tall double doors. They paused at the threshold and peered inside.

Jacob and Columbus, seated on the floor in front of a cheerful fire, were bending over a playing board. Malinda saw immediately why this was called the music room. There was a pianoforte against one rose, damask-covered wall. Beside it stood a tall, gilded harp, and two dulcimers lay atop a round mahogany table. A banjo rested on a nearby stool.

Malinda gasped when she saw the harp. "I've never seen a real one before," she whispered. "Isn't it just about the most beautiful thing you've ever seen? Who plays it?"

"Louise does sometimes," Elizabeth's tone was ever so slightly softer. "Her back gives her a lot of trouble so she doesn't do it that often. I've learned to finger it a bit myself."

Was there the trace of a smile?

"Jacob wants to learn but he's still too young. He does quite well on the dulcimer and the banjo. And I told you he's learning the pianoforte." Lowering her voice. "Samuel's buying him a fiddle for Christmas."

Columbus looked up and beamed. "Look, Ma, Jacob's teachin' me how to play jacks. And next we're gonna play checkers."

"That's very nice, Columbus. You be a good boy now while Ma helps your Grandma. And don't go disturbing Aunt Louise and Uncle Samuel."

"We won't. Jacob says they're readin' in the parlor. They always read after supper."

"Dinner," Jacob corrected.

"Huh?"

"What we just ate was dinner. Supper's what you eat real late at night."

"Oh?" Columbus pondered this new information. "Back home we eat supper early. I reckon we just skip dinner."

The women turned and walked back down the hall to the kitchen. "I'm glad to see they're getting along so well," Malinda said. "Jacob has certainly blossomed, hasn't h—" She was interrupted as a blast of wind rattled the windowpane. "My, that sounds fierce."

"I think we're in for a gale." Elizabeth lifted a kettle from the Glenwood stove and poured water into a large pan. Then she opened the door of the stove and threw two more pieces of wood inside.

"I hope the boys won't bother Louise and Samuel."

"Jacob knows not to disturb them." Elizabeth prodded the fire with an iron poker, keeping her eyes on the flames as she added, "Columbus seems better than I had expected."

"Better?"

"Considering what he's been through I expected to find him disturbed. It wouldn't be at all surprising."

Malinda's jaw tightened, but she remained silent.

Elizabeth closed the stove door, instinctively clutching her back as she straightened. "James has taken your bag upstairs. You'll be sharing a guest room with Columbus. There are two beds in the room, and I thought he would be less frightened staying with you rather than being in a room by himself. The house is so much bigger than he's used to. James will make a fire so you'll be comfortable."

What a strange choice of words. Why should Columbus be frightened? Or was it intended to be cruel? Malinda covered her thoughts with a smile. "Comfortable? Ma, everything about this house is comfortable, and I'll bet the beds are a lot more comfortable than my old pallet used to be."

Elizabeth grimaced. "I'd rather not talk about that. It was a long time ago, and best forgotten."

"Forgotten? But that was our home, Ma. Where I grew up. Don't you ever think about it? Don't you ever think about Pa?"

Elizabeth handed Malinda a drying towel, then plunged her hands into the hot water. "I try not to," she said shortly. "This is my life now."

Silent, Malinda picked up the delicate crystal glass Elizabeth handed her and carefully dried it. "Then I guess you don't plan on coming back to Caldwell County?"

It was Elizabeth's turn to look surprised. "Land a Goshen, why would I do that? I have everything I need right here. And Jacob has all the opportunities a child could ever hope for—in spite of the hard times. He'll grow up to amount to something." She looked squarely at Malinda. "He'll have the kind of life I'd hoped you would have. And you *would* have had it if you hadn't married wrong."

Again, Malinda bit back the angry words fighting for release, and answered instead, "There's nobody to say I don't have a good life now. Or that I couldn't have a good life in the city either."

"Really, Malinda!" Elizabeth scoffed, "the years haven't taught you anything, have they? You still float in some kind of dream world. If you lived in a city your husband would have to earn a living somehow, and these days there's not much call for gunslingers."

Malinda slapped the towel down on the sink board. "Why are you being so cruel, Ma? I had hoped that we … that you and me … that we could …"

"Mend fences? After the humiliation you've heaped on my head? Have you any idea what it's been like for me when people find out my daughter is a notorious outlaw? There are some things, Malinda, which can't be mended. Certainly not as long as you are tied to that … that *MAN,* there will never be a chance for a mending between us."

The cold wind rattled the window above the sink.

"I'm not an outlaw Ma," Malinda said quietly. "I was a civilian scout for the Union Army. I think I'd best check on Columbus." She walked to the doorway. Turned. Swallowed hard. "I've had it in my mind to … to leave that 'man', as you call him." At last the turbulent feelings had found a voice.

Elizabeth studied her suspiciously. "I thought you were pregnant."

"I am pregnant."

"And this is the time you chose to cut and run?" Elizabeth gave a small rasping laugh. "Don't tell me you're expecting your uncle—or *ME*—to take you in!"

"I'm not asking for anybody's charity," Malinda snapped. "Least of all yours!" She stormed from the kitchen and down the hallway toward the music room, feeling as if her body would explode with rage. Why had she come here? What had she hoped to find? She'd been a fool to think that Ma would be anything other than the bitter old woman she'd shown herself to be in her letter!

* * *

"Ma says your folks were bushwackers during the war." Jacob said mischievously.

"What's a bushwacker?"

"They're folks who go around burning down other folks' homes and stealing all their food and stuff. Everybody knows about what your mother and father did. Sometimes the boys at school tease me about it."

"Why?"

"Because they found out your mother's my sister."

"Oh."

"Everybody talks about your parents. But my mother doesn't like them much."

"Why doesn't she like them?"

"Like I told you. They were bushwackers and did bad things during the war."

"They did not!"

"Yes, they did. Everybody knows it. They even sing songs about them."

"Did not! What songs?"

* * *

"Do you hear anything?" McCaleb whispered.

Keith cocked his head. "Nothing but the wind."

"I thought I heard somethin.'"

Keith walked to the window. "It can't be much longer, it's coming up on two a.m. He peered out but all he could see were ghostly clouds skittering across the moon. All else was black shadow against an even blacker night.

"Think maybe they changed their plans?"

McCaleb's words echoed Keith's own anxiety. Maybe they had. Something didn't feel right, but he tried to speak reassuringly. "We'll soon know. I think it's time you head for the roof." He read the distress in McCaleb's face and regretted letting him be a part of this—but it was too late to turn back now. Kirk and three of his men were spread out in the barn, five more were hidden behind stumps and boulders around the front yard and along the wagon path leading from the road into the dooryard. Two of Keith's men were in the stone stairwell leading to the root cellar, three more were in the loft, and the remaining two were seated at the table. Waiting.

"I know what you're thinkin,'" McCaleb said, "but don't you worry, I'll do my job."

"I know you will, Uncle, but remember to stay low. You'll need to hug that roof like a woman's tit."

"I may be scared, but I'm not stupid!" McCaleb chuckled. "Uncle Webb used to say, 'God didn't make any stup—"

He was interrupted by the sound of hoofs entering the dooryard. Stealthily, Keith peered out the window. "There's a dozen of 'em," he whispered hoarsely. "Get to the roof. You know where the trapdoor is in the loft?"

McCaleb nodded, dropped to his knees and crawled to the ladder. He picked up a blanket wrapped object laying at the foot of the ladder, tucked it under his arm, and pulled himself up with his other hand. Keith stood near the door, back to the wall. His two men crouched beneath the window. A breath later reflected flames danced across the windowpane as an oil soaked cross was set afire.

For a long moment the only sound was the murmuring of men and the snorting of horses. Then a voice called, "Come on out Blalock. We know yer in there. We got y'all surrounded."

A tight smile flashed across Keith's lips. "Is that you, Jesse?" he shouted.

The question went unanswered. "We're members a The Brotherhood. Men a the South."

Loud hoots of "Yeah! Yeah!" followed as the gang rallied behind their leader.

"You're nothin' but a bunch of assholes hidin' under bed sheets!" Keith hollered back.

"We're here at the command a the Grand Wizard hisself! Drop yer gun and come out with yer hands up and there won't be no shootin.' Too damned bad that hellcat a yourn ain't here to see y'all take yer punishment."

They know Malinda isn't here? Keith edged a step closer to the door. Both pistols drawn. "Punishment for what?" he called.

"Come on out!" the voice yelled again. "Come out er we'll torch the house with y'all in it!"

Keith ran his tongue over dry lips and thought of McCaleb on the roof. He slipped the pistol in his left hand into the shoulder holster concealed beneath his shirt, threw the bolt on the door and slowly pulled it open.

* * *

Jacob leveled a knowing smile at Columbus and picked up the dulcimer. "Here's one of the songs they sing about your folks …

Oh they are vile bushwackers,
The thicket's their home.
And all through the mountains
These two do roam.
They butcher and plunder
And burn down your home.
Oh they are vile bushwackers,
The thicket's their home—

"Stop it!" Malinda burst into the room, her trembling hands reached for support on a wing back chair. "I want you to stop singing that song right now, Jacob!"

Two pair of startled eyes turned toward her.

"Jacob was tellin' me ab—"

"Jacob has no business telling you things he knows nothing about," she said sharply.

"What's going on?" Elizabeth stood in the doorway, hands on her hips.

"Jacob's singing a disgusting song that isn't right for Columbus to hear!"

"Oh? What song is that Jacob?"

Confused, Jacob replied, "I don't know the name of it. It's the one that goes …

There's a price on the head
Of each mischievous thief.
In case you don't know

It's Malinda and Keith.
She rides like the wind with her child at her breast,
And never a night for the baby to rest—

"STOP IT, I SAY!" Malinda shrieked. "*Stop it you little beast!*" Darting across the room, she snatched the dulcimer from Jacob with one hand and with the other pulled Columbus to his feet. "Come on, Columbus. We're getting out of here!" As she sailed past Elizabeth she cried, "How can you allow him to do such a thing?"

"I don't know what you're so upset about. The child is just singing one of the more popular songs from the war." Her voice rose an octave. "One I've had to *live* with!"

Malinda ran down the hall toward the foyer, dragging Columbus behind her. As she reached the foot of the wide staircase she encountered James, coming down.

"I … I need my bag. Where's my bag?"

"Upstairs Ma'am," the butler replied; disbelief mirrored in his eyes. "I'll fetch it for you if you wants me to."

"Yes, yes, I do want."

The envelope doors to the parlor slid open and Samuel stood in the doorway. "Why, Child, whatever is the matter?" Moving toward Malinda with outstretched arms he folded her to him. Momentarily, she let herself go limp against his chest.

"Oh, Uncle Samuel," she cried miserably, unable to stem the tears any longer. "I'm sorry to have disturbed you. And … and I'm so sorry we came. We shouldn't have …"

"There, there, Child. I'm sure things aren't as serious as you imagine." Over Malinda's head Samuel gestured his wife toward the music room, mouthing the words, "Please see what you can do."

Louise quickly obliged, heading down the hall toward Elizabeth who stood waiting, her hands resting on Jacob's shoulders.

Confused, Columbus hugged Malinda's skirts, sobbing but not understanding why.

* * *

Keith reached out the half open door and laid his gun on the doorstone. Then he stepped outside with his hands above his head. Twenty feet before him stood the flaming cross and gathered around it the group of now silent, masked men staring down at him. All were armed. His first glance had been correct; there weren't more than a dozen. He had expected more. The wind abruptly stilled.

A moment later the heavy silence was broken as the leader dismounted and slowly walked toward him. He carried a bullwhip in one hand, a rope in the other. "Keith Blalock, y'all been sentenced to a beatin' by the honorable members a the Ku Klux Klan."

"Honorable my ass, Jesse. There isn't one honorable man among you. As for a beating, you're the one who's in for it, you fucking, little weasel. Now take that sheet off your head and for once in your miserable life pretend you're a man!"

"Git him boys!"

Four men immediately dismounted and raced toward Keith. He knocked one cold with a swift kick to the chin and the second hit the earth from a powerful right to the jaw. Four others rushed forward, and then a fifth. The scuffling continued for several minutes, but when it was over Keith stood with two men on each side of him pinning his arms, another stood in back with an arm around Keith's neck. Two more, in the dust at his feet, were attempting to tie a rope around his ankles, but he was kicking with such force their efforts were in vain. Keith sent one flying with his boot.

The leader waited until he was certain his victim was sufficiently restrained then he slowly unrolled the bullwhip and walked menacingly toward Keith. When he was within range he raised his leg and kicked his victim full in the stomach. Keith buckled. As he tried to straighten he was caught with a fierce right blow to his jaw. Keith's head swung to the side with such force it knocked one of the men holding him to his knees. A fist to the stomach. Keith's vision blurred as the pain sent shock waves to his brain. On the verge of fainting he muttered with his last vestige of strength, "You pissin' little asshole, Jesse. You're too much of a coward to look me in the face." Another right to the jaw and Keith's feet spun out from under him. He fought to remain conscious. "I know it's you, Jesse," he sputtered, tasting his own blood. "I could smell you from all the way inside the house."

"All right, Blalock!" Jerking the mask from his head the man leered into Keith's battered face. "I wanna take credit fer this and it's sure somethin' I'm gonna enjoy."

Keith stared at his attacker in astonishment. Earl Eller! My God it's *not* Jesse! Then it all came clear. The small number of men. The fact they knew Malinda wasn't here. They'd figured out it was an ambush. Jesse must be laying in wait somewhere with the rest of the gang. They had set their own trap!

Then from the rooftop came the loud clamor of the supper bell.

Oh God, McCaleb, Keith moaned silently. *No! NOOO!*

* * *

The rain was torrential as James pulled the town coach up under the portico. He dismounted and hurried to the frightened horse in an effort to calm him. The animal was trying to rear on his hind legs; threatening to overturn the carriage as lightning ripped the black sky and loud claps of thunder crashed over the rooftop. In the protected doorway, Samuel stood with one arm around Malinda's shoulders, his other arm hugging Columbus.

"Child, I'm begging you," Samuel pleaded for what seemed the hundredth time. "Please don't do this. It's madness to go out on a night like this. I beg you to reconsider. Things will look better in the morning."

Malinda had regained her composure and stood resilient as the wind whipped at her cape and skirts. Louise hovered behind them clutching a shawl about her.

"No, Uncle," Malinda said firmly. "We're leaving now. We never should have come in the first place."

"But surely, you must realize your Aunt Louise and I are concerned about your welfare. Can't you wait—"

"Uncle Samuel, I can't wait. And truly we do not need the carriage. We'll be all right." Then added bitterly. "During the war we learned how to survive in foul weather."

"If you must go I insist you allow James to drive you to wherever you're going." Temper was edging Samuel's voice. He felt furious and despairing. "In all conscience I cannot have it otherwise!"

"Ma, I'm cold," Columbus moaned, huddling closer to Samuel. "Can't we go back inside?"

"The child is talking sense," Louise interjected.

"Hush, Columbus," Malinda snapped, ignoring her aunt's remark. My God she felt as if she were in an enemy camp. "All right, Uncle, we'll take the carriage," she conceded.

Reluctantly, Samuel offered his arm to Malinda and led her down the few brick steps to the open door of the coach. "I would give anything if this hadn't happened," he said. "I will have a talk with Elizabeth."

"That isn't necessary," Malinda replied as James boosted Columbus into the coach through the other door. "Ma and I see things differently and that isn't going to change."

"But I *will* get to the bottom of it and find out what happened," Samuel said firmly, helping her up the step. "My sister can be quite stubborn on occasion."

Mustering courage, Malinda leaned out to give him a kiss on the cheek. "So can her daughter."

"Yes, I can plainly see that." Samuel managed a tight smile.

In the doorway, Louise was waving a lace handkerchief, and intermittently using it to dab at her eyes. Samuel returned to his wife's side and put an arm around her misshapen shoulders.

James was again attempting to calm the nervous animal and as they waited Columbus tugged at Malinda's sleeve. "Ma? Ma? Was that true what Jacob said about you and Pa being bushwhackers? You didn't do bad things, did you Ma? Like in that song? Huh? Ma?"

"Oh, be still, Columbus. Oh, please, please Son, do be still."

The boy slumped back into the seat as James climbed up onto the driver's bench. Malinda waved to Louise and Samuel. The wind was pulling Samuel's coattails straight out behind him.

Elizabeth suddenly appeared beside Louise. She was holding Jacob by the hand. Then motioning her son to stay, she walked determinedly down the steps and across the portico to the carriage. "Where will you go?" Her eyes were as cold as the wind.

Malinda looked down at her with contrived amazement. "Why I'm going home to my husband, of course," she said sweetly. "Wherever else would I go?" Then lifting her chin she called up to James. "Take us to the train station, please."

"Yes, Ma'am." The colored man flipped the reins and urged the recalcitrant animal out into the fury of the night.

Malinda's last view of Elizabeth was as she stood under the portico, arms folded across her chest. Watching them go.

* * *

At the sound of McCaleb's signal Kirk's men opened fire. It was all wrong. Keith had instructed McCaleb to ring the bell when he got Jesse to unmask. That way the others would know who not to shoot. He wanted Jesse for himself. But in the darkness McCaleb couldn't see who had unmasked, and he'd heard Keith call him Jesse.

"Get 'em men!" Eller yelled, wrestling to pull his gun from beneath his sheet. The men holding Keith released their victim and raced for their mounts. Two were caught in the crossfire between their own men and those firing from the window of the house.

Keith grabbed the bullwhip Eller had dropped, pulled back his arm and with one artful swing encircled Eller about the chest and arms. Then he reeled him in like a fish on a line. A trick he'd learned from Daniel Ellis.

Kirk's men were firing from their various hiding places, and just when they'd thrown caution to the winds and exposed themselves, a dozen more masked riders came thundering into the dooryard. Rifles blazing. Three of Kirk's men fell in the first seconds and Keith cried out in dismay as he saw Kirk himself topple from the second story of the barn and land in a hay-laden wagon.

Crawling on his side and using one elbow to pull himself along, Keith dragged the struggling Eller after him as he edged his way toward the house. Gunfire was exploding all around him, but he had no free hand to draw his hidden weapon from the shoulder holster.

When he reached the doorstone, the door swung open and he scampered inside, still dragging Eller. A flurry of gunfire peppered the door and several more balls sped through the open doorway into the cabin. But none found their mark.

The two men inside the house were returning fire through the broken window. Keith pulled Eller up against the far wall, knelt over him and with one swift move knocked him unconscious with a right to the jaw. He then untangled his feet from the rope, drew his gun and headed up the ladder toward the loft.

The men stationed at the window were firing rapidly. The night was alive with the cries of horses and the screams of wounded men.

Keith reached for the next ladder which led to the trapdoor. He had to get McCaleb off the roof. Cautiously he peeked his head out of the opening just far enough to see. Spotting a dark hump disturbing the sharp incline of the roof, he hissed, "McCaleb! It's me, Keith. Come on down."

There was no response.

"McCaleb!"

"I can't," came the anguished reply. "I'll fall off." At that moment the sky was sliced by lightning followed by crashing thunder. The clouds opened and the rain that had been threatening for hours poured down. "Oh, no!" McCaleb cried hoarsely, "I'm slipping off!"

Keith holstered his gun and hoisted himself to the roof. Lying on his belly, arms and legs spread wide for traction, he began inching his way toward McCaleb. He worked his fingers under the shingles in an effort to find something to hold on to. He had built the roof with a sharp incline so the snow would slide off easily; now he cursed himself for being so practical.

McCaleb was a good five feet away, and the rain was quickly becoming a deluge. They were on the front side of the house and if they fell they would be cut to ribbons in the crossfire. "Dig your fingers underneath the shingles," Keith urged. "Get as good a grip as you can and work your way toward me."

There was no response. And no movement from McCaleb.

"Uncle, goddamnit, work your way over to me!"

Another roll of thunder broke overhead and McCaleb let out a tortured cry. "I'm afraid! I'm afraid!"

"If you stay where you are you're going to get washed away. Now dammit, *MOVE!*"

There was finally a slight motion from McCaleb and Keith reached out his hand, reassuringly. "That's right, Uncle, come this way."

Ever so slowly, McCaleb inched toward him. Each time he groped nearer, Keith withdrew his hand a little more. Coaxing him onward. But something was wrong. McCaleb was hanging by just one arm. He was holding something in his left hand and using only his right hand and his two feet to cling to the rain soaked roof. "What in the hell have you got in your hand?" Keith hissed.

"The bell!"

A rumble of hysterical laughter bubbled up from Keith's gut. He bit his lips to squelch it. "I think you can let go of it now," he said.

"But it'll fall and make a terrible racket. They'll know we're up here."

"I think they're busy enough with what's going on down there to take much notice."

"Okay. Okay." McCaleb released his hold on the bell and it hit the ground with a loud clamor. Unknown to Keith and McCaleb, it nearly fell on one of the Klansmen crouched beneath the splintered window. The man was so surprised he momentarily lost his concentration and took a shot in the stomach from one of the men inside the house. He fell backward across the bell as it clanged his death knell.

McCaleb was now less than a foot away from Keith. Keith began reversing his direction, but didn't risk turning his head. The roof was getting so slick he knew neither of them would be able to hold on much longer.

Finally, he felt the rim of the trapdoor. The fingers of his right hand squeezed around it just as he saw McCaleb start to slip downward. "Grab my leg!" Keith cried, thrusting his left leg out toward McCaleb.

McCaleb made a desperate try and Keith felt a tug on his leg. "Use both hands!" Keith hollered, and McCaleb let go of the shingles with his other hand and grabbed Keith's boot. Keith could feel his grasp on the frame weakening. He was now supporting his own weight and McCaleb's with one arm. McCaleb was dangling precariously and Keith felt sure both his arm and leg were being pulled from their sockets. With a final surge of strength he swung his left arm above his head and grabbed the frame of the opening, and pulled with everything in him. He was now chest high with the opening. His right hand reached blindly for the top rung of the ladder. Although McCaleb was hanging onto his rain slick boot with both hands, Keith could feel him slipping. He took a deep breath and heaved his shoulders through the opening. Then with his left hand he grabbed the next lowest rung of the ladder. He was now positioned headfirst down it. Two more rungs and he felt the weight on his leg break free as McCaleb grabbed the frame of the opening. With the counterbalance gone Keith tumbled headlong down the ladder onto the floor of the loft. A heartbeat later McCaleb fell through the opening and landed on top of him.

Spasms of pain shot through Keith's abused body. McCaleb moaned, and rolled off of him. Keith flopped onto his back, gasping for breath.

"My God!" McCaleb panted, "I didn't think we were goin' to make it."

"Have faith, Uncle," Keith gasped. "Have faith."

Keith wasn't sure if he could stand. He lay on his back, the cold rain pouring down on him through the open trapdoor. After a long minute he slowly, painfully, groped his way, first to hands and knees, and then to a standing position. He tried focusing on the men at the window slits. They were still firing. He fumbled his way over to them and ventured a glance outside. The cross, drenched by the pounding rain, was gasping it's last breath, but it still gave off enough light to show white draped bodies, oozing life, strewn everywhere around the yard. There were so many dead horses it looked like a slaughterhouse. Several of Keith's own men lay dead beside them.

Gunfire was still coming from the barn so that meant at least some of their men had survived the counterattack. But there were still a half dozen or more white sheeted men firing from behind boulders and tree stumps from vantage points throughout the yard.

Keith turned to McCaleb. "Are you all right?"

"Yeah, I think so. Did somethin' go wrong?"

"I'll tell you later."

Keith climbed down the ladder to the main room and crouching low, made his way to the window where two of his men were still firing. "How does it look?"

"All right if they don't send in more reinforcements, but we've taken some heavy loses."

Keith pulled his gun from his holster, took up a position at the side of the window and began firing intermittently. Moments later he became aware that the sound of gunfire coming from the loft had abruptly changed. Then there were loud thumps on the floor. One. Two. Three. Bodies falling?

Startled, he turned, and in the deep shadows he saw McCaleb come sliding down the ladder. There was a rope around his neck and the other end of it was in the hand of an unmasked Klansman. As the two men hit the floor the Klansman pointed his pistol at McCaleb's head and shouted at Keith, "One move outta you or them others and this ole man's head turns into a smashed pun'kin."

"*Jesse!*"

"Put yer gun down, Blalock."

My God, he must have come in through the trapdoor! Keith gave a quick look at his two men and in the split second it took for him to glance away, Jesse fired twice, shooting each man in the back. In tandem they slumped to the floor.

"You bastard!" Keith lunged toward Jesse and McCaleb. Jesse took a step backward, dragging McCaleb, and holding the smoking gun to McCaleb's temple.

"Drop yer weapon, Blalock. I mean it!" Jesse shrilled.

"You put *YOUR* gun down, Jesse," Keith said through steel lips. "Put it down and I'll let you go."

"Back off, Blalock! Yer in no position to be givin' orders. Ole McCaleb and me are walkin' outta here, and y'all are goin' to stand back and let us do it." He rammed the gun deeper into McCaleb's temple and McCaleb emitted a strangled gasp.

Jesse was holding all the cards. Keith felt certain if he put the gun down Jesse would shoot them both—but there didn't seem to be anything else he could do. He had to risk it. Slowly, he placed the gun beside his boot.

"Kick it over here to me," Jesse ordered.

The shooting outside was becoming less frequent. The battle was nearing its end. And Jesse had won. *Mother of God!*

"Kick it over here er he's dead!"

Keith pushed the gun with his boot and it slid across the rough hewn floor and slammed against the wall. Outside, there was one last halfhearted pistol shot ... then nothing. The only sounds now were the drumming of the rain and McCaleb's strangled attempts to breathe.

"That's more like it Blalock," Jesse crowed. "Now come on ole man. We're walkin' outta here. Open the door Keith."

Keith didn't move.

"Goddammit open the fuckin' door!"

Keith stepped backward three steps and pulled the latch.

"Open it wide godda—"

A woman screamed. The three men froze. It came again. "*JESSEE! JESSEE!*"

Jesse pushed McCaleb ahead of him to the window, using him as a shield. "Ma?"

From where he stood Keith could see a bent figure standing beside the smoking cross. *Zinnia!* She moved to the right, staggering through the drizzled maze of dead bodies, both hands clutching her head. In the sky the first fingers of gray light were warring with the rain.

"Jesse? Jesse? Son? Son where are you?"

Walking sideways to the door, McCaleb shuffling with him, Jesse motioned with the gun for Keith to step outside. "Do it or I'll blow his brains out!" he said through gritted teeth.

Keith stepped out onto the doorstone. Took one more step into the yard.

"I'm here, Ma!" Jesse hollered. "I'm okay!"

"SON! Oh my Son!" Zinnia rushed forward.

She had taken three steps when a dark figure sprang from behind the chopping stump, grabbed her and wrestled her to the ground. Jesse fired, the ball sailed above the heads of the two figures squirming in the mud. Keith was now parallel to Jesse and McCaleb. He took one giant step back, pulled his Bowie from his belt, and thrust it into Jesse's side. Surprised, Jesse's hold on McCaleb weakened. McCaleb broke free and hit the dirt. Jesse staggered and tried to lift his gun to point it at Keith. Keith pulled the knife free and plunged it into Jesse's back. Zinnia screamed as Jesse pitched forward onto the ground. Keith leaped on Jesse, pulled the knife out and again plunged it into the back of Jesse's neck severing his spinal column.

For a breathless moment everything was deadly calm. McCaleb rolled to one side. Keith leered down at his fallen prey. The man in the yard released his hold on Zinnia and stood up. Kirk. His face was covered with blood and his left arm hung limp.

Mouth agape, eyes bulging from their sockets, Zinnia stumbled to her feet. Hunched over, grappling forward. The men stood motionless. Silent and watching.

"Son?" Zinnia lurched toward the shattered body. "Son? It's Ma, Son." Then she shrieked and fell forward over the lifeless form, sounds pouring from her that defied human utterance.

McCaleb was the first to move. He reached out a trembling hand to Keith. Keith stared at him, then stepped around the sobbing woman and took his uncle's hand. Pulled him to his feet.

Suddenly, Zinnia reached her bloodied hands upward to Keith. "Don't you know what you've done? Don't you see? You've killed your own brother!"

Keith stared at her. Speechless.

"Carroll confessed it when he lay dyin' in my arms. But I always knew. I always knew … I always knew," she babbled. "A wife knows when her man lusts after another woman."

The strange words finally penetrated Keith's brain. He shook his head to clear it. "No, no," he murmured. "Carroll wasn't my father."

"*He was! He was!* And you've killed your own brother! You killed my boy!" She began rocking to and fro on her knees.

Keith looked at McCaleb. Begging for support.

At last McCaleb found his voice. "It's true, Keith," he said. "I've known for years. Carroll told me about it before you were even born." He lifted a bloody hand to his forehead. "I swore I would never tell." His shoulders began to shake, and a sob was torn from his heart. "I swore I'd never tell and now I have. Carroll was your real Pa, Keith. So help me God. And may God forgive me."

The indigo embers of the cross lost their battle to survive. The gray clouds began rolling away down the valley. The rain was dissipating and daybreak was pushing its way over The Grandfather.

Keith looked from McCaleb to Kirk, then his eyes took in the butchery around them as figures of his remaining men began to emerge from their hiding places. My God, why hadn't he died with these others? Why had he been left alive to suffer this torment? The humiliation of believing he was the seed of William Coffey could only be made worse by knowing he was Carroll Moore's son. *Jesse's brother!* People he had hated for a lifetime were his own blood?

The pain exploded in one primal scream, and Keith dropped to his knees beside Jesse. Blood soaked leaves swirled about them. He doubled over, burying his head in his hands. Kirk and McCaleb exchanged looks of despair, then turned and silently walked away. Zinnia's cries and Keith's racking sobs were the only sounds left to welcome the new day.

EPILOGUE

Malinda bore three more sons; John, Willie and Samuel. She died at the age of 58, of what was termed "natural causes." Keith lived to be 76. He died a violent death when the rail car he was hand pumping overshot a steep curve and plunged into a chasm. The handcar landed on top of him crushing him to death.

Was it a cruel joke? Could it have been ignorance on the part of someone who didn't truly know the man? Or was it a final act of vengeance? Whatever the reason Keith Blalock's gravestone reads:

L M BLALOCK
NORTH CAROLINA
PVT CO F 26TH REGT NC VOLS
CONFEDERATE STATES ARMY
NOV 21 1837 JULY 18 1913

WRITER'S NOTES—

The relationship between Austin Coffey and his brothers was real, as was his relationship with Carroll Moore. Austin was a devoted stepfather to Keith Blalock. Austin's murder at the hands of a gang, which included his former friend, Carroll Moore, is true, as was the discovery of this act by a stray dog. Jesse Moore and Keith Blalock were born enemies. Jesse did burn down Keith's house and he did shoot out Keith's eye, and Keith did eventually get his revenge by killing his lifelong enemy. Keith was also responsible for the killing of his uncle, William Coffey. Alfred Pritchard's murder at the hands of the Home Guard is also true.

Malinda successfully posed as Keith's brother, Sam, and was inducted into the Confederate Army along with Keith. Keith's romp in the poison oak and Malinda's subsequent release from the Rebel Army, signed by Colonel Zebulon Vance actually happened.

Captain Will Thomas of "Thomas's Highland Legion," was, as a boy, adopted by Chief Yonagushka and just before the Chief's death was made a Cherokee Indian Chief, the only known white man to receive such an honor.

Colonel George W. Kirk, Daniel Ellis, "The Old Red Fox," Colonel Zebulon Vance, Robert Green, John Boyd and William Woods Holden, are all part of recorded history, as are their relationships with Keith and Malinda Blalock. Keith took revenge on Robert Green in the manner told, and gunned down John Boyd in an act of revenge for the murder of Austin Coffey.

Dr. John Whitehead was my grandfather. His first wife died following the birth of their tenth child. He then married 18-year-old Margaret Meiz and they had seven children. My mother, Winifred, was the Dr.'s. seventeenth child. He was 70 when she was born. It was from stories he told my mother, which she later related to me, that I learned of Lonnie, and his unfortunate, "Halt three times or I'll shoot." Bud Riggs and Harold are products of this author's imagination.

The true identity of Keith's biological father remains unknown.

Printed in the United States
217217BV00001B/12/P